Spiraling Waters

The End of The Phoenix

Spiraling Waters
The End of The Phoenix

By Robin A. Clark, PhD

Copyright

ISBN 979-8-9899465-1-8

Written by Robin A Clark, PhD

Published by Amber Light Publishing
www.AmberLightPublishing.com

Editing and Book Design by Nita Robinson-Lewis
Nita Helping Hand? www.NitaHelpingHand.com

Cover Design by www.KAM.design

Other Books by Robin Clark

Naked Without a Hat
Battling Adult Philadelphia Positive Acute
Lymphoblastic Leukemia, The Real Fight for Those with
Ph+ALL
Shhhh, BREATHE

Part Two, The Aftermath of The Great Reset - sequel to
Spiraling Waters is coming up!

Phoenix Energy: *Invisible nefarious vibrations have afflicted Earth and humanity for eons. This 138-year cycle of resurrection and destruction, orchestrated by negative entities, keeps the human life cycle under secret control, perpetuating a constant struggle and the elusive hope for the American dream.*

It's now time to lift the veil and end the cycle before it's too late.

Chapter One

Pearl arrived in Athens eager and excited for the four-day seminar, *Botany, Ancient Discovery, and the Future of Healing* that was ahead of her. For the first time in history, Egyptologists, botanists, archaeologists, scientists, physicists, medical doctors, and healers from all over the world collaborated on a seven-year study of ancient herbs and healing remedies found inside King Tutankhamun's sarcophagus and in the tomb of Pharaoh Psusennes (Sou-sen-ess). What was found in the tomb with Pharaoh Psusennes is what intrigued Pearl and the collaborators the most. And now, for the first time, his sarcophagus was going to be opened and what lay within the casing would finally be revealed to the world. The grand opening was scheduled to take place on the first evening of the four-day seminar. News stations from around the world vied for a spot at the event, hoping to cover the exclusive story of the contents inside the pharaoh's sarcophagus and tomb, as well as the first to release pictures of the enigmatic pharaoh himself.

Passed down through oral tradition, this pharaoh, coined *The Silver Pharaoh*, had lived millions of years ago and he himself was well over a million years old upon his death. It is said that he lived in a time before the angels. His legacy in mythology is the "Keeper of Immortality". Now he and his sarcophagus were on display at the Megaron Athens International Conference Center in Greece. It was here that the sarcophagus was going to be opened and televised in front of millions of viewers around the world. The burning questions were, *Does he have the secret to immortality within the belongings found in his tomb or are they inside the sarcophagus with him? Or is it all just a fantastical story handed down through the ages for entertainment? If he does, is the world ready for immortality?*

Four of Egypt's most distinguished Egyptologists were on standby to do the honors. Media from around the world flooded into Athens for this remarkable event. Every hotel room in the area had been booked solid for over a year in anticipation of the greatest discovery ever. Every airport surrounding Athens had been jammed packed for days, flying in academics and the curious from one end of the globe to the other.

Pearl was thankful she was just a 45-minute flight from her home on Ikaria, one of Greece's small islands south of Athens. Her friend Harry had his own small jet engine plane that did the honors. The excitement and anticipation in Athens had been palpable for days, and it was pretty much the only story being covered on television. Pearl was thrilled to be a part of it.

Pearl's grandmother, Julia, one of the most renown healers in Greece who was known for her research in botany and ancient alchemy, had spent her life studying the myths surrounding this very illusive pharaoh. The volume of research Julia had uncovered throughout her lifetime filled the shelves in her library. The biggest question in Pearl's mind was why she was presenting her grand-mother's dissertation on the Silver Pharaoh and the biology of immortality instead of her grandmother.

Pearl grew up with Nonnah Julia telling her many bedtime stories about this pharaoh. She would sit on the side of Pearl's bed each night, and by the soft light of the tiny princess lamp she would tell them to Pearl as she gazed off into the distance as if she was in the room alone. Pearl loved hearing them as she watched her Nonnah tell her stories with such mystery in her voice. Julia's stories about Psusennes were like great adventures filled with secrecy. Psusennes' legacy was plagued with unusual conspiracy theories, and as Julia shared her interpretations of his fantastical life, it was almost as if she was putting a puzzle together in her mind, trying to make sense of the secrets that surrounded him. For reasons unbeknownst to Pearl, her Nonnah was obsessed with this pharaoh and his story.

One story that stuck with Pearl over the years was one that Julia's mother, Sophia, had told her when she was a little girl. This story that had been passed down through the ages, said that Psusennes was born out of chaos, a time before there was time. It is said that he manifested himself into being and was one of the first beings on Earth. He was immortal and had brought with him the secrets of immortality. As time passed, he yearned for others, companions to share the beauty of the earth with. Through alchemy he created others into being from the ethereal realm, then he created her, his companion, the perfect female. She came from the energy within the chaos that always soothed him and calmed him before he was flesh and blood. This energy, this woman, he named Priya, his queen, his love. They fell in love, but after a time on Earth, she wanted to return to the peaceful nature of the ethereal realm, which she did.

This devasted Psusennes so he put himself into a catatonic state and planned to remain that way until she returned. Those around him believed he was dead. They buried him – with all his treasures and his other worldly secrets – in a silver sarcophagus, never to corrode, in Egypt, buried deep within the sands of time. It was believed by some that he was alive inside his silver tomb and would awaken from his catatonic state when Priya someday returned to open it.

This story was the cause of many nightmares for Pearl. The thought of being buried alive in a tiny box made her shiver, but she listened intently, never asking questions. Pearl just watched her grandmother as she gazed off while sharing the many tales and scientific possibilities, as if all the myths of achieving immortality were indeed true. Through these stories, Pearl became just as intrigued with the possibility of an immortal life and decided her life's work would be to follow in her grandmother's footsteps as a healer, researcher, and scientist.

Pearl loved her Nonnah almost as much as she loved her own mother, Charlee. She giggled and told them it was a "toss up" as to which of them was her favorite. She was the jewel in both of their hearts. These days the three were like peas in a pod, all embarking on this incredible moment of a lifetime.

Finding The Silver Pharaoh's sarcophagus was world news. For decades, treasure hunters had been scurrying and searching the desert sands for this illusive piece of antiquity. In 1939, on the brink of WWII, Psusennes' sarcophagus was found by an archaeologist named Pierre Montet in an intact royal chamber in the buried sands of Tanis, Egypt. With escalating tension and an impending war in sight, Montet confiscated the chamber's contents and had them shipped to a secret, secure location in Cairo to be stored and studied later. When Montet died unexpectedly, the whereabouts of the secret location died with him, but in 2010, the hiding place was discovered. What made Psusennes' sarcophagus so special was that it was made of solid silver, which gave him the name The Silver Pharaoh. His was the only silver sarcophagus known to exist. The myths claimed that *inside* the sarcophagus was a vast hoard of jewels, gold, and many other precious treasures, the most important one being the recipe to immortality. Unbelievably, the vast amount of treasure that Montet found with the pharaoh's sarcophagus in the sands of Egypt was never looted. It was completely intact. Found in the hidden chamber with the silver sarcophagus were many scrolls, jars, and wooden crates. It was leaked to a reporter that a recorded history of medicinal cures for every disease known to man and the planet was found in the contents of the treasure. When the story hit the papers, the frenzy began. Everyone wanted to be a part of this archaeological find of the century. And now, after years of detailed study, the results were going to be televised on a global scale.

Many of the most renowned healers from all over the world were advancing on Athens for the first conference of its kind. Pearl, being a member of one of the most famous healing families in Europe who also owned and operated the most visited healing center in Therma, Greece, The Sacred Rock Healing Center next to Julia's home she called Agriolykos (Ag-ree-o-lee-kos), received one of the first invites. Julia was to be a keynote speaker at the conference, but at the last minute she was called back to Egypt. For the life of Pearl, she couldn't figure out why Julia would let anything get in the way of her being present at this event. Whatever pulled her away was so intense that she left in a hurry with Pearl's parents, Charlee and Mathias, in tow, leaving her extensive dissertation for Pearl to present for her. This would be Julia's third trip to Egypt in a short period of time. These trips were arranged through a phone call by a strange woman who kept her identity hidden. This strange woman coerced Julia into each trip, promising information regarding The Silver Pharoah. The first trip left her with a story so bizarre she questioned herself for falling for it. The second trip began with another strange phone call in the middle of the night. This anonymous phone caller claimed that four scrolls were circulating in the black markets in Egypt and were from the original cash of treasures Montet found within the chamber in 1939. The caller also stated that Julia's family name, Kaya, was on the outside of the clay jars that the scrolls were found in.

Two hours after this phone call, Julia, Charlee, and Mathias, Julia's daughter-in-law and son, were on their way to Egypt. Mathias was used to his mother's shenanigans revolving around this pharaoh, and when he married Charlee, she too became a believer of the greatest myth ever told. Julia's passion was infectious.

When the three of them arrived in Egypt, waiting for them at the airport was a woman in a dark burka with only her emerald-green eyes exposed. She was holding a sign with Julia's name on it. When Julia approached her, she quickly took Julia's hand and placed a large, heavy manilla envelope bulging at the seams in it. The covered woman pulled her in close and, without words, conveyed mentally through her thoughts that the scrolls inside were destined to be opened by Julia at this time in history. The woman's hand was uncomfortably hot. When Julia tried to pull away, the woman continued, gripping her hand tighter saying, *Inside contains the secrets you have been searching for. They exist. It is time to return them to you, Julia. Inside you will find the answers to the questions you seek. The alchemy for immortality is within. You must remember your place and who you are. You must decipher the code. As above, so below. The time of chaos has finished in the ethereal realm; now it is finished below, in your realm. He will come to help you.*

Julia looked down at the envelope then at Charlee and Mathias. When she turned back to ask the woman who would help her, the woman was gone; she had vanished into thin air. The last thing they remembered of this woman was her mentally telling each of them to decipher the contents and fulfill the prophecy. Julia looked inquisitively at the envelope then back to Charlee. Charlee looked at Mathias and together they looked at Julia and said simultaneously, "Alexander!"

Mathias asked, "Mom, do we know an Alexander?"

With a blank expression, her eyes trailed between Charlee and Mathias and back before she slowly said, "No. Should I know an Alexander? And how do you two do that? It amazes me every time."

In a split second they were transported back home on the island of Ikaria at the exact same time they had left hours before. They were standing in Julia's driveway in front of her car, stunned and staring at each other, trying to wrap their heads around this gap in time, how they got back home, and who the woman was.

When Pearl arrived home, she found them standing in the driveway, in suspended animation, not knowing how long they had been there. She had dropped them off at the airport and knew for a fact that they had boarded the plane. They weren't expected home for days. Panicked, Pearl tried to get information out of them, but nothing she said or did could break them from their unresponsive state. She gently took each one by the arm, slowly escorted them to the courtyard, and carefully seated them into side-by-side chairs facing the sea. When they were all seated, Pearl took a seat in front of them and asked question after question, "What happened? Why are you here? Why are you not talking to me? Are you OK?" No one made an attempt to answer her.

At one point, Pearl became concerned enough to suggest calling the local doctor. When she did, Mathias looked at her and said, "Pearl, let us be for now, sweetheart. We are OK." They didn't talk, eat, or sleep for days. They didn't even get up to urinate. It was if their bodies had stopped in time and these necessities were no longer needed. For one week they sat barefoot in Agriolykos' courtyard, staring out at the sea in silence.

Pearl was beside herself with worry. She spent days preparing meals and protein shakes, anything to get them to eat or drink, but nothing appealed to them. She covered them at night and uncovered them in the morning. On the seventh day, Julia spoke first, "It is time to work; let's do this." It was as if the three of them came to a shared epiphany at the same moment, knowing intrinsically what to do next; there were no spoken words needed. They stood up, walked to the Sacred Rock Healing Center, began emptying everything from the second story, and put all the existing furniture in storage.

The second story of the healing center had been designed as a large conference room for the many seminars that took place there each year. The three of them gutted the room and replaced all the chairs with rows of stainless-steel tables. Mathias boarded up the windows and installed natural lighting that lit up each table. Julia gathered all the equipment needed for this type of delicate research; computers, microscopes, and a variety of fine surgical instruments. They worked together as if in a choreographed dance, knowing what the other was going to do before they did it.

Pearl watched in disbelief, unable to ask questions. No one even acknowledged her when she spoke. She spent her time watching and helping when she saw it was needed. When their appetites returned, Pearl finally breathed a sigh of relief. She made all their meals and made sure they slept. If they were eating and sleeping, she was content.

Pearl knew a researcher's mind. In research mode, a kind of madness sets in, resembling unbridled desire unquenched by anything other than an answer. She too had found herself in this frame of mind many times throughout her career. It's a field that sends the researcher down a deep rabbit hole. Heaven forbid anyone interrupt the moment when this state of hypnotic determination happens! Day in and day out, Pearl kept quiet and watched the dance in awe. Her love for the three of them was etched even deeper in stone as she marveled at their ability to stay so focused. And, indeed, her curiosity was just as intense.

The second story of the healing center was being transformed into a sterile research lab. Each scroll was carefully placed and covered on the long tables in chronological order. The scribe had placed small black dots on the bottom of each scroll that represented the page numbers. Every scroll was logged and recorded by Julia. Microscopes, Ott lights, and computers crowded the wall-to-wall counters that surrounded the specimen tables in the center of the room. Hours were spent in this room as Julia's frustration mounted over the task she had been given.

The language used throughout the scrolls was an ancient language not found in any database or book. It was a combination of several ancient languages, along with musical notes interconnected into confusing combinations. Even piecing words together didn't help with a proper translation. The one and only clue Julia accidentally uncovered was that the alchemy presented in the scrolls was based on a vibrational system. Haphazardly throughout the scrolls, without any distinguishable pattern or logical reason, numbers were placed after words; numbers between 0-9. Next to each number was a small musical note. Julia remembered that numbers have vibrations. In this case, the number vibration matched the musical note next to it. She tried to sequence the notes with the numbers, then the notes by themselves, then the numbers without the notes, but nothing made sense. They spent hours staring at the tattered scrolls laying before them, hoping something would click and a pattern would emerge.

Finally, one morning after five cups of coffee, Charlee clapped her hands and started jumping up and down, startling Julia and Mathias. Charlee said, "Julia, the book! The book we brought back from our first visit to Egypt – where is it?"

Julia's face went blank as she searched her own mental databank for an answer. Julia stared at her, trying to remember. Slowly, she regained her composure and said, "OMG! Charlee, that is it. That is it!" She turned and left the research lab as if wild dogs were on her tail.

Mathias asked, "What is this about, babe?"

Charlee reminded him of the book that was given to Julia at the airport prior to boarding the plane home from her first visit to Egypt. What they thought was a wasted visit now seemed to have been a diamond in the rough. On that day, Julia strolled through Egypt's airport, disappointed that the trip turned up nothing when a woman suddenly stopped her, asking if the book she had in her hand belonged to Julia.

Julia glanced at the book in the woman's hand and pleasantly said, "No, it is not."

The woman asked again, "It is your book, is it not?" She opened the cover and showed Julia that indeed her name was written inside. In astonishment, Julia took the book from her and thumbed through it quickly. When she raised her head to ask a question, the woman was gone. Julia looked around, but she was nowhere in sight. Julia returned her attention to the book. It was on ancient languages that were no longer in use. Why was her name in this book? Until this moment, it had remained an unanswered question.

When Julia returned to the lab, she had the book with her. Over dinner Julia, Charlee, and Mathias scanned the pages forward and backward, looking for a chapter or anything resembling the languages on the scrolls. There was no perfect match, but what they did discover was that this vibrational language was ancient and considered a myth; an ancient language of the fallen angels. Julia began to realize the significance and importance of these scrolls. The fear of someone finding out she had them chilled her to the bone. They had to remain a secret or else they would be confiscated. As far as Julia could gather, there was a missing link to the secrets within the scrolls, and she was bound and determined to find it before someone else did.

Two days before the anticipated unveiling of Psusennes' sarcophagus, Julia received a third anonymous phone call asking her to return to Egypt. It was the same voice with the same unique hum that had her scrambling around Egypt looking for clues on her last two visits. Julia knew it was her, the woman who had handed her the manilla envelope with the scrolls in it. This time the woman said, "The time has come. You must be present. The answers will be given to you. I will be waiting for you."

Julia knew what she had to do. She needed to be in Egypt, and she needed to go now, so she asked Pearl to attend the conference and present in her place. She had spent years teaching Pearl the story of the illusive Silver Pharoah and knew that her granddaughter would do her proud. As Pearl dropped off the three of them at the airport, Julia left her with extensive instructions and a list of materials she wanted emailed to her as soon as the conference was over. Pearl was in shock, trying to wrap her head around what was happening, but she knew her Nonnah well. If Julia was willing to choose Egypt over The Silver Pharoah unveiling, the magnitude of her ask was well accepted. She was a bit nervous about their trip, but knowing her father was going calmed her jitters a bit. Her job now was to present Julia's work and find out as much as she could about the contents of the sarcophagus after the unveiling. The excitement of being a part of it all was overwhelming to Pearl. For the first time, the Silver Pharoah's secrets would soon be revealed to the world in a one-night extravaganza on live television, and Pearl would be there to witness it all.

Chapter Two

Pearl was up for the challenge Julia had given her and she was looking forward to her time in Athens. She had spent many semesters in the city while getting her Masters and multiple PhDs within the science and biology fields. She had made a lot of friends, but for the most part she was well known through her Nonnah Julia, her late grandfather Daniel, and their children, Melena and Mathias. Her Auntie Melena was famous in all of Europe and the United States since her face was on the cover of every magazine and newspaper, perfume bottles, and the Hollywood screen. It was Melena that gave her the name Pearl. Pearl's father, Mathias, was one of the most skilled masons in all of Europe and the Middle East. The entire Kaya family was quite infamous and well connected, and Athens had become her second home.

After Pearl arrived in Athens, she settled into her hotel room overlooking the Parthenon. She loved this hotel and knew the owner well. She stayed there whenever she visited the mainland. They always gave her the room with the best view and prepared her favorite meal when she arrived. It was only eight blocks from the conference center, which was perfect. The walk over would give her some exercise and time to clear her head before each day's events.

Starving, she took the elevator to the eighth floor to the outdoor restaurant. Here she could take in the sights, sounds, and smells of Athens as the sun set from her rooftop table. Her usual glass of red wine and a basket of bread were waiting for her. A large bowl of Kakavia, a delicious soup combination of fish, shellfish, vegetables, and a variety of herbs, was being prepared for her. She claimed it was like heaven in a bowl. As she waited for her food, she sauntered around the restaurant with her glass of wine, conversing with the staff and a few locals that she knew well.

Well into her bowl of hot Kakavia, her phone rang. "Hello? Yes, this is her. May I ask who this is?"

Pearl set down her spoon and listened as he answered, "I am a distant relative, kind of. Is Julia available?"

Pearl said, "A distant relative, *kind of*? And no, my grandmother is in Egypt. Can I help you?"

"Are you going to the conference?" the calm voice asked.

"Yes, I am going to attend. What is this about?" she asked.

"My name is Alexander and I have a package for your grandmother, Julia. I have come from Qatar to deliver it to her. It is very important that I see her as soon as possible. I was told she was speaking at this event, but I have since been told that you are presenting for her. Do you know when Julia will return?"

"You are a relative, you said? What does 'kind of' mean?"

"Well, yes, and no. I am Dimitri's son. I am aware this does not make me a blood relative, but through the stories my uncle shared with me, your great-grandfather, George, and his best friend, Dimitri, called each other brothers. I feel as though we are related, at least through a pseudo family history, if that makes sense..."

Pearl replied, "Yes, it makes sense. I have a few pseudo aunts and uncles."

Alexander continued, "I have never met your family but have spent many hours sitting next to my Uncle Qaseem's bedside, reliving the time he spent with Dimitri. These stories are very sacred and very secret. I am the only one besides my mother who knows the true story of my existence. I assume Julia knows a portion of Dimitri and Qaseem's story. It was long ago but only recently that I found out about Dimitri, my father. I need to talk with Julia. I am in Athens now. I know this is short notice, but my intention was to attend her conference and present the information I have to her after. Will she be back soon?"

Pearl took a long sip of her wine, eyebrows knitted, feeling a bit perturbed and wondering where this was going. She finally had a moment to sit and rest to clear her mind of all that had happened over the past couple of weeks and now that didn't seem possible. She sat down her wine glass and leaned back in her chair while gazing out at the Parthenon.

When Pearl didn't answer, Alexander continued, "Dimitri, as I am told, never knew about me. My mother, Gabriella, is the sister of my uncle, Qaseem. He was the Emir to Qatar. He and Dimitri were very close and spent a significant amount of time together many years ago. My uncle has since passed, and I have been given the task of giving your grandmother Dimitri's belongings and inheritance. You see, my uncle was in love with Dimitri and his love never faded. Their love was a forbidden love in my country. This was very difficult for Dimitri because his love for Qaseem was all consuming. He was in constant despair about being the hidden lover as he watched Qaseem, the Emir, take many women companions as a facade. After many months of this and in a complete state of sorrow, Dimitri disappeared and no one ever heard from him again. After years of searching, Qaseem found out that Dimitri had died along with his wife, Katrina, and your great-grandparents, George and Sophia. This made Julia, your grandmother, the successor to Dimitri's inheritance. This is really confusing and very convoluted, I know. But it was Qaseem's dying wish to give Julia Dimitri's inheritance. Please, can we talk in person? Can you meet me after the conference?"

Pearl sat up straight, took a sip of wine, and pondered this thought. She knew Dimitri didn't have a son; this was a fact. So, who was this guy? She stared up at the Parthenon as the evening floodlights surrounding it flashed on, bringing the ruins to life. It was so calming to see the soft lights playing on the walls of the Parthenon as the stars woke up each evening. She could sense every tourist in town marveling at the great sight before them. The magical mountain with giant white pillars made the bewitching hour more mystical.

As the silence became uncomfortable, Alexander said," Hello? Are you still there?"

"Yes, yes. Sorry. So, I know for a fact that Dimitri did not have a son. Are you sure you have the right family?" and before he could answer the question she said, a bit agitated, "I guess you must because you just named them all, huh? How did you get this number?"

Alexander took a long breath, "Pearl, please – can we meet tomorrow? I have some things I want to show you. I promise this will all make sense after we meet. I just sent you my info. You can research me and my family, and I am sure you will feel differently about our meeting after you do so. OK?"

Alexander's tone seemed desperate, but the conference was more important to Pearl than meeting with a stranger on a quest to meet her family. Everyone wanted to meet Julia. Could this be just another paparazzi with an elaborate story who wanted an autograph and a picture with her? It had happened many times before. But the curiosity of Alexander's story intrigued her. She answered, "Fine, I will look at the information you sent and decide if I want to meet with you. If I do, it will be after the conference. This is putting me in a hard spot. My obligations and schedule this weekend are pretty tight already. Text me your contact number and the number to your hotel. I will get back to you tomorrow evening." Pearl hung up and ordered another glass of wine. She leaned back in her chair and looked up into the fading night sky. The sun had set, but dusk was still hiding the stars. It was her favorite time of the day. She listened to the street cars below and the faint voices and laughter from the patrons around her. Her phone chimed several times; it was Alexander sending her his information as promised.

One of the waiters, a dear friend, joined her, "Pearl, are you OK, love?"

"Yeah. The strangest thing just happened. I received a phone call from a man named Alexander. He is in town wanting to meet with my Nonnah Julia about an inheritance of some kind. He says Dimitri, a friend of my great-grandparents, is his father. I have heard many stories about Dimitri over the years, but none about him having a child. My great-grandpa George and Dimitri were inseparable growing up. Dimitri and his wife are actually buried next to my great-grandparents in a small family cemetery next to my home, along with my grandpa Daniel, Nonnah's husband. Anyway, the phone call caught me off-guard. He said he would send me some personal info. I will look him up and figure it out later. No need to worry, really – I am good."

Pearl shook it off and changed the subject, "I am so excited about tomorrow's seminar! I need to go over Julia's work one more time before tomorrow morning. I am presenting for her. She is in

Egypt, and I am sure I am going to be asked a million questions by a million people, first being, *Where is she?"*

Her friend said, "Wow! You know what? I will be right back." Pearl watched her disappear into the kitchen. When her friend reappeared, she was holding a bottle of cold ouzo, the famous Greek liquor known as heaven in a glass, "Nightcap, my friend?"

Pearl's smile widened as she exclaimed, "ABSOLUTLEY!" They giggled as the clear liquor was poured over the ice, turning it into a milky white, delicious treat.

When the meal was done, Pearl headed back to her room. All she could think about was this Alexander character. *Who was he really? Was his story true? Was he really Dimitri's son?* As she entered her room, she quickly found her tablet and typed in the information Alexander had forwarded her. Page after page she scrolled through saying, "Holy shit! Are you kidding me? What the hell? No way! Oh my god!" with her hand over her mouth.

She had to talk to Julia. She knew Julia and her parents would be asleep at this hour, but that didn't stop her from calling. There was no answer, so she left a message saying, "Nonnah, this is Pearl. I had a very interesting phone call today from a man by the name of Alexander from Qatar. He is looking for you. He claims to be Dimitri's son. He is here in Athens and has a package for you. He said his uncle, the Emir to Qatar, was a good friend of Dimitri's. He wants to meet with me. Do you know anything about this? Please call me when you have a chance. The first speaker takes the stage at 9:00 a.m. tomorrow morning. I will have my phone off for most of the morning and afternoon so call before 8:00 a.m. or after 10:00 p.m. I am going to text you Alexander's information. I love you. Tell Mom and Dad hi." She hung up. Exhausted, she plopped back on her pillow with her hands behind her head, staring up at the ceiling. She thought, *Emir of Qatar? What the hell! These are some good family secrets. What did I miss?* As the exhaustion, wine, and ouzo settled in, Pearl fell asleep.

Chapter Three

Julia woke up bright and early to the obnoxious sound of her phone alarm. As she silenced it, she noticed she had a missed call. *Pearl*, she thought, and sure enough it was. She swiped up, pressed play, and listened to the voice message. When it was over, she looked at Charlee then back at her phone. She swung her feet from the bed and onto the floor then began wandering around as if she were in the dark. "Where is the computer, Charlee? I cannot see anything on this phone; the screen is too small. And where in the heck are my glasses?"

Charlee stretched and yawned then sat up to see Julia fumbling around the room, "What's the matter? Are you OK?"

"I am not sure. Pearl left me a weird voicemail last night. Here, listen to it and please turn on the computer while I go to the bathroom."

"Is Pearl OK? What happened?"

"Yes, yes, she is OK. She sent me some information about a man claiming to be Dimitri's son and something about needing to talk to her or me. I do not know. I need to look him up. But first I need to pee!" As Julia headed to the bathroom she asked, "Where is Mathias?"

"He got up early to go for a jog. He'll be back in about an hour," Charlee replied.

Charlee scrambled through her tote for her laptop. She set the computer on the desk and powered it up. She made two cups of coffee and joined Julia at the desk as she thumbed through the text messages on her phone. Julia took a big swallow of coffee, then started typing the information Pearl had sent her into the computer. With a gasp, she looked up at Charlee.

"What? Julia, what?"

Julia sat back in her chair and said, "Oh my god, Charlee! Dimitri, well, I am really not sure... but I think... it cannot be... I mean... NO!"

Charlee reached for the computer to see what the heck was going on.

Julia continued to stutter, "I am not sure how, or I mean *how* but… oh for crap's sake!" She turned to face Charlee, and in true Greek fashion she got up and paced the floor, talking with animated arms and hand gestures as she proceeded to tell the story. "Pearl got a phone call from a man claiming to be Dimitri's son. As far as I know there was no child, there is no child. He and Katrina tried for years, but she could never conceive. BUT, the story goes, Dimitri had a lover in Qatar. At the time, this lover was a very important prince, and this prince went on to become the Emir of Qatar. His name was Qaseem, if I remember correctly. Charlee, much of our early fortune comes from Dimitri. My parents never really knew how or what actually took place between the two of them, but it was definitely a romantic relationship. Dimitri left a note and a lot of money, gold, lose jewels, and artifacts for my grandfather when he died. Charlee, it was enough to run a small country. Anyway, this man called Pearl, looking for me." She held out her phone to Charlee, "Here, just listen to her voicemail."

When Charlee heard the name Alexander she paused, knitted her eyebrows, and cocked her head to the side as she stared at Julia. "There's that name again. Julia, do you know an Alexander?"

Before she could answer, Mathias entered the room. He was sweaty and clearly ready for a shower after his morning run. Both women turned and looked at him with confusion on their faces. He looked at his watch and said, "Babe, I did say I would be back in an hour. It has only been 55 minutes."

Charlee chuckled, waved him over, and said, "No, honey, come here and look at this."

Mathias sat down and listened to the phone message from Pearl. When he heard the name Alexander, he quickly turned and looked at Charlee. She knew exactly what he was thinking. He took the computer and read the first few paragraphs about the Emir named Alexander then said, "Mom, is he talking about our Dimitri, the one buried next to Pop?"

Julia shrugged her shoulders and said, "Yes, I assume so."

Mathias listened to the message again, "This is either some bizarre synchronicity or a very strange coincidence. I think we need to meet this Alexander. This is the second time this name has crossed our radar. Do we know an Alexander?"

Julia shook her head no.

Chapter Four

The next morning Pearl got up and spent an hour trying to decide what outfit to wear. For the first time in her career, she was going to be one of the star speakers at a very prestigious conference, one that would be televised worldwide. This was going to be her moment. The academics in this field were known to be very exclusive and very pompous, so she needed to stand out enough to be recognized, yet conservative enough to warrant respect. First impressions amongst her peers could make or break her career. Her attire had to be just right.

Pearl had the body of a supermodel; a long, elegant neck, broad shoulders, perfect B-cup breasts, and a slim waist. She walked tall with conviction, and many times appeared to be unapproachable. She was like a box of chocolates; you never knew which Pearl you were going to get – the woman, the warrior, the lover, or the girlfriend. She had the keen ability to read the room and become the aspect of herself that fit the circumstances. Her presence changed the vibration wherever she was. She made you forget what you were thinking about when she stepped into your presence. It didn't matter what outfit she chose; she would look fantastic in a paper bag.

She chose a dark navy suit with a soft pink blouse and a string of pearls, her favorite, of course. Before she left the room, she did a quick review of her speech material and a last brief glance in the mirror. She took a deep breath, gave herself a big smile, and left her hotel room. She was ready. She had a nice breakfast up on the terrace restaurant then walked the eight blocks to the conference center while practicing her speech.

When she arrived, she took her seat near the front and texted Alexander, agreeing to meet with him late Monday morning after the weekend events ended. The excitement of the conference was now overshadowed by this new information from Alexander. She thought her Nonnah and parents running around Egypt was weird enough, and a bit crazy, then to throw this in the mix was mind boggling. For now, she needed to concentrate on each presenter's material for Julia. Each presenter had a different twist on the same subject matter; who was The Silver Pharoah and did he truly have the key to immortality with him in this box? She thought it strange that the syllabus was set up to have a series of academics state their theories about the myths surrounding this pharaoh when it could all be a moot point when the lid was removed. To her, that was a lot of unnecessary work if proven wrong. She couldn't help but remember the terrifying nightmare she'd had for months claiming that the guy in the box might still be alive. It made her shudder. As with all puzzles and great secrets, a little drama and a scary story kept this myth intriguing and nail-biting while waiting to find out if it were true.

As she sat in the dark listening to each speaker present their research on the pharaoh and his life, she found herself staring at her phone, going down the rabbit hole on Google, consuming everything there was to know about Alexander and his family. She no longer noticed the crowded room filled with media, TV cameras, and the hundreds of people from all walks of life who wanted to know the secret to immortality.

At one point her name was called. When she didn't answer, the lights went up in the house to find her. Completely absorbed in her Alexander research, she didn't hear or notice the change in the room and the lights going up.

A bystander tapped her shoulder and asked, "Are you Pearl?"

Startled, she looked up and said, "Yes. Yes, I am." She looked around and realized every eye in the room was on her. She stood up, collected her thoughts, and walked on stage toward the podium.

Behind the podium was a large pull-down screen. Julia's face was being shared with a caption, *Renowned author, herbologist, physicist, and chemist, Julia Kaya from Ikaria.* Pearl had planned for this moment for weeks, sharing the spotlight with Julia, but now she walked to the podium alone. She was presenting material from the recent peer reviewed studies Julia had just finished for publication.

She began, "Hello, ladies and gentlemen. My name is Pearl Kaya, and I will be presenting for Julia, my grandmother. With the recent information that was obtained from the treasures found in The

Silver Pharaoh's belongings, we know that we are on the cusp of something spectacular. Today I want to talk to you about what true immortality would look like and how the human body could successfully function as it does today, but for eternity. Is it possible to transform the bodies we live in now, with their existing chemical makeup and biology, into a body that lives forever?"

Julia's research was geared toward the biology of the human body and its relationship to nature. No one else was covering this area. Pearl had everyone's attention. She read the room and knew what to do. She wanted to be remembered, and this was her moment to shine. Smiling inside, she ended her speech with the fantastical story her great-grandmother Sophia had shared with Julia about Psusennes and Priya's mythical love story, and the couple's connection to the heavenly realm. After she finished, she looked out into the crowd. Every mouth was open, and the room was silent. Slowly, she scanned the audience with a contemplative look on her face. Knitting her eyebrows and cocking her head to the side, she could see the anticipation building in the audience's faces. When she had everyone transfixed, she said slowly with an edge to it, "Angels do not die. The myth suggests that Psusennes is still alive, in suspended animation. Alive, in this sarcophagus, right here on this stage, waiting for her. There is not one documented curse wrapped around this pharaoh as was King Tut, but it is said that only she, Priya, is to open this box."

Pearl snapped out of her acting moment, smiled big, and said, "Ladies and gentlemen, I am as anxious as you are to see what is inside. Let's hope he is not too upset, if he is alive, that it was us who opened his box and not Priya. Thank you!" Pearl stood at the podium for few seconds longer, staring out at the speechless crowd. You could hear a pin drop in the room. Several people squirmed in their seats. Pearl smiled, pleased with herself as she gathered her things and turned to exit the stage. If there was one speech that would be remembered at the end of this four-day conference, it was going to be hers! There was silence in the room for at least ten seconds after Pearl finished, then a standing ovation and a round of applause filled the room. Ten seconds later, the room was abuzz, everyone talking to each other at once. After a few bows and a big *thank you* to the audience, she returned to her seat. Her whole life, Julia had prepared her for this seminar, whether she knew it or not. Every bedtime story was about The Silver Pharaoh and now she was in the same room with him, giving the biggest talk of her career, and all she could think about was Alexander and his story and, of course, a healthy curiosity about whether or not the pharaoh *was* alive.

When the final speaker of the day approached the stage, all the lights in the house were turned off and a gigantic movie screen was lowered from the ceiling. The speaker, a distinguished Egyptologist with over forty years of experience working with mummies, clicked the handheld device and filled the screen with eleven different x-rays and CT scans of the pharaoh in the sealed sarcophagus. Interestingly, it showed his hands sitting crossed on his chest, but no other bones were present, as if he was wearing a cloaking device. Where his skull should be was a metal mask and a round metal box with a cord protruding from it, connecting it to the hands of the mummy as if he was holding it in place. The speaker had no explanation for it other than it might be an anomaly caused by the scanners. The speaker turned the photos on the screen in several different directions as if playing a video game, but unfortunately, they didn't give a clear and concise picture of what was in the sarcophagus other than two hands, a mask of some sort, and a round metal box with a cord.

Many of the audience members took this time to take a bathroom and beverage break while the last speaker finished his presentation. Pearl decided to join them. She took a few minutes to email Julia the entire syllabus of the conference and the research material being presented by each speaker, along with the file containing the x-rays and CT scans. She spent the next 45 minutes nursing a glass of wine and answering questions about the myth her Nonnah told and its relevance to the unveiling. By the time the break was over, Pearl realized she had planted such huge expectations in these people's minds, and she hoped she hadn't ruined the whole experience for them. There was a true possibility that the unveiling would be anticlimactic. Most of the mummies found were just that – mummies wrapped in old rags with stretched, dried up skin, bones protruding through bandages that came loose and, for the most part, it was like, "OK, there it is, a mummy," then taking a few pictures and everyone was off to the next big adventure. These people were now expecting this pharaoh to get up and walk away. Yikes!

When the final speaker was finished, Pearl and the rest of the academics, along with a huge equipment crew, spent the next two hours preparing the stage and auditorium for the unveiling. Ladders, cranes, pulley systems, cameras, tools of all sorts, and lighting systems were put into place. Large suction cup structures were placed around the sarcophagus, gripping the lid to pull it off in one giant tug. The equipment was bulky and enormous. The media scurried around on the floor taking pictures from every angle, and electrical cords snaked everywhere. By the time the stage was ready, the only way the audience was going to see the unveiling was from the large, elevated monitors surrounding the auditorium ceiling.

By 6:30 p.m. the doors were opened and the crowds returned. Over 1,500 people were packed into the auditorium where there was standing room only. Everyone was trying to get as close to the stage as possible. Pearl made a quick sweep around the room, vying for a place of her own. The only people allowed on the stage were the crane operators and the Egyptologists with their photographers.

Pearl looked up and scanned the ceiling area of the stage. High above the stage was a scaffolding system used for maintenance purposes, lighting systems, and the big projector screens. "Yes!" she said out loud. That was to be her spot. It gave her a bird's-eye view directly into the sarcophagus with no obstruction. And it was hidden enough to take as many pictures as she wanted without having to share her photos with the Egyptologists prior to leaving the seminar. *So ridiculous*, she thought, *that everyone has to sign a waiver claiming any photos taken during the unveiling was subject to confiscation.*

Her new hiding place was perfect. The air conditioning system was running at full capacity, keeping the room at a consistent 68 degrees. 1,500 cell phones with cameras engaged were snapping up memories as they pushed in even tighter to get the best view. Pearl wondered how the authorities were going to take even one of the 1,500 cell phone cameras. Talk about an instant riot!

At 7:00 p.m., the moment had finally arrived. The archeologist who found The Silver Pharoah's secret hiding place prepared the audience for the unveiling. He asked that everyone stay calm and keep their focus on the screens above them. Staying out of sight, Pearl navigated the dark hallway to the stairs leading to the precariously hanging metal walkway dangling high over the stage. When she got to the top of the stairs, she looked down, not realizing how high her secret viewing platform was. She could feel her heart pounding as she took a big breath and squeezed herself through the railing onto the scaffolding. When she secured herself in place, she got comfortable.

Indeed, she did have a direct view right above the pharaoh. She held on tight to the railing and leaned over, her hair dangling down the sides of her face with her eyes wide open as she carefully balanced, waiting with her camera ready.

The speaker looked back at the crew and got a thumbs up. He turned to the audience, "Ladies and gentlemen, please turn off your cameras!" He gave the audience a big smile then, with a theatrical countdown, he started, "10, 9, 8, 7, 6, 5, 4, 3, 2," and when he got to 1, the lights dramatically shut off. The crowd squirmed as the anticipation was at its peak. The only glint of light came from the hallways of the open doors. Just as dramatically, the floodlights snapped on. The audience gasped as the stage and sarcophagus lit up like the Northern star. A loud "OOOOOOH" came from the audience. The suspense was almost unbearable. The crane engine started with a loud grinding sound as the suction cups gripped tighter onto the lid. The audience was reminded again to stay calm as the lid began to move. No one breathed, not even Pearl. Slowly, the lid separated itself and when it did, it was as if someone opened the emergency door in an airplane in full flight! All the air in the room rushed forward with gale force winds into the sarcophagus. People were abruptly thrown forward, tumbling onto each other in piles on the floor. A split second later, a loud piercing bang with a blinding light exploded from the coffin, sending a shockwave through the room, reversing the energy and throwing the audience backward on top of the people behind them. Everyone was holding their ears, screaming and running to get out of the room, trampling anyone beneath them.

Pearl grabbed the metal bars of the scaffolding and held on for dear life as she watched the lid fly off and land on the side of the crane, dangling precariously. Everyone standing on the stage was thrown off their feet, landing ten feet away, equipment tumbling all around them. Pearl, eyes wide open, stared down into the box as the light diminished and the atomic bomb-like energy settled down.

Staring up at her was Psusennes. Pearl didn't blink an eye. She was paralyzed, her eyes glued to his. In her mind, she heard him say, *You are the chosen one, Pearl. Thank you. We will meet again when The Phoenix returns. You are safe. Find Alexander.* He then evaporated into a fine mist as his essence shot up into the air toward Pearl. Pearl gasped as his spirit raged through her. She instantly felt pain at the back of her neck and fell onto the narrow beam of the scaffolding she was balancing on. She had been holding her breath, and when she let it out, she leaned back against the railing and watched Psusennes' swirling white energy engulf her and the scaffolding as it left the room abruptly through the ceiling. All that was left in the sarcophagus was a golden pharaoh's mask that had been covering his face, along with a brilliant shimmering white sheet that was sparkling as if diamonds were woven into it.

When he was gone, Pearl looked down at the chaos below her. People were frantically running over the top of each other, shoving, pushing, and yelling. Many people stood motionless while crying, in shock. The security guards were trying their best to help people up and bring order to the room. It was if an earthquake had occurred and people were running for dear life. Pearl's colleagues got up from the floor and ran back to the sarcophagus to get a look inside. At the moment the lid flew off, one of Pearl's colleagues on the floor had looked up and saw her dangling high above the sarcophagus. Pearl was the only one who'd had a bird's-eye view of it all.

Dizzy and nauseated, Pearl slowly made her way down the ladder to the back of the stage where her things were. She quickly collected her purse, briefcase, and bottle of water then left the building unnoticed. She stumbled eight blocks back to her hotel in a daze, her head pounding. When she got to her room, full of fear, she rushed in, locked the door, then leaned against it as she slid to the floor. *What had just happened?* A piercing sound began in both ears and the spot on the back of her neck felt as if it was on fire. She reached back to feel the area and although painful to touch, there was no blood. Had she bumped the back of her neck on the scaffolding when she fell? She couldn't remember. Fumbling through her briefcase she found aspirin and downed two of them with her water.

She could still see his eyes and hear his words as he permeated her while disappearing into the ceiling. *Where was he now? Was he looking for her?* She started to cry, holding her legs close to her chest while trying to get as small as she could. When she heard a knock on the door, a woman's voice said, "Open the door, Pearl, you are safe." She started shaking, fear overtaking her. Pearl's head was splitting and the nausea was intense. The room was blurry and her vision was chaotic. Pearl stood up and turned around as a woman appeared in front of her with emerald-green eyes, speaking words that were in-audible to Pearl's ears. She took Pearl's hand and placed something in it. Then she was gone. Pearl fell back to the floor and held her head in her hands as she moaned in pain. Her mouth started salivating and the tears began to flow harder. She knew she was going to throw up. She tried to stand, but the pain increased. She got on all fours and slowly crawled toward the bathroom. Her eyes clouded over and before she could make it to the commode, she passed out.

Chapter Five

When Pearl awoke, she was on the floor in a pile of vomit with the sun shining on her through the hotel window. Her headache was gone, but the brain fog was still there and the spot on the back of her neck still burned. She tried to remember the details of the conference, but all she could piece together was everyone screaming and running, and his voice in her head. She remembered someone knocking on her door shortly after she arrived back in her room, but she couldn't remember who. It didn't matter; all that mattered was that something in that sarcophagus was alive and he had looked into her eyes and said, *"You are the chosen one, Pearl. We will meet again when the Pheonix returns. You are safe. Find Alexander."* Over and over, she heard his words. But what frightened her most was hearing, "You are safe." Safe from what?

She found her phone and was startled to see it was Sunday morning. She had been on the floor for over 36 hours. She had slept straight through Saturday and into Sunday morning. Her phone had ten voicemail messages, a string of emails, and pages of text messages with several videos, all from Friday night. She opened one of the videos and watched Friday evening's horror take place. She put her hand over her mouth in shock. Message after message, her desperate and frantic colleagues were asking where she was, if she was all right, what had happened, and what it was she had seen. When Pearl was done reading all the messages, she looked at the time stamp. They all came in between 8:00 p.m. and 8:30 p.m. Friday night. After 8:30, there were none.

Pearl cleaned up the dried vomit on the floor then took a long hot shower, washing the remnants of vomit from her hair. With a small mirror, she tried to see the spot on the back of her neck that had been bothering her, but all she could make out was a large red area that resembled a burn mark. She put on some ointment she had in her purse and when she was done, she wrapped herself in the hotel robe and laid back on the bed. Slowly, her strength was returning and she could hear her empty belly calling for food. But it wasn't food that was motivating her at this moment, it was her wanting answers to a ton of questions.

Pearl called Doris, one of Julia's closest colleagues that had been present at the conference. Doris was also in a daze. She said she left the event Friday night, went home, and got sick. She said she spent most of Saturday in bed, flipping through the news stations, trying to recall exactly what had happened. But there was nothing. Not one station was covering the event or what had happened.

Doris said, "Pearl, I called every one of our colleagues yesterday, I mean the whole damn crew, and no one can piece together what happened. When they showed up to the conference hall late Saturday afternoon, there was nothing on the stage. No equipment, no sarcophagus, no audience chairs, nothing. It was empty, and no one took responsibility for cleaning it all up. I mean no one, not even the hotel staff or security guards. No one can wrap their heads around it! All we can remember in detail was people running, pushing, and shoving each other as they screamed, trying to get out of the building. As far as we can tell, no one was hurt or taken to the hospital. It is so crazy! It is as if there was a time warp of some kind." Pearl shared her story of two nights on the floor with the same outcome, along with a fuzzy memory. Pearl asked her what everyone's plans were for the remainder of the conference.

Doris let out a quick laugh then said, "Everyone left. They all went home! It is as if it never happened. I am going to have to see a therapist next week. I feel like I am going crazy!"

When the phone call ended, Pearl lay back on her bed, trying to remember. As each minute passed, her memory got weaker. It was like waking from a dream. The details were memorable upon waking, but within a few minutes, the memory and the details were gone. She thought about calling Julia but decided not to. What was she going to say?

Chapter Six

Starving, Pearl got dressed and went upstairs to the terrace restaurant for some air and an early lunch. On her way up, Alexander texted, asking for a time on Monday when she would be available to meet. She ran her fingers through her hair, thought for a minute then decided it was the perfect opportunity to take her mind off current events. She texted back, asking to meet with him today if he was interested in an earlier appointment. She had been so irritated with this man on Friday, but for some reason today she felt it necessary to meet this man named Alexander. They planned to meet at 1:00 p.m. on the stage at the Acropolis, the huge outdoor stadium that was built centuries ago. She felt safe meeting this stranger in a wide-open space. If she needed to scream for help, all of Athens would hear her. The Acropolis theater has some of the best acoustics in the world!

At 1:00 p.m., with the sun shining hot onto the giant, ancient theater, Pearl found her caller sitting in the shade in the middle of the stage. Papers, photographs, and letters were scattered, yet in somewhat of an organized mess. When he saw her coming, he stood and waited then stuck out his hand as she got closer. With the sun blocking his view, he said, "Pearl?"

She replied, "Yes, that is me." She shook his hand and looked up into his eyes. She was immediately transfixed. She stood staring at him, almost paralyzed as strange emotions emerged from the depths of her soul. His eyes were a very light, mesmerizing emerald green. She felt as if she knew him and suddenly felt unusually comfortable in his presence, yet the vulnerability that began to overwhelm her made her uncomfortable.

Alexander strangely felt the same way. Something about her made him feel as if they had met before. He quickly searched his memory with no results.

Realizing she had been holding his hand for an uncomfortable amount of time, she abruptly pulled her hand back and regained her composure. She quickly looked down at the organized mess of material at her feet. He just stared at her. She was beautiful. Her soft blonde hair had tiny ringlets that trickled her face and cascaded down her back. It glowed as the sun blanketed her from behind. She was 5'5'', very petite, and had eyes the color of a clear, turquoise ocean. Without a stitch of makeup on, she looked like an angel, but her demeanor didn't match her lovely appearance. She dropped her bag, and with her hands on her hips she said, "Now tell me what is going on. What is this about? Why so secretive?" She waited about ten seconds as he tried to formulate his words. Just as he was about to speak, she continued, "Why could you not tell me any of this on the phone? I had a very important engagement this weekend, and your mysterious phone call really messed with my head. I needed to be on top of my game, and you really screwed that up! I have not been able to think about anything else since you called. My mind is all jumbled up because of you!" As soon as the words came out of her mouth, she realized she was deflecting and being unbelievably harsh to this man standing before her.

Alexander crossed his arms and just stared at her with a confused look on his face. He was a handsome man with slightly darker skin and jet-black hair with a few strands of grey peeking through. He had it pulled back in a ponytail, and it looked to be about shoulder length. He had a dark, groomed mustache and a strong, chiseled jawline with a slight five o'clock shadow. He wore a crisp white, button-down shirt, black tailored pants, and shiny black loafers. He stood staring at her blankly, startled at her demeanor. Why was she yelling at him? He was thankful she had dropped her purse instead of whacking him with it!

It was a standoff. Who was going to talk first? He wasn't sure what to say to her. At this point he was more concerned about how to start the conversation regarding his presence in Athens. He stood staring at her while trying to find and choose his next words carefully. Feeling the air thicken around her, Pearl took a quick breath as she took a step back. She stuttered nervously, not saying anything co-herent, lowering her eyes, bending down then started sifting through the pictures before he had a chance to answer her questions. As she moved the piles around, she recognized the people in the pictures. She calmed herself and slowly said, "These are pictures of my family. This one looks like Dimitri." She held up the pictures and looked at them closer. The pictures were old and her family was very young in them. She realized these pictures were taken well before she was born. "Why do you have these?" She stood back up slowly and nervously looked around as if she was being watched. She immediately felt uncomfortable. The pit in her stomach she had been carrying around since Friday was back.

Alexander collected himself, brushed his hands together as if something were on them, and firmly said, "You are safe, Pearl, I promise! Please just sit down and listen for a minute."

This got Pearl's attention. She said harshly, as she looked around, "Safe from what?" She instantly felt fear at this moment. This was the second time in two days she was told she was safe. Everything was a jumbled mess in her mind. She lowered her eyes as he raised his hands, showing her that he didn't have anything up his sleeve.

Guardedly, she did as he asked and sat down. As she did, she noticed a box sitting off to the side. It was old, tattered, and had enough old yellowing tape on it to wrap four packages. She reached over and started to pick it up when he yelled, "Wait!"

Startled, she whipped around and said, "WHAT? What the hell?" Her mounting anxiety was getting the best of her. Her instinct at this moment was to run, to leave and wait for Julia to deal with this.

He saw the fear in her eyes and was concerned. He said quietly and calmly, "Just sit for a minute, please. I have come a long way to be here with you and I have spent years researching your family. Please slow down and just listen."

Feeling his sincerity, she took a big cleansing breath and said, "OK, OK. I am sorry. It has been a strange few days, and I am already on edge." She took another deep breath, relaxed, sat down, and got comfortable amongst the paperwork.

Alexander, relieved at the change in character, smiled softly then told her a story she had never heard before. He carefully began the story saying, "Pearl, I am looking for information about Dimitri and his life. He was my father. When Dimitri was 18, he met my Uncle

Qaseem, who was a wealthy prince in Qatar at the time. They had a very secret love affair. In my country, this type of relationship is punishable by death. When people began to question Qaseem's relationship with Dimitri, my uncle took on a harem of women as wives to mask his love for a man. This destroyed Dimitri and he abruptly left the country, but not before he had a drunken 'one night stand' as you call it, with my mother, Gabriella, the prince's sister. Unbeknownst to Dimitri, Qaseem had already spoken to Gabriella about giving him a child by Dimitri. This way Dimitri's presence would remain unquestioned in Qaseem's world.

When Gabriella found out she was pregnant with me, she knew it would thrill Qaseem. She knew of Qaseem and Dimitri's affair; she had actually helped hide the affair and became the liaison for them. When she told Qaseem of her pregnancy, he was quite joyful that Dimitri had a blood heir to his fortune and a solid place in the family tree. But, of course, this could never be professed out loud. Out of wedlock and with Dimitri gone, Gabriella needed to hide the pregnancy, so my uncle found a suitor for her and they married immediately. As far as anyone knew, she went into early labor and had me. Your great-grandmother, Sophia, and her best friend, Katrina, helped my mother through her pregnancy. They were all very close. Sophia and Katrina were like mother-figures to Gabriella.

Unfortunately, my mother died in a plane crash when I was two, and her husband died from cancer shortly after so my Uncle Qaseem raised me. For years I watched my uncle secretly search for Dimitri, the love of his life, and when he finally found out where he had been, Dimitri had long since passed away. He was devastated at the news of Dimitri's death. At this point in his life, my uncle's health was declining, and I truly believe it was the search for his long-lost love that had kept him alive as long as it did.

I am the only child that came from that union. I sit before you today, the son of Dimitri and the heir to his lover's fortune, my Uncle Qaseem's, but this is not the only reason I am here today. It is to explain all this to Julia and to give her what is in these boxes and the envelopes that go with them."

When Alexander was done with his story, Pearl was speechless. She sat down and started examining each picture slowly while

Alexander sat beside her. Her anxiety of meeting him was waning. As he talked, she felt his sincerity and it calmed her. She said, "OK, let's back up a bit on your story. Dimitri had an affair with the Prince of Qatar. Are you a prince?"

Alexander handed her an old journal. "This will explain everything. It was Dimitri's journal. Katrina, who became his wife, found it years ago. She knew his heart was with Qaseem, but she married him anyway. That is another story that will make sense after you read his journal. Take a few minutes to read a couple pages while I am gone. I am going to go get us some coffee across the street. Is there anything else I can get you?"

She said, "Thank you, no, coffee is fine. Cream and sugar please."

He stood and started to leave, turned, and said, "What I am about to say will make sense after you read his journal. Your great-grandmother, Sophia, had a very illusive and somewhat scandalous past in Qatar. She and Katrina, the woman who took care of my mother while pregnant with me, and who married your great-grandfather, George, were the keys that helped me find your family and to somewhat make sense of all of this. Like you, I was kept in the dark about our families until recently. When my uncle's will was read, I knew I had to fulfill his wishes. Before you start reading, I warn you; you must have an open mind. It is both a beautiful and shocking story at the same time. I hope you realize, as I have, that the love they had for each other was very special and it lasted a lifetime. Our families are intertwined in ways that are somewhat remarkable and un-believable. I am here for answers, Pearl, nothing else." With that, Alexander turned and walked away.

Chapter Seven

The journal binding was made of soft old leather. Pearl ran her hand over the binding then smelled it. She loved the moldy smell of old books. A frayed string, tightly knotted, kept it closed. The pages were yellowed, and some of the writing was smeared but legible. Pearl leaned back against the upper step and turned page after page as Dimitri's words tugged at her heart.

I am Dimitri, and this is my story…

I have never thought about journaling, putting my thoughts down on paper. My thoughts are so confusing and sinful that I could not bear sharing them with a piece of paper that someone else might read. I figured they were safer inside my head. But my head is full and the sorrow I feel in my heart is quite heavy and deep. If I could, I would cut a hole in both my heart and my head so the pain could pour out onto the ground, absorbing into the soil. This would be my wish. But knowing this is impossible, I have no choice but to rid this chapter of my life from my throbbing head by writing it down, removing the story, from beginning to end, from my brain in the hope of starting fresh… or to just end it all….

After months of working in the Persian Gulf, reshaping and rebuilding the submerged, crumbled foundation of an old abandon fortress, I decided to treat myself to an afternoon at the races. The unbearable heat beating down on me each day as I worked the stones was exhausting. The only relief from the penetrating heat was the sea. Being a mason with underwater skills was a blessing. The cool waters keep me from having sun stroke daily. Thank God for the sea! I have spent years working as a mason with my father on the edge of the oceans, restoring ancient castles, walls, boat docks, and riverways. Any job that required a mason with expert skills in the use of under-

water dynamite was a job we were called to do. Very few of us have these skills – actually only nine men that I know of – and together we work these jobs around the world. Qatar is by far one of the hardest places to work due to the heat, but it pays the best.

Besides the beautiful Persian Gulf, Qatar is home to some of the best Arabian horses in the world. My dad used to take me to this place when I was a boy, before the racetrack even existed. It had been a barren land of rolling hills blanketed with dry, wheat-colored grasses. Radiating waves of heat rising high above the ground scorched anything green that dared to grow. Not a bug was in sight. Yet, like a far-off oasis, a small swath of green peaked up out of the dry, brittle land. It was quite an anomaly.

It was here that years ago my father built the most exquisite family estate for the Emir. Everyone thought the Emir was crazy, but he had a secret. He knew what was under that patch of green. He knew that water was in abundance there. Once built, the estate was vast with several large buildings. Fronting the enormous house and buildings, a huge Arabian horse racetrack was built. I love the horse races and learned how to bet on them years ago with my father. The excitement of the packed crowd on their feet cheering, "Go, Go, Go," spilling their drinks, and shoving and bumping into one another while cheering on their favorite horse is electric! When the horses 'round the last bend on to the final stretch, the roar of the crowd intensifies as they wave their hopefully winning tickets in the air. The loud, thunderous rumble beneath our seats as the horses pass us in full stride, thrusting their heads forward and backward, nostrils flaring, hooves kicking up dust, eyes focused, and their coats glistening with sweat is exhilarating!

As usual, I did not have a ticket to get into the stands, but I knew the back way into the arena. I squeezed through the chain link fence behind the bleachers. Its opening was just big enough for me to get my head through, allowing my body to follow. I found a shaded seat in the bleachers and watched the horses prance around, getting ready to race as the early morning sun cast its penetrating heatwaves down onto them.

As the horses and trainers prepared for the next run, my eye caught the prince, the son of the Emir, standing on the racetrack and looking into the stands. He looked up in my direction and tipped his chin for recognition. I looked around as if his eye contact were near me. I was alone. I looked back toward him; he was still looking up at me. He made a hand motion and a woman appeared next to him. She leaned in to listen then turned to look up in my direction. She nodded and headed toward me. I did not know whether to run or stay. I had an uneasy feeling that I was in trouble even though I was not doing anything wrong. I had not talked to anyone since I arrived. I was just as innocent as the rest of the spectators in the stands but without a ticket. How would the prince know I did not have a ticket?

Nonetheless, I gathered my things and headed toward the crowds and away from the back stable entrance. As I passed the stable doors, a large man with a handheld radio abruptly stopped me. He grabbed my arm and gruffly said, "Be still."

I swallowed hard and was about to ask why when the same woman talking to the prince was at my side. Softly she said, "Hello – welcome. The Prince would like your presence in the inner stables. He is anxious to meet with you."

"Am I in trouble?"

Sweetly she said, "No, no. This in an honor. No one is allowed into the stables except his Excellency's private personnel. Will you join me? Will you join him?" She stood smiling at me like a little girl looking for a playmate in the schoolyard. I stood in disbelief, con-fused. I nodded as she took my arm. "He will be arriving shortly; in the meantime, I was given permission to give you a tour. Are you interested?"

I nodded again. Her nametag read 'Gabriella'. She was at least 6-foot tall. As she stood in front of me, I could look directly into her dark indigo eyes. I had never seen eyes this color, the color of the Aegean Sea in its depths. I lowered my eyes before she did. She had a pretty smile and a gentle demeanor. Her hands and fingers were soft and delicate as she moved them through the air like a ballerina on the stage. Her dark, shiny hair was tied in a tight knot at the base of her neck. By the size of it, her hair must have fallen to her waist when relaxed. Soft chestnut, sun-steaked trendles framed her face and gently danced around her temples in the warm afternoon breeze. She wore the traditional riding garments that accentuated her small waist and

41

broad shoulders. I guessed her to be about 20 years old. In my entire 18 years, I think she was the only woman I ever felt the desire to kiss.

"My name is Gabriella. I am the Prince's sister. I love the Americans so forgive me for holding your arm as we walk. I have seen this in the movies. I quite like the idea of a private escort that holds the arm of the person you are 'strolling' with. Did I say that right? I also learned English through the American movies, and my brother, of course. He is a master of English and the American ways. Did you know it is forbidden here for a woman to touch anyone but her husband? But Your Highness has suggested I do this to keep you from running away." Then she whispered, "And I am not married!" She giggled as she snuggled into a comfortable gait. "So, big fella, what is your name? I heard that line in the movies too," she said, pleased with herself.

I replied, "I am Dimitri."

She giggled, "Yes, Dimitri, I know who you are. I know all about you. I was just teasing. I wanted to say that line and see how it sounded. Kind of funny, 'big fella'. How is your father?"

"My father?"

"Yes, your father."

"He is well. And so is my mother," I emphasized. "They are both well."

She giggled once again, "Yes, your mother is excellent. She and I have been acquaintances on more than one occasion. Your father has been employed by the Emir, my father, on many of his projects. Did you not know he helped build this estate?"

"I do remember but not a lot of detail. I was pretty young."

"Oh yes," she continued. "His knowledge of the largest underground aquifer located right here under your feet is why this empire of the Emir exists. Your father built the canals and designed the engineering that brings up the water from below. Did it occur to you that the only oasis of lush green pastures is effortlessly found here in this arid part of the country? We do not need to bring water in, which is essential to the horses when in training. The water just bubbles up like tiny spirals and keeps the ground moist, but not wet. And it helps keep this unabating heat down."

She was so animated and bubbly as she talked, perfectly ignoring the sweltering heat. We both had small beads of sweat running down our necks and backs. It was 107 degrees as the sun blazed down, scorching everything that moved. It was 11:00 a.m. and the temperature was still rising. It always amazed me that the Arab men could wear the long Thobe and turbans in such heat.

Gabriella continued to talk as if we were long lost friends, "We can talk about the designs of this place another time, though it is interesting you did not know this. Your father and you are quite famous, yes? How is it you did not know?"

Surprised, I just shrugged my shoulders, "I came here with my father when I was a small boy, but most of this was not yet built. I vaguely remember it, but I do remember my father talking to the Emir on many occasions."

"Yes, yes. Let's walk, shall we?" She returned her arm through mine, and we headed to the largest indoor equestrian facility I had ever seen. From the outside it looked like a giant bike helmet sitting on top of 20-foot walls. The huge building was surrounded with bulletproof windows located just under the overhang of the giant helmet.

I began to question her about her knowledge of my family. She put her finger to my mouth and said, "Shhhhh, another time, I promise." She continued as if this issue was benign with no additional conversation necessary. I started to rebuff when she took my hand and spoke over the top of me as we walked toward two magnificent ornate gold, crimson, and white entrance doors painted in the country's flag colors. When we arrived at the door, she turned me around with the doors behind us and pointed out the vast array of buildings, grandstands, racetracks, and the unique walls that surrounded it all.

"Dimitri, this estate was built throughout the late 1940s into the '50s. It was built as a fortress to protect the family. The walls that surround this fortress — my brother hates it when I call it that — are impenetrable and of course embedded with security cameras. When my brother showed interest in horses, our father gifted him this place and it was transformed specifically for housing, breeding, and training the Arabian horse. The Prince showed an interest in horses when he was quite young. Our father knew his son's empire would need to be

diverse from the family's oil empire, 'Oil will disappear, horses can be bred to last.' he would say. This estate houses between 60 and 80 purebred Arabian racehorses at all times, of which most are known and ranked best in the world. The Prince is only interested in the Arabian. His horses have won year after year in Normandy, France, the Americas, and Britain. He is somewhat of a horse whisperer, the Prince is. You will see." Gabriella let out a small giggle.

As she continued to give me the tour, she pointed in all directions and communicated her knowledge. I observed and nodded as she continued her history lesson. "You will soon understand what I mean when you see the Prince with his horses." She continued, "This is a state-of-the-art facility. Its horseshoe shape encompasses over 360 acres inside and over 5,000 acres outside. The land surrounding this estate, for as far as you can see, is also owned by The Prince. It not only represents the literal footprint of what lives here, a horseshoe, but it is known for its security and surveillance systems. With only one entrance into the complex, the horses are safe, and the atmosphere is docile and extremely compliant, which is important when training a horse. No one likes a spooked horse!" Gabriella chuckled at her own humor. I smiled at her, and she smiled back with a little girl twinkle, showing me her beautiful, white, perfect teeth with a small gap between the two front teeth. To most men it might be a reason to send your gal to visit the dentist, but it was a signature hereditary imper-fection in the Emir's family. It was something to be proud of and I found it cute. She continued, "The outside is made of impenetrable walls, as I said, and it resembles many of the fortresses of antiquity, do you not think? I hear you too have become a legendary mason like your father and grandfather. You know of these things?"

Feeling a bit puffed up with her compliment I said, "Yes, my father and I, along with seven other men, are the best in the world. We actually recently received 'Expert' recognition in the UNESCO literature. I began working with my father when I was seven years old. Our specialty and talents lie in underwater repairs. It does not surprise me that my father designed the water system here." As far as the eye could see and to the edge of the cliffs, the land was a dry, golden yellow without a stitch of greenery. Yet within these walls trees grew, flowers bloomed, and lizards did their pushups on the hot rocks while eyeing a future mate. The buildings were constructed to cast a shadow on each flowerbed at the height of the summer sun. No vegetation wilted. It was thriving with color. It was an oasis in the middle of a dry, arid hell hole. This must have been pretty special water to do this, or my dad was a genius. People traveled miles through the heat just to watch The Prince and his famous Arabians race, but mostly they came to gamble and experience the green environment.

"How old are you now, Dimitri?"

"A bit over 18."

"Hmmmmm, nice age. Dangerous job being underwater?"

"Yes, not many of us have these skills nor do they seek them out. My friend George and I are the youngest. George's father is the best of the bunch, teaching both of us how to use TNT underwater. It is considered one of the most dangerous underwater jobs, besides welding."

"I am impressed, Dimitri."

We walked through the outer stables first. They were covered with a lean-to style roof. It was a blessing to be in the shade. From the vantage point of the stands, the people could view and cheer on the horses as they left the inner stable to the outer stables. The cheering began here as the horses pranced around, preparing themselves for the next race and the move onto the track. The 1 3/4-mile track was made up of lush green grass cut very close to the ground. The track was wide enough for seven horses to race at once. In the center of the track was a large pond with a waterspout shooting high into the air, and its gentle spray could be felt in the stands if the wind was just right. Every time the wind was just right, the people in the stands cheered as if it was a sport in itself. At least fifty flagpoles surrounded the track, waving the Qatar maroon and white flag. The horseshoe-shaped stands cozied up to the track with a four-foot-high metal railing painted in white, separating the people from the horses. With the 107-plus degree temperatures, no one touched it, let alone crawl-ed over it.

There was enough seating in the stands to accommodate 1,400 people. The bleachers were covered in another lean-to style roof with a huge announcer's box on top. As we walked into the inner stables, it was like walking into a professional soccer training camp. It was the size of the Colosseum in Rome but covered in a state-of-the-art heat reflecting roof. I am pretty sure you could see this roof from space on a hot day. As we walked inside, a burst of cool air hit us, causing both of us to sigh and smile as we enjoyed the change of temperature. With most of the horses working out, the air smelled of manure and hay yet not a bit of either could be seen. It looked as if you could actually eat off any surface in the building.

Gabriella said, "Is it not beautiful? I love it here! I could live in here. I actually did spend the night here a couple of times, just to make my brother mad. He is a bit overwhelming sometimes. Dimitri, he has been waiting for you to show up here for months. He is very happy today. He knew you were coming." I quickly turned and looked at her just as she touched my arm and said, "Wait here for a minute or just walk around if you like. I will be right back," and she jotted off to meet with a trainer who had motioned her over. I was standing there in shock. Why did he want to see me? How did he know I was coming? I did not even know I was coming! I did not feel like I was in trouble, so I thought maybe he needed to reach my father, although he had the resources to contact him. As I stood there contemplating, a trainer holding the reins of a horse in tow asked me to step aside as they passed.

I decided to walk around while I waited for Gabriella to return. The inside of the building was segmented into different training modules with long walkways in between. Each state-of-the-art module contained all the apparatus possible for that particular exercise. Horses were in pools swimming against a spiraling current within the water. Each seemed happy, enjoying the cool water surrounding their massive muscles. Treadmills were set up around the perimeter and horses were running on them in a casual lope. Groomsmen were tending to hooves, brushing out long manes and tails that reached the ground, and a plethora of medical examinations were being perform-ed. Some were just grazing and relaxing as if their day in the gym was done.

Gabriella returned and startled me from behind. She giggled, returned to my side, and crossed her arm within mine again. "Come on, I will show you more." She continued to explain the daily routines to me over the next half hour. "In this heat, many days the horses stay inside and train until the sun sets and the breeze cools the air. These horses are trained to run for over 50 miles at a time. They can stay on the treadmills for hours without exhaustion. Today is a race day so those not racing get a casual day inside, if you can call it that." She smiled big, giggled, and said, "What do you think?"

"This is amazing! I had no idea," I said as I scanned the enormity of the building and the complexity of the training program with adoration. These horses were treated like kings!

"Dimitri, as I said before, this is an honor not only for you, but for the Prince too. He has waited many months to finally be in your presence again." I looked at her quizzically, ready to address this comment when she turned her gaze away from me. I realized the Prince was watching us from a slight distance with a smile on his face. Gabriella lowered her eyes and head, and dipped into a slight bow or curtsy, maybe both. As he approached us, she said, "Your Highness, wonderful day you have had. Congratulations once again. If you need anything, I will be available. Dimitri, I am sure we will talk and walk again. Thank you for a lovely afternoon. Good day!" The Prince tipped his chin at her, and she was gone.

The Prince turned and causally leaned against a structural pillar with his arms folded in front of him and said, "So, Dimitri, did you enjoy your tour?" His voice was low and strong, even captivating. He wore a crisp white shirt with the sleeves carefully folded to a 3/4 length sleeve. The stark white color made his skin look even darker than it was, bronzed and shimmering with the sweat from the heat. He wore riding boots to his knees, and his pressed khakis were tucked in tight. His small waist and broad shoulders made him look like a seasoned body builder. He was over 6 foot tall, strong, and in control of every move. His hair was shiny black, slightly wavy, all one length, and rested on his shoulders. I wanted to run my hands through it. I was speechless and a bit shy all of a sudden. I thought I was looking at a model in a magazine. "Dimitri, did you enjoy your tour?" I heard him repeat.

Quickly I said, "Yes, I did – very much. Gabriella was very gracious. Thank you. Congratulations on your win today." I could feel my cheeks flush as he faced me and stared into my eyes.

The Prince's deep emerald-green eyes were piercing into mine. His body was so close. I could smell his scent, an amber wood mixed with mint soap. I had smelled this scent before, but I could not remember where or when. I breathed him in. It was intoxicating, and every hair on my body felt alive and stimulated. Standing in front of him I felt exposed, as if I were naked. My mouth was so dry I could not talk.

He said, "Walk with me please?" As he waited for an answer, I nodded my head. He let out a small chuckle and smoothly said, "There is nothing to worry about, Dimitri. I will not bite." I smiled and lowered my eyes, at a loss for words. He reached out his hand as if expecting me to shake it. I took his hand in mine. Our hands were the same size and fit together comfortably. His hand was strong, with calluses at the base of the fingers yet it was soft and inviting against my dry, mason-callused hands. He casually shook my hand as I watched his upper arm muscles flex. His crisp white shirt was unbuttoned to the collarbone and exposed a few dark hairs. I felt as if he was aware of my every move. Staring into my eyes he said, "A man's handshake says a lot about the man. You squeeze too hard, you are considered domineering and controlling. You shake too soft, you are considered a coward, meek, unreliable. You shake firm yet soft with eye contact, and you are family, friends, and can be trusted." He pulled me in close and kissed each cheek. As he held my hand longer than I expected, he said, "How did that handshake feel to you?"

I glanced to the side then back at him. I could feel my erection growing, knowing it was visible to him. I quickly put my left hand down in front of me to cover it. He smiled as his eyes followed my hand down. "Like friends," I answered shyly.

He said, "Good – we are friends, Dimitri." He let go and leaned against the railing to an open stall and said, "I have known of you for quite some time. I have watched you work and have inspected your work for several months. Your talent and the confidence in your skills are remarkable for your age. And your ability to govern your crew is quite admirable. You were trained well. I am impressed. I hope to employ your talents for all my projects. Walk with me."

My mind was whirling. He has been watching me work. Was he my boss? *I raced through my memories.* Had I seen him before? *When the sheikhs wear their long white thobes with the trailing turbans, it is hard to recognize any of their details from afar.*

As we strolled through the stables, he introduced me to each of his horses, all Arabians. "Dimitri, did you know that the Arabian is one of the oldest breeds on the planet? They actually date back to before 4,500 BC. The Arabian stallion is the strongest, fastest, most refined horse there is. It is bred for its endurance and strong bones. Most horse breeds around the world today have the Arabian bloodline in them. Did you know?" I shook my head and he continued, "The Arabian was used over the centuries for both war and trade. In battle, they are a fierce and reliable warrior." He clenched his fist and shook it slightly, representing the strength and fortitude he felt within each horse. "I fell in love with them as a child. It took watching only one race and I was hooked. I now own 72 purebred Arabians. My stables have produced the most sought-after, strongest horses in the world. When people ask how I continue to breed such a winning stock, I say it is in the water, it is special. Because of this, my stables are well guarded. Trust me, if I could bring my horses into my home at night and lock them in, I would." He let out a hearty laugh and clasped his hands, laughing at his own joke.

I smiled and realized I was holding my breath. As we rounded the corner and headed out the back door of the stables, two horses were saddled and waiting for us with guards standing close by. The Prince pointed to mine and said, "You will fall in love with her. Enjoy." With help, I mounted the beast and settled into the saddle. Being raised on a horse, I felt at home on the back of the most beautiful horse I had ever seen. She was pure white with bulging, well defined muscles, and her mane draped over the saddle's cantle. As I mounted, she danced casually side to side, raising and lowering her head as I took the reins and squeezed her firmly with my thighs, letting her feel my strength and command. As she settled down, I leaned forward, stroked her shoulder, and whispered into her ear, "I am one with you." She whinnied, pushed up hard, and raised her upper body straight up into the air, standing on her back legs then gently set back down. Her body quivered between my legs. I felt myself sink into her as she shifted me and the saddle into place. She bounced her head, thrusting her jaw forward and backward until she was completely aligned with me. I felt alive on this horse. I could feel her eagerness to run, and I too wanted to bolt from the stables as soon as she set her upper body back to the earth. My heart was racing. It had been months since I had sat on an animal like this. Her power beneath me surged through my thighs.

I took a deep, lingering breath, calmed my nerves, and looked over at the Prince. He was sitting there with his arms crossed and a slight smile on his face. "I see you two have bonded. Her name is Thunder. I chose her for you. This is Lightning," he said. Lightning was pure black; even his eyes were pure black. He did not dance or move around. There was no showboating, yet every muscle was tense and engaged. Each breath was followed by a "Humph!" He seemed to be preparing for that slight kick in the side signaling NOW! He was exquisite, on fire under the calm exterior. I felt as though the horse mirrored its rider.

The groomsman addressed the Prince, "Your Highness, when should we expect you back?"

"We will run the back trails along the seawall and return this evening." The men tipped their heads as we handed them the reins. Both horses pranced perfectly as we were guided through the gates out onto the vast fields surrounding the estate. As we sauntered out, the Prince turned to me and said, "You are extremely fortunate, Dimitri. My stables are off limits to non-employees. A vigorous background check is required as well. Many men have not returned who felt these rules did not apply to them." He waited for a response.

I remained calm and listened as I looked out into the outer lush green hills that slowly merged into dry, brittle grass. I knew exactly what he was saying. It was a message of respect and he expected it from his employees. I am sure they did not return to the estate or their own homes. I am sure the word "Missing" took on a whole new meaning. For some reason, his words did not frighten me though. I was beginning to feel quite at ease in his presence. I am not sure if it was because I was sitting on this massive beast holding the reins and controlling its power or because the Prince was stunningly handsome while sitting erect, confident, and paying attention to me. I was at a loss for words. I was now alone with him, and I had no idea what was next. The excitement of running free and wild with this beautiful creature between my legs was spilling over. I wanted to run. I wanted to feel alive!

I also felt an ache in my groin that I had never felt before. I had spent years learning my trade. My father never allowed me to feel the longing for love and its pleasures. He would say, "A man's work defines him. It is his craft that provides for a future family. Work first, love after." I spent my youth learning my craft to become the best. I had spent hours with George underwater, learning how to detonate bombs and rebuild ancient walls, and I had dated only one girl, but never did I feel an ache or even experience an erection like I did then.

When the groomsman closed the gates behind us, I felt a surge of excitement from knowing I was going to ride this horse until its body glistened in sweat. The thought of feeling the freedom of the wind passing through my body at breakneck speeds invigorated my soul. I had spent years working tirelessly with my father to make ends meet. It was years of being away from home, living in foreign lands and foreign dwellings with nothing to look forward to but another day's work under the water and in the heat of the sun. The talented masons who roamed the globe repairing and restoring historic landmarks to preserve history received little recognition and the pay was limited. Most jobs were funded by UNESCO World Heritage Center who depended on private donations and grants, many of which gave most of their monetary funds to provide public information and awareness. The men doing the repairs and restoration received little compen- sation other than a blurb here and there in the tourist pamphlets.

This was my turn to relish in the attention, to trust, receive, and feel the joy of it. I was alive. I was ready to run, to fly on the back of this exquisite creature as if I was a centaur shooting an arrow with no landing spot in sight. I knew horses, and the Arabian was an ex- ceptional breed, yet I had never ridden one. It was bred for endurance, to run fast and furious, as if it was being chased by pure evil itself. The faster it ran, the more distance there was between it and the snare.

I could feel Thunder's thoughts. She heard me when I said, "I am one with you." When I whispered, she quivered. She too was ready.

The Prince had other thoughts as he slowly cantered next to me. He chose to continue our conversation. "These stables are guarded by the best security officers in the world. The men you see working the stables are some of the best horse trainers in the world and they are trained security guards incognito." The Prince looked at me as if waiting for me to say something. I smiled but said nothing. He continued, "Dimitri, did you know that it is said that Allah took a handful of southerly wind, blew his breath over it, and created the Arabian horse? Did you know this?" I shook my head as he continued to tell me of the many races and awards he had brought to Qatar throughout the years. The love for his country was palpable.

I relaxed in the saddle the best I could while listening. I had no words, and my head was spinning. His baritone voice was deep and rich, like chocolate slowly melting down my throat. His voice had a soft and gentle nature to it, filled with humility and kindness, yet a distinct confidence that almost seemed arrogant at times. I was mesmerized by all of him. Why had I been given this honor? Why did this very powerful prince trust me?

As if knowing what I was thinking, he said, "You must be intrigued by why I allowed your entrance into my property and stables."

"Yes, I am. Why me?"

"Dimitri, I think you are special. I think we are going to be great friends."

I stared at him, not understanding his meaning. Why were we going to be great friends? What did he know about me? How did he know me well enough to give me access to one of the most guarded places in Qatar? Why was he being so mysterious yet so casual and aloof? I felt as if he was toying with me, yet I did not feel fear or humiliation. Instead, I felt sexual sensations I had never experienced before. It was as if he was diving straight into my soul and searching for just the right emotion to pull out of me. I did not know whether to lean into his request to just relax or to stay alert and cautious. Knowing many men had never returned from his estate made me a bit nervous.

He turned to face me, put his hands on his hips and chuckled, "Dimitri, would you like to share with me what you are thinking? Cat got your tongue?"

"No, I mean... Maybe," I stuttered. I could feel the heat engulf my face as it undulated through my body from the back of my neck down to my toes. I could feel my face flush and a small stream of sweat slowly trickle from my forehead to the edge of my jaw. As the breeze hit my face, a small shiver raised every hair on my body. I was in a state of confusion, trying to take it all in. I just wanted to run with Thunder as fast as her massive body would take me. My heart was racing and I desperately needed to work out the adrenaline building in my body. Ahead of us were vast miles of rolling hills just waiting to be trampled, and the sea breeze lingered in the distance. I needed it against my face.

Thunder felt as I did. I could feel her muscles contracting between my legs, just itching to be given the signal to bolt. Yet the Prince pulled gently on his reins and stopped Thunder. He slowly came around to my right side facing me, with the horses side by side, head to butt as they flicked their tails in each other's faces while chomping nervously on their bits. The Prince's leg pressed against mine. He smiled, showing his perfect white teeth with the slight gap between the front two. He sat tall in the saddle as if it were his home. He was defined, causal, patiently staring at me. He asked, "Dimitri, I want you to feel relaxed with me. There is nothing to fear. Do you understand? Are there any questions you have for me?" He was so close I could see specks of gold in his emerald eyes. I swallowed hard, never breaking from his stare. He looked me straight in the eyes then lowered them to my mouth, down to my groin then back up to my eyes. I felt as if he were taunting me, seducing me. He reached out his hand and settled it on my knee. Without ever looking away, he slowly took my free hand and raised it slightly, pressing his palm to mine then swiftly spread his fingers and grasped my hand, intertwining our fingers. An electric surge raced through my body as I took a deep, startled breath. My groin was burning with an immediate sense of pleasure. He held this grip tight for a few seconds then swiftly pulled me to him, our mouths connecting as his tongue entered and slowly explored my mouth, gently lingering as he waited for me to kiss him back.

I was alive! I was transported to another dimension. I melted into him, kissing him with the same passion he was giving me. He let go of my hand and eased back to an erect stance on Lightning. I was frozen in my seat. He said, "Dimitri, I have wanted to do that for a long time. Are you OK with this?" I slowly nodded and began to answer when he slapped Lightning on the rump and took off like a bullet. Thunder, without hesitation, bolted forward, almost throwing me off her back. I pulled up tight on the cantle and reseated myself as she lunged forward into a full sprint on Lightning's heels. I felt a surge of excitement rush through me, finally being able to expel the energy welling up inside me. I tightened my grip on the reins yet gave Thunder the slack she needed to run like the wind.

The Prince ran Lightning hard, his hooves digging deep into the pale grass and sending dirt flying behind him as he lowered his body to round the corner onto a path that skirted the edge of the jagged cliffs. His shirt was billowing in the wind and his hair was flying free. I felt like a man in pursuit of his lover. The wide dirt path went on for miles. The lost shoreline below was only a few feet from the path's edge as the jagged cliffs plummeted into the sea and waves crashed endlessly against the rock face. Thunder let me know she knew this path and knew it well. She inched her way next to Lightning, pushing harder and faster with every dip of her head. Humph! Humph! Every breath she took expanded her girth, filling her lungs with the cool ocean air. The edge of the cliff was within inches. I cinched my legs around her belly and relaxed the reins. She was in charge, and I let her take me to where she was in an exhilarating burst of pure pleasure, free to ride the dangerous edge with skill and faith, no one controlling her. She was free. The horses, side by side, were inches from each other as our legs brushed against each other. The horses desperately maneuvered to lead as rocks spilled over the edge into the nothingness. My lungs were burning and my muscles were engaged, wrapped around this beautiful, elegant creature. We were one, both lunging forward and backward as she took each stride, clearing at least ten feet. Their manes flew frantically in the wind as they were in *a competitive battle to the finish line. There was no fear of the dangers below, just pure excitement in the race.*

When we came to a corner, Thunder eased up just enough to let Lightning dart ahead of her only to catch up again in two strides. The sea mist whisked over the edge into our faces, and I could feel the damp air saturating my shirt. My hair, once slicked back in place, now danced around my face as it captured the energy of the wind and mist. I felt so alive!

The Prince's shirt now clung to his arms and chest. Every muscle was pronounced and engaged. He was pushing Lightning, just as I was pushing Thunder, to win this race. We were both slightly off the saddle in a crouched jockey position, allowing the animals to be free of our rhythm, to push hard to the finish line.

The Prince turned to me and pointed. About a mile ahead was a building. I understood that it was our destination. There was a slight curve in the path up ahead, leaving the cliff's narrow edge behind us. A wide pasture led us to a straight stretch ending in the finish line. As we reached the straightaway, I felt Thunder make her move. Her stride lengthened, her head lowered, and every muscle, hard and tight, was pushing us forward. The power in her being was at full speed. I felt her desire, her passion, her drive to win. She was in her glory, and I was relishing it. She was going to win this race and I was now just along for the ride. I held my breath and lowered into her. In one giant stride, she thrust forward, breaking the imaginary winning line inches before Lightning. I wanted to scream. I yelled "YES" as she slowly eased her gait. I stood up in the stirrups with my hands in the salty air and just took it in. We had won! It was as if I was born again. Every hair on my body stood on end as if a lightning bolt had just shot through me. I sat back down, leaned forward and hugged her, congratulating her on her victory. She was covered in sweat just as I was. She pranced as her head darted up and down, catching her breath as if in a gentle tease with Lightning. The Prince rode up next to me and held up his hand as I slammed mine into his with a high five gesture. Smiling from ear to ear, we sat back into our saddles and took long cleansing breaths, shook the water from our hair, and started laughing.

After we caught our breath, we dismounted and let the horses roam free to cool down. The Prince grabbed me, gave me a giant bear hug, and slapped me on the back as he congratulated me on the win. Exhausted, I lay down on the lush green grass in front of a massive chateau engulfed in vast, extravagant gardens displaying every color of the rainbow. The Prince lay down with his head next to mine, his body lying in the opposite direction. I stared up at the clouds whisking by as I relived the race. Was I in heaven? This was a moment I would never forget. I crossed my legs, put my hand behind my head, and drank it all in.

The Prince did the same. After a minute of silence, he said, "You may call me Qaseem when we are alone."

I smiled, "Qaseem, that was awesome! Thank you."

He reached over and took my hand and held it saying, "It was my pleasure, Dimitri. You brought life back into me. I thank you." We lay there until our racing hearts calmed down, holding hands and staring into the sky. I now knew that the Prince liked me more than I could have ever imagined. Men of the East are forbidden to embrace a man like this, but here he was, relaxed next to me. I felt a comfort I had never felt before, and I knew he felt the same.

With a big sigh, Qaseem sat up, "Are you hungry? It is just us here. Can you cook?"

I replied, "Starving! And I have been told I am an excellent cook by the guy in the mirror." We both laughed.

"Good, let's shower and eat. I have an extra set of clothes you can wear. You can shower first while I start a fire."

The chateau was massive, more like a castle. It looked out of place for Qatar. It resembled a European design as did the massive gardens. It housed seven bedrooms and seven bathrooms, three large living spaces, an industrial-sized kitchen, and a banquet table.

Qaseem watched me as I walked through the ten-foot, ornate gold inlaid doors. I entered the waiting area and immediately noticed the white and cherry marbled tile only found in my family's quarries.

I looked at Qaseem who said, "Yes, from your father's quarry."

I immediately looked up to view the highest ceiling I had ever seen in a home. It was covered in a canopy of several large trees chasing the sun coming through the skylights. A large river of spiral-

ing water meandered throughout the expansive living rooms as if the chateau was built over a river. There were colorful fish in the stream, swimming in from one side of the chateau and leaving the other side on their journey elsewhere. The three large side-by-side living rooms were lined with floor to ceiling 20-foot windows looking out over the tops of vineyards, fruit groves, and rose gardens. It was a spectacular view. Roses and flowers of every color blanketed the gardens and around the trees. Beautiful vegetation spread out well into the distance until it disappeared over the cliffs into the sky.

Qaseem came up behind me, put his hands on my shoulders, and said, "This estate is home to over 10,000 roses of all varieties, as well as the famous "Royal Parks" rose from England. We lifted that rose, unbeknownst to The Queen." Qaseem chuckled then said, "That stays in this room!" I smiled as he continued, "This chateau and gardens were designed by my father's English lover. She was a painter who designed it to flow like a thick brushstroke with every color from the color wheel trailing behind it. From this window you can see the textures of each shrub, flower, and tree blending flawlessly into the scenery then falling into the ocean in the distance. There are over 60 water features and paths that meander through the beds. She took the design from a postcard of The Queen's estate and built this to resemble the gardens on the card. She added fruits and vines to fulfill my father's desire of sweet, juicy pleasures. It is very easy to get lost in the fragrance that permeates the air in the spring. There are lots of secrets in this garden. I suggest you never try to navigate it without me. It is very easy to get lost here. One of my favorite things to do is watch the hummingbirds and butterflies that migrate here in great numbers each year."

It was a spectacular view. Each flowerbed had its own variety of plants with walkways of soft moss in between. Small stone benches sat in front of each flowerbed to provide a place for contemplation or just a moment of rest to enjoy the beauty before them. The gardens were visible from every window. I turned to face Qaseem as he turned and said, "The gardens do not stop out there. She brought nature inside as well, as you can see."

In the corners of the grand rooms were floor to ceiling Empress trees, Tulip trees, and Willows growing, creating a canopy of beauty high above us. The room was filled with greenery and flowering vines that spilled from lazy flowerpots into the spiraling waters of the meandering creek as if they needed a drink. Throughout the room, water flowed from vases spilling down into water fountains then into the stream. It looked like a giant indoor botanical garden. The peaceful sounds of delicate splashing waters aerating the stream were serene. I had never seen anything so beautiful and cool in my life. I stood in one spot and turned a 360-degree circle. Plants, flowers, vines, trees, sweet smells, and an intense amount of color consumed the rooms. The tall windows showered the rooms with warmth from the sun, giving its life to every living plant. It was a palace of color that looked so fragile yet begged to be snuggled and touched all at the same time.

There were numerous lounging areas in each of the three large rooms. Each room was furnished with plump sofas and chairs covered in colorful, inviting cushions. Qaseem spoke from the opposite side of the room, "Living spaces this large can be so difficult to design, yet she made each room and each seating space luxurious yet comfortable. You can snuggle up with a pillow, feet up and stretched out, and relax on any piece of furniture. This was what my father wanted; luxury yet comfortable enough to enjoy no matter how old you are. It feels cozy in here do you not think, Dimitri?"

I nodded as I marveled at the large colorful rugs blanketing the cherry and white marble around each couch and chair. Throw pillows were everywhere. I thought about picking up one and throwing it at Qaseem. The thought of a pillow fight sounded exciting and daring, but I decided against it.

Qaseem approached me and reached for my hand as he described each plant and where it came from. I got the sense that this place was very dear to him. He talked effortlessly as I watched his face change expressions with each story. One wall was dedicated to family portraits. Qaseem introduced me to seven generations of men, each with a unique story of displayed bravery throughout the decades of war. Qaseem's portrait was the one directly at eye level. It captured him perfectly.

We walked through a set of huge archways into a large open kitchen gleaming with sunlight. The tall windows followed us through-

out the house. Nothing was spared; even the kitchen was completely stocked with everything a chef would need to throw an extravagant party. Long, cold black marble counters surrounded the perimeter of the kitchen, and next to the six-burner gas stove were large, towering stainless steel swivel spice racks filled with every spice on the planet. Baskets of colorful fruits and vegetables were placed at the end of each counter and in the middle of the banquet table. Knives of every size protruded from stainless-steel blocks, sharpened and ready for use, and were sitting next to the spice racks. A floor-to-ceiling glass wine refrigerator with a beautifully carved ladder next to it stood in the center of it all. It was like a game; pick the wine you want and watch the chef climb the ladder to find the delicate, delicious flavors to accompany each meal. A long three-foot-wide bar overlooking the stove allowed the guests to congregate and admire the skills of the chefs in front of them. This bar separated the guests from the kitchen, creating a boundary of sorts but also a perfect viewing spot. Directly behind the bar was a banquet table that sat twenty people. It was surrounded by colorfully cushioned tall-back chairs that matched the colors in the main room. The table was set with China, glassware, and polished silverware as if ready for the guests to arrive at any minute. Qaseem strolled behind me as I took it all in. "Where are your servants?" I asked.

"They have been let go for the day. Does that bother you?" he replied.

"No, not at all. I like the quiet. I live with masons. It is never quiet."

Qaseem smiled, "It is always quiet and peaceful in this house; it is why I spend so much time here. It allows me to think." Qaseem steered me down a long hallway covered in paintings by famous artists. Millions of dollars-worth of art was displayed, asking for recognition. Qaseem forcefully said, "Do not touch," then smiled at me and said, "I grew up hearing those words," and chuckled.

When we reached the first bedroom, Qaseem opened the door to a massive canopy bed sitting on a plush white area rug that filled the center space of the expansive room. You could walk all the way around it. The mahogany pillars were intricately carved in animal patterns, and the bed was blanketed in rich, royal reds and blues with tiny embroidered yellow flowers. The window on the opposite side consumed the entire wall with drapes made from the same fabric. The drapes were pulled back, exposing the wall of windows overlooking the gardens. The sun beamed in on white strands of light which illuminated the dark walls and stark white carpets.

My clothes and hair were still wet from the ride and the warmth was well received. I stood in awe, looking out the window onto the vast gardens below. You could see the enormity of the maze of box hedges and the path to the center. If anyone got lost within the maze, this was the perfect view to find them. It was the most beautiful view so far.

Qaseem went to the closet and with both hands he abruptly opened the floor-to-ceiling doors, exposing artfully arranged hangers filled with crisp, white shirts and dark pants on the left. Long white thobes were on the right, and casual clothing filled the back wall. In the center, an island of drawers separated the two sides. He opened drawers and took out undergarments, lay them out on the bed, and walked into the enormous pure white marble bathroom. A large white marble tub, big enough for four, sat in the center of the room just as the bed did in the sleeping quarters. To the right was a walk-in shower encased in glass with four shower heads protruding from the walls. To the left of the room were four side-by-side sinks with large swaths of counterspace between them. A full mirror extended the entire length, and four drawers rested below each sink. Four tiny seats sat to the right of the drawers. The 20-foot-long countertop ended in a room that housed the toilets and urinals. It was becoming obvious that nowhere in this house was luxury spared.

I looked at Qaseem and said, "Wow! My whole apartment could fit in this room. The mason dorms could use a bathroom like this!"

He smiled, went to the shower, turned on the water to two of the showerheads, and closed the door. He placed two large white towels on the seating chair outside the shower. "Dimitri, enjoy. I will return with a small dish of meats, fruits, and cheeses shortly. After, you can impress me with your cooking skills." He left the room. I took my time getting undressed as I admired the room and the obscenely expensive art that covered the walls even in the bathroom.

The water was inviting. I stood under the two showerheads, letting the jets massage my head then neck, shoulders, and back. It was *as if the water was washing away my aches. The ride had taken a toll on my muscles. With every minute, I felt better and more rejuvenated.*

As I turned to reach for the washcloth, Qaseem entered with a glass of red wine. "Dimitri, this is from the vineyard here on the property. I think you will enjoy it. He sat down the glass on the counter and turned to face me. I was standing facing him. He stood silent while looking into my eyes through the glass doors as the water washed over my body. I did not move or cover the fact that I was aroused by him.

He slowly looked down, and for a brief moment rested his eyes on my erection, then returned his gaze. He was as aroused as I was. I wanted to ask him in, but my words were lost. He smiled as I stood there like a stone statue staring at him, the water running down my body, caressing my every muscle. Neither of us moved. Neither of us said anything. With my penis completely exposed and fully engorged, I filled my hands with soap from the silver dispensers on the shower wall and began to wash my body. I was watching him as he watched me. I reached down and caressed myself, slowly massaging the shaft of my erection from the tip to the base over and over again. He watched my hand move faster and faster. The excitement, the danger and fear of not knowing exactly what he was thinking made the release that much more intense. I closed my eyes and leaned back against the shower wall as I moaned out loud, quivering in satisfaction while he watched.

When I opened my eyes, he was smiling, standing in front of the shower door. He reached for the door, opened it, asked for the washcloth, then told me to turn around. He gently washed my back then applied firm pressure to my shoulders under the slippery soap and massaged them. I put both hands up on the wall and let him work his fingers into my flesh as the hot water increased the relaxation. His hands felt so good. He then turned me around, face to face, and kissed me, slowly at first. Our lips barely touching then deeply and passionately he consumed my mouth. I returned his kiss. My whole body was alive. As he pulled away, he rested his forehead on mine, taking in the moment. He gently kissed the tip of my nose, smiled, and said softly, "I will meet you in the kitchen, my handsome prince. Take your time and enjoy the wine. I will shower next door.

See you shortly," and he left. What was happening to me? I felt so peaceful inside while at the same time a chaotic mess was consuming my every thought. I wanted more. And I knew he wanted more.

With a towel wrapped around my waist, I headed to the kitchen and scanned the fully stocked refrigerator, poured myself another glass of wine, and drank it in one gulp. I poured another full glass to drink slowly over dinner. My thoughts were not on dinner, but I was starving and had promised to make Qaseem a delicious meal. I was excited to please him. I decided on a nice rice dish with marinated meats and seafood sprinkled with lemon juice and rosewater with fresh fruits from the garden on the side. This dish was one my mother had prepared often and one I knew Qaseem would enjoy.

As the rice was cooking, I slowly walked down the long hallway into Qaseem's room with one of the bottles of wine he had chosen. He was sitting on the side of his bed, sheets turned down, waiting for me. When our eyes met, I stepped back outside the room and leaned against the wall, out of view. Fearful yet excited, heart racing, I knew what he wanted. I wanted it too. I had never been with a man before. I had never been with a woman. I had never felt this kind of animal passion in my life, but I knew I wanted him, and the excitement of knowing he wanted me made it crazier in my head. I drank from the bottle until half of it was settled in my stomach, wiped my mouth, took a deep breath, and walked back into the room. Qaseem was sitting there, still waiting. I handed him the bottle and he finished the last half as I had the first half. He sat the empty bottle on the bedside table, looked up at me, and held out his hand. I approached him slowly until I was within inches of him. With each step, my erection grew until it was hard and ready for him. He reached out, dropped my towel, took my engorged penis in his strong hands, and firmly rubbed it up and down then lowered his mouth to it. The warmth was overwhelming. I cried softly as he gently and rhythmically caressed me, tickling the base of the head with the tip of his tongue. My quivering legs were about to buckle as I released an explosion of semen into his mouth. A sea of emotions I had never experienced before engulfed me. I began to slide to the floor. He reached up and cradled my buttocks in his arms, preventing my fall. As I started to collapse over the top of him, he swiftly and gently swung me around to the side of the bed and let my head fall onto the pillow. He smiled down at me and softly stroked my stomach and pubic hair.

Qaseem asked, "Are you OK? Do you feel the same for me as I feel for you, Dimitri?"

I turned on my side, propped up on my elbow facing him and asked, "How do you feel for me?"

He said, "Dimitri, I am in love with you and have been for a while. I saw you a few years ago working in Turkey. You and your father were hired to improve the water ways of Hierapolis. I was there on site, talking with the engineers when I first saw you. You were with your father, working the stones from the sea back up to their original placement on an enormous ancient sea wall. I was mesmerized when I first heard your voice. Searching for you, I followed the sweet sound up and there you were, high above me, standing on a wall with no shirt on. Your broad shoulders merged into strong, pronounced muscles as you were staring down at me. So sexy and so sensual."

Qaseem closed his eyes, remembering the moment and smiled. "I can see this memory as if I were standing there now. Every muscle in your arms and back moved in unison with your body as you lifted the heavy stones into place. I found myself feeling like a voyeur standing beneath you, fantasizing you on top of me, rocking back and forth, wanting me as I was wanting you. I was transfixed. I desperately tried to figure out how to get your attention but soon realized, What would I do then? What would I say to you? *'Hey, you up there, come with me. I think I am in love with you, and I want you in my bed now!'* Would you have given me the time of day? It was as if I had lost my mind!*

I found a place to sit in the shadows to watch you. When you finished, I followed you to the cliffs, watched you take off your clothes and dive into the calm sea. I wanted to join you, but I knew I could not. I ached in my groin as I have never ached. I sat alone for a long time, trying to figure out a way to get your attention without exposing my-self within your secret hiding place. I was about to leave when you climbed up on the rocks and lay down, exposing your naked body to me as the sun blanketed you in its warmth. You ran your fingers through your hair as it dripped the ocean's salt into your eyes. As you did, you sang to God in the most beautiful voice I have ever heard. I was so moved I started sobbing. The words penetrated my soul, Dimitri. I could not stop the tears. It was as if I had saved them for just this moment. I cried for me, for the man I am. A man that can never fully be with another man. A leader of my family, who would gratefully stone me to death if they knew my secret. You changed me that day. After you fell asleep, I returned to the estate and asked Gabriella to find out whatever she could about you. When she told me you were well into 16 years, I was surprised. The boy in front of me had the chiseled body of a man yet was just 16 years old. And the voice, the voice of an angel. I have kept you close to me since, employing you and your father under business names most people do not associate me with. I am the one who pays you."

I looked at him with no words. When he saw my confusion, he reached down and kissed me passionately then lay beside me, his naked body next to mine. "Dimitri, please do not be upset with me. Do you feel the same way toward me as I feel toward you?"

I was not sure how to feel about what Qaseem had just told me. He had been watching, dictating my every move for a couple years? Why had I not noticed him? I looked into his eyes. They were soft and gentle, waiting for my reply. I wiped the thoughts from my mind, those telling me to ask more questions. Sitting before me was a prince, a man who could take the life of another without a second thought if need be. A man who could control a wild horse and bring it to its knees with a small whisper. A prince with the power to start wars with other nations. Yet he was bearing his heart to me as if a child wanting permission to love. Permission to be accepted for who he was and what he wanted – and he wanted me.

I turned to Qaseem and said, "I want to be here, and I know I want more."

He leaned in, putting his head on my shoulder and pulling my body close to his as he draped his leg over the top of my body, trapping me. It was a wonderful and comforting feeling. I could have stayed in his bed forever. I was home in this man's arms, and I never wanted to leave. We dozed off for a few minutes but were soon awakened by the rice timer.

I started to get up, but Qaseem said, "Stay. I will be back." I lay there staring at the ceiling and wondering if I should be upset with *him, but nothing in my heart would take me down that road. All I wanted was to be with him, now and forever.*

Qaseem returned with two full glasses of wine. This time I was on the side of the bed waiting for him. I reached for him as he sat down the glasses and stood in front of me. His body was so strong, his muscles refined, built to perfection. His chest was dark, sleek, and smooth. His shoulders were broad, his waist small, and his thighs were as strong as Thunder's. His dark hair framed his face as he looked down at me. And his erection was ready for me. I took him in my mouth, repeating the same motions he had just pleased me with. I was slower, enjoying a pleasure I had only dreamed of since I was a young boy. I ran my tongue up his shaft until I met the base of its head and played there while I stroked him firmly. He shuddered, reached down, and placed his hands on my shoulders then slowly and gently rocked his pelvis back and forth. I let him control the speed and motion as I teased his male clitoris. When he orgasmed, he threw his head back and moaned, "Oh, Dimitri I will never let you go." He stood there in ecstasy while I milked him with my mouth. When he was soft and fulfilled, he dropped to his knees and kissed me, exploring my mouth with his tongue and enjoying the flavor of his own semen.

When he released me, I looked into his eyes and said, "I love you."

He smiled, put his forehead to mine then kissed me again. "Good," he said sheepishly. "I am happy, Dimitri, for the first time in a very long time."

We made dinner together, talking about our lives, where we had been, and our dreams of the future. He asked me to move into the Arabian estate with him as a secret lover at night and an employee during the day. He explained that a prince could have many lovers, but male lovers are a crime against Allah, punishable by public execution. We would need to be very careful and quiet. Gabriella would be our only advocate. Signs of affection could ever be witnessed. If I agreed to this, I would have a place in his home but only share his bed like we did today at the chateau – in secret. I willingly, wholeheartedly agreed.

Days turned into months. At first, I was happy. Qaseem gave my father and I the best masonry contracts in the land. He contacted

UNESCO and paid handsomely for all contracts to cross his desk first. He allowed us to pick and choose each job then he negotiated the contracts, demanding a handsome paycheck in return. Our masonry business gained a reputation that exceeded our wildest dreams.

Qaseem's relationship with my father grew exponentially. Every job we took, we worked tirelessly and painstakingly to make it perfect. My father never knew my hidden relationship with Qaseem, and he never complained again about poverty. The money and prestige were all he had ever dreamed of.

As the horse racing season came to an end, we spent many afternoons at the English chateau. Racing to the chateau with Thunder and Lightning skirting the cliffs edge became a game. The adrenaline from racing at full speed built our passions to a height that would spill over into the bedroom. We no longer rested on the grass afterward; instead, we dismounted and raced each other to the welcoming shower and the four-poster canopy bed with the giant white rug under it. Panting, we undressed each other with fury to get to the presents awaiting us underneath the sweat-drenched clothes. Qaseem had a wine fridge and wine shelf built and placed next to the bed. We always had a bottle of wine with two beautiful crystal glasses waiting for us at the bedside whenever we visited the chateau.

Qaseem was always very gentle with me, slowly introducing me to the joys of intimacy. One afternoon he shared with me that his first encounter with a man was when he was a young boy. This man teased him for many months, brushing against him casually, letting his hand skim across his pants, whispering in his ear what he wanted to do to him. He had Qaseem watch him masturbate and "feel the firmness" on the ruse he was teaching him what all boys should be taught. One afternoon, he brutally raped Qaseem. The man apologized for his aggressive behavior, but it was not long before Qaseem realized it was his way. He was not kind or gentle, but rough and powerful, as if conquering his prey after a long fight. Qaseem was bruised and tortured for many years by this man, until he had the man killed in a presumed accident after finding out that this cruel man had done this to many boys. Qaseem said, "Lovemaking is to be experienced with joy and pleasure, not pain and fear."

On our fourth visit to the chateau, Qaseem did not race to the door, this time he abruptly got off Lightning and stood at my side, slowly helping me off Thunder. He drew me close and kissed me with love and compassion, pulling my waist into his and gently rubbing his hard bulge back and forth against mine. He then professed his love for me, "Dimitri, I have loved you for a lifetime, many lifetimes. You are a part of me. We are one. Do you feel it?" I nodded, looking into his soft, comforting eyes. "I have never loved anyone as I do you, Dimitri, and I knew it when I saw you years ago, sunbathing and singing softly from your heart to the God above. You did something to me that day. I have waited for you. I want you now and I want you forever. Can you feel this love I have for you?"

I kissed him tenderly and buried my mouth into his neck and kissed him again. Slowly he ran his hands up the sides of my neck and gently returned my passion. We stood outside with Lightning and Thunder, undressing each other then walked hand in hand to the front door. When the door opened, a gust of inside air filled our lungs with savory spices, warm and inviting. A wave of panic engulfed me. Scared, I looked around cautiously as if a servant was present. I pulled back on Qaseem's grip, looking around frantically for a place to hide my nakedness. My head was swirling with things to say if we had been caught.

The Prince pulled me close and said, "We are alone. Gabriella did this for us. She is gone."

My panic eased as my heart raced. I bent over in relief and took deep breaths. All I heard were chuckles from Qaseem, "Boy, this spooked you, did it not?"

I slowly shook my head as I stood up and let my body calm down. "Warn me next time, Qaseem, please! That was not good." He held me tight until I could breathe without the pain in my chest. He promised he would never frighten me like that again.

As we passed the banquet table, a place setting for two and an open bottle of wine were waiting for us.

Qaseem grabbed the bottle and downed the first half in one breath. He handed me the bottle and said, "This half is for you, my prince." I did as he did, downing the second half. I took a breath, wiped my mouth like a lumberjack and started laughing. We were both laughing. We could not stop. It felt so good to release the fear that had instantly consumed me when we opened the door. With our arms around each other, we walked down the hallway I knew so well; every painting, every signature, every face now had a name. The Prince had educated me on every piece of art in the chateau.

The bedroom was dancing with twinkling lights; a hundred candles flickering, their shadows reaching for the ceiling. The massive bed was turned down and a plate of meats and cheeses and an open bottle of wine waited. Qaseem followed me to the bedside. He faced me and pulled his waist into mine. We were both hard as rocks, wanting each other, softly caressing each other's manhood with gentle strokes. "I want you to penetrate me tonight, Dimitri. Is this something you are ready for?"

I shuddered, wanting him even more. "Yes, if you can do the same for me."

He kissed me tenderly, "I hoped you would say this to me, Dimitri." He kissed me then went to the dressing room counter, reached into a warm bucket of water, and brought out a cobalt blue bottle. He said softly, "Lie down on your stomach." He got up on the bed, knelt between my legs, and with his knees, spread my legs apart gently. He said, "This potion will help relax your tight muscles. You will feel a warm sensation. Relax and enjoy. If you want me to stop, I will."

I nodded, my body so alive and willing. My erection was pressed against the bed, wanting to explode. I could feel the warm liquid drip onto my buttocks and trickle down my hips. The sensation filled me with extreme anticipation. Slowly, I felt his finger penetrate me as he rubbed the oils around my opening and into the sphincter. As he moved in and out, applying the potion, he used two fingers then three. I felt pure passion as I began to move with him, rubbing my hard penis against the bed under me. When I could not take it anymore, Qaseem entered me with a slight force that made me lift my upper body off the sheets and gasp. He stopped, fully inside of me, and waited. I lowered my head as he lowered himself onto me. As we both sank back into the sheet, he whispered what he was doing to me into my ear. Pure erotica, relaxing me and my tense anal muscles. He slowly rocked back and forth, and with each full thrust, he let out a moaning breath in my ear. I was in a dream world, oblivious to everything except the man on top of me. He whispered. "Do not cum, Dimitri, hold it, hold it, my love. Hold it, hold it." Faster he moved, his breathing louder and louder. I knew he was ready when he breathlessly said, "Oh, Dimitri." He stopped, let out a soft moan, thrust himself deep inside me, and exploded. I could feel him pulsating inside of me, filling me up.

I started to move under him, wanting to explode into the sheets "Wait, Dimitri!" He pushed down hard on my lower back, activating sore muscles, changing my thoughts, relaxing my desire for one split second. He pulled out and in a swift move, raised my hips until I was on all fours. He grabbed my erection in his mouth and got it wet, rolled under me, and said, "Show me how much you love me now." I spread his buttock and entered him. I let out a gasp, threw my head back, and moaned, moving with him faster and faster. It was glorious, warm, and so soft. I felt feelings I had never felt. It was a closeness that was so different than being in his mouth. I moved faster and harder as he moved with me, driving me deeper into him. I grabbed his hips and pushed hard into him, both of us letting out an animal cry. I fell more deeply in love with Qaseem at that moment. This man was all I yearned for, all I thought about, all I wanted. I did not need food or water, just Qaseem.

On our sixth month anniversary, Qaseem gave me a jewel encrusted dagger. He had it engraved, For my love, wear it in peace. *I felt like the luckiest man alive.*

When we were at the chateau, we made love and learned everything about each other. Qaseem had only been with two other men before the age of 18. There was a moment when he was 17 that his brother became wise to his sexual preferences and threatened to expose him, but Gabriella saved him. She introduced Qaseem to a woman who became his friend, teacher, and confidant for several years. She was breathtaking. She had shiny, straight, jet-black hair reaching to her waist, sea green eyes, and a body that belonged in a granite sculpture. She was refined, educated, and came from the second richest family in Qatar; Qaseem's was the first. She had a secret too; she was in love with a woman. He never questioned her, and she never questioned him. They paraded around and professed to be lovers. His brother, extremely jealous, soon gave up on what he thought he knew about Qaseem's sexuality.

I asked him how much Gabriella knew about him. He replied, "Everything." I was so thankful he had her. She was special. I had never felt sexual energy toward any woman until the day she took my arm and escorted me around the property that very first day. I felt a kinship toward her that day and a curiosity that surprised me. Knowing she was on our side made me happy and gave me a sense of relief.

When Qaseem and I were in the presence of the rest of the world, he was my worldly teacher, my mentor. He educated me on how business worked and the legality of contracts, business partners, and investing. He, like my father, emphasized the importance of the English language and all its nuances. He explained the different dialects of the English language and its many interpretations. He explained that people from one state to the next, from one country to the next, speak English differently yet say the same thing. He showed me how to greet the world. I learned the proper Hello, *with the 'Not too firm, eye contact' handshake. He taught me the proper way to greet just about anyone, until I was proficient and professional. He showered me with lavish gifts and showed me an abundant life.*

When we were together, I was happy, but when we were apart, he loved others to honor his people. When Qaseem traveled abroad, I would not see or hear from him for weeks. Over time, I became lonely for his attention, for his hands to be caressing me. I became jealous of those around him. I even began to feel jealous of the horses. It began to take its toll on me.

One evening at the chateau, I was upset and expressed the animosity and pain that was welling in my heart. He reminded me of our initial agreement, "Dimitri, we will never be able to be together. Our relationship will always be one of secrecy." My heart sank. I had fallen so deeply in love with him that seeing him with others created an ache in me so deep it took my breath away. Many nights when Qaseem did not show up to the chateau as planned, I sat on the floor in a tight ball rocking and in tears. I felt a loneliness so deep I could not eat, and many days I could not work. This ache became all consuming.

One night after Qaseem failed to meet me at the chateau for the third time, I drank until I could not see. When I woke up the next morning, Qaseem's sister, Gabriella, was in my arms asleep, naked. My massive headache turned into fear. What had I done? I carefully got up, went to the shower, and let the hot water pour over me as I tried to remember the evening before. When had she arrived at the chateau and what happened? I was so ashamed. What if Qaseem found out? Would he send me away? I sat on the shower floor sobbing. Gabriella knocked on the shower door, opened it, and entered with a towel. My head was throbbing and the nausea in my throat was making me sick. I could barely see out of my swollen eyes. I apologized profusely. She did not say a thing, she just took my hand and carefully nudged me out of the shower. She dried me off and put me in a large white robe that matched the one she was wearing. She took my hand and with a big smile on her face, escorted me back to bed.

"Dimitri, lay down. I want you to just breathe in and out slowly. I would like you to calm down so we can talk." She fluffed my pillow and gently pulled the covers over my body. I began to cry again as I realized she was nurturing me, trying to help me through the pain.

When I finally got control of my emotions, she handed me a small glass of black liquid and a white pill. When I started to ask what it was, she put her fingers to her lips and said, "Shhhhhh, just drink, and drink fast! Oh, and plug your nose," and started giggling in her cute, girlish way.

It tasted awful! The tar-like substance coated my mouth but quickly absorbed into my gums and cheeks. It was the strangest feeling, a tingling that slowly numbed my entire mouth. She said, "Dimitri, just breathe." She towel-dried my hair, and within five minutes I was feeling like a million bucks.

I looked at her in amazement, "Wow! OK, that was good. Thank you."

She said, "I am magic. Now when you are ready, we shall eat. The food is ready." She bopped me on the end of my nose and walked away. The fear of Qaseem finding out and the sheer feeling of panic was completely gone. It was as if my brain had been washed clean. Whatever was in the black liquid was magic. With my mind clear, I knew what I had to do. I needed to leave Qatar.

As Pearl turned the next page, a few loose pages fell from the journal. She tucked them back in and sat quietly with her thoughts. She was overwhelmed with emotion as she felt the tears well up and trickle down her cheek. She wished she could hug Dimitri at that moment.

Chapter Eight

Pearl took a big breath and let it out slowly as she lowered the journal to her heart with tears streaming down her face. She took a big cleansing breath and realized that Alexander was sitting one step down, looking up at her. He handed her a cup of coffee and said, "I know – it is a lot to take in."

Pearl wiped her tears and took a sip, just staring at him. She was speechless. After a few moments she said, "I have never read anything like this in my life. This is the most beautiful, uncomfortable, yet saddest love story I have ever read. My grandmother Julia does not talk about the past. It is as if it were a secret. I figured something must have happened that caused her too much pain. I do not know. It is funny – I have asked my mother, Charlee, about her past and she too does not share it with me. She just lowers her eyes and changes the subject. What happened in this family that has created such secrets?" Pearl was just jabbering while working through her thoughts. Alexander listened as he sipped his coffee.

"OK, so what now? You found us. What is next?" she asked.

Alexander said, "I think we should put all of this away for now and go get some dinner. We can resume this conversation over a glass of wine. How does that sound?" Pearl nodded as she helped him pick up all the scattered material. He called the Spondi Restaurant, and after a few minutes of conversation they were in a cab and on their way.

"I am impressed," she said. "There is a waiting list two years long. Do they know you?"

He looked at her with a slight grin, and said, "Very well – I own it. No one knows this. I go by a pseudo name and my chef covers for me."

Pearl raised her eyebrows, "Wow, OK. I have always wanted to eat there. I will expect a standing reservation from here on out, yes?"

She giggled as he responded, "Absolutely! From now on you are my guest whenever you are in the mood for a fantastic Spondi meal and, of course, it is on the house." He held out his hand as a gesture for 'it's a deal.' She shook his hand with a giant smile.

When they were seated, Alexander removed everything from the table; menus, salt and pepper, and flowers. He ordered a bottle of 1954 Cabernet Sauvignon from a vineyard she had never heard of. He spread out a pile of pictures with several notebooks and the vigorously taped-up box and envelope he was so protective of. She was shown the linage of her family, the one she didn't know, through the old pictures and letters Alexander brought to the table. The one elephant in the pile was the large envelope addressed to Julia Kaya. It contained a section of Qaseem's will that pertained to Julia. Pearl would be the first to read it since its printing, besides Qaseem.

Alexander ordered their meals and an appetizer as she read the contents. Flabbergasted, she dropped the papers to the table when she was done reading. Grandmother Julia was the recipient of George and Dimitri's fortune worth $922,000,500.00. "Alexander, this is incomprehensible! This is very hard for me to believe. Why? How did Julia become the heir to this, this… uh, ALL of this?" she questioned as she gestured with her hands and eyes over the pile of stuff.

Alexander didn't answer but instead looked over at the larger envelope then up at Pearl as he crossed his arms and leaned back in his chair.

She realized this was her invitation to look in the large puffy envelope in the pile. In the bottom were two boxes, one small and one much larger. She took them out and looked at Alexander. He nodded as she slowly opened them. The small box had a ring in it. It was Sophia's. She recognized it from the pictures from her great grandmother's early days before she married George. It had a 5-carat diamond in the center and several jewels of different colors set around it. "Oh, my god! Jeez, it is so heavy and the most beautiful thing I have ever seen!" In the larger box was a matching necklace, bracelet, and hair pin. There were so many diamonds and jewels she couldn't begin to count them all.

Alexander said, "Those are yours, well actually your grandmother Julia's. As you have read, they were to be passed down to

Dimitri's son, if he had one; if not, on to his first daughter. Dimitri professed in his writings that Julia was like a daughter to him. His fatherly relationship with her and his fondness for her showed Qaseem that Julia was the rightful heir to his inheritance. These jewels are priceless. There is more and I hope to share them with Julia." Pearl put on the ring and there it stayed.

He continued, "In the taped-up box are the Emir's ashes. He stated, in his dying breath as well as in his will, that he is to be buried with Dimitri. Do you know where he is buried?"

She looked up and said, "Yes, he is buried just outside my home, my parent's old home, on the far side of the island. There is a small graveyard on the property. This is where Dimitri is buried, as is Katrina, George, Sophia, and my grandfather, Daniel. There is an empty grave site next to Dimitri. I do not plan on using it for myself; I have other plans with my ashes. So, it is now Qaseem's resting place. Nice coincidence, do you not think?

Alexander smiled, lowered his eyes, and said, "Not at all. I am sure it was planned a long time ago. It is interesting how the universe works. Nothing surprises me anymore." The food arrived with the bottle of 1954 Cabernet Sauvignon. Alex poured them each a glass, raised his, and made a toast, "To new friendships." They clinked their glasses together and took a lingering drink.

Pearl said, "Oh my god, Alexander, this is delicious! I have never tasted Cabernet so buttery before. It almost tastes like an aged Zinfandel, which is my favorite. Thank you! I could get used to this…"

Alexander smiled and said, "Oh yes!" They talked through dinner and well into closing hours. Still on the heels of so much more to learn, they decided to walk around the streets of Plaka as Alexander continued filling her in on the family's stories. They bought an ice-cold bottle of ouzo with two small tourist souvenir shot glasses, then found a tucked away bench to sit on just outside the bustling main street. Greece came alive after 10:00 p.m. and the streets were starting to fill up with locals. Tourists, by this hour, were normally sound asleep. It was the best time of the day in Greece; it came alive with street bands, vendors selling warm roasted nuts, and hungry, loud locals drinking the famous red wines and ouzo by the bottle. Alex poured the first shot of the thick, syrupy drink, and with a small clink of the glasses, they both said 'bottoms up' at the same time then laughed as they consumed the cool drink. Alexander said, "OK, are you ready for more of the story?"

Chapter Nine

It was a beautiful evening. The stars blanketed the dark sky and the ouzo was helping to abate the slight chill in the air. Pearl nodded when Alexander asked if she wanted more of the story. She got comfortable in her seat as she watched the patrons meander over their late-night menus.

Alexander took a big breath and began, "The story goes that Qaseem was extremely distraught and fell into a state of depression when Dimitri left. It was as if Dimitri took his heart with him. He stayed at the chateau for almost a year, waiting for Dimitri to return. He refused to leave, even when the Arabian Nights racing season returned. In the beginning, Gabriella took care of him as best she could. She prepared his meals, made him bathe, answered all his phone calls, and squelched the many inquiries into his mental health. She took care of all his business transactions, from corporate to horse racing. As her pregnancy with me began to show, Sophia stepped in to help her.

Your grandmother Sophia was in an arranged marriage to Qaseem's younger brother. In truth, she was sold to him. She spent her youngest years as a child bride, tortured and beaten, raped, and shared by drunken men that hung around the house. Many nights she was found crouched in a corner in a catatonic state with her eyes rolled back in her head, chanting words no one understood. When she would not stop, she was beaten more. Drinking in Qatar is illegal, but what happens behind closed doors is anyone's guess. Sophia was Qaseem's sister-in-law. Sophia's best friend was Katrina, who became Dimitri's wife. Sophia's original name was Maryam. She changed her name at some point, I am not sure when. Both Sophia and Katrina helped Gabriella through her pregnancy with me and also helped take care of Qaseem through his many dark, emotional nights. He was so mentally upset after Dimitri disappeared that his love for

Dimitri came into question by many of his staff. The ladies managed the barrage of negative press reports in the daily news and constantly dealt with damage control.

When Sophia's husband, Husam, Qaseem's brother, began forming the conclusion that the Emir's interest in Dimitri was more than as just a mentor, Qaseem's life was on the line. Pearl, homosexuality is seen as a hideous crime against Allah. It is punishable by death. A very public death. Husam would be next in line to the throne if Qaseem's secret got out. Sophia hated her husband with all her being. When Husam's secret plan to expose Qaseem started circulating, a bounty was put on the heads of the terrorists that were plotting the attack against Qaseem. You see, Sophia found the documents in her husband's office days before, detailing the time, day, and the event where Qaseem's assassination was to occur. She notified Qaseem of Husam's plan and told him of her own plan. It was time to deal with Husam herself. The amount of hate in her heart needed to be released and she had a plan to release it. Qaseem gave his blessing. She called her own execution team and prepared them. Husam had a list of men who wanted him dead, so they were easy to persuade.

That night, she drugged Husam and opened the door when the execution team arrived. It was in all the papers. A picture of a hooded figure holding my uncle's severed, dripping head while being fed to a pack of wild dogs in the moonlight at the edge of town, was on the front page of every newspaper. His headless body was dragged by the ankles through the back alleys then left to the same dogs hours later. Many townspeople watched in horror. When Qaseem got word of the incident, he returned to his royal position and never spoke of Dimitri again.

On that same night, Sophia and Katrina disappeared. No one knew what had happened to them for several weeks. Gabriella finally got word that both Sophia and Katrina were OK and hiding in Turkey.

When their whereabouts came into question, Qaseem reported that he'd had Sophia and Katrina return to Katrina's family home to grieve in peace. No one knew who or where her family lived, and no one questioned this. No one talked about the incident from that day forward. Fear had gripped the city, but the news quickly died down and life returned to normal.

When I was born, Qaseem took me in his arms and never let my feet touch the ground until I was three or four years old. I was his link to Dimitri and in his mind, I became his son. Qaseem searched for Dimitri for years but could never find him."

Pearl was captivated by the story and in shock. This was her great-grandmother he was talking about. The story she knew painted Sophia as a gentle, kind, and funny woman. Her thoughts were consumed with, *Does my mom know this story? Oh my god, I cannot wait to tell her! And I thought my life was boring!* Pearl was exhausted. She wanted to hear more, but it was close to 2:00 a.m. She looked at Alexander, yawned, and said slowly and dramatically, "I need to sleep. Please, can we reconvene tomorrow?"

They made plans to see each other again for dinner the following evening to go over Julia's return schedule. Plus, there were binders of legal paperwork that needed to be signed so Julia's inheritance could be forwarded to her. As they walked toward her hotel, she stopped, pointed up, and said, "This is me. Have a great sleep, Alexander. I have to say, this all seems like a storybook novel that is hard to put down. But knowing this story is about my family, well, there are no words to describe my shock right now. I will meet you back at Spondi's at 6:30 p.m.?" He nodded.

Just as she was about to turn around to leave, a man approached them and said, "Dad, I am taking off to the outdoor concert. Yanni is playing. Want to join me?"

Alexander looked at Pearl then at his son, "Adeem, this is Pearl, daughter of Charlee, granddaughter of Julia, great-granddaughter of Sophia."

Adeem looked Pearl in the eyes, slightly bowed his head, smiled, and said, "Wow! Pleasure." He looked at Alexander, smiled then looked back at Pearl, "Have we met before? You look familiar." Pearl blushed and looked away as if something had caught her attention. She was immediately in lust. Her jaw was on the ground, and she needed to pick it up. She was momentarily speechless. Never had a man rendered her speechless before. Now two men had in one night and the strangest thing was that they were father and son. She collected herself then met his eyes for the second time. Confidently she said, "No, but it is very nice to meet you." At that moment she too felt a recognition but couldn't place it. She prayed he didn't ask her any other questions. She feared stumbling over her own words. He looked just like Alexander without the salt-and-pepper highlights and was a little more stoic in build. And he smelled so good. Pearl found herself instantly wanting to know what he looked like under the big coat he was wearing. *Yikes! I am in trouble* was all that registered in that moment. Her brain was going to be festering over this man for sure. He was gorgeous. She instantly had a premonition that this was the beginning of something big, she just didn't know what yet.

Chapter Ten

Pearl's libido was totally engaged, and now she was wide awake. She too had an uncanny feeling like she had seen this man before. She tried to figure out where they may have crossed paths, like at one of the local events leading up to the unveiling. She searched her brain looking for something that would jog her memory, but nothing surfaced. Now that she was fully awake, she entered her hotel wondering how she was going to sleep after meeting Adeem. Her mind was full of possibilities. She still had Dimitri's journal, and curiosity was getting the best of her. She wanted to know more and, to be frank, she needed a distraction. Being alone would only bring Friday's bizarre events back to the forefront of her mind, and she didn't want to go there. Not now – not ever. But meeting Alexander made Friday's events seem coincidental for some reason.

She ran upstairs to the rooftop restaurant, ordered a small bottle of ouzo, and took in the warm evening air as she gazed at the Parthenon. She thought, *I do not know what it is that is so calming about this monument at night. It is just a peaceful feeling that over-whelms me. I love Greece!* She grabbed the bottle, a glass of ice, and a little bag of sweets the chef had quickly prepared for her. She kissed his cheeks and headed back downstairs to her awaiting fluffy pillow. She had brought four large vanilla-scented candles and a sage smudging stick with her as she always did when traveling. She lit them, placed them on the nightstand tables, and watched the shadows dance on the ceiling as she took a long sip of the ice-cold ouzo. She fluffed up her pillows and opened Dimitri's journal to where she had left off.

Over breakfast, Gabriella explained her presence in my bed. She said she was out riding when the weather turned, so she decided to stay at the chateau. She found me crying on the floor with several empty bottles of wine. She said she put me to bed and consoled me as she listened to me profess my love for Qaseem. I had gotten up to go to the bathroom and stumbled back to bed naked. She said I asked her to undress so I could hold her like I did Qaseem. One thing led to another, and we had sex. She said, "Qaseem will not mind, he will be happy for us. And, by the way, the whole time you made love to me, you talked in my ear as if I was Qaseem. It was quite erotic and sweet too."

She took my hands and said, "Dimitri, look at me." I kept my head down; I could not look at her. "Dimitri, there are things you do not know. Things Qaseem has discussed with me in detail that I thought he had discussed with you, but seeing you like this I assume he has not. Dimitri, Qaseem loves you desperately! He wants to give you a wonderful gift through me. I have agreed. I love my brother very much. There has been some talk around the arena about your relationship. It is a rumor we need to hush."

I did not understand what she was trying to tell me, but what I did hear was that there had been some talk. "Who is talking about what? I do not care. I am afraid, Gabriella! I am afraid I will lose him!" I cried, got on my knees, and begged her not to tell Qaseem. I feared if he found out, he would never see me again. How was I going to face him? How could I look him in the eye ever again? Tears rolled down my face. Gabriella tried to console me, but I could not hear a thing she was saying. My mind was distraught, and my body was ravaged by grief. Gabriella held me to her breast like a child who had just fallen from a playground swing and rocked me gently until I stopped crying. She fed me then gave me another, much larger dose of a yellow potion before she put me back to bed. As I mumbled my sorrow, I could feel my head becoming distant, and before I knew it, I could not remember why I was crying. Everything went blank. She stayed with me until I fell asleep. She left me a note telling me not to leave then headed back to the estate.

Upon arrival, she found Qaseem and told him of how she found me in a puddle of tears and a pool of wine bottles. Gabriella had known of her brother's secret love for me since he had confided in her the day she caught him secretly watching me sunbathing and singing to Allah on the rocks. He had Gabriella watch over me for two years *until the day I snuck through the gates of the racetrack. Qaseem knew his prayers had been answered that day and Gabriella knew what she needed to do. They formed a plan together. Qaseem wanted a child that he and I could raise as ours. It would have the blood of his family mixed with the blood of the man he loved. Her job was going to be so much more important than keeping a secret. Qaseem wanted her to carry his secret.*

The day Gabriella left me at the chateau after giving me the yellow liquid, telling me to rest and not leave, Qaseem left for the UK. His stables had been vandalized, several of his prized horses had been kidnapped, and a steep ransom was being demanded. The Prince was out for blood.

When I awoke the next morning, I knew what I had to do. I packed up my things and left. I searched for my father and found him on a jobsite not far away. I explained that I would be moving back home. He asked for my help to finish up his last job then we could return home to Turkey together. Against my better judgement, I stayed.

When Qaseem returned from the UK and realized I was gone, he was heartbroken. He showed up on the jobsite and begged me not to go. He said, "Dimitri, just stay a few more weeks. Everything will be better. I promise you will never want to leave me. Just wait! Please, I need a little more time."

But I knew my place and it would never be with him outside of secrecy. I would always be sharing him with others. He held me and professed his love for me, asked me to return within the month, and gave me a satchel of treasures. He told me that his heart would always be mine. I could not even speak as the Prince pleaded with me. I hung my head in shame as tears dripped to the floor. My heart would always be his.

Before I left, I tried to find Gabriella. I was told she had asked her father for permission to marry a man she claimed to be in love with. This came as a shock to me. I had not known her to be with any other man, but many of the marriages were arranged so I did not bother asking for more information. I wrote her a short goodbye note and left the Arabian estate. I gave the heavy satchel to my father and told him it was a gift from Qaseem. My father would never work again as Qaseem's gifts were grand.

For the next few weeks after my return, I was devastated and ached for Qaseem. I lost my desire to work with the stones. I stopped eating and bathing, and I could not sleep. Vodka became my best friend. I could not tell my parents about Qaseem, so I changed the story, using Gabriella as the culprit instead. My parents were beside themselves with worry as they watched me wither away in my own heartache. They called the church, counselors, and my friends, but I would not see any of them. I no longer had the will to live. When I could no longer live with the sorrow, I knew what I had to do. I made peace with myself and my God, and decided to jump off the bridge. Life without Qaseem was no life at all so ending it was the only answer. It gave me a sense of peace knowing this pain would soon be gone. I left a note explaining everything – Qaseem, Gabriella, and the chateau – on my bed and readied myself when suddenly there was a knock on the door. This knock changed my life forever.

Four Turkish military officials forcefully entered our home. They were dressed in full body armor, guns at their waists and ankles, and the rifles that hung from their shoulders were slung across their backs. Their faces were blacked out with paint so all you could see was the whites of their eyes. My mother slowly backed into the hallway as my dad talked to them. They handed my father an envelope stamped Top Secret *in red. He was ordered to sit and read the contents immediately. As he read the message inside, the officers stood at attention, bodies fully erect with their heads held high and arms at their sides, staring into space.*

When my father finished reading, he put the paper back into the envelope and told the officers, "NO." All four officers surrounded him and demanded to know where I was. My father stood tall and said I was out of town.

The soldiers turned to leave but not before the leader said, "We will be back." After they left, my father came to my room and told me what had just transpired. The Turkish government was looking for the nine masons with underwater TNT skills as well as advanced underwater masonry work. My father and I were two of the nine. My father said they became aware of us through the UNESCO restoration organization. He looked at me with fear in his eyes. I told my father I did not care about any of this. I did not care if the government needed people to push stones around for them. All I care about is Qaseem, *I thought to myself. I would never see him again. I wanted to end my pain. I wanted to rid myself of it all. My father was irate. He could not understand the changes in me, my depression, my anguish. He stood there at the door of my room yelling then pleading for me to snap out of it. "Dimitri, this is serious! George and his father, myself and you, are the only ones left out of the nine. The others have been killed or died in some strange accident over the past two days. This is not something you can run from on your own. Your mother and I talked; she is going to pack tonight. We are all leaving in the morning. We are taking the ferry to Samos then on to Ikaria. It is a Grecian island off the radar. I want you to pack immediately!"*

I pushed past him, went into the kitchen, and took a full bottle of vodka then stormed out the front door. I told myself, I am not going anywhere but to the bridge, and this information settled it once and for all. If I am going to die, it will be on my terms! *I crossed the street where darkness evaded the streetlights as I drank gulps of the clear Russian liquid from the bottle. Each swallow burned my throat and took my breath, but with each swallow it got easier, and I began to relax. I could see the bridge in the distance under the soft floodlights that enveloped the bridge at night.*

I began to talk to Qaseem as if he was standing in front of me, "Please forgive me, my love. You are everything to me and if I cannot be with you, I would rather die. Thank you for the love you showed me. Thank you for taking care of my family. Thank you for being my lover. Thank you for everything."

As I drunkenly stumbled down the street to the bridge, talking to a ghost and ready to end my life, my house exploded with my parents in it. The sound was deafening. I instinctively ducked and grabbed my head. I watched the vodka drop to the ground and shatter at my feet. A second explosion hit as I dropped to my knees then a third explosion followed. The energy wave from the last explosion shot out at me, almost knocking me over. The explosions rattled the city, sending a mushroom cloud into the night sky. The whole neighborhood lit up from the flames as if a million floodlights were just plugged in. I ran back toward the house, but it was gone. I dropped to my knees as I watched the flames whip across the dark sky, leaving trails of black smoke and flying embers in all directions. The heat was so intense it stung my face, neck, and arms. It was as if the bombs were dropped from the sky. They demolished the entire house and the houses next to it as the parked cars nearby melted into the streets. People were running in all directions, yelling, screaming, and burning while on fire. I sat helpless, in shock, as the flames got closer. My mind was numb from the vodka. Qaseem and now my parents were gone. I stared into the inferno with tears rolling down my face as I watched the horrific scene in front of me.

George lived across the street and down four houses. He was running to me yelling, "Dimitri! Run! Run!" It was as if I was under-water, hearing my name all mumbled and full of panic. George grabbed me, pulling hard, "Get up, Dimitri! Get up!"

I pushed and punched George as if I was a wild animal. "No, George! Let me go, let me go! Leave me alone!"

George grabbed my hair and yanked it back hard, gritted his teeth and said, "Dimitri, my parents died tonight too. Shut the fuck up and listen to me! We need to go NOW!"

I stumbled to my feet watching, almost numb to the chaotic scene in front of me. People were on fire, running and flaying their arms, provoking the fire that was consuming them. As they lost the battle and succumbed to the flames, they dropped to the ground in a fiery heap. Neighbors were dousing them with water as the trees and landscape burned with a fury so fierce and hot that you would have thought hell had arrived.

George and I ran to the bridge and slumped over the railing, trying to catch our breath when George said, "Dimitri, did anyone visit your house over the past two days?"

"Yes, why?"

"What did they want? Do you know?"

"Yes, they said they needed masons with underwater TNT skills for a secret operation in Greece."

"They came to my house too and the other seven houses of the men who have these skills. Dimitri, we are now the only ones alive out of the nine! My parents were killed in a hit and run accident tonight. The others accidentally drown in their tubs, died of food poisoning, and a freak boating accident. We need to hide!"

"How do you know they are dead, George?"

"My father told me about the others. They had all talked to each other right before the 'accidents'. When my father realized that he, you, your father, and I were the only masons left, he fanatically started stuffing everything in bags and preparing to leave tonight. He screamed like a wild man at my mom and me to hurry up, taking only what we needed. When my mom tried to take makeup and a brush, he hit them out of her hands and yelled, 'ENOUGH! Get the passports, the money in the top drawer, all our medicine, and the address book!'

My mother dropped to her knees crying, scared. He yanked her up by the arm and said, 'We have very little time so cry later – NOW MOVE!' We drove to the petrol station. I got out to help with the pump when a black SUV with a large metal grill barreled into the station and smashed into our car. I saw my dad's head smash against the window before he was thrown over to the other side of the car. The SUV backed up, almost hitting me as I stumbled to the edge of the station and fell to the ground as the car screeched away. I stood up, ready to run to my parents when our car exploded with the same intensity as your house. I ran for cover as fire swarmed around me and I watched the station blow up, leaving a hole in the ground ten feet deep. I just stood there in shock! My arms were on fire, so I brushed off the flames and dropped to the ground to put it out. We are being hunted and killed, Dimitri. But why?"

There were no words; we just sat there staring at each other. I put my head in my hands and started to cry when George noticed the burns on his arms and the burns on my neck and right arm. He said, "Dimitri, these are bad. We need to put something on them. Mine are really painful." I had not even noticed the burns. I felt nothing.

George stood and held out his hand, "Come with me. I have a place where we can hide for a while. It has supplies and water for a few days."

As we stood, two officers yelled our names and raised their weapons. We froze. They yelled again, "Raise your hands!" They were wearing full military uniforms with guns at their waists, ankles, and backs. They had black knitted head covers that only exposed their eyes and lips. When they approached, they gave us each an envelope, never lowering their weapons. The contents were the same as the ones our fathers were given. When we finished reading the proposed contracts and placed them back into the envelope, four black SUVs arrived. Two drove up next to us and two parked, blocking traffic from entering the bridge on either side. The two officers holding us at gunpoint swung us around, told us to raise our arms again, and placed the end of the gun barrel to our temples. The approaching SUV's bright headlights blinded us.

A woman in a military uniform got out and stood in front of one of the headlights of the SUV, blocking it. She looked to be about 50 years old with slick, pinned back hair. She wore a pistol at her waist, had a rifle slung over her shoulder resting on her back, and two hand grenades dangled from her belt. She was tall, stocky, and looked as if she could pick us up at the same time and dangle us from the bridge. She sounded like a stern schoolteacher asking a simple question, "Boys, you are about 20 years old?" We nodded yes. She said, "How long have you been working with underwater TNT?" We both said eight years. She told us to lower our arms. She leaned back against the car, looked over her shoulder at the driver, and snapped her fingers loudly. The headlights dimmed. The only light was now coming from the soft lights on the bridge. She stepped forward and walked around us, sizing us up as if deciding if we were worthy of such a contract.

When she noticed our burns, she immediately started barking orders for a medical case in the back of the van. Her demeanor quickly changed to almost maternal. She opened the medical bag given to her and gently cleaned and dressed our burns. We stared at her, not knowing if she was friend or foe. If George had any pain, he did not show it. When she was done, she cocked her head to the side to inspect her work, smiled, and stood up.

Without a hiccup she returned to her previous apathetic self, put her hands on her hips and barked, "Stand up!" Her entourage of scary military men immediately raised their guns, loaded the barrels, and aimed. Seven more anxious renegades stood, guns aimed and ready, in the shadows of the SUVs. She leaned against the car, crossed her legs and arms, took a deep breath, let it out, and continued asking us questions, but now in a tone that was patronizing and mechanical, "Boys, the government of Turkey needs your help. You will be doing us a great favor and you will be providing protection to the people of

Turkey. This is a very honorable job. You will be paid well for your services. Do you understand?" Was this the same speech she had given the others before she killed them? We nodded 'yes' to her question. "Good! Wonderful! This is a top-secret job, do you understand? You are to tell no one, do you understand?" We nodded.

Good, this is going well." She paced back and forth in front of us, her eyes never leaving ours. Back and forth she shifted her glare from me to George. "Now, George and Dimitri, do you accept the job? Before you answer, I think you should know that you two are the only qualified masons for this particular job. Yes, there were others, but they had unfortunate accidents. It is really a shame..."

We looked at each other, knowing exactly what the other was thinking. If we did not accept this job, we would probably be involved in an 'accidental' drowning under this bridge. We nodded 'yes'.

"Great! Both of you sign these documents – NOW!" We both jumped, knowing she was not friend but definitely foe. She handed us the envelopes with a pen. We each signed and gave them back to her. She smiled, patted the tops of our heads, took the papers, and handed them off to a man hidden in the shadows. We heard the double-click of a briefcase, a moment of silence, and a final double-click. She approached us quickly, as if she was about to push us over the side of the bridge. We both stumbled backward, slamming into the railing. She grabbed our shirts, almost yanking us off our feet, pulled us together, and shoved us hard against the railing. Her chin was tucked down and her eyes were slightly looking up at us. I felt as if a rabid dog was going to bite off our faces. The men gathered around her with their guns still launched and the barrels so close that we could smell the gunpowder from a previous kill. We held our breaths, closed our eyes, and waited. My heart was racing, and the vodka was long gone from my body. My mind was as clear as a cloudless day. I thought, This is it. I am not jumping off this bridge, I am going to be shot and thrown off this bridge with George next to me.

There was no gunfire, only the threat. In a slow, evil, controlled voice she said, "If you tell anyone, I mean anyone, you and they will not have a happy ending, do you understand, boys?" She was about four inches from our faces. We nodded. She stepped back in unison with the soldiers, smiled, and returning to her patronizing demeanor, *slapped us playfully then said, "Fantastic, your work begins right now. Good boys! Now get in the FUCKING CAR!" Startled, we jumped and started for the cars. As we stumbled forward in complete shock, black hoods were put over our heads. In the darkness under the hood, I envisioned Qaseem's face. I would never see him again. He would not know where I was. My tears began to fall silently to my chest. I had lost my parents and Qaseem. I had no idea where they were taking us, but what I did know was that my life would never be the same.*

Pearl laid the journal across her chest and stared at the dancing flames on the ceiling. She didn't know what to think. Her brain was having so many conversations with itself. Mostly she just wanted to cry for them. When she turned the page, the several added pages fell out again. The first loose page had George's name on it, but the penmanship was very different. She assumed they belonged to George and for some reason Dimitri had put them inside his journal for safekeeping. She tucked the loose pages back in between the previous page to read later.

Dimitri started the next page with, *I found these under the desk in the office inside the cement building. I asked George about them, and he said he had forgotten about them long ago. I asked if could add them to my journal and he just waved his hand at me and said, "I was made to write that crap down or they would have never let me out of that asylum. It is just a bunch of memories I let go of a long time ago. I forgot I hid them here. I did not want Sophia to see them. She probably never would have married me. Keep 'em, they are yours.*

As much as Pearl wanted to read more, it was late, and the bottle of ouzo was empty. Her thoughts were swimming as she blew out the candles, and before she knew it, she was asleep.

Chapter Eleven

Charlee and Mathias listened to the voicemail on Julia's phone twice, then looked at Julia and the computer screen with Alexander's information staring at them. Mathias said, "Mom, what is this all about? Is there a problem with this man claiming to be Dimitri's son? Is this something we should worry about, especially if he is with Pearl? The coincidence of an *Alexander* showing up is a little unnerving at this point."

Julia sat back on the bed and motioned the two of them to sit down. She said, "When I was a young girl, I found out that my father and Dimitri had a secret life. They were hired by the Turkish government to build an underwater storage facility for a weapon of mass destruction. I never told my mother I knew about it. It was my understanding that Dimitri and George were just simple fisherman." Julia got up and poured another cup of coffee. "Charlee, this is one big story. Honey, what do we have planned this morning?"

"We have nothing planned. We were going to go over the information Pearl was supposed to send us regarding the results from the seminar. Did she send anything?"

"Yes, she did. It is in my email. I glanced at it, but it is not what I was hoping for. There is nothing there that I do not already know. We can give her a call in a bit. So, I guess we have time for a story. Are you two ready for a fantastical story?"

Charlee replied, "Yes, I am. I have a hunch that we're going to need more coffee and some breakfast. Right?"

Julia nodded, got up, went to the bathroom and got dressed, then went onto the balcony of their hotel room while Charlee ordered room service. The sun was high in the sky and it cast a warm blanket of sunshine over her body. She hadn't thought about her younger years in a long time. Charlee handed her and Mathias a refill and both sat down next to her on the balcony.

Julia began, "For many years I was so confused about our family history, but I just wrote it off as my parents not wanting to relive their past. So, if this story gets confusing, just stop me and I will do my best to make sense of it all." Charlee and Mathias nodded and got comfortable in the balcony chairs as Julia began, "My mother was an avid writer. She journalled every day right before my father came home from work. After she passed, I found her journals in the attic and read them. There was a short story about Dimitri having an affair with the Prince, soon-to-be Emir of Qatar. I knew he'd had an affair, but I was not sure of the extent. I have all of this written down in so many of my journals back at the old house. I wonder if Pearl ever found them now that she is living there. There must be over twenty of them all together." Julia went silent for a moment and looked at the hotel room door just seconds before a knock was heard, "Food is here."

Charlee giggled, "How do you do that?" Julia shrugged her shoulders and smiled. A rolling table of fresh fruits, hot spinach pies, yogurt drizzled with honey and walnuts, and a large pot of coffee was being wheeled into the room.

As Charlee tipped the server, Julia and Mathias made themselves a plate and returned to the balcony. Julia continued, "Right before Katrina died, she gave your grandmother Sophia a large box containing her journals and I believe a few of Dimitri's, along with some private papers. I was not sure why she did this. The next morning, Sophia had the journals boxed up and the mail carrier took them off. My mother was so secretive and mysterious about her family history. Many times, I found her in deep thought, just staring at the wall. I would ask her a question, but she would not even register that she heard me, and I was standing right in front of her. I do not know how she and Katrina met, but they were very bonded.

Charlee, one day I was rummaging through the old attic. In the corner was an old chest of drawers. The drawers were empty, but in the back of the bottom center drawer was a small box. It had a ring in it that I am sure was worth at least a million dollars. It was exquisite. There were a few pictures of my mother when she was younger wearing it, but I never saw her wear it and I never asked about it. She was so closed off. I always wondered where she got it and from whom she got it."

Charlee looked at her and said, "I know about the trunks. I put several of my journals in one of the trunks for safekeeping when I moved into Agriolykos."

Julia looked at the two of them, "You know, I have a photographic memory. Give me a second and I will share with you what I read in my mother's journals. Let me think for a minute." She closed her eyes, sat back in her chair, took a deep breath, and found the memory, the memory of the day she read her mother's first journal.

She began and spoke almost monotone as she recalled its contents. "It seemed as though she was running from something or someone. She started her journal with… After World War II and through the 1970s, Turkey had been plagued by military coups, creating a series of unstable government regimes and fractured economic systems. Martial law was declared in all providences. Social and economic decline created countrywide poverty and distress. Secret black op military groups worked under the radar to prevent war between Turkey, Russia, and Greece, and secret military bases were necessary to hide bombs of mass destruction. If military force required them to be deployed, they needed to be strategically and locally located. Several of the isolated and poorly populated islands fronting Turkey were chosen to house such devices. The bases needed to be underwater and camouflaged, and required an extremely skilled worker to carry out the work.

There were only nine qualified men in the world. Seven of the men declined, and they died shortly thereafter of 'accidental' causes. The two remaining were the youngest of the nine. With permission, to retain a somewhat normal life while carrying out the work, they agreed to take the job. They were told that their service was honorable and necessary for the good of the people and if they spoke of their duties to anyone, due to the classified nature, they and those they told would be killed. The two men, George and Dimitri, understood the severity of the punishment if they were to leak any information of their duties and job descriptions. They were then moved to an isolated part of the island of Ikaria.

George and Dimitri were inseparable. They had worked most of their lives side-by-side with their fathers. They were especially skilled masons and were offered jobs all over the world. When they took the mission given to them, they were given homes next to each other and began a life on Ikaria. The townspeople only knew of them as fishermen living on the opposite and more deserted part of the island where the sea was deeper and colder. When they came into the village for food and personal supplies, they kept their conversations short and their personal lives to themselves. The journal said, *One day we saw them; we saw Dimitri. At first, I was panic stricken. Katrina and I were hiding on the island, not far from where the two men lived. We felt safe on this island. We knew this island was off the radar, but when we saw Dimitri, we began to make plans to leave as soon as possible. A few days later, Katrina and I ran into George and Dimitri at the market. They had been following us. At first, we thought we were recognized, but it soon became obvious that Dimitri did not know me. We were both relieved. I realized if I stayed with Dimitri, I would be safe – Qaseem would never let anyone hurt him, or me for that matter.*

Katrina and I decided to become friendly with the two men. This life would be a veiled life. We knew what we must do. I changed my name to Sophia and erased all traces of our past existence. Nothing to link us to Qatar. Nothing to link us to Qaseem."

Chapter Twelve

Pearl got up early and smiled as she thought about the evening with Alexander. She thumbed through the news to see if the events of the conference had made the headlines. There was nothing. As Pearl again tried to recall the events of that evening, it seemed almost like a fading dream. As the days went by, she was forgetting more and more, as if it was all made up. She opened her phone to the videos to pull one up to remind herself of what had happened. Every video was gone. Every text message and email were gone, as if it didn't happen, as if it *was* just a dream. *How on earth could all of this just disappear? This was a world-wide event. This pharaoh was going to change the dynamics in every field of academia – immortality! How could the two thousand people in that room all suffer from amnesia? It should be all over the news. Who was this pharaoh really? Who erased this and why?*

She shook it off, got dressed, and tried again to see the burn on the back of her neck with her small mirror. The pain was gone, but in its place was a large scab. She left it alone, put a small scarf around her neck to cover it, and headed downstairs for the best continental breakfast around. It was one of the reasons she always stayed at this hotel; the best rooftop restaurant and the best morning buffet. The cafeteria counters were full of hot spinach pies, meats, cheeses, nuts, olives, yogurts, and several freshly squeezed juices. She had some freshly squeezed orange juice, Greek yogurt with honey and walnuts, and a large slice of spanakopita, her favorite breakfast of all time. When she was done, she took two apples, three buttered rolls with some cheese and meat slices, rolled them up in a napkin, and put them in her bag to go. With an apple in her mouth, she texted Alexander, cancelling the evening's dinner plans, and made plane reservations to Ikaria, which was departing in an hour. She invited him to join her saying, "We want answers, and I think they are in the attic in a giant trunk. As much as I would like to enjoy another meal with you at Spondi's, my curiosity to know more about my family is calling me home. With everything I have been through these past few days, I need to be home in my own bed, in my own quiet space. And I need to try to remember what happened on Friday night. Something really strange is going on."

Alexander understood and agreed to go with her. He wanted information about his father, Dimitri, and she wanted to know her family history better. It hadn't occurred to her until now that what she did know about her family history was superficial. The depth of her existence was much more exciting than she had ever thought.

When she arrived at the airport, she found Alexander and Adeem waiting on the tarmac next to a helicopter, a beautiful jet-black bird with no identification on it. With no plane in sight waiting for her as she had expected, it seemed obvious that she was traveling to Ikaria via helicopter. Alexander had hired a driver to pick them up at the Ikaria airport and drive them to Pearl's home on the far side of the island when they landed. Pearl said sarcastically, "Well, this is so much more convenient, is it not?"

Alexander smiled and said, "Have you ever ridden in a helicopter?"

"No, I have not, but I have always wanted to."

Alexander said, "It is a good thing because I canceled your plane ticket."

Pearl shook her head and chuckled, "Yes, I can see that. No plane is waiting for me. Should I say thank you, Alexander?"

"From now on I would like you to call me Alex. All my friends do, even Adeem."

Adeem winked at his dad then turned to Pearl and said jovially, "This is your lucky day! I will be your pilot. I promise to get you to the island in one piece. Once you enter the ride, I will need you to put your hands and feet inside the vehicle and fasten your seat belt. Upon landing, please exit to the left." He laughed out loud, "Get it? Get it? Like in Disneyland?"

Pearl clapped her hands with excitement and said, "Yes! Lovely!" then rolled her eyes at Alex, who in turn laughed out loud.

Adeem helped her into the helicopter, handed her a headset, and swung the mouthpiece around until it almost touched her lips. He strapped her in and gave her a pair of bomber glasses to wear. He instructed her not to take off the headset and explained that through the mouthpiece, everyone would be able to communicate, even over the noise of the rotor blades.

She said, "And the sunglasses?"

He smiled and said, "I thought they would look good on you, and they do." Pearl felt her face flush and quickly looked out the window to hide it.

Adeem smiled as a twinge of excitement raced through him. He started the engine, flipped a multitude of switches and gears, and communicated with the tower. When the blades started to whirl, the noise became so loud that Pearl was indeed happy for the headphones. As the helicopter lifted and tilted forward, she began to laugh like a little girl. The excitement of it all was exhilarating. Alex and Adeem started laughing with her. She looked from one to the other and gave two thumbs up.

Pearl yelled into the headset, "THIS IS AWESOME!" Both men jumped as her voice screamed through the mouthpiece, then they laughed even harder. She just smiled at them as she stared out the window for a while, watching the land disappear and the ocean emerge beneath them.

Through the headset, Adeem announced, "The flight will take about two hours, so sit back and enjoy the ride. Cocktails and lobster will be served shortly."

Pearl and Alex looked up and laughed. Pearl noticed Adeem had adjusted his inside mirror. She could see him and he could see her. She thought, *Thank god for the glasses!*

When the helicopter was well on its way, Adeem watched her from the mirror. Her skin was white like a pearl, and her hair looked so soft and wispy as the curls danced around her face. Every so often, she would scratch her nose as the ringlets tickled her. She was one of the most beautiful women he had ever laid eyes on. Something about her was different, different enough to make him wonder just how far this adventure would take him.

At one point, she looked up and saw Adeem looking at her, and she smiled then looked out the window. The Aegean Sea sparkled below. Her heart was beginning to soften and fill with warmth. Ikaria did that to her. It was home, where she belonged. When she looked up again, Adeem was still watching her, at least it looked that way. She couldn't see his eyes behind his glasses, but he was definitely not looking through the windshield. Normally she would look away and so would he, but they didn't. They were transfixed, looking into the mirror at each other while hiding behind their safety net; two pairs of bomber sunglasses.

Alex looked up and saw what was happening. He smiled, bumped her elbow and said, "How do you feel about Dimitri's story?" Pearl looked over at him as he lowered his sunglasses and said, "Cat got your tongue, missy?"

She blushed and said, "Stop! I have read the first part of the journal. I am at the place where Dimitri inserted George's handwritten papers. While we are flying, I would like to read George's papers. Do you mind?"

Alex said, "Perfect! I have some work to do and can use this time to finish it up." They both dove into their satchels, pulling out the paperwork they needed. Pearl removed George's papers from Dimitri's journal, got comfortable, and began to read George's story.

After a couple of pages in, Pearl realized George was insti-tutionalized at some point. She asked Alex about it, and he said, "Yes. It is quite a story. Read on."

December 23
Today I am 18. Happy Birthday to me. My big present was a tablet with blank pages and ten ballpoint pens. Not the best present, if you ask me. The pressure to fill these pages has angered me to my core. I have spent every Tuesday for the past seven months in therapy. I was told that if I did not agree to counseling sessions for at least a year, I would be placed in a mental institution. This feels like a threat to me. This place is bad enough. I do not remember getting here; all I know is that I woke up here. My room feels like a jail cell. My view inside is a set of metal bunkbeds, a sink with a metal mirror, and a small drawer to put a toothbrush, toothpaste, a plastic comb, and writing pads or books in. My view to the outside is a barred rectangular window and billions of acres of dry grass and dirt. If anyone tried to run for it, there would be no place to hide. And this dingy grey

jumpsuit they make me wear rides up my crotch, pinching my balls all day long. I hate it! These suits are made for short people! Nice logo too – SDDC, which stands for Step Down Detention Center. I can leave my room, but I cannot leave the premises. I was also told that I had to write at least two pages a day on this stupid pad of paper. Not the best birthday present. What am I supposed to say? What good is writing your thoughts on paper? How could that possibly be a cure for what is going on in my head? I am angry! I am mad! I am sad! I cannot eat or sleep. Why can I not just work? It is the best possible thing for me right now. But I am told, "NO! You could injure some-one; hell, you could kill someone. Get your head on straight, son, and we will let you go home." I am the most skilled TNT man on the planet. I feel this is just a way to torture me. If Dimitri had not left, if Sarah had not left, I would have been fine. Are we not allowed to grieve? They were everything to me. They were my family, my best friends. Now I have no one. I have my parents, but they do not under-stand. They have had friends leave and friends die. They know I am hurting, so why are they making such a big deal out of all of this? I said I was sorry. I was not in my right mind. It was an accident. I am punished every day when I look in the mirror, so just leave me alone for a while. I just want to sleep....

December 28
It is almost the new year, and I am stuck here in this cell of a room. All night I hear people screaming, crying. Last night, Kaan was beaten badly by his roommate. I am not sure if he is OK. No one will tell me anything. I sit on my bunk with my head in my hands, and the only thing that makes me feel better is rocking back and forth. It drowns out the noises all around me. Now I understand why Kaan does this all day. He rocks and moans out loud, sitting on the floor in the middle of his room. Kyrone told him over and over to "SHUT UP!" but he would not listen. Half of Kaan's hair is on the floor all around him. He pulls out his hair little by little every day. His head has old bloody scabs and scars as if he has been doing this a long time. His eyes are black and glazed over and his face is without emotion; just rocking and moaning. The only thing he will eat is chicken livers with ketchup on them. It is the only time he looks normal. He eats each one care-

fully and looks around the mess hall at everyone, smiling, yet he really does not make eye contact, he just looks at people who are not there, or maybe they are and I cannot see them. If he had a knife and fork, I am sure he would cut his livers into little pieces and eat them like a sane person. It is the strangest fucking thing. He never talks to anyone but is always talking to himself as if he is at war with a ghost. Sometimes he jumps up and wails out loud, scaring the shit out of me.

Kyrone is constantly yelling at him. Everyone then yells at Kyrone to SHUT UP! It is a circus. Kaan is in his own world, and it is a dark world. I was told he drugged his parents, put them in their car, and set it on fire. He then pushed the car off the mountain near where he lived and told no one. Two years later they found the charred car and remains at the bottom of a ravine below his house.

Kaan had gone mad. The papers said that he killed two of the four officers that came to the house to arrest him. The other two had multiple broken bones but lived. Kaan left them for dead and was later found walking nearly naked down the old frontage road about ten miles out of town. All he had on was a sock, a knife, and an old, dried-up penis in his hand. Some speculate it was his father's.

I heard Kyrone beating Kaan again last night. Everyone did, but no one came to his rescue. I think most of us are getting tired of the endless beating rampages that have turned into melancholy sounds day in and day out.

I do not understand why my counselor put me in this hell hole, just because I would not obey her and her stupid rules. To get out of here, I have to write down everything about my past and I have to talk about Sarah. Why? She is gone. The love of my life is gone, and I cannot bring her back. WHY WILL YOU PEOPLE NOT JUST LET ME BE? I JUST WANT TO WORK!

January 5
Once again, I had my privileges taken away because I did not write what I was told to write. I can no longer go outside. All I got was the Old Testament thrown at me, "Here, this should help the time pass if you cannot seem to use your words correctly." I hate it here! I cannot believe my father allowed this. It is not my fault. I will not take the pills, I WILL NOT. For TWO WEEKS you put that shit in my food. I

refuse to walk around like a zombie, pulling out my hair and moaning on the floor!

Kaan was released from the hospital today and ate with us at lunch. His face was almost unrecognizable. They slit his eyelids so he could see, and his blackened face is covered in stitches. His wrists are in short casts, and he has the words SHUT UP carved into his arm. When Kaan looks down, he can read it. I guess if it was on his fore-head, he could not see it every minute of every day. They put him back in the same room as Kyrone. That is bullshit! God, I hope he shuts up.

At breakfast, I asked one of the guys in here – who is sleeping with the staff nurse – what Kaan's story was. I was told, whether this is true or not I am not sure, that Kaan's parents used him as a sex slave in their sex movies since he was old enough to walk. The nurse said that when they arrested Kaan, they found hundreds of tapes and photographs of him and his sister together in sexual acts, as well as with adults. The tapes began when he was about four, I was told, and the old, dried-up penis he was found with was his. He cut off his own penis. The nurse said he has a little nub and probably almost bled to death when he did this. She said his sister has saved his life many times. She was the one caring for him and would take him to the hospital every time he tried to end his life. After the last trip, she killed herself. I listened to Kaan's story, and it almost made me sick to think of what is in his head. The demons that he is living with must be monsters. What I do not understand is why am I in here with Kaan. This is not right AND YOU PEOPLE KNOW IT!

January 7

My father and grandfather came today. My counselor called them. My father sat on my bunk, took my hand, and looked at the floor for a long time. When he sniffled, I realized he was crying. I have never seen anyone in my family cry.

He said, "George, if you cannot speak out loud what is going on inside then you must write it. If you do not write, you will stay here longer. This is a new way to heal, and they tell me this journaling method really works, son. You must trust they know what they are doing here. George, it is very simple; write, my son, and rid yourself of this pain. If you do not, I cannot trust you with explosives. You almost killed Eli too. He is still not the same, but he is getting better. His hearing is returning slowly. You are my best man, George, but I need you to be focused and alert. I need you to stop playing games and be responsible. What we do for a living is not to be played with or even challenged. If you cannot come to terms with all of this, I have no choice but to remove you from the business altogether.

Dimitri is coming home. Together you two are the best there is underwater. We have trained you well. Let this all go – write and be well. Come home to us. Your mother is crying every night. She feels she is to blame for you being here. It is killing her, George. Please, son, just write, get it out. Stop writing about this place. We all know it is not where you should be, but it is better than being in prison for the rest of your life. It was an accident. We all know this. George, you must write about Sarah. Let it go, son. Let it go."

My father held me while I cried, and my grandfather soothed me with his loving words. I love my parents. I love my grandfather even more. I cried all night. The release kind of felt good until Kyrone yelled across the way, threatening to scalp me at breakfast if I did not SHUT UP. David, the guy next to me, said Kyrone's father used to yell and beat his mother because she cried all the time. My tears dried up after that.

I sit here in this locked room with a Bible, a pad, and several pens. I have been told to write. OK, I will write. I counted the blank pages in the journal. There are 369 pages, and I am supposed to fill them up. If I do, I get to go home. My father said that Dimitri and his father would be home in three weeks, and there are two restorations that start in March. Dad said we will all work the sites together as usual, but this time we will get paid five times more than we ever did. Something about Dimitri doing business with a guy in Qatar. I hope he was not telling me that just to get me to write. I could use the money, we all could. So, I will write my story, because I WANT OUT OF HERE! And you people reading this, you made a deal with my father; no pills, just pen and paper then I am released from this hellhole. I will write, so just leave me alone while I do. 369 pages is a lot of pages to fill up so I will write from the beginning and with the best penmanship, like my grandfather taught me. When I am done you better hold up your end of the bargain. No more putting medications in my food!

6:00 p.m.
I am finally feeling better. My head is clear, and my thoughts are not so jumbled. The medications were making me stupid, so for the first time since getting here, I feel normal. I will write if you continue to stop medicating me.

4:00 a.m.
My thoughts are keeping me awake. 369 pages... here is my story.
My father, grandfather, and great-grandfather are all masons. They are skilled in all facets of masonry and are best known for their talent in explosives and underwater detonations. Most masons are skilled as either builders, cutters, or quarrymen. Builders work with all materials; wood, brick, or stone combined with clay or mud then made into a mortar for stabilizing the stones when they set them in place. They are hired to build anything from walls to houses to government buildings. These structures have clean lines, simple geometric designs, and serve the simple purpose of keeping those inside warm and dry. Cutters are craftsmen who cut the stones for the builders from the quarries or from other pieces of stone. They are hired to cut stones to fit like puzzle pieces or to simulate the broken stones that need to be replaced or repaired. Some of the best cutters are found along the Aegean Sea. They rebuild the ornate carvings and pillars found in the great marble buildings of Athens, Greece and Hierapolis in Anatolia, Turkey. They are also skilled in making stones from different materials. If they make the stones from scratch, they stamp them with their personal Banker's Mark. A Banker's Mark is a personal symbol that identifies the work of a particular stone mason. These marks are passed down through the generations of stone masons in the same family. This is invaluable to historians studying the works of masons throughout history. Our mark is two overlapping circles creating an inner circle. In the middle circle is a large 'G'. Some ask if it stands for God, but it stands for George. It is pretty cool.

Quarrymen cut the stones away from the earth and ship the enormous blocks of marble or limestone off to the cutters. Quarrymen are the baddest of all. These guys are monsters. They are huge with muscles and strength equivalent to five men. Owning three quarries has made the men in my family powerful men here in Turkey. Once, my father and grandfather picked me up from school. The kids that made fun of me took a step back when they saw us all together. I think for the first time they realized that my family was a source to be reckoned with. A family of giants!

Then there are Masons, the men who lay the stones in complex geometric patterns and designs to last centuries, like those we see in the great cathedrals across Europe. I am part of this group of masons. These masons are mathematic geniuses and architects. The masons in my family are skilled in all facets of masonry and own three of the largest marble and limestone quarries in Turkey. Our Banker's Mark can be found on thousands of blocks around the world. My family and the work we do and have done across the east is very well known. We are all educated in design engineering and contracting, art and religious history, as well as skilled architects and proficient sculptors. But the skill that has made us extremely valuable and sought after by the many government restoration societies is our expertise in working underwater with TNT – dynamite. Many of the historical estates / castles were built on the edge of waterways and the cliffs surrounding the oceans around the world. Many succumbed to the moist, salty air and foundational deterioration, tumbling into submerged piles of stone that eventually settled into the sea floor. Each incoming and outgoing wave covers them with sand and debris. The only way to break up the piles, lodged together like a beaver's dam, is to use dynamite. My grandfather George learned these skills from his father when he was twelve years old and he taught them to his son George II when he was twelve years old. I was also taught these skills when I was twelve. Our family's specialty is the complete restoration of ancient historical sites dating back to the 1200s.

My grandfather owned and operated three of the first marble quarries in Turkey and employed over 500 men. Two of the quarries produced a unique cherry-colored marble called Rosso Levanto. Cherry-colored veins run through this marble, giving the marble its cherry pinkish and red hues. As soon as it was discovered, it was immediately in demand and exported by ship to several countries including France, India, Qatar, Spain, and the United States. It is seen in homes, businesses, and even in the United States' White House. It has been used in interior designs around the world.

The third quarry produced Opium marble, a black, yellow, and gray mixture that resembles an artist painting. Countertops, pillars, and flooring were made from grandfather's Opium marble. His business skills and fair reputation preceded him, and he treated his laboring employees as if they were his children. He watched them work long and brutal hours in the dust-covered fields and mines. They never complained and they never had to ask for anything. The money brought in by the mines and quarries was so vast that employees' paychecks represented the wealth that the quarries brought in. Each employee was given a percentage of the sales, allowing them to pro-vide for their families without worry. No one ever quit, yet it took a special man to work the quarries. They had to be strong, have a solid constitution, and be built to move hundreds of pounds of rock day in and day out. Most of all, they had to work as a team, a family. No one was more special than the next, and if anyone felt they were, they were simply told to go home and not return. This is how our business continues to run today. We are all a family. I love my grandfather and my father.

When I turned seven, my father asked me if I was interested in following in the family's footsteps. My first question was, "Can I learn how to blow up the rocks?" The answer came with a hearty laugh, "Well of course you can!" My big present that year was my grandfather's toolbox and tool belt. I was a tall, lanky kid. I had no hips, but I was determined to wear that tool belt. I could barely pick it up with a full load of tools and I had to hold it up on my hips with both hands or it fell to the ground, along with my pants. This hap-pened on many occasions. One day, I took off my shirt and tied it around my waist then put on the tool belt above my shirt. It was a miracle! The thing stayed on all day.

Over time I grew into a feisty, strong man resembling both my grandfather and father; tall with shoulders, arms, and thighs so big we had to hire a private tailor to make our shirts and pants fit correctly. The girls at school always teased me saying, "George, take off your shirt. Show us what a real man looks like." Whenever they asked, I did take off my shirt just to anger the guys who had always pushed me around. I got a Valentine's Day letter one year, and several of the girls at my school read it before it was handed to me. It did not take long for it to circulate around the school. After that, every guy in my class hated me. The letter was from Sarah. I cannot remember every word, but it went something like this:

I love the way you wear your long, black, shiny, and slightly wavy hair, pulling it back when you work and letting it loose to impress me. I love your dark, sun-kissed skin covering your massive muscles and how they glisten when you sweat.
I love your crystal blue eyes, and your teeth as white as alabaster. You look like a movie star from Hollywood.
I love the way you look at me and how my tiny hand feels in your strong, callused hands. They make me feel safe.
Someday, I would like to have my first kiss with you.
Roses are Red, Violets are Blue, I want to be your Valentine, Will you be mine too?

I still have this letter. I miss her so much. I need to stop writing now.

January 8
This morning when I got my tablet back, my social worker said, "George, remember you are writing these things down for you, not necessarily for me. For many people, writing is so much easier than talking. I am proud of you. You are opening up. Keep up the good work." This morning I was not handed a cup of pills, just a large glass of juice. It was freshly squeezed and so cold. It was like a treat. I drank it slowly, tasting every drop for as long as I could. I asked if they were going to put the pills in my food. I was told, "Not anymore, as long as you continue to cooperate." I asked why the regular med nurse was gone and I was told she had gotten fired for sleeping with the patients. I think that is my fault, and I am sorry. At breakfast, Kyrone told everyone that Kaan was dead. When Kaan was in the hospital, recovering once again from a beating from Kyrone, he stole

*a pair of scissors and put them under the inner sole of his shoe.
During the night he put them to his temple and slammed his head
against the wall, embedding the scissors into his head. This really
upset me. I had to leave the cafeteria. All I could do was cry. It was
like someone had turned on a faucet. I found myself rocking again
to calm myself down. I knew this place was not right for Kaan. He
needed a lot more help, and keeping him in a room with Kyrone was
so wrong. I will always wonder why or how he was placed here
instead of a real mental institution. All I did all day was cry. The
small amount of hope I had, trust I had, is now gone. I just want
out of here!*

January 10
*The last two days have been hard on me. Everyone is shaken up over
Kaan, and no one is socializing or even talking at all. They shut down
the work schedules and announced over the intercom, "This is a great
tragedy. We hope this is a wakeup call. Everyone can spend the day
in silence, contemplating your lives and situations." We then got a
lecture on gratefulness. I am sure Kaan might have wanted to hear
that speech before he decided to stab himself in the head. It is so hard
to focus on this writing. I am so tired.*

1:00 p.m.
*When I was at school, I craved attention from the girls. I hung around
with the pretty girls which made the other boys hate me even more.
This brought me great pleasure. Many times, I would wink at the guys
as they passed me in the halls, taunting them and purposely making
them uncomfortable. This created balled-up fists and red, angry faces
that were always followed with name calling. I did not care when the
jocks made fun of me at school, calling me names like mastodon,
monster boy, humongous ape, freak. I just walked right up to them,
looked down at them, flexed my biceps, and eventually they walked
away disappointed that they could not get a rush from me. Many times,
I saw fear in their faces when I did this and it gave me great joy. As I
got older, I eventually learned compassion with the help of Sarah. I
think I fell in love with her the day she sent me the Valentine letter.*

For the most part I hated everyone at school. My comfort came from Sarah, my family, and the quarry workers.

When I began working the quarries, I met a lot of great people. Many days I worked alongside them. They invited me to their family parties and social events, so I saw how the other side lives. My family was so stringent on perfection, but the quarry families taught me how to enjoy the fruits of our labor with swimming pools, playing team baseball, backyard barbeques, and always with the best meat on the grill. They taught me how to feel the stones, to become one with them as if they were alive. It was a gift to work with the stones and I felt a connection that most people outside the business might think strange. Most boys my age worked in the factories after school. Not me – I sat at the dinner table every night while my grandfather pushed book after book in front of me, meticulously teaching me mathematics and pouring over engineering and contracting blueprints. I learned the history of architectural design dating back to the 1200s and the secrets behind the mason's stonework that still stand to this day. These studies began when I was seven and continue today. It was a given that I would follow in my family's footsteps. At seven, I tagged along with my father to the many ancient historical sites.

When I turned nine years old, I met Dimitri. Dimitri's family had moved in across the street four doors down. He was the new kid on the block. His family returned to Turkey from Qatar where he spent many years with his father working for the Emir. He had learned many skills from his father that began at the age of nine. By the time he was 12 he was working side-by-side with his father.

Dimitri had skills that I did not have. He is proficient in work-ing with water. His father was a master of aquifers and knew how to bring fresh, clean water to the surface for all kinds of uses. He was also the youngest mason in the field of explosives. It was in Qatar that Dimitri learned the power of TNT – dynamite. His skills at 12 were impeccable and unbelievable. He knew how to handle it, pack it, and detonate it with such perfect precision that nothing was damaged except for what he intended to blow up. His father and grandfather were two of the best explosive engineers in the world, and Dimitri was close behind. But working with dynamite is not a frivolous task. It requires a strong mind, a steady hand, and a lot of faith, let alone a personality that did not dawdle on the mundane things in life. Dimitri was quiet, intense, and aloof. He did not play games or run around with the other kids. He was a silent observer and if you were lucky, every now and then you just might see him smile.

It was a block party that brought our families together. A night of celebration – National Sovereignty and Children's Day, a Turkish celebration to bring joy to the children who had lost their families during the war. Over the years it had turned into quite a festive event. The whole day was spent with the children playing games, eating, laughing, and uniting with other family members. Members of the community shared food, stories, and fun.

Dimitri's father began working with our family. He had so many wealthy contacts around the world that before we knew it, Dimitri and I were taking on bids for work all over the place at the age of fourteen. It was awesome! We knew we were good, and so did all the kids at school. As we got older, we became the most popular guys in our class. We always brought the beer and the food to all the parties. There was never a party that we were not invited to. We were like kings! After a while, Dimitri started turning down invitations, so I was now "the guy". All the girls wanted to kiss me and date me, and all the guys wanted to be me. It kind of went to my head. Then it happened.

January 12

I can feel my mind becoming clearer and clearer. The drugs are no longer in my system, and now I remember. For two days, all I could do was cry and rock. They made me stay in the infirmary on watch for two nights.

I am only going to write this once and I do not want to talk about it out loud yet.

Sarah was the only one who really knew me. She knew when I was hurt or scared. She knew when I was nervous or anxious. She knew when I needed to be held without talking. She touched me and kissed me as if it was the first time every time. She never pressured me, but she made me "tow the line" as Grandpa used to say. She had a way about her that was always, well, she did not treat me like everyone else is all I can say. She had a look – you know, like that

Mom look that told me to knock it off whenever I got a little too into myself. I trusted her with my thoughts. Many nights she held me when all I wanted to do was cry. When my dog died, she was there night and day, just holding me and caressing my face and head as I lay in her lap. She was the first girl I gave myself to, and I was her first. We were inseparable after that. I did not care about anyone but her. I bought her a ring and asked her to marry me. She said yes, but not until she graduated from high school. I was so happy. We could sit and talk for hours. I wanted to make her the happiest woman in the world.

Whenever she commented on a pretty dress she saw and liked or really anything she liked, I bought it for her. Her eyes would light up, then she would lower them and say, "George, you must stop doing this. It is too much!" I never listened to her.

On Christmas Eve we all went to the beach. Jerry had an old VW Bug on his parents' property, just rotting in the field. Its engine was made of magnesium. When you light one of these engines on fire, it glows so brightly for hours that you can see it from space. A group of us guys towed it to the far side of the beach where no one would see us and invited everyone. We had been drinking all day, getting ready for the party of a lifetime. I called Sarah to make plans to pick her up. She was going to an anniversary dinner with her parents and said she would come out after. When we got to the beach, we dug a huge hole in the sand and tipped the car over into it. I had stolen some dynamite from the quarry and brought it with me. I knew it would be the biggest, baddest fire ever. When it got dark at around 10:00 p.m. or so, we decided to light it up. Everyone was begging me to light up the car.

They did not know I brought the explosives. I put the dynamite in the car under the engine and ran a long fuse up and over the sand dune. We all hid, drank more beer, and after a while I lit the fuse.

Sarah was on her way out to the dunes. She did not see us, and we did not see her. We had ducked down so we would not get hit by the exploding sand. Sarah saw the fuse, and not knowing what it was, she walked over to it as the flame traveled down the hole to the car. She yelled, "Where is everyone?"

Eli jumped up in front of me and yelled "Sarah, run!" I looked up. I was so drunk, but I remember.

Sarah looked down and slid into the hole as the sand buckled under her feet and the dynamite exploded. Eli lost his eyesight and hearing. I lost my Sarah. Oh my god, I killed my Sarah. What did I do? Oh my god...

Pearl set the journal papers in her lap. Her head was in a whirl with tears flowing down her cheeks. Alexander saw her tears, touched her hand, and said, "Yes, I know. That was a hard read. These two really went through a lot in their young lives. It took me some time, but I finally pieced most of it together. It appears George stayed in the detention center for an additional two weeks after his memory fully returned. He was heavily medicated for most of that time. Sarah's parents were called in and the records show that they forgave him, and shortly after that he was released. He spent two weeks in outpatient therapy learning how to forgive himself. Not long after, he and Dimitri reunited. But as I calculate the dates, it seems it was the night both their parents were killed that this reunion took place. There is a huge gap at this point."

Pearl took a big breath, wiped her face with her hands, and leaned her head back as she folded George's papers and returned them to the journal. She looked up and saw Adeem in the mirror. He had his glasses off and was looking at her, his eyes full of compassion. She looked back at Alex and lowered her head in thought. Just a few days ago her life was so simple, actually a bit boring, just going through the motions; getting up, making breakfast, and skimming through the local newspaper and highlighting her horoscope and the weather report for the day. Without this information, no one knew if a sweater was necessary or not. Living so close to the sea always brought a mixture of wind, mist, and sun. She always told her friends, "Bring layers. You can take off or put on as the weather changes."

The rest of her days were filled with long hours of studying within the piles of college books filled with potions, tinctures, and healing modalities, along with Nonnah Julia's research papers and articles that cluttered her entire kitchen table. But now, this simple, boring life had a wakeup call and the words, 'You are the chosen one' was still gnawing at her. She looked out the window of the helicopter as she watched the island of Ikaria come into view. At that moment, her body took on a whole new feeling. A warm blanket of calm over-rode the sorrow she was feeling for both Dimitri and George. Knowing she was almost home was all she needed to wash away these feelings. The island's gift of love and peace permeated through her. Just flying over it made Pearl feel safe.

Chapter Thirteen

Adeem landed the helicopter safely and, sure enough, there was a driver and car waiting for them. Pearl pulled Alex aside and requested an overnight stop at Agriolykos. She needed to check on The Sacred Rock Healing Center and Agnes before heading to the far side of the island in search of the journals. Agriolykos and the healing center were next door to each other in Therma, only a few miles from the airport. Alex said 'no'. He was determined to get to the journals and didn't want to stop for any reason so Pearl took another tactic. As Alex dealt with the driver and the rental car, she approached Adeem and skillfully gave her pitch, slowly and seductively, "Adeem, did you know that Therma has some of the most ancient healing waters in the world, and for thousands of years people have traveled here to bathe in them to heal their aliments?"

Adeem watched her as she ran her finger along the side of the helicopter as if she was carefully feeling for a flaw. He said, "No, I did not."

She looked up at him from a distance and said, "Did you know that Agriolykos has the best masseuse in all of Ikaria?" She walked closer to him.

He stuttered, "Uh, no, uh, really? No, I did not know this."

She got close enough to shake his hand if he reached out to her. "I would really like to take a swim and go to Haman tonight for a sauna and soak in the thermal waters before we start rummaging through the old journals in the dark, dusty attic. Haman is a really cool, huge natural hole in a rock mountain. Inside it is like an intense sauna with hot dripping water coming from inside the mountain. Sitting in there takes all the stress out of your muscles. I would also like a massage after. My brain is so heavy with all this information, I do not think I can sleep if I do not relax a bit. Would you like to take a sauna and swim with me?" She was close enough to unbutton his shirt as she looked up at him with a slight smile.

He said, "Oh yes!"

She said enthusiastically, "Good! Tell Alex, and I will make a quick call to Agnes." Pearl bounced off, almost wanting to laugh out loud but dared not to. She had gotten her way and that was all that mattered.

Agnes was elated that they would be staying overnight. She began planning a nice dinner on the patio for 9:00 p.m. Alex completed his business transactions with the rental car company and said, "OK, we are ready. Time to go."

Adeem said, "We are staying at Agriolykos for the night. Pearl has decided for us. We will have dinner on the patio after a nice swim and sauna. I think this is a great idea. I have decided you will join us, so put those keys away." Adeem caught up to Pearl and took her hand as they headed to the car, leaving Alex in a stupor. Pearl glanced back and winked. Alex put his hands on his hips and just shook his head. He knew she was going to be a force to be reckoned with.

As they began the drive to Therma, Pearl gave the men a quick overview of Ikaria and its wonders as if she was a tour guide. She had been a tour guide for several summers, so the information rolled off her lips effortlessly. "Ikaria's population is just over 8,000, with Therma's population just 300, give or take one or two. Most of the island is made up of rough terrain; brown and dry with crumbling shale rock that is mostly uninviting. If you look out the windows you will see many old homes and buildings from centuries ago; fallen ruins that have succumbed to time. But as you head inland and over to the beaches on the other side of the island, the land becomes lush and green. And the building styles change. They are much more modern.

Most of the island is a nature preserve. Many of the plants, flora, insects, birds, and reptiles here are found only on this island. There is also a species of dolphin that only swim the waters around Ikaria. Is that not cool?" Both Adeem and Alex nodded as they scanned the terrain from the windows. Pearl continued, "Ikaria is best known for its honey and teas, and both are sold all over the world. The diets are very simple, not a lot of fuss, but very nutritious." Pearl turned and looked at the men and said, "Did you know that Ikaria is called the island where people forget to die?" They shook their heads. "Yes, because of the rough terrain. The amount of energy it takes the body to navigate the steep treacherous hills, tend to the land and gardens, and grow fruit trees and vines amongst the slippery slopes is exhausting. But the people love it. They are always exercising; very fit, hardworking, not lazy. Most live well into their 90s, still working as if they were 20. Another part of their fountain of youth is coffee, very strong, along with homemade wine, which they drink every day, and a lot of sex, of course." Both men looked at her and smiled. She smiled back and continued, "Yes! Even in old age, sex is a priority, along with a daily nap and church. I love it here!"

Both men looked at each other and smiled. Adeem asked, "Do you live by these rules too, angel?"

Pearl quickly turned to Adeem and said sternly, "You are not allowed to call me that. And yes, I do!" Alex chuckled.

Adeem said carefully, "OK, I will choose another name when the time is right." She smiled and returned her gaze out the window.

Therma was only twenty minutes from the airport, and Pearl was so excited to be home. As they drove around the last corner before the road took a steep dive to the shoreline of the Aegean Sea, Pearl saw Harry. She quickly sat forward and asked the driver to stop. Pearl had made friends with Harry years ago. She didn't see him often, but when she did, it was always at the sacred spicket. Harry was 72 years old and originally from Ikaria. When he turned twenty, he moved to New York City and started a financial business that became very successful. He married his high school sweetheart and they had seven children who eventually took over the business. Harry and Mrs. Harry returned to Ikaria to retire. Pearl met him when she was 12 years old. She was scurrying around in the bushes with Nonnah Julia, looking for the yellow tea flower that grows specifically around the freshwater springs. Harry was filling his water jugs when Pearl jumped out of the bushes and yelled, "Peek-a-boo."

Both Harry and Julia jumped, shrieked, and grabbed their hearts. Julia yelled, "Pearl, how many times have I told you not to do that? You are going to be the death of me, child!" Pearl and Harry laughed and laughed until they cried. That day, Harry fell in love with Pearl and Pearl fell in love with Harry. From that day forward, Pearl was Harry's little "angel".

Today, Harry was at the spicket filling his water bottles. The spicket protruded from a tiny little shack hidden behind the overgrown vines, flowers, and shrubs that steal the healing waters for their own nutrition. It looked like a pump house for a well, standing room only, with a small door. From this spicket comes the purest, coldest water on the island. Everyone travels the length of the island to fill water containers every month.

Pearl rolled down her window and yelled to Harry as the car came to a stop. Pearl was so excited, "Adeem, have you ever been to Mount Shasta in California?"

Adeem said, "Yes, many times. A group of us go every spring solstice."

"Does your group stop at the spring below the mountain to fill up water containers before you climb the mountain?"

Adeem nodded and said, "Every time."

Pearl said, "Well, this is our Mount Shasta. Come, let's say hi and take a drink."

When Harry saw Pearl, he opened his arms and greeted her with a big hug, "How is my little angel? And who are your friends?"

She introduced everyone and got caught up on all the recent gossip. Harry filled a jug of fresh water for her to take with her. He gave her another big hug, a kiss on the cheek, and said, "Goodbye, my sweet angel." When she turned her back to leave, Harry looked sternly at both men, shook his finger and said, "No funny stuff. I will find you, heh?" The men nodded, understanding the meaning.

When they reached the beachfront, Pearl let out a big sigh, "Home sweet home." The driver dropped them off at the entrance to the Sacred Rock Healing Center. The guys grabbed a quick snack from the restaurant in the center while Pearl picked up the mail and checked on the staff. When she was done, she gave everyone hugs and kisses and they headed up the stairs to her sanctuary on the hill, Agriolykos. When they got to the top of the stairs, Agnes was waiting with open arms. Pearl ran to her and embraced her with a giant hug. Agnes was her favorite person in the whole world next to her Auntie Melena, Nonnah Julia, and Mom, of course. She was the live-in caretaker when Pearl's grandmother was gone. Her grandfather had passed away a few years back, and Agnes was hired to help Julia take care of the guests. Agriolykos was an Air B&B during the busy summer months.

Agnes looked up at the men and said in her strong Greek accent, "You share Room #3, and Pearl, you stay in the big house with me. Put your things away and we meet in the courtyard." Adeem and Alex looked around for Room #3 as Pearl and Agnes headed for the big house. Agnes looked back and hollered to the men, "Are you good swimmers?" They nodded yes. She said, "Good – put on your swimming shorts. We go to the thermal baths now."

Both men looked at each other as Alex said, "I do not have swim shorts with me."

Adeem answered, "Just wear a pair of shorts – it does not have to be a bathing suit."

Alex shrugged and said, "Huh, I have a pair of shorts." Adeem smiled and hit him playfully on the arm.

The women continued to walk and talk until they were out of sight. Agnes probed her about the men, especially Adeem, "You know I worry about you, my flower. You are studying so hard, long hours, and no romance. You want to be 85 like me, strong and sexy? You must have sex and lots of wine. No sex flower makes petals fall off." Pearl busted up laughing. Agnes said it like it was, with no filter. She got more graphic as they reached the big house.

Pearl finally said, "Agnes, stop! We just met and I might be related to him. Hell, I do not know. But he has been flirting with me. And I him. So, there you go!"

"Related? No, I do not see it. You will have sex with him, I insist!" she said. They both giggled. While the men were busy with luggage and changing, Agnes asked Pearl to get her caught up on what she had been up to and wanted to know all about the men. "Sit, quickly tell me everything," Agnes said with a demanding tone. Pearl couldn't talk fast enough. Every time she started a sentence, Agnes followed with another question. She explained everything from being interrupted with the phone call at the seminar, to the strange conference incident and Dimitris' affair with a prince, to Alex looking for his father, and the big reveal, finding out that her great-grandma might have had a man's head cut off and fed to wild dogs. When Pearl was finished, Agnes looked at her and said, "NO, you are telling me the truth? NO. Oh, jesus, oh, mother of Mary. What have you all gotten yourselves into? We go to Haman and soak. We get rid of evil spirits. We go now!"

Pearl nodded, "I know, right?! It is so confusing."

Pearl put on her swimsuit with a pretty cover up and headed to the courtyard to find Agnes and the men waiting. Agnes handed each of them a beach towel and said, "Come, we go the way of my special rocks. Follow me."

Pearl looked at Alex and Adeem and said, "Be very careful. Do not do as Agnes does. The rock paths are made up of loose shale, very sharp and very dangerous." At 85, Agnes flew down the slippery rock path like when she was 15 years old. The rest of them made each step count, slow and steady so as not to fall and break their necks.

When they got to the edge, Agnes said, "I do not go by the way of the beach, I go the way of the cliffs and swim. I am an old woman, and I do not want the people to see me. Boys, turn around for a minute." She put her finger in the air and swirled it around. When they turned, she took off her dress, exposing her bright banana yellow string bikini with all her voluptuousness rolling out around her tiny suit. She said, "OK, you can look now." As the men turned around, she said with a giant smile, "They might look at me and think I am a James Bond girl, yes?" They all cracked up, laughing with her as she turned and jumped off the rocks into the sea.

Adeem took off his shirt and stood before Pearl as if waiting for her to say something. Pearl looked away, took off her dress, squared up with him and stared back. His body was strong, tight, and rippling with muscles. His skin was smooth, and his chest was naked with no hair. Her eyes gravitated to his arms. His biceps were huge and slightly flexed as he moved. She thought, *Oh my god, his arms could hold me for hours if need be.* A man's arm says a lot about him, and it was the one area, besides teeth, that she looked at first when sizing up a man. Her belief was, the stronger and bigger the arms, the safer she was. Many men are disgusting creatures, so cleanliness was also a virtue.

Pearl felt so petite in front of his massively muscular body as she looked up at him. Realizing he wanted her to look at him and admire his physique, she exaggerated her actions and looked him up, down, and all around as if he were on display. She then put her hands on her hips as if to say, *OK, so you look good.* He was doing the same thing to her. When the moment was over, they both let out a laugh, but underneath Adeem was mesmerized. Her swimsuit was small and didn't leave a lot to the imagination. Adeem was speechless when she had dropped her dress. Her breasts were slightly visible on both sides of the bikini top, creating a perfectly soft, puffy cleavage. His eyes followed her toned, slim stomach and curvy waist down to her tiny, sexy feet with painted pink toenails. With all his being he wanted to reach out and pull her close to him.

Alex watched the two of them admiring each other. When their eyes met, neither gave up the glance. Alex said, "OK, let's end the staring contest and go for a swim, shall we?"

Both slowly looked over at Alex then back at each other as if they had forgotten he was there. Agnes yelled, "Alex, jump in," and he did, leaving the two of them alone.

Adeem walked closer to her and reached out to move a thin curl of hair covering her eye. He ran his finger slowly down her cheek to her mouth then touched her lips. "I want to kiss these lips someday, Pearl." She closed her eyes and waited. She felt like she was in a dream. She knew what she wanted, and she prayed he would give it to her. Adeem pressed his body against hers, pulled her waist into him, and tenderly brushed his lips against hers as she shuddered. Every goosebump on her body was alive and engaged. With his lips barely touching hers he said, "Not now, flower, I want to be alone when I devour you."

Pearl abruptly pulled back, opened her eyes, knitted her eyebrows and said, "You are not allowed to call me that! What is wrong with you? Oh my god! Jeez!"

Agnes, watching the encounter, threw her hands and yelled, "Jump, Pearl." And she did. Adeem lowered his head in defeat. He stood there staring at the ground wondering what had just gone wrong. He rearranged his erection and jumped in after them.

From the cliffs, the thermal baths were about a quarter of a mile away. When swimming in the Aegean Sea, it is almost as if you are swimming in the Dead Sea. The body is like a bobber on top of the water, making swimming effortless. One of Pearl's favorite pastimes was floating in the sea with her ears below the surface in a pure state of silence. It was so profound and her favorite place to meditate. She was so happy to be back in the sea. She ignored them all while she lay back in the water, ears submerged, and slowly backstroked as the three of them talked. All she could think about was how insensitive Adeem was, calling her pet names that didn't belong to him to call her. Not realizing she was talking out loud with her ears underwater, she gave Adeem a huge verbal lashing about respect and etiquette. Agnes, Alex, and Adeem humorously listened to the rant.

Agnes looked at Adeem, "My dear, you listening? Pearl is special. Tough like her grandpa was. Fight she will to the death if she loves you. Chew you up if not. Yes? You hear me, yes?"

Alex said, "I think this one is worth fighting for, son." Adeem just stared at Pearl and continued to listen to her express out loud her disappointment in his pet name choices. Pearl was oblivious to the audience.

As Agnes bobbed up and down, completely enjoying the entertainment she was getting from Pearl, she watched the two men as they listened intently to her. Alex had a huge smile on his face and laughed out loud a couple of times.

Adeem looked at Alex and said, "Thanks for the support, Dad."

When Pearl finally finished her rant, there was silence again. The two men looked quizzically at Agnes when the one-way conversation ended. Agnes burst out laughing. She said, "She does that to me all the time. I am always laughing when Flower is around. And NO, you cannot call her that, Adeem. What is wrong with you?" He raised his hands in defeat then slapped them down on to the water, which in turn broke Pearl's concentration as she rose out of the water to rejoin the group's conversation. No one said anything to her when she emerged from her floating tirade, they just turned and continued to follow Agnes to the thermal baths.

As they enjoyed their slow swim, Pearl shared the history behind the thermal baths. "From the time of antiquity, people from all over the world visited these waters as a curative treatment. Ikaria's hot springs are the most radioactive in the world and are super-hot, with temperatures reaching as high as 136 degrees. They treat all kinds of ailments from arthritis to infertility. There is also a rare Hamman located on the island. It is a natural cave that drips steaming hot water from its walls. It is the island's natural sauna. Very relaxing." As Pearl talked, the men listen intently. As they swam closer to the springs, the water became warmer and warmer. When they reached the small cave, they each found a seat on the submerged boulders that surrounded a large sitting area just inside the opening. Agnes said, a bit hysterically while waving her hands in the air, "Move your feet or the little fish will eat from them! Like this. I do not like it! You like fish eating your feet?"

Pearl put her hand over her mouth so as not to start laughing. She knew of Agnes's huge distaste for the fish that schooled around the boulders waiting for the next foot to nibble on. The men looked into the crystal-clear water and, sure enough, little fish were heading toward them. Agnes kept her feet in motion the whole time saying, "I do not like it!" The way she said it was like a little girl trying lemons for the first time and realizing it was not sweet and enjoyable. It was so cute and funny at the same time.

Alex jumped and yelled out, "Oh, oh, oh," while looking in the water at the fish surrounding him. He started moving his feet fast and furious, just like Agnes. They were like two peas in a pod, fighting off abusive insects.

Pearl couldn't contain her laughter. It was hilarious! Adeem started laughing with her. Her laugh was so infectious. While Alex and Agnes focused on keeping the fish away and trying to have a conversation, Adeem was watching Pearl. He didn't mind the fish. All he could think about was the moment on the rocks when her body leaned in and connected to his. The way her warm skin felt against his had to be repeated. He closed his eyes and relived the moment he brushed his lips against hers, the moment he felt her breath against his cheek.

Pearl was unaware of his thoughts and his gaze. Two locals had entered the cave, and Pearl spent the next five minutes catching up on the shenanigans of Therma while she was gone. Her attention was brought back to the crystal-clear warm waters when she felt Adeem's foot against hers. He carefully lowered himself into the hot water and slid over to sit next to her without saying a word. He placed his hand on the small of her back which was under water. She abruptly sat up straight and looked at the others as if being caught in the act of doing something inappropriate. No one was paying attention. They were all laughing and discussing the foot pedicures they were receiving. He didn't remove his hand but continued to talk with the others as if both hands were in his lap. She looked at him. He was completely involved in a conversation about a possible fishing trip with Alex while they were on the island. Without looking at Adeem, she put her hand on his thigh. Her breath was shallow and her heart was beating a hundred times a minute. Adeem pressed his thigh against hers, smiled at her then returned his attention to the group.

Alex said, "It is pretty amazing how these little fish can live in this hot water. You would think it would cook them."

Pearl said, "It is a conundrum, is it not?"

They all nodded in agreement as Agnes stood up in her little yellow bikini and authoritatively stated the rules of thermal waters. "The rule, no sit in the radioactive water for longer than 15 minutes. The heat becomes not good after 15 minutes. We go back now."

Slowly they said their goodbyes to the locals then the four of them swam back to the rocks. It was an invigorating feeling as the hot water slowly merged into crisp, cold water as they got closer to the rocks they had jumped from earlier. Agnes said, "All those poisons leaked out and are washing away as we swim into the cold."

Alex smiled and said, "I needed a cleansing like this. Just wonderful. I could do this every day!"

Pearl chimed in, "Right? That is what I love about Therma. It washes away all the bad. It is a place to detox and feel the wonderful energy of life as it permeates your mind, body, and soul. It is perfect here." With towels wrapped around them, they made their way back up the precarious shale path to Agriolykos.

At the top Agnes said, "Your meal is in the kitchen. Eat, we will go to Hamman after. Eat light." She kissed Pearl on the cheek and said out loud for all to hear, "I saw, I saw. I told you that you need sex. You both do!" and she walked off.

Pearl said, "Oh my god, Agnes. Really?" Agnes just waved her hand in the air as she headed to her room. Alex and Adeem laughed out loud as Pearl put her hand on her hips and said, "Do not encourage her!"

Both men said quickly, "She is right!" as they walked off to Room #3 to change out of their wet suits.

Chapter Fourteen

Pearl headed to the kitchen and turned on the oven to warm the meals Agnes had made for them. She set the timer for a thirty-minute warm up. She went to the patio and drank in the beauty of the place she called her second home. The courtyard was so inviting with its combination of hammocks, soft material lounge chairs, Adirondacks of every color, and quaint, round metal tables with seating all around them. Large blue and white flowerpots flowing with color from different varieties of flowers and vines were everywhere. A trellis covering the patio with lush vines and Bougainvillea in bright pink and sand whites kept the hot sun at bay. Beautiful trees dotted the entire property, and the view was breathtaking. Agriolykos was situated at the far end of town and sat perched high on a cliff secured by a retaining wall made of a million plus strategically placed stones. At more than fifty feet tall, you could see all of Therma, the entire cove, and the islands across the sea. It was a spectacular, picture-perfect postcard view. A small three-foot stone wall surrounded the upper property. When you looked over, it plunged several stories right into the crystal-clear sea scattered with sunken boulders below.

Pearl arranged a beautiful table for dinner. She brought three wine glasses and a large carafe of Julia's best wine to the table, along with a large plate of meats, cheeses, olives, and breads, and a small crystal bowl filled with olive oil and sweet balsamic vinegar to dip the treats into. With several minutes left on the timer, she took a quick shower and found a cute floral dress and a pair of rhinestone-covered sandals to wear for dinner. She left her hair wet and hanging free. As it dried, the soft curls became full and framed her face tenderly. She poured a small amount of virgin olive oil into her hands and carefully rubbed it into her feet, legs, and arms, and the remaining into her hair. The curls glistened in the evening sunset. She placed a dot of Talia vanilla oil drops on the back of her neck, between her breasts, and the back of each knee. She finished with a soft pink gloss on her lips then admired herself in the mirror, nodding with approval. She knew exactly what she was dressing for, and she was hoping her efforts to seduce would be noticed. Maybe Agnes was right – she needed sex, and her body was definitely telling her the same. And her eyes were telling her that Adeem was her catch.

Pearl could hear the men talking. She went to the balcony of the big house, looked down, and saw them enjoying the view of the island of Fourni across the bay. It was a stunning view and the men were mesmerized by it.

Pearl cleared her throat just loud enough for the men to turn and look up at her. She said, "Gentlemen, I will be right down with dinner. Please pour yourselves a glass of wine, but be careful, as it is much stronger than you are used to – and enjoy some fresh hors d'oeuvres. I will be right down."

As she started to leave, Adeem said, "Wait!" She turned around and looked back down at him. He said, "My Juliet, I shall wait for you patiently as I drink your wine."

Pearl smiled and said, "Juliet? OK, that works," as she turned and walked away.

Alex said, "Oh boy, you are in so much more trouble than I thought you were, son." He chuckled and smacked Adeem on his shoulder then headed for the wine.

The dinner was delicious. The men wiped up every bit of sauce and oils with the homemade rolls. Two more carafes of wine were consumed over dinner. When they were done, Agnes returned, cleared the table, and said, "You drink too much wine tonight. No Hammam. Another time. There is ouzo in cold box in kitchen. Goodnight, see you in the morning."

Pearl apologized and thanked her with a big hug as the dishes were cleared. Agnes whispered, "You look pretty, Flower. You have protection?" then she laughed a big hearty, Greek laugh and walked away. Pearl just stared at her with her mouth open in disbelief. The men, again within earshot, raised their eyebrows at her then lowered their eyes with big smiles on their faces.

"Unbelievable, Agnes!" Pearl barked. Pearl threw her hands up in the air, shook her head, and walked over to the cold box to retrieve the ouzo and the small glasses next to it. She motioned for the men to follow her to the far end of the courtyard to her favorite place to sit and watch the evening sky turn flaming colors of reds, oranges, and yellows. Alex found a comfortable Adirondack chair, and Adeem and Pearl sat in a hammock like a chair, side-by-side, and let their legs dangle to the dirt. They propped up the end pillows as a headrest and Adeem carefully rocked the hammock back and forth with his toe on the ground. It was a peaceful evening. No one spoke for a while. They watched the sky as the stars started making their appearance. As the sun set and the night darkened, little lights in the homes embedded in the mountain beyond the cove slowly started making their appearance like Christmas lights being turned on one by one. The restaurants came to life as Greek music started playing softly in the distance. People began showing up and the town, at 10:00 p.m., came alive.

Alex finally broke the silence, "Pearl, do you know where the journals are?"

"Yes. They are in the back of the attic in my home. The last time I was up there was during the remodel. I had one of the contractors push the trunks to the back end so we could use the front space for storage. If I remember correctly, there are two trunks. I have looked in them, but it was quite a while ago. I think my mom was the last one in them. I remember she put her journals with the rest for safekeeping. But yes, they are there. How long are you planning on staying in Ikaria?"

"Good question. Until I know my father's story. Until I have read all the journals, unless you will let me take them with me?"

Pearl sat up straight and looked at Alex resolutely, "I do not think Julia or Mom would allow that. Shall I plan on you being here for at least two or three days?"

Alex hesitated then said, "That sounds like a plan." Adeem shook his head, agreeing that would be fine.

Pearl said, "I will have to say, my recollection of Dimitri and George, the stories Nonnah told me, were pretty awesome. But as far as I remember, it was a mundane existence, very quiet, not a lot of excitement. At least, not after they ended up on the island. What more can you add to the story?"

"My Uncle Qaseem gave me a great life," Alex said. "I never really thought about my parents much until Qaseem took ill. He was exposed to a virus that infected his lungs. We were told it was a simple virus that is found in dirt and dust. It settled into his lungs and eventually weakened his immune system. He no sooner got well than he got sick again. When I knew his end was near, I started asking a lot of questions about my mother and father. Every time I asked, he would tell me wonderful stories about my mom, what a jewel she was and how her kindness was a blessing to all. I believe he loved his sister more than anything. And, of course, he told me she loved me very much.

But when I asked questions about my father, he would get quiet and stare out into space. One night during a bout of pneumonia, his temperature rose to 102.9 degrees. The doctor was dealing with an emergency in town and was unable to come. He gave me instructions on how to get the temperature down and told me to push the herbal tea he had made to help break up the phlegm in his lungs. I was changing the cool cloth on his forehead when my uncle began talking about Dimitri. At first, I thought it was a dream or a story he had read. He almost seemed delirious, rubbing his hands together and shaking his head from side to side. He was telling me things that were so obscene that I was shocked and uncomfortable listening to him. Acts punishable by death flowed from his mouth. As he talked, I tried to stop him, afraid of who might be listening, but I could not stop him. He had a story he needed to purge.

I stayed in the room for hours as he rambled on, crying and rolling over into a fetal position and saying things like, 'It is all my fault. What have I done?' He told me the story that is in Dimitri's diary but in greater detail. When he was done, he got up while in a fevered stupor and stumbled to a small picture on the wall. He pushed the center of it, the picture moved to the side, and a wall safe appeared. He opened it and handed me his will, Dimitri's diary, and the jewelry boxes. I sat by his bedside and read it out loud to him for several nights in a row, over and over again as he cried. It was after reading the diary that I began my extensive search for Dimitri.

Reading their love story made me realize that all my life I had been living in an empty space filled with anger, animosity, and grief over my father leaving me. I turned my reason for living into Adeem. I pushed him hard and taught him everything I know and ten times more. The night after he moved out on his own I had a dream. I was told in this dream that it was time, time to realize my true purpose and it was time to find Julia because Adeem was going to do something spectacular once I found her. When Julia's name came up in one of the diaries, it was a sign for me. I have had many unexplainable events happen to me in my life. I am a believer in gut instincts and synchronicity. I am not one to shy away from it. I spent months reading over archived documents from old newspapers, magazine articles, and restoration projects hosted by UNESCO, hoping to find Dimitri's name and whereabouts.

I looked for travel documents and ticket sales from every seaport and airport, looking for Maryam and Katrina, hoping they would have answers for me. I was looking for a needle in a haystack, but I finally found travel documents for a Sophia and Katrina. They had flown from Qatar to Cairo then on to Turkey. They stayed in Turkey for a while with some military family Maryam knew. After that they took a ferry to Samos then on to Ikaria. This research took over five years to find. Then I found the death certificates for all four; Dimitri, George, Katrina, and Sophia.

I went to Qaseem with the news. He was very ill by this time. He had spent most of his later years in bed fighting infection after infection, although some months he was as healthy as a horse. It was strange; he would ask me to take him to the spiraling pools the horses cooled off in and would float there for hours. After, you would have never known he was sick. But in time, he would become ill again. In these later years, he was thin, pale, and feeble. One night as he coughed up blood, he instructed me to have his body-double killed. Many great leaders have several body doubles. They use them in times of civil unrest when assassination plots were expected. Qaseem had only one. In detail he told me exactly what to do. He explained to me that upon his death, I was to kill his body-double then switch the bodies. I was instructed to then take his body and bury it next to Dimitri's. I and Dimitri were his only living heirs. He died three days later. Just as he asked me to do, I had his body exchanged with the double, and the double was buried in a grand ceremony. No one knew.

I had Qaseem's body cremated. It was the only way I could get his body to Ikaria and get away with it without documents. So, I put his ashes in a box and here he is in Ikaria." Alex rested his head back on the chair, took a deep breath, and said, "Pearl, I cannot keep my eyes open. Let's talk more tomorrow."

Pearl had been so captivated by the story that she didn't realize Adeem had fallen asleep on her shoulder. She said, "Yes, the three bottles of wine and the ouzo has made its way to my head too. But one question – how did Julia become Qaseem's heir?"

"That part is a bit confusing to me too. Um, so Qaseem's only brother and sister were dead. All he had left was Dimitri and me. At some point in time, I am not quite sure when, Dimitri returned to Qatar. It seems his return was around the time his wife Katrina had died. On her deathbed, Katrina supposedly told Dimitri that she knew all about his alternative lifestyle. She confessed who she was and told him all about her past life in Qatar with Sophia. She told him to return to Qaseem one more time, that Qaseem needed him. Qaseem was unaware that Dimitri was coming and when he arrived, Qaseem was in the UK on business. Dimitri left a letter telling Qaseem about his life over the years, but left out where he had lived his life, and said that his family was now George, Sophia, and Julia. He shared that he never had children, and Julia was his daughter in his heart. He said his sorrow was abated by living vicariously through Julia and her silly exploits on the island, always bringing him bugs and asking for advice about a boy in her class. He loved Julia deeply. So, when Qaseem found out that all four had passed away except for Julia, he did what he thought Dimitri would have wanted him to do with his share of the estate. And here I am in Ikaria with it. There is a bit more to it, but I feel like I am not making any sense right now."

"Wow! Yes, you are making sense. This is such an amazing story and I guess I am still shocked about the amount of money that Julia has inherited. That is a lot of money. It is not even fathomable. I truly cannot wrap my head around a billion dollars. I definitely want to be present when Julia finds out," she replied.

"I am the heir to much more than that, Pearl, much more. Adeem will inherit it when I am gone. Qaseem's estate is worth more than three trillion dollars. This small drop in the bucket that he has given to Julia no one knew about. Much of his money is distributed throughout several corporations, multiple projects and investments, his vast Arabian horse racing teams across the country, and so on."

Adeem readjusted his body to a laying position in the hammock and pulled Pearl down with him. He said, "Guys, it is time to sleep." It was a warm night and sleeping under the stars was a perfect ending to a perfect day.

Alex yawned and said, "What is a hangover like on the wine Julia makes with added ouzo on top?"

Pearl snuggled in to Adeem and said, "There is no hangover with the wine. She does not put any bad chemicals in it. Now the combination of ouzo and the wine, I am not sure. I have been drinking the combo since I was young so for you, we will see."

Everyone closed their eyes and were asleep within seconds. Agnes got up for a nightcap and turned off all the patio light when she noticed the sleeping bodies. She put blankets on all of them and placed six small glasses full of ouzo on the table with six white pills next to them. "Hair on dog," she whispered and smiled as she left them to their dreams.

Early in the morning, Pearl awoke. The sun was nowhere in sight and the stars were still twinkling in the night sky. Adeem snored softly, almost like a purr next to her. She smiled and snuggled in tighter and fell back to sleep. A few hours later, they all awoke to the roosters crowing from across the bay. When Adeem sat up, he quickly ducked his head and held it tight between his hands, moaned, and lay back down. Alex was in the same condition with a splitting headache. Pearl said, "Alex, hand me three of the little white pills and two glasses of the ouzo." He did. She then said, "Now take the three remaining pills and chew them up until they dissolve in your mouth then wash it down with the double shot of ouzo. And do not ask me what the pills are; I have no idea, but they are a miracle made by Julia especially for occasions like this." She handed Adeem his pills and the two glasses of ouzo then motioned 'bottoms up'. They both did as they were told.

Pearl looked at the men and said, "Do as I do." She took a slow breath in and a slow breath out with a pause then did it again. The men watched her and did the same.

Within two minutes, they were dumbstruck at how great they felt. "Amazing!" was the only word she heard, but it soon followed with, "What is for breakfast?"

Pearl giggled and said, "Good boys! I am impressed!" then headed toward the kitchen to help make a famous Agnes breakfast.

Alex checked on the rental car as Adeem talked on his cell phone, pacing the courtyard in a heated conversation. "That was not the plan! The decision was made that both horses were being bought together; not one but two."

Pearl met Agnes in the kitchen who was already preparing the morning meal. She gave Agnes a quick peck on the cheek and propped herself up on the counter. Agnes asked about the night and gave Pearl a sneaky smile. Pearl asked innocently, "What? What is up?"

"I put blankets on you last night. Adeem's hand was quite happy."

Pearl laughed and said, "Yes, so was my bosom." She caught up Agnes on their evening conversations. She expressed her concerns on how Mom and Julia would feel about letting these two strangers read the journals. After a long discussion, she decided to call Julia.

Chapter Fifteen

Julia was sitting in the library of Alexandria, Egypt with about 20 books stacked in front of her. Every book was opened with bookmarks and yellow stickies everywhere. She was frantically searching for one last clue to the puzzle as she sifted through the multitude of library books and the material Pearl had sent her. She had a pile of pens and notepads, a pencil behind her ear and one in her mouth as she typed away on her laptop. She didn't notice or give any attention to the magnificence of the building. Today its modern structure with its tall pillars and high ceilings was a marvel. Not as unique and architecturally breathtaking as the original one, but Julia would say, "It is all about the books and what is in them. If you need to find the needle, this is the haystack you want to find it in."

Julia looked up to address Charlee who had just come back from fetching another handful of books Julia had requested. As she wrote down a series of numbers on a sticky pad, she raised her finger and said, "Just a minute, my love…" Charlee dropped the heavy stack of books she had in her arms next to the return pile. As Charlee began to sit down for a moment of rest, Julia handed her another piece of paper, "Here is another list, babe, I only need four, and I think this will be the last. Thank you, my dear." Charlee sighed and started for the shelves when Pearl called. "Wait a second, babe. This is Pearl calling. I will put her on speaker." Charlee sat down to listen to the conversation. "Are you there, Pearl?" Julia asked.

Before Pearl could speak, Julia said, "Pearl, we found the two men who were with the archaeologist when he found Montet's Silver Pharaoh's secret hiding place. They were hesitant at first, but they told us the most amazing thing; Montet did not just find one sarcophagus, he found two. The second one, much smaller, was also made of silver. Montet was able to open the smaller of the two sarcophagi, but not the larger one. When he opened it, something strange happened. The two men that were with Montet had left the tunnel to get more equipment prior to him opening the sarcophagus. As the two men headed back toward the tunnel that Montet was in, they saw a flash of light then a massive gust of wind that almost sucked them back into the tunnel. Immediately after they experienced a reverse gust that threw them off their feet outside the tunnel opening. When the two men re-entered the tunnel to check on Montet, they found the sarcophagus open and the mummy inside. It was a female. Montet's body was several feet away on the ground, dead. Presumably he died on impact when his body was thrown against the rock wall.

They gave me several more scrolls to look at. I have been able to decipher a couple of them. Within the scroll they talk about a white, powdery substance called Ormus or Mana, I am not sure yet. But this white powder was found in jars inside the sarcophagus and under the mumification wraps. The female mummy was covered in it. Her body was so well preserved that DNA samples were collected from soft tissue as well as bone marrow, all viable and ready to tell the secrets to a long life. The most amazing thing was, when they added saline to the DNA material and viewed it, there was no cell structure. No nucleus, no mitochondria, no chromosomes, no DNA. But what they did see was pure osculating light. The slide under the microscope burst into light which illuminated itself above the slide and created a wave-like dance above the extracted material.

I remember reading a story years ago about a group of angelologists who traveled to Bulgaria in search of a tavern deep in the earth. The author states that many of the fallen angels were supposedly captured and chained to dwell in darkness for eternity. When one of the angels escaped, trails of his blood were found throughout the caverns. It was a trail of pure light like the one on the slide. When the other chained angels were questioned, the only thing they said was, 'It is imperative for him to find Kaya.' Eventually these angels took on the name of Watchers. I do not know why my name keeps coming up and why The Silver Pharaoh has been burned into my family's psyche, but for some reason we are being called to find out. This is now on the top of my list to research. The documents are incredible, Pearl. I wish you were here. You would love this. I will fax a copy of them for you to read at your leisure."

Julia hadn't slept much since their last phone call, with her main source of nutrition being coffee, black and strong. It took every ounce of energy Pearl had to keep up with her. Julia was already writing her next book.

"How was the seminar?" When Pearl didn't say anything, Julia said, "Pearl, are you there, honey?"

"Yes. I am. I am about to leave Therma and head back to the house, but I have something to tell you. It is a bit confusing now and the series of events are all jumbled up in my mind, but when Psusennes' sarcophagus was opened, the same thing happened. A gust of wind and a flash-bang." Pearl told Julia the events that occurred Friday night as best as she could remember. In truth, her memory of the night's event were continuing to slowly disappear.

"Nonnah, you know I have an excellent memory. Heck, you are always asking me to remember things from ten years ago and I usually can, with ease. But this is different. Even the pictures and videos on my phone have disappeared. I truthfully cannot recall much of the night. Some of it has come back in my dreams, but I am not sure what is real and what is not. The only part of that night that I remember and which keeps replaying over and over in my head and in my dreams is when the sarcophagus was opened, Psusennes looked straight up at me and said, 'You are the chosen one, Pearl. Thank you. We will meet again when The Phoenix returns. You are safe. Find Alexander.' Then Alexander showed up and I am in a daze about all of this. I am really sorry. I know you were depending on me. I called Doris to help me out, but it seems that most of the people that were in the room Friday night are having the same difficulty remembering what happened. I am so thankful I got that info faxed to you when I did because it is no longer on my phone."

"Pearl, darling, this whole situation is strange and it is getting stranger by the minute." She left Pearl with an interesting question, "There was an x-ray showing a round object inside the body. Was there any word on that?"

Pearl said, "Now that is an interesting question. It took me a while to remember this, but a woman came to my room right after I returned from the conference on Friday night. I was pretty dazed. I do not remember much other than she handed me a round metal pot.

She said you, Julia, had been looking for it or needed it. She said to give it to you immediately. I was in a hurry because right after she handed it to me, I threw up all over the floor then passed out for 36 hours. I think she was one of the speakers, but I cannot remember seeing her at the conference. The weird thing was, she did not stick around for me to ask questions. She actually disappeared, I think. But now that I remember this, I think she said to give it to Alex. I had not yet met Alex. I do not know, I am so confused, Nonnah, but I will have it with me when I see you next. I have not unpacked my luggage yet, but I assume it is in there."

Julia listened intently then said, "That is great news! I cannot wait to see it. But yes, something very strange is going on. I do not know why we are in Egypt just yet. It is like we are waiting for something. We got a message that it was urgent to be here to meet an archaeologist that knew secrets about The Silver Pharaoh, but we have yet to meet with this person. We have only met these two men that gave us the little bit of info I just shared with you. But when asked, they do not know anything about an archaeologist or anything else other than what I just shared with you. Anyway, I will figure it out. Thank you, darling, for all your help. Here is your mom."

Before Pearl could say anything else, Charlee said, "Hi, babe. How're you doing?"

"Hello, Mom. All is well. How are you doing? Coming back soon?"

"Julia is obsessed, as usual. The information you sent her has her on a worldwide shopping trip. I had to tell her to eat and shower yesterday *and* today. If not, she works right through until sunrise. If I had an IV set up, she would have me put coffee in it and hook her up. It is ridiculous! That woman is so driven! How are you doing and what's going on with the Alexander story?" Pearl spent the next hour going over everything that had transpired since the last call. She took a picture of Sophia's ring she was wearing and a picture of the necklace and bracelet and sent it to Charlee's phone.

Charlee was shocked. "Wow! So, this is a true story? What's the end game?"

"Well, that is why I am calling you. Alexander is the Emir of Qatar, a good guy. I think this is the first trip in his life that he has not been surrounded by bodyguards, but the subject matter precludes him from having them around. This whole story is quite amazing. I wish I had known Great-Grandma Sophia. You are not going to believe her true identity, and Nonnah is going to flip her lid. I will let Alex tell you that part of the story when you meet him. He has been very transparent and even won over Agnes, if you can believe that. Agnes likes his son Adeem even better. Mom, she has talked continuously about sex openly in front of them. She actually told me that I needed sex – in front of both men! Can you believe her?"

Charlee started laughing so hard that she had to take the phone to the bathroom to pee. When she collected herself, she started laughing again and said, "Do you need sex, my love?"

Pearl rolled her eyes, "I knew you were going to laugh at this. It is not funny. She is embarrassing!"

"Honey, I'm not laughing at you, but with you. Come on, you know Agnes – she talks about sex to everyone. She believes it's the elixir of life; they all do on Ikaria. I think the men stay in Therma just because she's there," she said laughingly.

Pearl dropped the phone from her ear and said, "Agnes, talk to Mom. I am going to check on the guys. But do not hang up; I have not asked her about the journals yet." She knew Agnes would fill her in on the men and what she thought of them, good guys or bad guys. But it was a given, she would gossip with Charlee for at least another hour.

The rental car had arrived, along with a second car and driver. Alex was putting his suitcase and things into one car and Adeem into the other. "What is up? Are you not going with us, Adeem?" Pearl asked.

He looked at her as he loaded the trunk with his things and said, "Trust me, my Juliet, I do not want to leave, but I must." Adeem stepped back, smiled big and all proud of himself, "I like the name Juliet. Do you?"

Pearl smiled, "As long as it does not conjure up ideas to poison me."

He walked over to her, took her hands and said, "I have business that needs my immediate attention. I must leave, but I will return. I have unfinished business here."

"What unfinished business?"

"You, my lovely Juliet. I will return for you as soon as I can. In the meantime, I hope you can help Dad get the answers he needs about Dimitri. Pearl, I think he just needs to feel him, know his life, connect a face to a story. It was really hard on him when he started this journey into the unknown. But in the end, I think it was the love Qaseem and Dimitri had for one another that he is clinging to. He has been with women, of course, but he has never felt what his father felt. He talks about an 'uncanny feeling,' as he calls it, that something big is going to happen. I do not know. He has been a driven man all his life, looking for whatever it is that haunts his nightly dreams. Maybe if he finds what he is looking for in your attic he can finally move on. It is hard to see him like this, to tell you the truth. I want the best for him."

"I will do the best I can. *I* do not even know the whole story, it seems. Hopefully the journals will answer his questions," Pearl said as she looked up into Adeem's eyes. He held her look as his mind wandered down her neck to her breasts, imagining lightly brushing his lips against her bare skin.

"If you want to play the game 'staring contest', I must say, you will lose," she said coyly. He moved a small lock of hair that was curling into her lip. He bent down and kissed her softly, slowly, then with a quick tug, he pulled her waist in tight against his and kissed her deeply, exploring her mouth with his tongue as she returned the passion. Every hair on her body was alive and wanting him. When he let go, she almost fell backward.

He smiled and said, "I will do that again when I return, if you like." She just stared at him in a daze and nodded. He smiled, got into the car, and waved as he left. Alexander was standing against the rental car, legs and arms crossed, watching.

Pearl collected herself, brushed down her blouse with her hands and said, "What? So maybe I do need sex. What is your story, mister?"

Alex laughed, "I will tell you my story on our ride to your house. It is boring, but it is mine if you want to hear it." She nodded and returned to the kitchen to finish up her phone call with Charlee.

Agnes was still talking a mile a minute when Pearl returned. "Aww, here she is. You coming home soon?" she asked Charlee.

"Yes, in a couple of days we should be finished. It was a really good trip. Thanks for the update, Agnes. Keep our Pearl safe."

Agnes handed Pearl the phone and said, "She knows every-thing, I told her. She has talked with Julia already." Pearl took the phone and gave Agnes a thumbs up.

"Hey, Mom, Agnes says she told you everything. I am not sure what her 'everything' is, but I am sure it is juicier than my story would have been. What did Julia say about Alex reading the journals?" Pearl asked.

"We talked about it in depth after we received your last call. She's OK with it, and she's OK with you claiming her mother's ring. You really should've asked her first, my dear. That ring is priceless. Be careful where you wear it."

Pearl said, "I am sorry. I know I should have asked, but to tell you the truth, it is a little small. I cannot take it off – I have tried. It is stuck and it must weigh a pound!" Pearl held her hand in front of her face to admire the ring. "It is the most beautiful ring I have ever seen, except for Aunt Melena's ring. Anyway, what did Agnes tell you about Adeem?" she asked as she twisted a ringlet around her finger.

Charlee took a breath, smiled, and said, "Agnes said, 'Charlee, it was meant to be. These two are from the same mold. She, Aphrodite, and he, her Adonis. The two are in so much trouble when they finally figure it out.'"

"Mom, it is really crazy! I have known this man a minute and he is all up in my business. He is all I can think about. I do not know if I can trust him yet. Frankly, this could just be lust. Maybe he is just that guy to have sex with, you know, then it is done. Agnes would be pleased. Or, maybe he will just toy with my emotions then leave and never look back or visa-versa. Then I am crying and cannot sleep because... Oh I do not know, you know?" Pearl rambled on.

Charlee let out a sweet giggle, "Pearl, you are so honest and surprising at times. The fact is, the minute I saw your father standing on the scaffolding the day I arrived in Therma, I knew I would marry him. And all I thought about for hours after I saw him was how to work my way into his arms and bed. Yes, love is a crazy thing. Just be careful. No grandchildren until you marry, kapish?"

Pearl chimed in quickly, "Do not get your hopes up, Mom. Children are not on my radar. What else did Nonnah say about the journals?" she asked, changing the subject.

"After you emailed us the information on Alexander, she did an extensive search. Plus, she found one of your grandpa's old friends that worked in Qatar with this family and called him. It seems that Alexander never married. He had a short relationship with Adeem's mother, and during that time she got pregnant. I guess he met her in a college class or something like that. She didn't want his lifestyle and made it abundantly clear that she was just in it for the gifts and material pleasures. When Adeem was born, she signed him over to Alexander and moved to The States. Sometime after Adeem turned three, Alexander got word she had died in a drug rehab center in New York. Since, he hasn't been with a woman steadily. He raised his son alone, just as Qaseem raised him alone. Did you know about this?" Charlee asked.

"I know about Alexander being raised by Qaseem, but I did not know about Adeem's life."

"Pearl, it's quite an amazing story. Adeem never went to public school or university. Supposedly he can speak nine languages, and at the age of twelve he took the SAT college test, just for fun, and got a perfect score. He owns four financial institutions and an Arabian horse business. He's built multiple housing units in Qatar for the elderly with no family and he pays all their bills. He's earned an international humanitarian medal, owns several aircrafts, and has no girlfriend. There isn't one negative thing said about Adeem or Alexander in any newspaper, magazine, or on the internet. Pearl, this man is beyond belief. Alexander taught him everything. And Alexander's credentials are three times bigger than his son's. When Julia started digging, the printer was going nonstop for twenty-four hours. She has enough information to write four books on these two men. And yes, she said it was OK for them to read her journals, but they are not to leave the house under any circumstance. If that's made clear, you're good to go, my love."

Pearl's jaw was on the ground. She knitted her eyebrows, shifted to one foot, and stared up at the ceiling.

"Pearl, are you there?" Charlee waited.

"Sorry, yes. Yes. This is interesting. Wow! I had no idea. Are you sure? Adeem does not come across with a lot of intelligence, but more of a player, or at least a guy who has been around the block a few times. He *is* very good looking, Mom. Are you sure?"

With that, Julia took the phone. "My princess, smart men need smart women to teach them how to be vulnerable and loved. They tend to act a little juvenile in that department until a good woman comes into their lives and teaches them. Love is scary when your heart is consumed with it. It is a dangerous place to be for a man, but a powerful place to be for a woman. Be careful. If you like him, take it slow. He has learned from the best when it comes to his career and life's material pleasures, but you can be the one who teaches him how to love from the heart and not the zipper." She laughed.

"Oh my god, Nonnah! You and Agnes have lived together too long." They both laughed out loud.

"Pearl, I have lived a good life. There is nothing in those journals that I am afraid to share with you. I love you very much. Now listen – go have fun, do not think about The Silver Pharaoh. Let me deal with this. I will fill you in when I get home."

Alexander had the car packed and was ready to go. Agnes put together a care package for them with a nice lunch and dinner, along with Julia's favorite wine and some sweet cakes for dessert. Agnes gave her a big hug and said, "Lunch is easy, dinner is great. I put bottles of wine, fruit, and veggies like you like, and some anise rolls for sweet." Agnes nodded toward Alexander and said, "He might be your father-in-law one day. Exciting for you, huh? So, you know how old he is?" She turned to Alex who was about two feet away watching them and winked.

Alex laughed and said, "74! OK, woman with many names – Flower, Angel, Juliet, Pearl, let's go! It is getting late."

Agnes said, "74, I am surprised. You know Harry? He drinks from the fountain of youth too. You need to meet Julia!"

Pearl was putting her things into the car when she heard this. She swung around and said, "AGNES! Oh my god! Do you have no shame?"

Agnes winked at Alexander again. He reached over and gave her a quick kiss on both cheeks and whispered in her ear, "Yes, I hear Julia is wonderful." He hastened his walk to the driver's door as he said, "Agnes, it has been a pleasure. Thank you for your wonderful hospitality."

Chapter Sixteen

It was half past one in the afternoon when the two finally got on the road. It was a long drive to the far side of the island, and they still needed to stop at the grocery store in Christos. Pearl hadn't been home in so long so she knew the cupboards were bare, and who knew what might be growing in the fridge. Christos had everything she would need. Pearl loved Christos, a small village in the mountains surrounded by winding roads, pine trees, terraced hills, and vineyards dotted with dilapidated ruins of days gone by.

By midafternoon, the sun was high in the sky, shining its warmth on the pine trees and releasing a calming smell of pine sap into the air. It was such a clean smell, and Pearl loved to drive the winding roads with the windows down so she could breathe it all in.

Lefteris lived in Christos. Pearl loved Lefteris, a retired, single veterinarian who liked to speak English to whomever would indulge him. He now owned the small grocery store in the center of town. It was a quaint little village with cobblestone streets that all led to a center square filled with tables and chairs to sit and relax. It was not uncommon to see men sitting and playing a game of Backgammon or enjoying a meal from the bar or pastry shop. Lefteris' store was in the center of it all. It was getting close to the end of the tourist season, so many of the surrounding stores were closed, but Lefteris' grocery was never closed. At midnight, all his buddies would show up in the square and kibitz until all hours of the morning. Many times, when Pearl spent the night in Christos, she had to wear earplugs to sleep. The entire group of men were semi-deaf, so their conversations were always loud and boastful. They shared their secrets of who made love to whom and who got caught with who, thinking no one could hear them. By morning there was always a dispute between husband and lover from the not-so-secret secrets anymore. And these men were all over eighty years old. Amazing!

Alex settled in behind the wheel and said, "Show me the way," and off they went. The conversation started out small with Pearl asking him where he lived and what hobbies he enjoyed. "How long is this drive?" he asked. "Am I to answer one hundred questions along the way?"

Pearl smiled, "Yep, that is the plan!"

He turned, smiled at her, and said, "I live at the estate that I grew up in. It belonged to Qaseem, and now it belongs to me. I run most of my businesses from there. I lived at the chateau for many of my younger years, but Adeem lives there now. I love the chateau; the grounds are magnificent. I made some changes, like there is no longer a river running through the inside of the chateau. That was a bit much. When Adeem was small, he would feed the fish every five minutes and track water through the whole house, so I tiled over it. But almost everything else is the same. I hope you can visit one day. Really, Pearl, you should visit sometime. I think Adeem would enjoy that." Pearl had her hand out the window, feeling the breeze and smelling the clean air as it blew in through the car windows against her face as she listened.

She looked over and agreed it would be nice. He continued, "As for my hobbies, to tell you the truth, it has always been Adeem. So many of the young heirs in my country are pompous, entitled, and arrogant. They have minimal education, spend most of their time playing video games, clubbing, and spending money on ridiculous things. For example, recently in the news, one of those entitled boys had his sports car studded with diamonds – the whole car. The funny thing was, one night he parked it outside one of the popular clubs downtown and when he got in it to leave, half the diamonds had been pried off. Unbelievable!"

Pearl looked at him and exclaimed, "REALLY?"

Alex nodded and continued, "Qaseem taught me how to run the world and I taught Adeem the same. Adeem has been a challenge, but he is a great student. Sometimes I think I pushed him too hard. But in the end, I feel confident that his future is set. He is brilliant, you know. When you get to know him, you will understand. Just ignore his Tom Cruise persona. I think it comes out when he gets nervous." Alex laughed, "It is so funny to watch him when he is acting this way."

Pearl smiled, looked at him, and said, "OK, I get the hint. Between you, Agnes, my mother, and Nonnah Julia, I have a feeling you all have our wedding planned. Now do not get me wrong, I do feel a strong attraction to Adeem, which is very unusual for me, but let's take it one day at a time, please. Julia said he speaks nine languages. Did you teach him?"

He turned to her with a big smile, showing his beautiful white teeth with the small gap between the front two. He was even more handsome when he smiled. He said, "Julia did her homework. Interesting. And we will all keep our fingers crossed on the wedding idea."

Alex smiled again and looked over at Pearl, gave her a wink then continued, "Qatar is a small country but a big country as well. We do business with people all over the world. It is out of respect that I learned and taught Adeem the languages of the world. So many things are lost in translation, and I simply cannot afford this in my line of business. Knowing the language of the people you are talking with makes for more trustful business partners. I speak twelve languages and yes, Adeem speaks nine. In addition to his nine, I learned Navajo, Vietnamese, and Icelandic, just because they were a challenge.

Adeem, not so much. He is a good man. He is business oriented, disciplined, wise in many ways, and a boy in others. He is not interested in gaming or clubbing or drugs. He has dated two women, and the last one was many years ago. Actually, this is my fault. I gave him a taste of success and now he chases it. Not in a compulsive way, but in a goal-oriented way. He is very creative and an amazing humanitarian. He has really good ideas and when he comes up with one, he details the budget then works hard in his day job to make the money to fund the ideas. It is his passion. For instance, there are a few areas in Qatar where most of the residents are ailing and aging. A lot of families have split up, sending the youth to other cities or countries to make money. More often than not, the family members that leave to make the money do not return. Adeem has built many self-sustaining neighborhoods to house these people that no longer have families to take care of them. He hires a staff of people with different skills to manage and live within the neighborhoods. The staff live there for free. In return, they manage the residents' care, their meals, the gardens, the livestock, healthcare, dentistry, etc., and they maintain a harmonious environment. They grow the food, cook it fresh, and in return they enjoy a peaceful, beautiful environment. Adeem built several complexes on a five-hundred-acre plot and designed everything down to the safety handrails throughout the gardens. He amazes me every day."

Pearl was watching him talk. She was captivated. This Adeem was way too good to be true. She asked, "So, what is the catch?"

"Excuse me – the catch?" he asked.

"Yes, the catch. No one is that perfect. What part of Adeem do you shake your head at? You know, like, 'Oh my gosh, that boy still has some lessons to learn.' What might they be?"

"He knows nothing about love or women. He tries," Alex chuckled, "but he still makes me shake my head when I see him trying to be some Brad Pitt or Tom Cruise character. As I said before, I saw him do that with you a couple of times. But you impressed me with your comebacks. He needs that in his life; someone who will treat him with respect and demand it in return. I like that about you." Pearl smiled as Alex continued, "I think if you gave him a chance, he just might surprise you. I think he *will* surprise you. I am not playing matchmaker, but I have thought about it about ten or twenty times since I met you. You are the kind of woman that I think will pair nicely with my son." He looked at her with a huge grin. Pearl playfully hit him on the arm. They both smiled.

For the next ten miles neither talked. They were in their own worlds. Pearl's life was flashing before her as she watched the rolling hills of tea flowers and bee boxes pass her by. She had strategically planned her life when she was about ten years old. She was brilliant and had graduated from high school with honors at the age of fifteen. By the time she was thirteen, she was already enrolled in evening college courses. She was now finalizing her PhDs in biology, chemistry, herbology, and botany. She had spent her entire teenage years with her face planted in books, absorbing every morsel of information they offered. Her weekends were spent listening and watching Nonnah Julia create medical treatments out of Ikaria's lush gardens that grew on every rock, within every crevasse, and on every hill throughout the island. When they weren't studying or concocting together, they were hiking the hills and valleys on the island, collecting specimens that ultimately became part of Julia's next article or treatment plan. The grand plan was for Pearl to take over Julia's teaching work and classes at the institute. Up until now, nothing or no one had interrupted this goal.

Pearl had never fancied dating or getting involved with any activity outside of her grand plan. She found most men distracting, without common sense, needy, and lacking motivation. Ikaria and most of Greece was known for its laidback atmosphere. Mornings start at 11:00 a.m., naps or sex in the afternoon, dinner at 10:00 p.m., and businesses are open from midnight until dawn. It is a great place to grow old, but it is a bit mundane for young people. Going to Athens for university is number one on a teenager's bucket list. It is their way to escape, really. Pearl was raised in a family with movie stars, writers, travelers, expert educators, and some of the best craftsmen in the world. She was going to continue in the successes of her family, one of the most notable families in Greece. The idea of falling in love was novel, to say the least, but not in the plan. At least not yet. A one-night stand here and there was much more appropriate for now.

After stopping in Christos for supplies, they continued to the other side of the island. The old family home was miles from town, and there were no road signs naming the many dirt roads that turned off the main, narrow, double-lane highway on the way to Pearl's house. Alex looked at her asking, "You will tell me when to turn?" She nodded as she ate from a bag of grapes sitting in her lap. As they got out of town, the dirt road became windy and full of potholes. In some sections, Alex had to drive beside the road through the low-lying vegetation to get around them.

Alex was beginning to wonder what this place was going to look like being this far out of town and in such a desolate area. To his amazement, it was not old and dilapidated but a beautiful, modern-looking, two-story home with vegetable gardens, prolific fruit trees, and a small vineyard with ornate walkways throughout the beautifully landscaped property. A four-foot wall built from slate encompassed the entire estate. The entrance had a remote-controlled iron gate with the words *Sacred Healing* embossed in it. He looked at her as he stopped the car in front of the gate. "You live out here alone?"

She said, "Yes. It is my home. It is the best place to study. No one ever stops by for tea, so I have been able to write four dissertations in two months. I love it here!" She pulled a small remote device from her purse, aimed it at the gate, and pushed the small white button.

When it opened, Alex slowly drove up to the house and parked. He got out of the car and looked around in amazement as he took in the beauty.

"My father and grandfather remodeled the old house for me years ago, after they finished Agriolykos. They thought about tearing it down and selling the land, but I convinced them to give it to me instead.

Of course, their biggest concern was me being so far out of town, but it is safe here. All of Ikaria is safe. You can walk anywhere, any time of day, and not worry about your safety." Pearl continued to point to different places on the property that were extra special to her while she helped Alex bring in the luggage and groceries.

On the last trip in, Alex walked over to the family cemetery and ran his hand over Dimitri's gravestone. He knelt down and stared at the writing as he traced the letters with his fingers. Pearl came out and was about to say something when she noticed Alex kneeling. He had tears in his eyes, so she walked back in and waited. Alex sat down with his back against the gravestone, his knees bent up with his head in his hands crying. He was talking softly to Dimitri. Pearl couldn't hear his words, but she knew, in his own way, he was connecting to the man in the ground.

When Alex walked inside, Pearl handed him some water and a moist washcloth for his face. He didn't try to hide his sorrow. He looked her in the eye and said, "Thank you, Pearl, for allowing me into your home." He drank the water as he looked around. He was impressed; the inside of the house was just as modern as the outside. Stainless steel appliances, double pane windows, marble floors, and the bathrooms had walk-in closets and showers that drained into Jacuzzi-jetted bathtubs. The walls were double insulated for the cold of the winter and the heat of the summer. And if an unidentified object should hit the earth, a secret fallout shelter was available under the home as well. Pearl had her own Shangri-la all to herself on this isolated part of the island. Alex was pleasantly surprised.

Pearl showed Alex to his room, gave him a set of towels and a glass of wine, and asked him to meet her for an early dinner when he was done washing up. She flipped the two switches on the bathroom wall then headed to the kitchen to put away the groceries and prepare the spectacular Ikarian dinner Agnes had made for them.

Alex sat on the edge of the bed and smiled as he scanned his room decorated in old lace, beautiful flower watercolor paintings, and antique furniture stained in dark walnut. He realized he was in the most feminine room he had ever been in. To his astonishment, he felt very comfortable. The room had a slight vanilla scent to it. He laid back on the pillowtop bed and took in a deep breath through his nose as he closed his eyes. He felt as though he was being wrapped in a woman's arms; soft, supple, and inviting. It had been a very long time since he had been in a woman's arms. For the first time in a while, he felt lonely. He lay there staring at the ceiling, wondering what he would find in the journals that were most likely directly over his head. It was the only part of the house where the old roofline was still intact with an attic space. He finally got up, washed his face and hands, drank the whole glass of wine in one gulp then joined Pearl in the kitchen.

When she saw him, she saw a different Alex. She asked, "You OK?"

He nodded, "Yes. I am experiencing a feeling I have never felt before, and I am grateful. I know this must sound off or amusing to you, but I am more comfortable here than I have ever been elsewhere. It is very peaceful here. And I am looking forward to delving into the journals, wondering what I will find."

Pearl smiled. "Thank you. Yes, it is peaceful, and it is why I love it here. Knowing my family grew up here makes it pretty special to me. I have heard a lot of stories about this place, especially from Nonnah. I guess she was quite the pistol growing up. Lots of shenanigans went on here!"

They talked through dinner, planning the trip to the attic and when to bury Qaseem. When they were finished eating and the dishes were done, Pearl showed Alex the staircase in the ceiling to the attic.

A small knob on a short rope hung down just low enough for Alex to reach it. He pulled hard yet it wouldn't budge. After a trip to the tool shed and a ladder was put into place, Alex climbed up and was able to unhinge the folded ladder stuck in the ceiling. The sun had set and the attic was dark. Pearl got them each a headlamp that strapped around their foreheads. They made their way into the large, dusty room full of boxes and old furniture. A very narrow walkway separated all the furniture treasures on one side and a four-foot-high row of boxes on the other. In the very back corner sat two large trunks with blankets stacked on top.

Alex said, "We are never going to be able to get these trunks out of here. We should take the journals out of the trunks and take them downstairs. We can put them in chronological order down there." Pearl agreed.

It was well into midnight when they were finally done. The journals that were in the trunk labeled 'Julia' were put into one pile and the trunk labeled 'Kaya family' were piled into another. There were also two journals labeled 'Charlee'. Pearl took those and put them by her bed to read later. By the time they were done going up and down the narrow stairs, it had been over two hours, and both were exhausted and filthy. They agreed to call it a night and begin reading tomorrow. With a quick goodnight, they headed to their rooms.

Alex was exhausted. He thought of just going to bed and showering in the morning, but when he took off his shoes and went into the bathroom to urinate, his feet were instantly warm. She had heated floors in the bathroom! The whole room was cozy and inviting. When he looked in the mirror, he laughed. His face was streaked with grime that was smeared with sweat. Bathing was definitely in order. He took a long hot shower and was practically snoring before his head hit the pillow.

Pearl sat on the edge of her bed staring at the journals. Her mother never talked about her childhood; she always evaded questions by deflecting to another subject and being very secretive. Pearl was a bit nervous as she stared at them. What would she find? She tucked herself into bed after a long hot shower then propped her head on her elbow as she contemplated whether she should begin reading tonight. After a long discussion with herself, she decided to finish Dimitri's journal and the pages George had tucked in then start her mother's journal at sunrise, before Alex got up. She poured another glass of wine, propped up her pillow, and began:

George and I sat in the car in complete silence with black hoods over our heads, listening to instructions. When we tried to speak or ask questions, we were smacked on the top of the head with a blunt object and told to be quiet. The female leader continued to talk to us in a stern yet patronizing tone, toying with us as if we had just ruined her evening. We sat rigid and scared. "You boys are going on a great adventure. It is a great honor to serve your country."

I thought, If this is a great adventure, I want off the ride now!

She took a breath then continued, "Your mission is simple – you will be building an underwater base with a monitoring building above it off the island of Ikaria. This base will house a large nuclear submarine. Does that bother you?" We shook our heads. "Good – you are pleasing me. Now I assume you are aware that we have had some very unpleasant neighbors lately, yes?" We nodded our heads. "We just cannot have that, now can we? No, we cannot! It is our job to prevent any kind of war or harm to our country and its people, and if that means being prepared for a nuclear strike then that is what we will do. We will be prepared. Do you both agree?" We nodded again. "Great! We are off to a good start. Before we go over your job descriptions, I want you to know your country will pay you handsomely. It has been determined that with your skillset, this mission will take you approximately three years to complete. It will be just the two of you. Each month a plane will land at the Ikaria airport at 3:00 p.m. It will be unidentifiable; no markings, no windows. Either of you will wait until the stairs are lowered from the plane. You will then go to the bottom of the stairs; some-one will exit the plane and give you your monthly checks. No words will be exchanged. You will deposit your checks into an ATM in front of the bank. The money will be forwarded from a bank in Turkey. This account will always show a small balance on your end but the correct amount on our end. Think of it as a savings account. No one will suspect you of foul play. Do not worry, you can trust us with your money. We are honest and we are fair. When your mission is complete, you will continue to man the station indefinitely. You will never leave this island. Boys, we are not cruel people. You are working for us and your country. We do appreciate it – really, we do.

So, when you have finished with construction and the station is operational, you can enjoy your lives on the island, but not before. You can then find wives, have children, whatever you want. You will be known as the two strange fishermen that live on the dark side of the island where the waters are cold and deep, and the currents are volatile most of the year. You are to keep to yourselves. No fraternizing with the locals, ever. Do you understand?" We both said yes. "Good boys! Now, a crew of carpenters have built two modest homes for you on the island, one mile from the station site. There is a dirt road that will take you to the main highway into town for personal incidentals. Your safety gear, construction materials, and tools will arrive in crates via submarine, below the construction site. Later we will set a date and time for delivery every three months for as long as you need them. You will be provided with a fishing boat that will suffice as your day job. You will fish one day a week and sell your lot in town to maintain the persona of two brothers making an innocent living as fisherman. You will not engage with the locals other than simple pleasantries. If you choose to disobey, whomever you conversed with about your true identity will be punished severely. Do you understand?" We both nodded.

The car came to a stop, the doors opened, and our hoods were removed. We were at the airport, parked outside a small cement building. There were no windows, just a steel door. The building was surrounded by a tall, solid fence. The only view was looking up to the dark sky where the stars and moon were shining brightly down on us. The woman flipped a switch on the wall next to the door. It opened and out popped a camera. She stood close to it as a red laser beam scanned her eyes. The other captors did the same. When the door opened, we all stepped into a large cargo elevator; George, me, the female leader, and three of our captors who were all holding machine guns. The leader pushed the button labeled L12. We immediately began to descend – fast! George and I grabbed the handrail in the elevator.

When it came to a stop, it was gentle and unnoticeable. We looked at each other for the first time, and it was obvious that George was just as terrified as I was. We were sweating, red-faced, and fearful. When the door opened, we entered a large command center. The only light was coming from the technology surrounding the room. Gigantic computer screens hanging from the walls around the room were covering every inch. Each screen represented a different location and set of coordinates. Several had active maps of multiple military bases all over the world and underwater submarine locations. A few screens showed the inside of hallways with cameras monitoring the building inside and out. Five rows of cubicles faced the screens and each cubicle had personnel wearing headphones with a secondary monitor in front of them. The room was filled with voices and animated movements coming from each staff member as they communicated remotely through their headsets. It reminded me of the New York Stock Exchange like I had seen on TV but with less people.

In the middle of the room were two long tables. One had a 3D model of the Greek Islands and the other had a 3D model of just the island of Ikaria. Above it was a hologram of Ikaria that was being manipulated by just a finger, turning it left then right then sideways. The hologram even depicted the sea floor around the island. The seven military personnel surrounding the table were concentrating on the far side of the island and the rock face that was submerged below the sea, approximately where the new nuclear submarine station was to be built. Each of the men surrounding the table had a large yellow number on the front of their shirts. As they spoke, they referred to each other by these numbers. We were escorted to the table. On the table were engineering designs planned for the nuclear substation that we were to build.

The female leader addressed one of the men futzing with the hologram, "Team, this is George and Dimitri. They are the architects that will build the station. Please begin."

Team member #6 asked us to join him on the other side of the table. "This is the island of Ikaria." He pointed to the hologram as he moved it around in the air, showing us all sides. "It is approximately 250 miles from the Turkey border, and its elevation reaches just under a mile high. You will be stationed on the far side of the island – here – which is mostly flat and uninhabitable. This side of the island has a plunging face that is covered in sharp shale rocks that are not stable. We have lost several men before you who were trying to navigate the treacherous conditions. Your job will be to build a simple cement command station here, and a deep-water channel here to house a 572 foot long, 48,000-ton nuclear submarine. Your homes are here, approximately one mile from the building site." Number six continued to point and spin the hologram as he spoke.

For the next two hours we were instructed and familiarized with the exact designs and expectations of the project. When the team and the leader were finished, we were asked if we had any questions or concerns. George and I looked at the men around the table then back at her. I knew what George was thinking – there was no way in hell these designs were going to work at this location. Neither of us spoke. Who knew what would happen to us if they knew we did not approve of their plans. She saw our hesitancy and walked over to stand between us. She put a hand on each of our shoulders and said, "Speak freely, boys. This is your time to shine." We looked at each other and began to talk at the same time. George swung the design plans around so we were looking at the cliffs from the water view to the island and not the island to the water. It was obvious why they had lost men using these designs.

I started, "First of all, you cannot dynamite here with this shale face. There is no stability. As soon as the channel is dug, the falling shale will fill it back up. The inner tunnel will collapse onto the sub if you build here."

I turned to George as he continued, "We need to build a granite or cement underwater jetty the length of the entire sub. Also, granite walls will need to be in place straight up to a platform where the monitoring station will sit. This station will sit directly over the top of the first 40 feet of the sub to deflect any falling rocks. We will need to move the coordinates over here. This is a stable rock face."

George turned to me as I pointed and spun the hologram around and said, "Yes, and we can build the upper station so it cannot be accessed from the water, which will be vulnerable. We can place a mountain of shale rock here so anyone who might become suspicious of the building and try to enter it will become a member of your departed workers from your first attempts."

George and I continued to pick apart the engineering designs and when we were finished, the project was moved south. It was now two miles on the other side of the two homes built for us. We requested additional men to work with us. There were several parts of the design that would require a bigger team.

The female leader said, "You will report to #6 and #9. They will be your contacts. They will get you whatever you need promptly, but the work will be done exclusively by the two of you. I have seen your work. I have no doubts that this project will be completed in the timeframe we have given you. We could put a large team on this and have it built in a shorter amount of time, but unfortunately it would draw attention to what we are doing. This is not an option. May I reiterate again that if, at any time, any of your identities – you too, 6 and 9 – are compromised, you will be terminated immediately. Do we have an understanding, gentlemen?"

#6 and #9 both stood at attention and said, "Yes, sir!"

George and I just stared at each other as she waited for an answer. We both nodded.

"#8, take these two to their quarters. You have two weeks to redesign the engineering and put together a six-month material list before you are dropped off on the island. At that point you will begin work the following morning. All material crates will be delivered on the same day via sub at the base of the underwater checkpoint."

Pearl was exhausted, and her eyes were starting to fade. She set down the journal, took the last drink of wine from her wine glass, and lay back down. Before she knew it, she was asleep.

When she woke up, the smell of eggs and hot coffee permeated the air. It felt so good to be back in her own bed. Her Auntie Melena had bought her this mattress from Milan a few years back. It had been a source of being late to work on many occasions. It was like sleeping on a cloud. She stretched and elongated her whole body, her toes reaching the end of the bed and her fingertips touching the headboard. Every muscle was happy, which made it even harder to get out of bed.

She wanted to go back to sleep for another hour, but the smell of coffee wafting into her room was intoxicating. She needed a big cup of coffee and she needed it now, but she didn't want to get out of her warm, cozy bed, so she sat up and yelled, "ALEXANDER!" There was no answer. Again, "ALEXANDER!"

He came running to her room. "What? Are you OK?"

With a soft little girl voice she asked, "Will you please bring me a cup of coffee?"

He said, "Are you kidding me? You scared the shit out of me, Pearl!"

She grinned a childish smile and said, "Pretty please? I was up until 3:00 a.m. reading." He rolled his eyes and left the room. She giggled and yelled, "Thank you – you are the best! Cream, no sugar!"

He returned with a cup of coffee and let her know breakfast was ready. Knowing it was going to be a long day of reading, he put the roast in the oven with the vegetables they had picked up in Christos. This way dinner was ready when they were. He had gotten up early and put the journals in chronological order and was anxious to get started but didn't know how Pearl wanted to begin the process. He started to explain his morning chores when Pearl asked if he had read all of Dimitri's journal and if so, what his thoughts were.

He had. He sat down on the end of the bed and said, "What are my thoughts? Well, for the most part, I realized that he was a very lonely man. This saddens me because I watched my uncle live a very lonely life without Dimitri. It is horrible when you think about it. Two people in love yet so lonely. Life is such a gift, yet I too feel lonely. Sometimes I wonder if they unintentionally passed that energy on to me. Adeem seems to think that we are surrounded by an energy force that is much stronger than Allah. Of course, he mostly keeps these beliefs to himself, only sharing these ideas with me. But when he sees me in this depressed state of mind, he informs me that we bring into our lives the emotions of our thoughts. So, I am working on it." He smiled, slapped his hands down on his thighs, stood up, and said, "Get up. It is time to eat, and I am starving!"

Pearl got up, washed her face, and put on some comfortable clothes. She met Alex in the kitchen, drinking a cup of coffee contently while reading the morning news on his phone and patiently waiting. When she saw the spread of food, her smile went from ear to ear, "Wow! You can stay! I need a cook. This looks great. Thank you!" She smacked her hands together and rubbed them vigorously, so excited for her breakfast. She filled her plate with scrambled eggs, biscuits and gravy, and a variety of cut-up fruits. She refilled her coffee cup and made a new pot before she sat down. She took her first bite, "Mmmmmmm, so good." As she prepared the next bite on her fork she asked, "Alexander, what are you hoping to find out about your father?"

Alex put down his phone, sat back in his chair, and ran his fingers through his hair. He stared at Pearl as if looking for the right words to answer her question. She fixed her eyes on his and waited. He sat back and shifted his gaze out the window. He continued to stare out the window as he said, "Well, that is a good question, young lady. I am not sure. I do not know how to explain it, but I am looking for a feeling, a feeling of belonging. For most of my years, I believed my father knew about me, knew I was alive. There was never a day that went by that the thought of him abandoning me did not cross my mind. I was an extremely disappointed and angry man for many years." Alex got up and topped off his cup of coffee. Pearl watched him and his body language. She could feel his sadness; his loneliness was palpable, penetrating her. He even looked older and more tired as he answered the question. He took a slice of orange and ate it slowly, looked at her, and sat back down. "As a child, I was raised by the women in the house and adored by Qaseem. He was the greatest father I could ever ask for. I bombarded him with questions about my father over the years, but all I got was, 'He disappeared, not knowing you were ever born.'

In my late teens, anger found its place in my heart, and I began acting out, a real rebel. Qaseem viewed my behavior as destructive and self-sabotaging. I never shared with him my unwavering search for my father. I must have written what I had planned to say to Dimitri a million times, and it was not pleasant. I wrote letter after letter, stacks of them, professing my animosity toward him. Qaseem, unbeknownst to me, read every letter in that stack one day while I was away at school. He was so upset with me as his eyes were boring through me like a laser beam ready to tear me apart, yet he had tears in his eyes as he spoke to me, 'Pack a bag and meet me in the fourth stable in the second arena in a half hour. We will be gone for a few days. I do not want to hear your voice until I ask you to speak, do you understand?' He did not wait for me to answer. He turned on his heels and walked away, taller than I had ever seen him. Needless to say, I was a bit humbled at that moment.

When I got to the arena, there were two horses saddled and ready. Qaseem was already mounted, looking off into the distance. I got on my horse and just as I got settled into the saddle, he scowled at me then took off like a bat out of hell. His anger or pain or maybe both was radiating from him. We raced the cliffs side-by-side to the chateau. When we arrived, he dismounted, bent over with his hands on his knees and cried. He was different. The man that served Allah and his country – strong, capable, intelligent beyond belief, fierce, and sometimes even a little scary – was not at the chateau with me. Qaseem left that persona behind and showed up a broken man yet a man of conviction. I took the horses into the barn, fed them, giving him some time in the house by himself. I was confused, to say the least. I went in and sat down at the kitchen table across from him and waited.

Qaseem told me the truth about his and Dimitri's relationship and what had happened between them, but it was not until he got very sick that I learned the detailed truth. This day at the chateau, I understood that the two of them were close, closer than brothers. He did not tell me they were sexually active, but I understood by his words that they were in some way or another. He said their relationship was preordained, that it was an eternal love. He said Dimitri would have a son and that son was me. He paced the room as he told me the story, staring at the floor as he spoke with great grief in his voice. He explained that he was told in a dream by a strange woman that this son would change the world and that it was his job to teach this son of Dimitri and blood of Qaseem everything he knew. He came to the table with an open heart and a lot of tears. Much of what he said, I did not comprehend at the time. It took many months for me to wrap my head around the stories he filled my head with that weekend. He took a big chance telling me about their relationship. He knew I was a hothead and that this information could ruin or even have him killed if I were to ever tell anyone. But I believed him and I witnessed his years of painfully lonely days without Dimitri by his side. As I had spent hundreds of hours looking for Dimitri, he too had spent hundreds of hours looking. We shared our information with each other and I promised to look until I found him.

So, long story short, Pearl, I am looking for closure and I want that closure to be full of love. Love to replace the years of pain that Qaseem and I shared over losing him. And, I am hoping to understand his dream. I hope that makes sense."

Pearl had stopped eating and had given Alexander her full attention. She had tears in her eyes as her heart felt his pain. She didn't say a thing.

Alex got up, drank a glass of water then sat back down. When you are done eating, will you be ready to start the journals?"

She nodded, wiped her eyes, and smiled at him, "Yes, I am as curious as you are. Let's do this."

Alex had put the journals in piles. Each pile represented a person – Julia and Sophia. Pearl put Dimitri's next to the rest of them.

Sophia's journal was locked and the writing on top was in Arabic. Pearl didn't want to destroy the journal's binding, so she decided to look for a key later. They made another pot of coffee and brought the bowl of fruit into the living room with them. The sun was warm and sent beams of light from the windows into the room where they decided to take up shop. Pearl chose to read her mother's journals first so she went to her bedroom to retrieve them, and Alex chose Julia's. He assumed that because Julia had lived with or around Dimitri for most of his years, within her journals he would find his father and answers to so many questions. They got comfortable, with Pearl in the big puffy reclining rocking chair in front of the window overlooking the gardens, and Alex in the matching chair opposite the coffee table between the chairs.

Alex asked Pearl the same question she had asked him, "What are you hoping to find out about your mother?"

Pearl leaned back in her chair and looked up at the ceiling then back at Alex. "Well, I have had an extremely wonderful life. My family has always supported each other through the good times and the bad. When we get together and reminisce, my mother leaves the room. She finds reasons to get snacks, water, or a glass of wine. She never talks about her past. I have found her many times staring out at the sea as if in a dream, her eyes glazed over. I always say to her, 'Penny for your thoughts,' which she replies something like, 'Pearl, your father changed my life and made me the happiest woman ever. I want for nothing. The past is the past and for some of us, we are very grateful that it is gone, but unfortunately not forgotten.' I have asked my father many times about her childhood. He always says it is not for him to tell. So, I wonder why the secrecy. Why she runs from it whenever she is asked about it. She is an amazing woman with the heart of an angel and the fortitude of a lion. I want to know who she was and what made her the woman she is today. I love her so much. Julia researches the heck out of everything, but my mom seems to just know things intrinsically. A wonderful gift. Together they are a force to be reckoned with."

Alex reached over and shook Pearl's hand and said, "Let's learn about our parents, shall we?" She smiled as they each took a journal and began reading.

Pearl began Charlee's journal:

For as long as I can remember, I've felt as if I've lived ten lives in this lifetime. I've lived through divided adversities and challenges most people never experience. And I'm not yet done. Truth be told, I think there's so much more to my life than what I understand. As a three-year-old, I'd already discovered what survival of the fittest meant. I understood the dynamics and emotional composition of the people around me, and I knew that these people wouldn't be in my life for long. I knew intrinsically how to behave and how to fit in; to be recognized yet aloof enough to have those around me enthralled and intrigued but to stay far enough outside their radar so as not to be examined. I learned early on how to navigate this life with my assets, those being my eyes and the ability to listen. I was told once, I don't remember by who, that to understand how to listen is the meaning of love. People want to be heard and when you make eye contact and give a minute of your attention to those speaking, they can't help but tell you their life story, even if they don't know who you are. When they're done, they're unburdened and lighter, as if they just saw a shrink and got the services for free. This gift I have, I recognized very early in life. Indeed, since I was very young people have told me things, some things I felt they shouldn't have shared.

I was conceived in the backseat of a car at an outdoor drive-in theater. My mother was Hungarian, barely 19, and my father was a 23-year-old Ukrainian Navy man. One day his ship docked for repairs in the San Francisco harbor. My mother, his high school sweetheart who he'd been estranged from for a few years, happened to live close by. After a phone call and a quickie date, she found herself pregnant after a one-night stand, losing her virginity. I think I swam around in her embryonic fluid knowing this was going to be a difficult life.

The next day my father returned to the sea. My mother returned to her life as one of nine children being raised as a strict Catholic. Oh, the surprise and angst when she found out that in a short seven months she would be a mother. Sent away in the dead of the night, her sisters and brothers woke in the morning to find she'd disappeared, along with their father. Several hours later, he returned without her, and the children were told not to ask questions. I grew in her womb in a sea of emotions; fear, anger, disappointment, and sadness. Most of all, I already felt abandoned. I believe it was here that I decided to make the best of this life, knowing I'd never see her again. At 1:07 a.m. on December 17, 1961 in a sterile hospital room, I saw only a glimmer of what she looked like.

I didn't cry. I awoke from my long incubation, looked into the eyes of my grandparents who held me at arm's length, I guess to get a good look at me and maybe ease their guilt in the years to come. At that moment, looking into their eyes, my maternal grandmother said, "You weren't meant to be with us. You have somewhere else to be and a different life to live. Goodbye." I said my goodbyes. The shame of it all. Me, their dirty little secret. As I remember, my mother didn't really participate much in giving birth to me. She was in a drug-induced dream, her endocrine system never allowed me to feel her emotions during my birth. No fear, no happiness, no pain, just a blank slate. I'd already prepared for this moment. I'd basked in a sea of warm nothingness for nine months. I knew she wouldn't be a part of my life.

My first home was a Catholic orphanage. The nuns placed me in my own little bassinet amongst several other bassinets with babies

*crying and waiting for someone to pick them up and take them home.
I didn't need to cry. I was born ready for this new world. My only
concern was how long it would take before I could stand, balance, and
run. It's interesting what goes through your mind when you lay in a
bassinet amongst others that aren't wanted. When we were all quiet,
bellies full and the nuns of the orphanage resting while getting a
second wind, we communicated with each other, sharing our fears of
the unknown. We weren't given names or identities; we were just
numbers based on our day of birth. I was #17. Our little homes were
made of see-through plastic. I could look to the left and see #9, and to
the right and see #3. I connected with #9. Our eyes locked and we
found refuge in those moments two feet apart. All our bodies could
do, swaddled so tight, was turn our little heads and merge into each
other's mind, comforting each other as we lay in wait. #3 left first
and then me. #9 was left to find comfort in the next arrival. Sometimes I wonder what happened to #9.*

*The day I left my plastic see-through home, I was cleaned,
dressed in a white cotton dress, little soft booties and gloves, and a
pink hat, all wrapped in a tight flannel blanket. The nun didn't say
much to me. She was in her own world, like a robot carefully going
through the emotions of discharge and NEXT. Comfortable and ready
with a full belly, the nun handed me to my new mother. She wept as
she held me, as if I was a porcelain China doll. After waiting two
long years, my new mother had gotten the call, "If you're still
interested, we have a baby girl available for adoption." She didn't
hesitate; she was on her way. In her excitement, as she sat in the
courtyard waiting to be called to see her new baby, she scanned the
many books of baby names. From these books my name was decided –
Charlee. The name meant Freedom. She knew this baby, me, was her
freedom. Why, I'm not sure. My new mother had kind, deep brown,
and gentle eyes. She said over and over again, "An angel brought you
to me. She said you were coming."*

*Life was good and I had no complaints. I was cared for, loved,
and coddled as most mothers would do. Fifteen months later, I had a
baby brother. He too met my first handler, the robot nun from the
orphanage. We knew as soon as we met that life was not as it would
seem. We were destined in this life to be alone. He knew his journey,*

he shared it with me, and I shared mine with him. We didn't need to talk. We were always confined to small spaces together and we communicated with each other without words. We knew the life ahead of us would be a roller coaster ride. What most people don't understand is that as little children we can communicate without words, and we intrinsically have a knowledge of life's possibilities that await us at the moment of birth. It's a strange thing coming into the world with this much knowledge and not being able to share it.

By eleven months old, I was getting pretty good at walking from table to table, chair to chair, using them as my props. Everything I could reach I grabbed, until one day I reached for the cup of pain that would scar me for life: hot coffee. I reached for the handle on the cup and pulled it toward me. It fell from the tall table and its scalding contents spilled onto the fragile, thin skin on my neck and chest. I spent many months agonizing as the doctors and nurses peeled the burnt, dead skin from my neck as it healed, layer after layer. My parents were never the same. The blame became too unbearable and before long, Dad's days of work, afternoons playing sports, and nights spent in college left Mom alone and lonely with two children and her guilt.

Before long, my brother and I felt sorrow, confusion and, once again, the feeling that we weren't a source of joy but a source of inconvenience. This time we weren't given a plastic see-through home but a dark, quiet pen that we shared in our wet clothes, continuously hungry. Our mother could no longer stand the sight of us. She just left us alone in the dark. We stayed quiet. We made no noise. We had each other and that was our comfort. We spent many nights like this, with me forever my brother's protector.

At the age of three, my dad began coming home to my brother and me alone in the dark playpen, drenched in our clothes. He would change us then buckle us in the front seat next to him in Old Yeller, an old Ford pickup, and drive from bar to bar in search of my mother. Our father never hurt us. He was always kind. Our father was our knight in shining armor. It didn't take long after that they divorced. We now had two homes, one with our mother and her new boyfriend, and the other, Dad's new apartment.

My first memory of being in my dad's new home, an apartment complex, was from the bottom of a pool. His legs were running toward me in a pair of Hawaiian red and black swimming trunks. My next breath choked me, being full of chlorine and water, but I wasn't alone in the bottom of the pool. I felt calm. It was surreal, like in slow motion. I wasn't afraid at the bottom of the pool. I was just at the bottom with air bubbles all around me, sparkling as the sun glistened through them. I knew I might be in trouble for being at the bottom of the pool. I had gotten too close to the edge and slipped in before anyone knew I was there.

After that, my dad moved in with my grandpa and we stayed with him whenever we visited Dad. Grandpa lived on a small tri-angular piece of land in the middle of the city. He owned the whole piece. He grew olives and cured them in an old cement washbasin outside. He was a World War II veteran who had married young and had two sons. When my grandmother went into labor with their daughter, complications occurred and they both died. Grandpa never remarried. He went off to war, giving his sister the two boys to raise.

Grandpa was my light. He called me his "little glamour girl, his little angel." I sat on his lap many a night as he told his funny stories. He drank sweet and fruity port wine which he shared with me and my brother, always saying, "Don't tell your dad." We would look into his sunken eyes filled with love and warmth and promise to never share the secret.

His home was small and dark, and the rug was very thin, very worn, and very cold. My brother and I slept on the floor in our sleeping bags. We would play with the spiders that crawled across the floor at night, staying very quiet so Dad could sleep. Food was scarce, but we were never hungry. Dad lived with Grandpa for a few years.

My brother and I loved to roam the yards, all unkept with stuff laying all around. We found refuge in the old barn and shed, finding treasures to play with. Being in the open air without supervision was glorious!

One day when we were walking and exploring together, my brother disappeared. He was next to me then he wasn't. He'd fallen into an old septic tank. I looked in and he was at the bottom, laughing.

I started laughing too. I found an old ladder and he got out. Thank God it was empty. I'll never forget that.

Mom was into her new boyfriend. She dolled up whenever she could with a giant beehive hairdo, tight pants, and painted lips. She'd met him at the bar. He was a swinging single; a tall, handsome man who liked his women, his drinks, and cars. He was a businessman who made good money but lived a life very different from my father's. He was the "bad boy", and my mom was smitten. Although she'd been raised a strict Catholic, I don't believe this new man in her life ever saw a Bible, let alone had ever stepped foot in a church. My mom fell in love with danger in the form of a sweet-talking, savvy man who was excited to exploit change, and steal her naivety and pureness. They were married shortly after they started dating.

On the weekends, the house was full of people; couples and singles with clothes everywhere, nudity, cigarettes, alcohol, and music. My mother and stepdad were happily enjoying life to its fullest. I watched from afar with my brother. We were sequestered to the den with the TV station fixed on cartoons. When the minutes turned into hours, we'd sneak into the hallway and watch the adults laughing, touching, and kissing as if they all belonged to each other with no contracts binding them. They were high on life.

After a while, the nights turned into yelling, questioning, loud thunderous noises from blows to the walls, and our mother being thrown about. The front door would slam and she would cry softly in the hallway, only a few feet from our bedroom door. Slightly ajar, we could see her crumpled on the floor with mascara running down her cheeks. We hid under our covers, sweating and fearful, trying not to make any noise. Some nights on his liquor binges, he'd come home with other women. I think he forgot he was married, only to be surprised we were in the house. These nights my brother and I closed our door and lay together, praying for the night to end.

It wasn't long before the boogie man started visiting our room. My brother and I shared a room that was divided by a short wall that allowed the room to be separated in two. We never knew which side of the room the boogie man would visit. I closed my eyes and pretended to sleep until he left, satisfied. Mom never came in to scare the boogie man away because she'd succumbed to the bottle. Her nights were spent in a drunken sleep, trying to escape her fate each night.

One year, on her birthday, with the help of my mom's friend, my brother and I bought her a pretty nightgown for her present. When she was found wearing it, it was torn from her and she was thrown outside to sleep for the night. I'm not sure how she made it through the cold night naked and alone on the cement step, but she did.

One summer my stepdad roasted a giant pig in a massive pit in the backyard. All the neighbors and people from work were at the house. My new uncle was there too. The music was loud and the adults were happily celebrating life, enjoying each other's bodies. When the night was over, my new uncle was given my bed to share with me. He was gentle and quiet as he touched me, but I closed my eyes and prayed for light. In the morning, he was gone before my parents woke up.

My brother and I kept to ourselves, and I never let him out of my sight. As we grew, he began to act out. He began taunting and teasing the kids in the neighborhood. Many times when we were outside playing, he would run and hide behind me as the group of boys trailing him yelled curse words and promises of a brutal ending if they caught him. I was a scrappy girl with the tongue of a razor blade and the heart and strength of a gorilla protecting her young. The boys would come to a screeching halt before me, all at once yelling the crimes that had just been committed and the punishment that was about to be inflicted on the crumpled-up boy hiding behind me. Never was a hair on his head touched. I took one beating and learned that I too had it in me to reciprocate the sentencing. When the first boy landed in a heap, the others knew that I had no fear and if they got within arm's length, they too would suffer the consequences. I was never the aggressor, but I was the defender if you got too close. Years of this made our bond deeper, and my need to protect my brother became ingrained in me as if he were my child. It caused great grief when I couldn't protect him from the boogie man.

When the boogie man from down the hall started visiting at night, my brother and I changed. The punishments for our childish behavior came in the form of a belt, a board, or standing in the corner for days. We took the punishments like champs, closing off *our emotions and fear, reducing the pain receptors' firing. We stayed silent as the blows connected. This wasn't accepted behavior, and only increased the length of the punishment. It was the guilt they felt afterward that gave us pleasure. I really think he beat us just to keep us quiet.*

One day we heard the neighbors were going to be gone for a few days. For the life of me I can't remember why, but we broke into the house, opened the refrigerator, and destroyed everything in it. There was ketchup all over the floor, broken containers, and food slung from wall to wall. When the refrigerator was empty, we left. Days later, we sat quietly on our beds listening to the disappointment and apologies coming from the living room as our mom absorbed the magnitude of our escapade. I don't remember the punishment much. I closed my mind and fell into a dream state. My body was at the hands of a madman who had just endured public humiliation and wasn't going to let it happen again.

The next day I examined the scars, bruises, and cuts all over my backside, legs, and arms. I hurt for days. My brother's punishment was to watch. I remember looking into his eyes. He locked them on mine until it was over. This is how I found the strength to get through my punishment. Our eyes were fixed. He'd learned to tune out everything, just as I did. Unbeknownst to him, he saved my life by staying connected to me during my punishment, my little body being beaten like a grown man. When I awoke late that night, he was next to me, holding me gently. He took care of me for days as the anger welled in his soul. I regret the moment of bad judgment when entering that house. The consequences of that act changed my brother, watching me being beaten as I stared him in the eyes with no emotion. He lost his ability to care about anyone or anything after that, except for me and the little girl that lived a few doors down and across the street.

Pearl lowered the journal, tears streaming down her cheeks. She couldn't believe the story she was reading. Alexander looked up and asked if she was OK. Pearl nodded and said, "Oh my god. This is horrible, Alex."

He said, "Pearl, it is a story from long ago. You know your mother now. She is wonderful and maybe that story is why she is so wonderful. Read it as an understanding of who she is now." He stood up and said, "Come here." Pearl did and he gave her a big hug and wiped her tears. "Here, have some fruit – it will make you feel better."

She gave him a big smile, blew her nose, and refilled both their coffee cups. She took a huge cleansing breath, picked up the journal, and began reading again.

My brother spent his days collecting bugs, playing in the dirt, and figuring out ways to impress the little girl down the street. His most daring act of love was when he pinned a towel around his neck fashioning a cape, propping himself up on the top of the fence, raising his hands in the air, crying out "Batman", and jumping. She was smiling, clapping her hands, and jumping up and down, coercing him to "fly" while giggling with glee.

It was a perfect landing. When he stood up fully erect from the perfect 10-point landing, his mouth began to ooze blood. He looked at me, stone-faced, looking into my eyes with the same emotionless stare we had come to sync with. I ran to him, grabbed his lower jaw, and looked in. He'd bitten through his tongue. In a muffled voice he said, "That was a good one," and smiled, showing me his teeth covered in blood. He looked at his lady who was jumping for joy, not even acknowledging the bloody teeth and saliva dripping from his chin.

I said, "Yes it was," and he was gone, in her arms, laughing and spitting. Many of the neighborhood kids witnessed the jump that afternoon. The respect for my brother grew exponentially that day. Did it entice the other boys to ignore the mouthy slurs he slung at them? Nope. Did it stop the weekend entourage of bullies from wanting to put him in his place as he continued to taunt them? Nope.

My brother never learned his lesson until he had landed himself in the Soledad Prison System at the age of 17. He was charged as an adult after using a gun to steal marijuana from a renowned drug dealer. Six years later, my brother left that prison, and all these decades later, I think he's said enough words to fill only two pages of binder paper. He became a man of very few words.

By the time I was seven, I had learned a lifetime of knowledge. Weekends were filled with backyard barbeques and all-night parties.

We were confined to the den on these nights, so many times my brother and I took turns sneaking out and stealing snacks and drinks from the trays and dishes around the house. We lived on the coast so the hors d'oeuvres were always seafood-related; smoked and raw oysters, smoked clams, sea urchin butter on crackers, crab, steamed calamari, caviar, and baked shark in a ceviche dip. Our mother was a horrible cook! If a tablespoon of spices was good in the soup, she put in four, and the salt was enough to attract a herd of deer. Her specialty was hors d'oeuvres, tiny bites of cheese with local fresh seafood, with no spices required.

Some of my best memories were watching my mother soak in the tub. She was a reader who escaped into novels. It didn't matter what they were about, she had hundreds from each genre. She'd pull out the cutting board that was tucked neatly into the cabinetry then put on a pile of potato chips, dill pickles, seafood of all kinds – depending on her mood – and a cocktail, then placed the banquet cutting board across the bathtub. She'd sink into the warm water and eat and read until the steamy water turned cold. I'd sit on the commode and watch her and try to make conversation. Sometimes I just stared at her and waited for her to share her food. Sometimes she'd talk to me, putting down her book and engaging in conversations wrapped around her life, ideas, and new creative projects.

She taught me how to use the sewing machine at five, and at six, I made my first quilt. My mother was very talented. She knitted and crocheted, was a professional wedding cake decorator, and an excellent seamstress. She taught me how to make all my Barbie's clothes.

At six I learned how to iron. I was given a stack of my stepdad's dress shirts and a can of spray starch. I actually enjoyed it because it made me feel grown up. As I got better, my mom stopped taking his dress shirts to the cleaners. He had a very high-profile job at McDonnel Douglas, working on the Gemini project – one of our first trips to outer space and the moon – and was expected to dress the part, I was told.

The day my stepdad found out that I was ironing his shirts, my mother left the bedroom with a chunk of hair missing from her head. As he passed me in the hall, he said, "You're doing a great job," touched my chin with his finger, letting it linger down to my nipple, kissed me on the mouth, smiled, and left. I was so happy he was happy with me. As I looked down the hallway, my mother looked at me with tears in her eyes, swollen from crying as she lowered her head. When the front door closed, I ran to her and held her tight as she sat on the floor looking at me. I brushed her hair back and kissed the spot where the hair was missing. There were many memories like this, but she never talked about them with me. She kept her thoughts to herself.

One summer, my brother and I boarded the PSA flight to the central valley to see my father and his girlfriend. We had six weeks to escape the chaos and the boogie man, and we were happy. My father's girlfriend had flaming red hair, which was always pinned up in a teased beehive, the hairstyle of those days. She had crystal blue eyes just like my father. She had four girls; the oldest girl was four years older than me, and the youngest was four years younger than me. They were nice enough at first. We looked very different. My dad's girlfriend had been married to a Lebanese bookie from Vegas. Not an attractive man, but a confident, rich man with many secrets.

I overheard my father talking one evening. The bookie had a little black book with names of all the prominent politicians, police commissioners, ministers, teachers, and TV personalities that he took bets from. He was a scary man with a lot of scary people surrounding him. His motto was to put fear into the people around him if they crossed him, including his wife.

I didn't understand most of the conversation I overheard once, but what I did understand was when my dad said, "I'll protect you to the death," he meant it. This made me love my dad more. His love for her was palpable every time she walked into the room. It wasn't long before his attention became focused mostly on her. The long conversations with my dad and I dwindled and his hours at work extended. He was preparing to marry her.

One day while visiting Grandpa on his triangle piece of property, a man across the street was playing with his kids. He picked up the little girl, threw her into the air as she giggled with joy, and when he caught her, he kissed her on the nose and hugged her. I smiled and said as I watched them play, "My stepdad kisses me on the mouth."

After hearing me say this, my dad's girlfriend came to me very slowly and sat next to me on the stoop. She said, "Oh, does he play like this with you?"

Not really paying much attention to her, I was in my head, trying to figure out how to run across the street and join in the fun. I said, "No, not like that, but in other ways. He loves me and makes me laugh, but sometimes he makes me scared, but not all the time. He scares my mom more." She put her hand on my hand. This got my attention. When I looked up at her, she was as white as a ghost. She was looking at me with a look I'd only seen in my mother's eyes after she'd done something that made my stepdad mad. I retracted and went to the car, pulling my brother along with me. Something inside me told me to run and hide.

By the end of that week, I'd been interrogated by several people. My father's brother was a family attorney, and his best friend a judge. I'd been examined by a social worker, a nurse, and several female doctors, and wasn't allowed to see my brother or my family.

The day I finally got to see my brother was the day my mother came to see me in the courthouse with a gift, a small white box. She'd been crying, was unkept, and looked like a little girl. She reminded me of the many occasions I'd looked in the mirror as I brushed my teeth after my stepfather went on a drunken rampage, leaving me frightened and battered. She said, "If you tell them you're lying, I'll give you this pretty bracelet." It was her beautiful charm bracelet. I used to play with her jewelry, always admiring this particular bracelet, always trying it on only to be told abruptly to "Take it off!"

I hadn't slept in days, and I hadn't eaten much. Worries of my brother without me plagued my mind. I asked over and over again where he was and to bring him to me, but I was told, "No. He is safe."

Fifteen pounds underweight with transparent skin, I could count the veins all over my body. I was as protective as a lioness, had the strength of at bull, and was about to explode. People were going to get hurt! I wanted my brother next to me.

Nothing mattered but my brother. I was sick with worry. I didn't understand the request from her for me to lie or not to lie about what-ever she was asking me to do. What I did come to understand was that the boogie man was a really bad man and that he'd no longer be hurting my brother, me, or my mom. He'd no longer be bathing me or visiting my bed at night. I'd no longer watch late night TV with him in the dark while he drank and played games with me. Sometimes the games were fun and felt good, but other times he hurt me and held me by the neck, a neck that was still painful from the burns. He'd hold me down and make me touch him in ways that frightened me. The next morning, he'd apologize and kiss me, reminding me that the drinking made him confused and that I was the only one who made him truly happy. This would temporarily take the fear away, but over time I learned to play the game to survive so I wouldn't end up like my mother. I'd lay in bed at night and wonder why she didn't just take us and run away. Most of the time she just disappointed me as she scolded us or beat us, only to brag about it when he came home saying, "I know it hurts you to discipline the kids, so I did it for you." This made him happy. On those occasions I didn't have to worry about a visit from the boogieman. I was left alone. He was busy making Mom happy.

When she asked me to lie, I looked her in the eyes, knowing what she knew, knowing she was asking me to return with her to my stepdad, and that the bracelet was a bribe. I walked away. That day, my brother and I were placed in the custody of my father on one condition – he had to be married. It was a time when men worked and mothers cared for the children. After a quickie wedding, we went home with our father. The courts gave my mother the same visitation rights that my dad had; six weeks in the summer and every other Christmas. We'd see her again.

With my father's vehement hatred toward my mother and my mother's disgust of my father and her overwhelming embarrassment, I learned by the time I was nine to be the best actress in the world. While we were with my dad, I proclaimed to hate my mom. While we were with my mom, I proclaimed to hate my dad and his new wife.

Life changed drastically after we were placed with my father. The boogieman left me alone when we visited my mother. A part of him died after the court hearings, the courtroom filled with his co-workers and friends there to support him, not knowing what he'd done. He lost his charm, charisma, and zeal for life, and became a broken man. My mother became more hateful and angry, and used every sober moment to shower me with guilt, claiming I'd destroyed her life. I never understood why she didn't leave him.

The summers were horrifying, and our mother stayed married to our stepdad. As per the rules of the court, we had to visit her every other Christmas and six weeks in the summer just as my dad's visitations were, but now I had no bedroom. I had to sleep on the couch so my brother had the room to himself. Many days, through the drunken stupor, my mom would hold my hair and demand that I say into a tape recorder that I'd lied. She lost all her friends and my stepdad lost his job. Liquor was their only sanctuary. No more parties. What little life my mother had was gone. They drank themselves to sleep by 8:00 p.m. every night. I used this time to sneak out, run to the beach, look up at the stars, and pray for all my wishes to come true. My biggest wish was to fall in love with a prince who would take me away like all the princes did with the princesses in the Disney movies. Then my brother and I would live happily ever after.

Living with my father and his new bride and her girls placed my brother and I at the bottom of the list, especially after my stepmom gave my father their only child together, a son. It was survival of the fittest, a perfect Darwin analogy. There were seven kids, a two-bedroom house, and my father working around the clock to provide for us. There were many good times, but it didn't take long to realize what was mine was no longer mine but ours. My quiet little world with my brother was gone. It was loud and noisy all the time with continuous fighting and bickering.

My stepmom took to staying in her room until my dad came home. If we needed a mediator, standing outside her bedroom door we would plead for assistance over our issues. Her response was, "Is anyone bleeding or needing to go to the hospital? Is anyone dead? You don't want me to me to come out of this room and deal with this!" We would scurry away to fight these battles by ourselves.

The day I was called Cinderella was a day I'll never forget. My new step-sister, only six months older than me, called me Cinderella as I was washing dishes in filthy water. I splashed it on her and she hit me square in the back as I turned. I made a fist and swung around with all my might. She ducked, and I hit her square in the eye. If she hadn't ducked, the blow would have gone straight to the shoulder.

That night I found out what picking a switch was all about. After a while, switching came easy for my stepmom. She was fed up with all the fighting. The mixed family and all its dynamics were changing her. Her fairytale fantasy had come to a screeching halt when my brother and I became a permanent fixture in her house.

A few years passed before she couldn't take it any longer. Her youngest daughter was sent away and so was my brother. He'd become the brunt of all that went wrong, while her new son was golden. My brother soon found his life amongst the undesirables and that was when he was incarcerated at 17.

I visited him in prison whenever I could and sent him care packages to help him manage in prison. He stopped writing so my letters became less frequent. By the time he was released, he was a shell of a man. He retreated into the horizon and I lost touch although I searched for years. One day a letter arrived with no address and all it said was, "Stop – I don't want to remember anymore, and you're my memories. Stop looking. I'm a ghost to you now." My heart aches for him, my only true family.

My high school years were typical. I became a cheerleader. It was expected for all the kids to become an athlete. I kept my head down during the high school years and out of my sisters' way, and all was well for the most part. I got good grades and upon graduating I was accepted into the college nursing program. I knew I wanted to be a healer. I studied apothecary, alternative medicines, and several other holistic modalities. My favorite thing to do is learn about the healing power of the flora and fauna on the planet.

Before entering the nursing program, I learned that my mother and stepfather, from years of partying, died of cirrhosis of the liver, both on the same night in the comfort of their home. They'd been sick for many years. It was at this time that my knight-in-shining armor father and stepmother began to suffer from different debilitating ailments. They began to require more and more help. It wasn't long after that my stepsisters then youngest brother left for college or disappeared into the night and I never heard from or saw them again. It was as if they never existed. It was extremely sad and unconscionable. I stayed behind and took care of my father and stepmom while I finished college. When they passed, there was no funeral or cele-

bration of life. I made the decision to mentally divorce the family. They no longer existed. It was the only way I could handle their disappearance. The relationships between us kids was simply a deception until high school was over and we could exit the nest. It was liberating, actually, when I realized everyone was gone.

I put the house on the market, packed up all my parents' belongings, and had hospice pick it up. I called a lawyer named Derrick to help with the house. I decided to give him the responsibility of finding the siblings to dole out the proceeds acquired from the house. He was gentle and kind, and before I knew it, we were having an affair. He was 68 and I was 22. He was married but estranged from his wife with no plans to divorce her. Their assets together made a divorce undesirable to both, so they remained friends but not lovers. I took that role for him and him for me. It was the first time in my life that I felt what love was. We adored each other and spent every waking minute sharing and contemplating the philosophical aspects of life and all its nuances. He had the wisdom I craved and a peaceful heart, just what I needed, and he let me be me with no expectations. It wasn't long before we finished each other's sentences and read each other's minds as if we'd walked the same path in another lifetime.

During the long and lonely nights while caring for my parents, I was able to accelerate my studies and get my PhD in biology and metaphysics. I found my relationship with Derrick defined by the theory of entanglement. Simply put as an analogy, when two people share the same space and time, and create strong emotional bonds with each other, their energy force becomes entangled and can never separate. Each feel and respond to the other simultaneously, no matter how far apart they are. This connection can never be broken. This is how I would describe our relationship. It was profound. He looked at me as if I was the only woman on Earth. He was enamored with me. He'd often sit back in his chair, cross his arms and smile as if he was trying to figure me out, wondering if I was real or just a dream, a dream he could only fantasize about. It was so much more than sex, friendship or companionship – it was magical. I became his teacher to the world of possibilities and he my mentor to the realities of life and the experiences and challenges we go through.

He quieted my mind, and I filled his. In the beginning I was hesitant to trust him, but after five months of dealing with legal data, he said, "I'm not sure if I can trust you with my heart, but I had a dream last night and we came this close to having an affair."

Before I even had a thought in my mind, I kissed him gently and walked away then turned and said, "Chew on that," a line I'd heard in an old black and white movie. Several days later, after an afternoon of coffee then tea then food then wine, we fell asleep fully clothed in each other's arms. For the first time in my life, I slept with no demons hang-ing over me like a mobile in a child's crib. Several nights later we stood before each other, two candles flickering their dance on the dark walls while, eyes locked, we slowly undressed each other. He touched me gently as if I was a fragile flower, pull-ing me close against his strong body. He kissed my breast softly and whispered, "You're the most beautiful woman I've ever seen, Charlee."

We made love every chance we got. We were inseparable. We bantered, joked, laughed, and shared our bodies, our thoughts, our dreams, and our fantasies. One night, our legs and bodies entangled while we snuggled in bed he said, "I'm indeed a lucky man. Your energy, your wit, your snappy dialog, the way you stand your ground, the way you bring laughter into my life, your vulnerability, and how you love so generously is all the reasons I fell in love with you." My heart, my brain, and my consciousness now knew what real love felt like.

When the legal matters of my parents' estate had been finalized, I didn't get a bill, I got the voice of reason. Derrick sat me down and said, "Go live, love, be, and know I'll always be entangled with you. Go to Greece and fulfill your dream. Feel and be with this energy that's calling you, Charlee. Someone awaits, I can feel it, and you're ready to give and receive now. I'll miss you terribly, but we'll see each other again, I know this to be true now." This was the night of my 23rd birthday. We made love and he gave me a bracelet with an infinity sign on it with two beads, one representing him and the other me, together forever in time and space. We said our goodbyes and I left.

We meet only a handful of people in our lives that make us feel as if they're a part of us, a part of our soul, born with us from the same mold. Derrick is the second, my brother was the first.

It took a few weeks to stop obsessing over our relationship. Many times, I picked up the phone to call him only to put it back down, take a deep breath, and walk away. He was right – it was time for me to venture out into this great big world and live again. I spent nights reading article after article about the island of Ikaria in Greece. I don't know why this tiny, secluded island entered my radar, but when I started reading about it, I knew that the energy of this island was calling me. How? I can't describe it. It had first been introduced to me through metaphysics, its mystical healing properties and thermal springs that attracted people from all around the world called to me too. Secondly, through the tabloids. Every grocery store had maga-zines with photos of Melena and Maximus, the two most famous stars of the film industry. She was beautiful, perfect in all aspects, and Maximus was the envy of all men and desire of all women. Together they built an empire. Melena was from Ikaria. I read in her bio that her father and brother, two masonry carpenters, were sought after around the world. Their skills employed them at ancient archeological sites that had succumbed to the elements over time. Her mother, Julia, was a renowned healer just as her mother Sophia was. Her expertise was in the tinctures, teas, and ointments she made from the flora and fauna on the island, and she was an attending professor at the university in Athens.

These articles possessed my dreams and my every waking moment. For the life of me I didn't know why. It was as if God herself was pushing me toward that island. Julia's family lived in Therma, a small Ikarian coastal town that, since antiquity, harbored ships full of people traveling to bathe in the natural, healing springs found only on this island. Melena's father, Daniel, and her brother, Daniel Junior, had built a home on the cliffs called Agriolykos. It was a pension with few rooms.

The summer after my 23rd birthday, I sold everything I owned and applied for a six-month visa to further develop my studies on the island of Ikaria. My dream was to work with Julia. There was nothing I wanted more. It was as if a force was pushing me to the island, push-

ing me to find Julia. When my visa arrived, I was on the first plane to Greece.

Athen's airport was bustling with people. I breathed in the excitement of vacationers from all ethnic backgrounds as they flooded into the baggage claim area. I grabbed my bag and headed to the next departing gate to Ikaria, and landed in the tiniest airport I'd ever been in. I'd rented a car prior to leaving The States and was thankful when I saw it waiting for me. I drove into the small town of Therma, not knowing where I'd be staying but prayed for an available room at Julia's hotel. When I arrived, the parking lot was on the beach. I got out of the car and looked up at the sun to greet him as I do every day with, "Hello, handsome." My eyes were drawn to the cliff overlooking the town. Something told me to go there NOW!

The only room in town that was available was now mine. I'd gotten the last room at Agriolykos. Julia greeted me in the courtyard, and when I looked into her eyes, I knew something big was happening; I wasn't there by accident. I felt as though I knew her but couldn't remember from where. It was a powerful yet warm feeling. Something was magically aligning in the universe, and I knew I was exactly where I was supposed to be.

Julia welcomed me into her home and asked what had brought me to Ikaria. I said, "Hello, Julia, my name is Charlee. I came here with no plan but to meet you, and here I am." She looked at me quizzically as she touched her chin and asked if we had met before. I told her we hadn't.

She said, "YES! We have met before, Charlee." She looked into my eyes, knitted her eyebrows then slowly gave me the motherly smile I'd only seen in the movies. At that moment, I knew she'd metaphorically meant "spiritually". I felt an immediate bond with this woman like I'd never felt before. I felt connected to her the moment I saw her. Her energy was so soft and warm, comfortable, and welcoming. I explained my background and studies and how I'd been following her work. I expressed my desire to learn from her and hoped she could find time in her schedule to mentor me. Julia smiled as she listened to me ramble, keeping eye contact. I began to feel as if she was looking straight into my soul, yet it didn't feel intrusive. The excitement of being in her presence was over-

whelming and I was so happy! She showed me to my room and asked if I was available this evening to learn more. We planned to sit and talk after I'd had some time to look around the small city and get my bearings.

I got settled into my room, changed into my comfortable baggy shorts and T-shirt, grabbed an apple, and headed out to explore Therma.

From the moment I began walking, something steered me in a different direction than I was originally headed. I felt so open and alive. With love in my heart and the warmth of the sun all around me, I set out on my first adventure. I walked about fifty yards and from above me I heard two men talking. Then I saw him on the wall. His energy was calling me. I felt him before I saw him, and I knew I was exactly where I was supposed to be. I raised my hand like a visor and watched the men work until my apple was gone. Standing high above me like a Greek god floating from the heavens was the most beautiful man I'd ever set eyes on. Both men looked like Atlas as they lifted the rocks above their heads and put them into place.

Holy shit! *was my only reaction. I'd read stories about this father and son team in my studies. This was Daniel and his son, Daniel Junior, nicknamed Mathias, Julia's husband and son. I looked at Mathias with his small waist, dark hair, and khaki pants with no shirt, exposing his very well-defined shoulders and arms.* Oh my goodness, *I thought,* look at him!

Without thinking, I brushed my hands together, making a clapping sound while dusting off the final remnants of my apple. Mathias turned and looked down at me. I froze. I felt like a peeping Tom who had just gotten caught. We stared at each other, neither saying a word. With my nerves on fire, I yelled up to him and asked, "Do you speak English?" He nodded yes. "Are you Daniel Junior?" He stopped and gave me his full-frontal view as the sweat on his chest glistened in the sun. I said, "I've read about you and your family. I'm Charlee. Can I make a suggestion?"

Shyly, he said, "Yes," as he fumbled, almost falling off the scaffolding. He was transfixed, and didn't even blink as he stared down at me. Daniel Senior watched as the scene unfolded in front of him. He turned toward his son, leaned against the wall, crossed his arms, and smiled first at Mathias then down at me.

I said, "It would be even better if you added different colors or designs, like a bird or a sunset, something like that."

Mathias didn't say a thing, and after a long, uncomfortable pause, I said, "Oh, but I like your work. It's beautiful. I'm just saying." He continued to just stare at me without speaking. I waited, but nothing. I said, "OK, well, have a nice day." I wanted to find a hole to climb in.

Daniel Senior smiled ear-to-ear while trying not to show it then asked, "Charlee, are you alone?"

I stopped, turned around, and said, "Yes, I'm here for six months. I'm here to study the fauna and flora for medicinal tinctures."

He said, "You come to dinner at my house tonight. Daniel Junior here will cook us a meal and we can talk. My wife will teach you where to go on the island to find what you are looking for." I robustly thanked him – maybe too robustly. I'd say almost embarrassingly so. Daniel Senior chuckled as he looked at me then Mathias. "We live at Agriolykos. Arrive at 7:00 with an empty stomach. Do you like wine?"

I smiled, "Funny, I just checked in to Agriolykos. I'm staying in your guest house. It was the only room available on the island. And yes, I like red wine."

Daniel chuckled, hit Mathias' arm, and said softly, "It is meant to be." He yelled back down, "Good, I will prepare red wine."

I looked at Mathias and asked, "Is this OK with you?"

He quietly said, "Yes."

I was shaking and so excited, "OK, should I bring anything?"

"Yes, a pad and paper – and be prepared to stay up late," Daniel Senior replied. With that, I turned to walk away when I heard Daniel Senior smack Mathias and say, "Wake up, boy. What do you feel right now?"

Mathias said, "Yes."

Daniel Senior laughed out loud then Mathias said, "I am done for the day. I will meet you at home."

His father chuckled and said, "Yes!

I giggled as I walked away. It was a perfect day! Then I panicked thinking, Oh my god, what am I going to wear? I'm going to be
sitting at the same table with this man. How am I going to breathe?

*I stopped in my tracks, turned around, and ran back to my room
to get ready. As I headed up the stairs along the back pathway to
Agriolykos, I saw a patch of flowers and decided to pick some for
Julia. I thought they'd look nice on the table. I quickly showered and
stared at my suitcase. I must have changed my clothes a hundred times
even though I only had a small suitcase. I finally decided on a simple,
silky, powder-pink dress with short sleeves. It was cute but still a little
sexy, exposing my neck and shoulders. I wore a pair of white sandals
adorned with tiny pearls and rhinestones. I loved those sandals! I put
my hair in a ponytail then in a bun, then decided to just let it hang
free. When I was thoroughly exhausted and my nerves were almost
shot, I sat on the side of the bed and slowly breathed until I calmed
down. I'd never felt this alive in my life. Derrick taught me how to love
and be loved, and I was truly thankful. At that moment, I felt that my
relationship with Derrick happened so I could open up my heart to the
next love, a love that would last a lifetime.*

*I was so nervous. I knew the people of the island had a
reputation for always being late to everything, but for some reason I
felt this wasn't the case with this family. I took my chances and arrived
five minutes early.*

*When Julia opened the door, her smile was from ear to ear.
She gave me a kiss on both cheeks and thanked me for the flowers.
She said, "Wait here – I will be right back." She went into the kitchen
and, with the door ajar, I heard her apologize to the flowers, "Oh,
my friends, I am so sorry you were picked today, but tonight you will
share our table. This will be my daughter-in-law." I felt horrible! I
wanted to crawl out of the house and slither back to my room, then I
realized everything she'd just said. The reaction Daniel Senior had
toward Mathias meeting me today popped into my mind. I stood there
alone wondering all of a sudden,* What does this family have in store
for me?

*Julia returned, took my hand, and showed me into the living
room where Daniel Senior was uncorking a bottle of wine. He pour-*

*ed us each a glass then raised his, waited for us to join in, and said,
"Here is to new friendships and grandchildren."*

Julia said, "DANIEL!"

*I busted up laughing and said, "OK, but not tonight." They
laughed and we all had a sip. I wasn't sure where Mathias was, but
after noticing his nervousness earlier, I figured he needed as much
time as I did, or he was a typical Ikarian and was late to everything.
Julia asked me a million questions about my schooling and intentions
on the island. As I shared my degrees with her and ideas on what I
wanted to do with them, I heard the patio door open, letting in the
warm evening air. Mathias was talking to someone with him. I was
thankful for the interruption since Julia had begun asking me questions about my family. This wasn't a favorite topic and I was very
nervous to share anything about my family.*

*I played it casual and took another sip of wine and a bite of
bread when Melena and Mathias entered. Standing before me was
a page out of a magazine. Melena and Mathias were stunning! I
stood up politely and extended my hand. Melena giggled, ignored the
hand, kissed me on both cheeks then said, "Have you met Mathias?"*

*I looked up at Mathias, our eyes locked as I swallowed and
softly said, "Yes." I was standing next to the most gorgeous man I'd
ever seen. I'm not sure if I was pale or fifty shades of red. I took
a breath, collected myself, and said, "I mean no, not formally."*

*Melena said, "Well, let me introduce you. Charlee this is
Mathias, and Mathias this is Charlee. Oh, and Charlee, I am Melena,
Mathias' sister." Melena stepped in and whispered in my ear, "I just
spent an hour schooling my brother on American women and gave
him a large shot of ouzo on the way to the patio. The only word he
seems to know tonight is Yes. He is a whole lot of nervous. Be gentle
with him."*

*I let out a nervous giggle as I extended my hand to Mathias.
He gently took my hand and took one large step toward me. I was
six inches away from him, staring straight up into his eyes that were
looking down at me. I thought my knees were going to buckle. He
leaned in and kissed each cheek slowly. His hair hung free, softly
brushing my face as he crossed from one cheek to the other. I could
smell his cologne just enough to want to search for its origin. When*

he backed away, I knew my cheeks were flushed and so were his. For the first time in my life, I was speechless. I swallowed again, looking into his eyes while everyone just stood in silence. Daniel and Melena had giant smiles on their faces, and Julia had tears in her eyes. The moment seemed like an eternity.

The moment ended when Daniel said, "I do not know, Charlee, maybe tonight is not too soon after all." I wanted to die; I was so embarrassed. Mathias looked at his father then at me.

Thank god Julia stepped forward and said, "Daniel, you are a terrible man!"

I quickly cleared my throat and said, "Uh, did you give any thought to my idea of the, the, uh, the birds?"

Mathias said, "Yes," and the room broke out into laughter, breaking the sexual tension. Mathias and I jumped as if someone had just yelled "Boo."

It wasn't long before we were all talking at once, sharing our stories and journeys. After hearing a watered-down version of my family life, Julia declared herself my new mother. By the end of the night, our bellies were full and six bottles of wine had been consumed.

I was so happy! I knew I was going to be a part of this family forever.

After the kitchen was clean, Melena went to bed first, followed by Daniel then Julia. I was so excited to be alone with Mathias. We went into the courtyard away from the house and sat in silence under the full moon, gazing at its beams of light sparkling across the Aegean Sea and up into the courtyard. I fell in love with Agriolykos that day and knew I'd never leave. I stood up, walked over to the short wall that surrounded the courtyard, and sat looking down into the dark sea. It was so peaceful.

Mathias walked over, took my hands, and raised me to my feet. I was standing in front of him, gazing up into his blue eyes when he put his hand on the middle of my back, pulled me in close, and gave me a soft, gentle kiss. It was so tender and sweet. He wrapped his arms around me and held me tight. I could feel his strong body next to mine.

I felt so petite next to him. He looked down at me and said softly, "Charlee, I have never made love to a woman. I have never been in the presence of a woman I wanted to share myself with. From the

moment I turned around and looked down at you from the scaffold-
ing, I knew you were the one. I have never felt this way before. I feel
very nervous yet alive right now. I am saying this because if you do
not feel the same way, then please tell me and I will back away. I am
not sure how this is done. This is the only way I know how to ask you
this – will you stay with me tonight?"

I felt my tears welling up inside. It was the most beautiful
moment in my life. Before I even thought about it, I said, "I want to
stay with you tonight. I want that very much." From the light of the
moon, I saw his eyes tear up as mine had. He held me tenderly in his
arms then reached down, picked me up, cradled me in his arms,
and walked me to my suite. When the door was closed, he lowered
me down and stood still in front of me. I reached up and slowly
unbuttoned his shirt, exposing his soft skin and powerful chest. His
breathing increased as he watched me. I pulled his shirt over his
shoulders and let it fall to the floor.

My hands gently touched his skin, and I leaned forward and
kissed the center of his chest then each nipple. He shuddered under
my touch without moving. I undid his belt and the button of his pants,
then lowered his zipper and let his pants fall to the floor. He stepped
forward toward me and out of them. All he had on were his briefs. I
leaned in and hugged him, allowing his body to connect with mine
completely. I felt his erection press against me. I was nervous yet so
alive. I could feel every hair on my body moving with emotion. I
reached down, lowered his briefs, and let them fall to the floor. He
again took one step toward me and out of them. I looked up at him,
seeing that he was watching me. As I touched his engorged penis, he
took a quick breath, lowered his head back then took another big
quick breath in. I started to lower my mouth to him when he stopped
me, pulled me back up, and kissed me with fury, devouring my mouth
as he pressed me backward into the wall. He pushed against me,
trapping me between him and the wall, kissing me as if he were an
animal yet tender enough to make me want more. I didn't want him
to stop. His naked body was wanting me. He stopped abruptly and
looked into my eyes as he ran his hand from my shoulders to my waist
then under my dress. He lowered my panties until they fell to the floor
then turned me around, unzipped my dress, and let it fall. As I turned

back around, he stepped back and looked at me from my eyes to my chest to my belly and down. He looked back up and said, "Charlee, you are beautiful. I want to be inside of you."

I stepped out of my dress and toward him, took his hand, and walked to the bed. His erection became soft. I could feel his nerves, his fear, his innocence. He laid back as I slowly ran my hand over his chest, feeling its strength as I lingered down to his groin. I touched him gently at first then firmly held his penis in my hand and rhythmically began to move up and down. He moaned as his power returned. I moved up and over, placing myself on top of him before I placed him inside of me. We were transported to another world. He moved with me, desire overwhelming us, breathing faster as we moved faster and harder into each other. When I was about to explode in pure pleasure, he swiftly grabbed my waist and turned me over onto my back with him on top of me. "Charlee, I want you. Can I, can I..."

"Yes, Mathias, explode inside of me!" I pulled him in with my legs crossed over the top of his back and held on tight as we both let go. He arched his back, thrust into me once then again, and together we let out a thunderous moan that I think all of Therma heard. This man on top of me, for the first time, felt unconditional love. He sank into me, laying against my chest. His body was trembling with mine. He rolled over onto his side and pulled me in close, kissing me slowly, lovingly, as he caressed my skin. We lay in each other's arms, touching and exploring each other's bodies until we fell asleep.

After that evening, we were inseparable. I studied with Julia during the day and made love to Mathias at night. On our many nights staring at the stars and moonbeams shining across the sea, I told Mathias about Derrick and how he'd saved me, how he taught me to trust myself and gave me the courage to take this journey to Greece. I explained that through Derrick I'd learned how to love and be loved. I explained to Mathias how grateful I was for the relationship. I also explained my family's dynamics. Originally, I told the Mathias I was an only child. I truly felt this way because I really felt alone. I knew I'd never see any of them again.

Mathias wasn't a jealous man. He was happy that through all my pain I'd learned to love. Now he could learn with me, together forever. I was grateful to learn about love with Derrick or I couldn't have trusted enough to let Mathias into my heart. And it was love at first sight! I felt with this man I could – we could – conquer the world together. He was my dream come true.

Two days before my six-month visa deadline, Daniel gave Mathias his mother's wedding ring, a perfect two-carat ruby on a diamond-studded band. That night as I slept, he put it on my finger. He lay there all night watching me sleep, knowing I'd accept. His heart was full of joy and happiness.

When I awoke, Mathias was lying next to me, propped up on one elbow, resting his head in his hand as he watched me sleep. I smiled and stretched then noticed my hand. I sat up, looked at it then at him, and said, "Mathias, is this what I think it is?"

He said, "Marry me, Charlee. I will love you forever!"

I started screaming, "Yes, yes, yes!" and jumped on top of him and kissed his whole face. I don't know what came over me, but I started dancing around the room laughing and looking at my hand yelling, "Yes, yes, yes!" It wasn't long before the whole family joined in on the excitement.

Melena went all out for the wedding. She took me to Paris and had me pick out the dress of my dreams. She planned everything as if it was her own wedding, and I let her. I would've eloped, but the family wouldn't have ever forgiven us if we had. She had some of the best chefs from the mainland catering the event, and a local band was hired so we could dance the night away. Agriolykos was draped in every color of bougainvillea, tiny white lights, and hundreds of white candles in small crystal jars. The wedding was to begin at dusk, and as the sun set, Daniel walked me down the aisle.

Mathias' wedding vows to me were:

"I felt you before I saw you. I could not speak; your energy stole my voice. I could not move, afraid to blink that you might disappear. You captured my heart and stole its power just by standing before me. I did not hear a thing you said, but with every pause, something told me to say, 'Yes'. Today I say yes now and forever. Will you be my wife?"

With tears of happiness, I said "Yes." When Mathias said, "I do," a roar of cheers and applause could be heard throughout

Ikaria. Mathias kissed me with passion, longingly and lovingly. It was magical!

We partied all night long as the island danced. The next day, when we opened our wedding gifts, one particular gift stood out. A thick, bulging-at-the-seams envelope that said, "Our gift to you." It was the last gift we opened. When we opened the envelope, it was the deed and title to the dilapidated building next door to Agriolykos.

In the 1950s it was a grand three-story hotel, but after the recession in the late 60s and early 70s, it closed and fell into disrepair. When the sea wall barrier was built to protect the natural thermal hot springs, the beach disappeared, leaving the hotel sitting partially in the water, its foundation still strong but slowly deteriorating. I'd been through this building, mostly boarded up, on my early morning walks, fantasizing about how I could buy it and turn it into a healing center for Julia and me. Now I had a deed in my hand with a 3-million- dollar check signed by Melena and a business card to an architect here in Therma whose grandfather had built the hotel. On the back of the business card, it said, 'Paid in full, fulfill your dreams, Derrick! My gift to Charlee and Mathias'. The tears flowed. I couldn't see the writing anymore.

Julia, Daniel, and Mathias surrounded me. Mathias spoke first, "Sunshine, we all met Derrick last month. He came here soon after he finished your parents' estate and bought the hotel. He explained himself and your journey to us. He said he does not know why, but he was compelled to do this for you, for us. He is a good man, Charlee, you chose well."

Julia interrupted, "Charlee, he has arranged for everything down to the furniture. Of course, it is up to us to design, but the city has accepted his proposal, and the engineering of the building has been approved.

The three million is just in case or a donation to start the business when the building is complete. That gift is from Melena." I cried and cried, so thankful to Derrick and Melena. A part of me was in overwhelming disbelief. I felt as if Derrick was in the room with us, it felt so strong. I knew his energy would always be with me.

Mathias softly chuckled and said, "Sunshine, what bothers you? Are these happy tears? Is this what you want?"

I said, "This is a dream."

I heard Derrick say, "No, it's a gift, my gift to you for the gift of sight you gave to me." He was standing next to me. He was here – right now! I stood, kissed Mathias, and reached for Derrick. Together we all cried, laughed, and hugged. We all shared a wonderful meal and I don't know how many bottles of wine. Throughout dinner, everyone talked at once about the designs of the healing center and the engineering feat that lay ahead. When the moon began its descent and the first rays of sunrise appeared, we finally called it a night.

Mathias and I greeted the new day with gratefulness for all the people who'd entered our lives, never asking for anything but trust and love. When we awoke late that afternoon, Derrick was gone. He had chartered a private jet back to The States.

I couldn't contain myself when I arrived for lunch in the courtyard. Sitting at the long table were five businessmen; two in suits, three in jeans and T-shirts. Mathias and Daniel greeted each one by name. Ikaria's a small island, with everyone knowing each other or of each other. Daniel and Mathias had already started the ball rolling a week ago. First on the list of things to do was to shore up the waterfront situation. The two men in suits sat with Julia and me. Julia asked, "Charlee, tell us what you see, what is your vision? What do you want the building to look like?"

The rest of the afternoon and over the next six months, we spent every day building a healing center in Therma. Everyone had jobs. The whole town became part of the project. Everyone's ideas were incorporated in one way or another. The healing center was named The Sacred Rock Healing Center. *When it was complete, Mathias and I took the upper third story for our private residence. The second story was a 200-seat theater hall for conferences. The first floor had six classrooms to be used for various healing modalities, a small café for coffee, healing tea, and a simple Greek salad or yogurt with honey, and a gift shop. A large deck extended out over the sea that provided seating for up to 75. Each table had an umbrella to block the hot summer sun. All additional food and supplies needed to run the center were strictly purchased from the locals at a discounted price for shares in the center.*

Together, the town of Therma owned the center, with everyone receiving nice fat bonuses at the end of each month. Speakers and healers from around the world entertained diverse audiences interested in a multitude of healing modalities. The locals of Therma were able to repair, expand, and fortify their homes and businesses so they could stay on the island year-round without worry. A large parking garage was built at the far entrance to Therma. No cars except the locals' cars were allowed in town. The tourists had to walk through town, admiring all the businesses when they arrived at their destination. This generated more jobs for the younger locals to transport tourists in and out of town. They made carts that connected to their bicycles to carry luggage, and the tourists always gave generous tips. Within two years, Therma had a new electrical grid, sewer system, and water treatment plant tucked away in the hills.

The population stayed relatively the same with the addition of one sassy little girl, Pearl, who had eyes as crystal blue as her father's and the soul of a lioness like her mother. We named her Pearl for Melena. Her memories of Maximus will live forever in Pearl. We made Melena Pearl's godmother. Mathias and I homeschooled Pearl with the help of Julia, Daniel, and Melena. Most days Pearl preferred Melena's company over everyone else's, and Melena preferred Pearl's.

Every day, I look into my little girl's eyes and thank God for blessing me with such love. Someday she'll read this and know how much I love her. She completed the dream I never thought possible. When I was a little girl, I always dreamed of a happy ending. I always dreamed of what it would be like to have so much love in my life, true love without expectations or disappointments. I've found my happiness here in Therma, in Mathias, and in my beautiful little Pearl. My life is complete.

Pearl turned the last page, closed the journal, and softly sobbed. Her mother's life was hard to fathom, so it was no wonder she never spoke of it. It gave Pearl solace knowing that her mother finally experienced a fairytale life full of love, family, and friends. She had a huge desire to hug her mother and decided to call her.

She looked over at Alex who was deep into Julia's story. Every so often he would laugh out loud and say, "Your Nonnah is funny! I am looking forward to meeting her." One time he put the journal down, tears streaming down his face, confused, and went out on the porch by himself. At the time he didn't want to talk about it. Pearl didn't pry; when he was ready to talk about it, she would listen. When he returned, she got up, stretched, gave Alex a big smile, and headed outside to the porch.

The fresh air felt good. The breeze was stimulating and felt almost cleansing with each big breath she took. It was as if she needed to purge her mother's story back out of her. She took five deep cleansing breaths and with each exhale she let it go. On one hand she wanted to have a sit down with her mother and ask a million questions about her past, but on the other hand, she knew that it was a story her mother needed to purge as well and maybe she did so in her journals. Pearl thought maybe it was enough to know her mother's past through the journals. She decided not to bring it up unless Charlee did.

Just as Pearl picked up her phone to check in with Julia and her parents, Adeem called. She saw the number on her phone and in an instant her heart was racing and a big smile burst across her face. It was as if she was a schoolgirl having her first crush on the boy who sat across the room, the boy she was scared to talk to but wanted so much to kiss. After reading her mother's story, her heart was full of love and possibilities. She answered the phone as if she had no idea who was on the other line, "Hello, this is Pearl. Oh, hi, Adeem. How are you? Alex and I have spent most of the morning in a pile of journals and about ten pots of coffee. I feel like I could run a marathon right now."

She giggled and let Adeem import his charm. Adeem's business in the city was done and he asked if he could return. "Pearl, I know you two are on a mission of discovery and it is a personal journey, but I feel that you and I have unfinished business of our own. I hope you feel the same…"

Slowly she answered, "Yes, I do." Her cheeks were flushed, and she began twirling a small curl of hair between her fingers.

"That is good to hear. I must tell you, Pearl, I have not been able to concentrate or focus since I met you. You have completely taken over my mind. I hope this is not too forward, but I need to be with you. I need to be next to you. It is all I can think about. I do not usually like people, but for some reason you are an exception." Adeem laughed out loud and so did she. He continued, "I can be back on the island early tomorrow morning. How does breakfast sound? I am cooking."

She was flustered and her mind was whirling. She had only known this man a few days, yet she was feeling the same. How could he possibly be so enamored by her in such a short time? Typically, men tend to be intimidated by her. Usually, she created the tension in the first place, causing the intimidation. Most men's approach was garnered with flirtatious gestures of a possible hook-up. Most men irritated her. What disgusted her more was a man who looked at her breasts first, then expected her to be enamored with them the moment after. Adeem obviously wore his heart on his sleeve and this was endearing to her.

She shifted in her seat and said, "Yes, breakfast sounds great. But I do not know how long Alex is staying. I am pretty sure he will leave as soon as he is done with his 'investigation' as he calls it. But you are both welcome to stay as long as you like. I have three guest rooms, so plenty of space. If you two have the time, I would like you both to meet Julia and my parents. They return in a day or two, I think. Also, we need to bury Qaseem."

There was a long pause. Adeem finally said, "And?"

She understood exactly what he meant. She smiled shyly, giggled and said, "I have not thought about you at all. I have been busy reading." She had a huge smile on her face.

He returned with a cocky tone, "Ahhhhhhh, I know you love me so give in, get over it."

Pearl immediately sat up tall, a little startled hearing those words in that manner, 'You know you love me so give in, get over it'. She was at a loss for the right response. She was searching her brain for a fast comeback. Was he just like the other men, pompous in his approach to asking her out or was he really into her? She traced back all the conversations they'd had up to this moment, searching for a pattern of arrogance – or was he genuinely wanting to spend time with her or possibly trying to be funny to distract from his shyness? Was he shy?

The silence became a bit uncomfortable. Adeem said, "Hello, Pearl, are you there? Or are you avoiding the question?" There was still no answer, but he could hear her breathing. He too was beginning to feel the possible interpretation problem. Did his cocky ego, as Alex called it, just get him into trouble again? He quickly realized how juvenile the statement was, presumptuous and lacking in respect.

Pearl was about to speak when Alex stepped out onto the porch with her. She was relieved and said, "Perfect timing! Adeem, here is Alex. You can ask him yourself on how long he is planning to stay." She quickly got up, rolled her eyes, and handed her phone to Alex. She turned and walked into the house, shutting the door behind her. When the door closed, she said, "Oh my god, what was that?" She bent over, letting the blood run back to her head while taking a deep breath. *That was the most awkward moment ever*, she thought.

Alex sat down on the porch with Pearl's phone in hand, waiting for Adeem to say something. What came next surprised him, "Dad, I think I just made a big mistake. What was Pearl's expression when she handed you the phone?"

Alex said, "She did not have an expression. She just handed me the phone and quickly left the porch. What happened?"

"She makes me crazy! She is all I have thought about since I met her. I cannot focus and almost screwed up the Coster account last night. I have never felt this way about a woman before and I think I got a little brash with her a minute ago. Now what do I do?"

Alex chuckled and asked, "How brash is brash?"

"I said to her, 'You know you love me, so get over it' when I asked if I could come back to the island and hang with the two of you."

Alex laughed out loud, "Son, this girl is different. She is not the typical woman after you for your prestige and money like the others that seem to flock to you. Be yourself. She will see you and when she does, you will know what to say and how to be the man you want to be around her. But for now, I will give her the phone back so you can straighten out the misunderstanding. I could use you here. I have been reading Julia's journals which are quite entertaining, to say the least, but have not learned much about Dimitri. It appears he became a quiet man after he left Qatar. I have several hours of reading still, but I should have Julia's set done by the time you get here."

Alex adjusted himself on the step and sat back against the wall getting more comfortable. "Adeem, son, you need to rethink the 'macho persona' you use with women in times of bewilderment. If I have said it once or a hundred times, it is embarrassing to watch you. Just be yourself with this one. Show her your heart, and the rest will follow.

A bit of wisdom, my son – the secret of life is about decisions, all decisions, even the insignificant ones that, whether you want to believe it or not, lead to the bigger decisions that will shape your future. Every word you speak will create a reaction. Think about the reaction you want to see or hear and make the right choices in the words you choose to speak. Some choices change everything, every single moment, for the rest of your life.

I watched Qaseem deteriorate for years over the decisions he made with Dimitri. He was a broken man, and it is coming to light that maybe Dimitri was too. Choose your words wisely with Pearl, Adeem. She is not your average woman.

Put your ego away and search for that vulnerable bone that I know is inside of you, and maybe, just maybe, you will have the pleasure in this lifetime to experience the one thing we are all here to experience, which is true love. Women are multifaceted, they are not black and white. And their gray area is filled with categories. Her mood depends on the category she wants to assign it to. They are unpredictable, yet very predictable. If you talk from the heart and put it in front of her, bare and exposed with deep borderline volcanic passion, she is putty in your hands. The trick is not to disappoint her after she gives you her heart. My advice is to pick your words wisely. Got it?"

There was a long silence followed by a big sigh, "Yes, I got it. Thank you. It is just that she makes me so confused, like I cannot find my words when I talk to her and, as usual, I screw it up. But I get it. Do you think she feels the same about me or am I projecting?"

"Listen, Adeem, love is scary until you do it, so why not just do it? After talking to her a bit about you, I would assume she does feel the same way about you at this point, so be careful. If she is anything like her grandmother Julia, you have got a pistol on your hands. I find Pearl very refreshing. So, are you coming or not?"

Alex met Pearl back in the living room. She was sitting on the floor skimming through the next journal in the pile. He handed the phone back to her. She was about to put it back in her pocket when Alex said, "Pearl, Adeem is still on the line." Her face flushed as she looked up at Alex. He whispered to her, "He knows he messed up. Give him another chance. He is sweating bullets." He winked at her and sat back down in his comfy chair to resume his reading. He smiled, wondering if he too might someday find love as Adeem had.

Pearl took the phone and headed back out to the front porch. She sat back down on the step and stared at the phone. Melena's voice clearly came back to her, "Pearl, my beautiful goddaughter, there will come a time when you will want a man in your life. You will know he is the right guy when you cannot stop thinking about him and all you want to do is touch him all over; kiss him, hug him, and feel his strong arms around you. You will desire to be with him every minute of every day. You will feel emotions throughout your body that are foreign but spectacular. Listen to your heart and not your brain, my sweet pea, and all will be as it should."

Pearl finally spoke into the phone as if there was no awkward moment. With a cheerful response she said, "I am back! Yes, Adeem, you are welcome to stay here with us. You are planning to return tomorrow? Do you know what time?"

Adeem cleared his throat and carefully chose each word, "Pearl, I really like you, but you must know you make me so nervous that I try to hide my nerves behind ridiculous humor, which Alex has explained to me is not funny. I am sorry if I was too forward with you. I was trying to make light of my feelings in a way I could handle my racing heart without passing out. I hope that makes sense. I would like to spend more time with you. I have a feeling I will be saying these words to you again and again until I get it right. With that said, would you be OK with me returning to the island and spending more time with you? If the answer is yes, I would like to be there in the morning to make you and Dad a nice breakfast. You could both catch me up on your findings."

Pearl had a smile from ear to ear. As quickly as possible she said, "I knew you loved me. Yes, you can make us breakfast. See you when you get here," and hung up the phone before he could respond. She started laughing.

Adeem looked down at his phone, smiled, and yelled at the top of his lungs, "YES!"

When Alex heard Pearl laughing, he smiled, raised his eyebrows, and mumbled, "I miss those days…"

Julia's journal hadn't said much about Dimitri yet, but her story was so fun, and Alex was truly enjoying getting to know her through her writing. Knowing within the next few days he would be having a long sit-down with her made learning how she operates before that meeting a blessing. But the one journal he felt had all the answers was the one that had *Sophia* embossed on the outer cover. It was closed by a locking mechanism that required a key. Pearl mentioned that Julia most likely had the key, so that journal was set aside for another day. He had a feeling that it was a very important journal and it frustrated him that he couldn't get into it. When he started his research, he was focused only on Dimitri, but the more time he spent with Pearl, the more it gave him an uncanny feeling that this family was going to be a part of his life for more than a weekend. And with Adeem head over heels in love with Pearl, he was beginning to like the idea.

Pearl entered the room, casually sat down in her chair, and opened up the next journal. She looked at Alex and said, "Oh, by the way, Adeem is making us breakfast in the morning if that is OK."

Alex laughed out loud and Pearl joined him. They were like two peas in a pod at this moment. The bond they were creating would last a lifetime. Alex cleared his throat, which got Pearl's attention. She looked at him and said, "Yes, what?"

He smiled, got more comfortable in his chair and said, "Well, I am not finding much about Dimitri yet, how about you?"

"No, not yet, but I do remember overhearing Nonnah talk about him a few times with Mom years ago.

There is an interesting story about him. I guess he died at sea, or at least that is what everyone thought. Then he was back in the picture. I remember it being quite gruesome, but I do not remember the details. I was pretty young. I am sure it is in Nonnah's journals somewhere."

"Pearl, tell me about your Nonnah. Tell me about Julia."

Pearl smiled, reclined her chair, looked up at the ceiling then looked at Alex with a gleam in her eyes, "Well, she is beautiful inside and out. She does not look her age at all. She has flawless skin and long, beautiful hair. She does not have a mean bone in her body, but she is tough. I think she was kind of a tomboy growing up. I believe that to be true because there is not a challenge she will not take on. She digs in no matter what. She says I remind her of her when she was young, and I take that as a compliment. She has taught my mom and me everything she knows about the nature of this planet and all that grows from her. And let me tell you, she teaches with passion! Her seminars are packed and there is a waiting list a mile long. When she gets on a roll, there is no stopping her, and the audience at her seminars stay for hours after just to talk with her. And do not get her started on The Silver Pharoah story. It is a passion beyond this world.

I heard a different story about this illusive pharoah every night. Her living right next door and my bedroom having a door and balcony that extended to her courtyard allowed her to sneak in and read me bedtime stories, always ending with another Silver Pharoah adventure. I loved nighttime stories with Nonnah!

I guess when her mother, Sophia, died, she took on the role of parent to my great-grandpa George and also Dimitri until he disappeared. Not sure what happened, but it was devastating to George. No one really talks about it anymore. Anyway, she grew up pretty fast after that. There are some bizarre stories about her life after Sophia died. I have asked her a few times to tell me her stories, but she seems to always change the subject. I do know she was a prolific writer so maybe her journals will bring her story alive to us. Alex, you will like her. Everyone who meets her falls in love with her. She is a very special woman. Right now, she is all about The Pharaoh and the silver sarcophagus and what is in it. Anyway, to truly answer your question, between Nonnah, Mom, and my godmother, Melena, I can say I have the perfect female role models in my life."

"How long has she been a widow?"

"About six years now. Grandpa died in his sleep. They say it was a heart attack, but we will never know since there was no autopsy. Nonnah refused to let them carve him up. They were the greatest love story of all time. I want a love story like theirs. Grandpa loved her beyond the universe and back. He was a great man, a good man. Why do you ask?"

"No reason really," he said.

Pearl replied, "Everyone falls in love with Julia, and you will too! I think she will like you. So far I do, and that is big!" They both laughed. Pearl filled two glasses with squeezed lemon and sparkling water and put a bowl of nuts on the table between them. "Should we get back to it?" Alex nodded, picked up another one of Julia's journals, and settled in.

Julia's Journal

My name is Julia Kaya. This is my new journal. If it was a diary, it would have a little key, so it is a journal. I am 14 years old. I love watching my mother write in her diary every evening before my father comes home from work. I asked her once, "What are you writing about?"

She said, "Oh a lot of things, my love. A woman must write down each day what is swimming in her head or she might go mad!" She tousled my hair, kissed the top of my head, and we laughed. Soon after this talk, she surprised me with a journal of my own, along with a bag of pencils and pens. I asked her why her journal had a little lock and key and mine did not. She told me that her diary was given to her by an angel friend who told her a diary is a special private place to store your secrets so it must always be locked and kept safe.

I do not think I have any secrets because I tell my mom everything. She is my best friend, really. I have asked her many times to tell me about her life when she was a little girl, but she says there is really nothing to tell. She said it is too complicated, and the story is confusing and boring. She always starts her story with the day she conceived me. Sophia, my mom, conceived me in her early twenties. She always says, "Your father, George, has made me the happiest woman in the world!" They were in love. I love to watch them look into each other's eyes and smile. Someday I am going to have a love just like my parents.

Today I spent all day in the stone pile. I found so many new beetles and bugs. I brought home twelve for Mom to name for me.

Mom knows everything. She tells everyone, well mostly Uncle Dimitri and Aunt Katrina, that I am a very curious girl and somewhat of a tomboy. I do not think I am a tomboy, but I do agree that I am much smarter than all the boys in my school. Most of them are embarrassing to be around. I find them to be exhausting most of the time. Sometimes they want to go exploring with me because I always bring the best creatures to show and tell at school. But when I am not in school, I like to spend most of my time turning over stones and playing with the bugs and lizards by myself. No one understands my imaginary friends except the plants and flowers around the island. They understand me. I do not have to explain myself to them. Mom always says that having a lot of friends can be tiring, but the living creatures and vegetation around the island will always protect and love me if I protect and love them back. Some days I lay in the dirt or grass and just stare at the clouds. I feel so good when I lay in the dirt. I feel things around me that I cannot see, but I know they are there. I call them my friends. Sometimes they take me on big adventures that get me into trouble. On these days, I end up with Band-Aids everywhere. Mom keeps a lot of Band-Aids for my scrapes and cuts. On these days, it takes all night for Mom to get the grass and sticks out of my matted hair and the dirt out from under my fingernails.

I love this time with my mom. She always explains things in a way that I can understand. Like Daniel. UGH! He is a boy in my class that Dad calls my secret admirer. My parents know his dad, Simon. He is a mason too. Daniel's mom died when he was very young. Mom says it was because of her "unnecessary death" that she became a healer on the island. There are no doctors living on the island. They only visit the island from the mainland if someone gets really sick.

There are only four kids in my class at school; Daniel, Voula, Mekel, and me. There are only eleven kids in the whole school. Voula is my best friend. She dates Mekel and they both think I should date Daniel. This is never going to happen! First of all, I am only fourteen and I do not like boys. But Voula is shy and Mekel is quiet, and they get along like two peas in a pod. They are always together either under the big pine tree staring up at the sky or walking the outskirts of town hand-in-hand, quiet and perfectly content. Mekel and Voula live in the same town near the school. I live on one end of the island where the water is deep and cold, and Daniel lives on the other side of the island where the fun beaches are. Voula and Mekel told me that Daniel is smitten with me and has been in love with me since the first day of kindergarten a million years ago. He does not know it, but I know he follows me and spies on me. I have seen him a couple of times when I have climbed the jagged cliffs into the sea to swim, and a couple of times when I was with my secret friends, talking to the flowers and bugs. As far as I am concerned, the flowers and bugs understand me better than anyone except for Mom.

When I turned thirteen, Daniel told me that he was going to marry me. I thought I was going to throw up. I have seen his grades since he sits right next to me. I get straight A's all the time and I do not even have to work at it. With grades like his, he will not amount to anything. Mom says I was blessed and that if I play my cards right, my life will be wonderful. I do not know what that means, but it sounds good. But Daniel, all he does is stare at me. He does not pay attention to the teacher, so it is no wonder he has bad grades. Every time I catch him staring at me with those big eyes I say, "DANIEL, WHAT?" He just turns around in his chair and says nothing. This happens EVERY DAY! He is silly and annoying. I kind of feel sorry for him sometimes. It is like he is sad all the time.

On the first day of school last year, I guess he finally got up the nerve and wrote me a note. He told me of his feelings and asked me to marry him. He had his hand behind his back, handed me a note with his other hand, then pulled out a big bunch of beautiful bougainvillea flowers he had picked. When I saw the picked flowers, I became irate and knocked his stupid note to the ground. He has watched me for years talk to the flowers, so he knows how I feel a-bout my flower friends living in the meadows. Without even think-ing, I yelled at him and lectured him for five minutes straight, demanding he tell me why he would kill such a beautiful living thing! I was so mad, standing there with my hands on my hips glaring at him. I wait-ed for an answer. Daniel was frozen, staring at me, speechless. I said, in a very firm and authoritative voice like my dad uses sometimes, "You WILL give them a proper burial, Daniel!" I grabbed his ear and pulled him across the playground into the grassy area and made him dig a hole and perform a proper burial ceremony. My heart was broken as I sat on my knees, eyes closed and hands in prayer while he gave last rites and a very clumsy, uncoordinated flower eulogy. When he was done, I stood up, looked him in the eye and said, "Never, ever do that again, Daniel!"

He was red-faced and embarrassed as the rest of the kids on the playground watched, speechless at what they were witnessing. As I looked around and realized everyone was staring at me with their mouths open, I stomped off, so angry that he made me look like a crazy person in front of everyone. The rest of the day, I turned my chair around so I would not have to look at him. After school, Mekel and Voula gathered Daniel and his injured spirit and went to the other side of the playground to console him. I watched as Voula put her hand on his shoulder while telling him something that obviously was making him feel better. He smiled and walked away, heading toward home.

Voula slowly walked over to me and told me that Daniel asked what he could do to make me love him like she loved Mekel. Voula said, "I told Daniel, I do not know. I told him you are different, very special." I was not sure what that meant but she continued, "You know, Julia, I know that you do not like boys, but maybe after you come into womanhood you will think differently about Daniel. My mother told me when I came into womanhood that I was beautiful and that men would see me differently, as a wife and a mother, as my father saw her. She says everything in life changes, especially how you see yourself and relationships. I know you have not started your menstrual cycle yet like the rest of us, but you will. And you will fill out like the rest of us too."

I did not know what to think about all this. I was a little embarrassed. All the girls started when they were like eleven and I am already fourteen. I went home and stared at myself in the mirror. It was true. I did not look like Voula with her breasts needing a bra and her hips widening, giving her a curvy, womanly appearance. I am lanky, thin, and still looked like the fourth graders. But Mama tells me all the time that I have the hair of a goddess – long dark ringlets with chestnut streaks and perfect eyes as blue as the sea.

She says my face is perfectly symmetrical without a single flaw, and my golden olive skin shines as if it was illuminated. She says I will have many suitors when my full blossoming arrives and I should not try to grow up so fast, "Once your youth is gone, it is gone." I love these talks with my mom, but at the same time I do not have any desire to even hold hands with a boy let alone want to be with one for any length of time. They are just so gross!

The next day, Daniel came to school with another note. When he got to school, he showed it to Mekel and Voula. Voula warned me, saying that he was up all night trying to figure out what to say to make me happy with him. She said it was a proper note this time and that I would be pleased.

I looked at her and said, "Voula, please do not encourage him," and before I could say anything more, Daniel was next to me with his note. He was nervous, apologizing for his bad behavior with the flowers. Without any emotion on his face, he handed me the new note and once again the last line read, "Will you marry me?" I do not know what it is about this boy. He is so irritating and determined to make me upset every day, it seems. Why can he not get that I do not like him? If this was my final moment to get my point across, I took it and yelled, "NO, DANIEL," then turned to walk away. Mekel and Voula stood in the background watching.

Daniel pleadingly asked me for a reason why not, saying, "Julia, is it because you have not gotten your womanhood yet?"

I could not believe my ears. WHAT DID HE JUST SAY? I swung around, looking at Voula who had her hand over her mouth in shock, and said, "VOULA!" I stepped forward and gave him a big push in the chest, sending him flying backward, but he did not fall down. I deliberately walked at him as he stumbled backward and firmly said, "DANIEL, why do you say these words to me? Do not look at me! Do not talk to me again, ever!" then I stomped off the playground and ran home. I was so mad at Voula and so disappointed in Daniel. All the way home I continued to yell, curse, and scream at both of them as if they were in front of me, flailing my arms like a crazy person. UGH! Anyone watching me probably thought I was out of my mind. Ugh, Daniel, with his idiocy and juvenile comments. I am not going back to school for a week!

*When I got home, Mama was in the kitchen kneading bread for
dinner. I told her I had stomach cramps and would need to stay home
from school for a week. She looked at me funny and smiled, "OK,
only a week. Since your grades are perfect and you are way ahead
of the school curriculum, I will write a note for you. Really, stomach
pains for a week?" I said yes. She smiled and said, "I must remind
you, Julia, that it is very important for women to get a good education
so a man will want her. It is the woman's responsibility to run the
household and the finances while the men work hard all day."*

*I listened to her advice as I drew little pictures in the scattered
flour on the bread table, but when she insinuated that a man might
not want me, I abruptly looked up at her and sarcastically said, "No
problem there. Have you met Daniel?"*

*We raised our hands in the air and looked to the heavens and
said, "Aye, yi, yi." After, we both laughed out loud. I love talking
to her about life and all the shenanigans of my friends at school
and the relentless Daniel with his never-ending notes. She always
seems to know what to say to calm me down. I love her and admire
her for all she does for the family, especially for my father.*

*Mama looked at me with a little grin and raised her eyebrow.
I knew she knew I was not sick. I lowered my eyes and waited for
her to say something. Finally, she said, "Julia, I am not sure what is
going on in that sweet, pretty head of yours, but your studies are
impeccable. A few days off will not hurt, I guess." She looked at me
again and added, "It will be nice to have you around during the day.
You can help me with some new tincture recipes. I have many that I
am re-vamping due to the flora and fauna being so different here
than in Qatar. Did you know that the environment that you live in
and the medicinal plants that grow in that environment are the plants
that can heal the body? It is truly amazing.*

*There is an ancient myth that a pharaoh by the name of
Psusennes, who was buried in a silver sarcophagus thousands of
years ago, holds the secrets to immortality. He alone was blessed
with the secrets of the universe, and the universe gave him this knowledge to share with the world, but unfortunately he died. It is said
from infected teeth, so brush your teeth every day." She giggled
and tousled my hair. I asked her where Qatar was. She stopped*

what she was doing and looked at me strangely. She said, "My goodness, you are a very good listener, my love. You will be a great mother someday and a very lovely woman. I will teach you everything I know."

I smiled from ear to ear. I am always so happy just being with Mama. She is so wise, so kind, and so smart. But I have noticed how tired she has gotten taking care of both Papa and Dimitri. She seems to be resting more often and her eyes are in a dream world as if she is somewhere else in time. Daniel looks like this all the time with his glazed over eyes, staring into space and daydreaming. At school he stares out the windows, not listening to the teacher, which gets him in trouble all the time. No wonder he does not get good grades.

I asked Mama once what Papa and Dimitri do at work. They leave for work every morning at dawn and do not return home until well after sunset. If they are really fishing, why do they only bring home one or two fish a week? All the other fisherman bring home lots and lots of fish several times a week. When I asked this, she looked at me with a strange face as if she was going to say something then changed her mind because she did not really know how to answer. She looked at the floor then back up at me. I crossed my arms just like she does and raised my eyebrows, just like she does, and waited for an answer.

Finally, she said, "Sit down, Julia," in a voice that kind of got my attention. She said, "I am going to be extremely honest with you, my love. And we will never talk about this again, do you understand? You are never to talk about this to anyone – and no more questions." I nodded. She wiped her hands on her apron, took a big breath, and slowly let it out. She sat next to me and looked into my eyes with all seriousness. It kind of made me feel as if I was in trouble and gave me an uneasy feeling in my belly.

Mama said, "I love your father very much, and Dimitri is very dear to my heart. When we started dating, we both knew we would be together forever. A woman knows this. Well..." She took a big breath, let it out, stood up, walked around the table, and started kneading the dough again as she spoke. "Your papa told me he could never speak of what he and Dimitri really do for a living, but he did say it was a good, honest, and honorable job. We were told that if anyone asked, to tell everyone in town that they are fisherman. Since there are no other fisherman fishing this side of the island, no one really gives us much attention or asks questions, which has always intrigued me because everyone knows everything about everyone on this island. I think they think we are a bit crazy."

We laughed, then Mama got really serious again. She pressed her temples with her fingers as she knitted her brows. Her face went pale, and she started sweating. I have watched her do this a lot lately. Usually, she takes her medicine and sits down for a while until the pain goes away. At night when I get up to go to the bathroom, I see her sitting alone in Papa's chair with her head in her hands. I asked her once if she was OK and she said she just could not sleep because she had too much on her mind. I have noticed her getting more tired lately. I think the demands of the household and Dimitris's growing neediness for Papa's attention since Katrina died has her exhausted. Dimitri is always with Papa. Mama makes his meals, cleans his clothes, and takes care of his house too. It is a good thing he lives next door.

Just as Mama was about to talk again, Papa walked in. He went to her, took her hand, and kissed her gently on each temple. Papa's love for her is so special. I hope when I marry, I find a man like Papa. He started to ask her a question and she interrupted him and said, "Dear, Julia is home from school with a sour tummy," then winked at him. I could feel my face getting red hot. She knew I did not have a sour tummy. I was caught red-handed. He sat next to me and asked me what was so bad that caused me to have a sour tummy. He was looking right into my eyes. I looked down at the floor then stood up and told him the whole story about what Voula did and what Daniel said. As I was telling my story, I got mad again, and when I was done, it felt like it had just happened all over again.

Mama put her hand on her mouth and tried not to laugh. Papa chuckled, gave me a big hug, and said, "I admire the boy for his tenacity." I was so mad at both of them. I stomped my foot and went toward my room. Does no one understand that Daniel is driving me crazy? At least Papa did not make me go back to school. He was happy that I was home for a few days to help. As I rounded the corner to my room, Papa yelled for me to return to the kitchen.

When I got there, Mama was admiring a gold coin dangling from a tiny gold chain that Papa had just clasped around her neck. She said, "George, we could use this coin; it is worth a lot!"

He said, "We are fine, my love. It will remain on your neck, and if ever we need it, I will know where to find it." He kissed her deeply and hugged her gently. I giggled and Papa turned around and said, "What is so funny, huh?" Before I could answer he said, "I have something for you too." He bent down and handed me a long silver piece of paper with something in it. He told me to open it. As soon as I did, the room filled with the smell of grapes. It was amazing! I looked at him, not sure what to do with it. He said, "You chew it, never swallow it, and it will stay the same forever. It is called chewing gum."

I popped it in my mouth and as I began to chew, my whole mouth exploded with saliva. It was delicious! I chewed and chewed, and it never changed. Mama gave me a little salt dish to sit next to my bed to put my gum in. I was so excited! I could not wait to show everyone at school what gum was. I have now chewed my gum for four days and it is still the same. Papa was right.

I decided to go back to school today. Voula and Mekel were waiting for me, and both said sorry about a million times. I gave them a hug then showed them the rubbery substance that never broke down. I told them all about it and everything Papa had said. By the time I was done, all the kids at school were next to us, wanting to touch it. Voula and Mekel took turns pulling it and wadding it back up. Daniel was watching from the swing set. I figured he was still wounded from knowing I was not happy with him. To be truthful, I was embarrassed by what he said, but I tried not to think about it. I was really happy sharing my new gum with everyone, so I just ignored him.

When I got home, Mama asked me to sit down, she had something to tell me. "Julia, today I went to town to pick up my medicine and had lunch with the ladies. They asked me about you. I told them you had an admirer – Daniel." I started to stand up to protest when she took my arm and lowered me back down. "Julia, they told me about Daniel, and I would like to share with you what I was told. Simon, Daniel's father, is a mason, and so was his father, and his father before him. They specialize in rebuilding the many ancient *ruins around the island. There are many times when his job takes him to the mainland in Athens to work for several weeks. Daniel learned early on how to fend for himself. He has spent many days and nights alone, and by the time he was ten, he knew how to cook, do laundry, take a shopping list to the grocery store to purchase food, and even make bank deposits. Everyone knows Daniel; the butcher, the banker, and all the old ladies in the village that look after him while his father is gone. To keep himself busy when he is alone, he does odd jobs for them. And I have an inkling, by all the notes he presents to you, that all his evenings are spent writing notes to you."*

I could not believe what I was hearing. I started to feel really bad about how I treated him. She said, "His father, every Tuesday, leaves a coin on the table for him to buy a little piece of candy for himself, but it appears he is saving up for a wooden race car down at the market. I guess he plays with it in the store then hides it behind all the other toys so it does not get sold before he has enough money. So cute. A couple of the ladies have threatened to buy it for him. But as far as they can figure, he has four coins saved and will have enough this Tuesday to buy it. Julia, I am telling you this because after all the shenanigans of Daniel's notes and the many times you have told me about his grades, I think we need to conclude that he is so smitten by you that he cannot function at school. Maybe you could find it in your heart to be a little nicer?"

I was so embarrassed. I felt so bad. All I could say was, "I am going to bed early tonight. My tummy really is sour." I decided I would ask him to show me his new car on Tuesday. I think that would be a good idea.

Today is Tuesday. Daniel has avoided me for three days. I looked all over for him, and even Voula and Mekel did not know where to find him. I figured he was still mad at me, but at recess as I was walking out to the big tree to be with Voula, she stood up and started pointing at me. She yelled for me to turn around. I turned around, and Daniel was walking toward me with determination in his stride. Mekel was running behind him. When he got to me, standing about a foot away, he got down on one knee and handed me another note. I read it. It was as if he took all the previous notes and combined them into this one note. When I finished reading, I lowered the note to find Daniel still on one knee. He held his hand out, and in his palm was a whole pack of chewing gum. My eyes lit up. I could not believe it was a whole pack! I was so happy. I turned to Voula to show her. She was staring at me like she was looking at a ghost.

Mekel said, "Look, Voula, Julia is happy. She does not even look the same." Voula just shook her head. I did not care if they were making fun of me because I had a whole pack of chewing gum in my hands. I looked at Daniel. He had a soft, tender smile on his face while looking up at me. I felt so vulnerable at that moment as I looked into his eyes. I had never felt that way before. He bought me a pack of gum instead of the wooden car he had been saving a whole month for. I was overwhelmed. He stood up and before I even really thought about it, I kissed him on both cheeks and politely said, "Thank you, Daniel." I turned around to show Voula, and she and Mekel were looking at me with a blank stare.

Mekel said, "Oh my god, you look pretty like Voula. I always thought you looked like a tomboy like my sister. It is like you are a different person because of this gum. Look, Daniel, she is pretty. Do you think she is pretty?"

Daniel just nodded as he stared at me with a smile from ear to ear as he touched his cheek with his hand. I could not stand it any longer, I had to open the pack of gum. There were seven pieces in it. I gave each one of them a piece, and all at once we popped them in our mouths. It was strawberry and it was delicious. We all just kept making the mmmmmmm sound as we chewed.

Daniel spoke first, "Julia, will you marry me?"

For the first time I said, "Maybe." His smile immediately went blank, and I swear I think he started to cry. I turned to Voula and said, "Is it not delicious? The piece my Papa gave me lasted ten days." I explained how to take care of it by putting it in a salt dish by the bed so it lasts longer. I do not think Daniel heard a word I said. He had that daydreaming, glazed-over look in his eyes. I decided right then and there that I was going to give Daniel a chance. One chance, but he was going to have to straighten up and do better in school.

Mama said he was smart, so maybe he can show me just how smart he really is. We all four played and sat by each other all day. Daniel and Mekel made us laugh so hard I peed my pants a little. It was a really good day today. I decided I liked the strawberry gum better than the grape.

Daniel left school early, and Mekel and Voula walked me halfway home. Mekel told me that Daniel said that for the first time in his life, he was truly happy. He said, "Now I understand what Papa felt when he fell in love with my mother. I now know for certain that Julia will marry me and I will never forget the look on my Julia's face when I gave her the gum." From that day forward, Daniel brought me a new pack of gum every fourth Tuesday of the month.

For the rest of the school year, I helped Daniel get his grades up so he could graduate. We all four got straight A's on our final report card. For his reward, I taught him about the laws and sensitives of nature and its magic on the island. And I finally came into womanhood. Over the summer, we spent every moment we could with each other. With Daniel living so far away, for many weeks we did not see each other but spent every moment counting the days until we did.

Mama started having blackouts and her health is failing. Many days I cannot write in my journal. I spend my time helping or taking care of her, Papa, and Dimitri. Sometimes weeks and even months go by before I remember to write. Sometimes my head fills up with so many thoughts, I wish I had a pin to pop it so all the thoughts poured out.

I help Papa and Dimitri as much as I can. I learned how to cook and clean, and Mama and Daniel taught me how to pay the bills and make bank deposits. I feel as though I am growing up too fast. When I look in the mirror, I see someone else staring at me. I wear a bra now and Voula has taught me how to use a little makeup. Daniel says I do not need it, but he always tells me I look beautiful when I wear it. He is starting to look different too. More like his father. He is now taller than I am, and his body is getting stronger and more defined. I like it. He still has not kissed me, but I feel it is coming. Voula said I should kiss him, but Mama says no; wait and it will be worth it.

It has been almost a year since my last entry. Mama became ill with tremors, headaches, and dementia. The doctor told Papa that the headaches were most likely being caused by an aneurysm in the brain and there was not anything they could do. Our job was to keep her quiet and comfortable. Papa reduced his work week to only three days, six hours a day, which left Dimitri having to spend more time alone. I tried my best to help with Dimitri, but as time went on, it became harder for us to give him the attention he was used to. I became the cook and the housekeeper, as well as a shoulder for Papa to cry on. Dimitri became despondent and slid into a great depression. He had built his life around my parents and now neither were available to him.

On the last day of the summer after a long night up with Mama, there was a knock on our door. One of the local fishermen found Papa and Dimitri's boat adrift on the sea. We never saw Dimitri again. It was assumed that his depression had gotten the best of him and he had taken his life and given it to the sea, the one place he felt at peace.

Papa was riddled with guilt. He cried for two days, and on that second day, Mama fell into a coma and passed in her sleep, her head in my father's lap as he wept and gently caressed her face.

I knew the time was getting near and the fear crept in like a tornado. I was so concerned for my father, and I was scared for me. Without her, Papa was less of a man. She was his joy, his everything.

After we buried her, Papa fell silent and sat in his chair, day in and day out. The day Dimitri went missing, Papa stopped going to work. The day after Mama's funeral, Papa gave me a letter and instructed me to take it to the airport and give to the man who exited the airplane with no windows. From that day forward, on the first of each month, I went to the airport and met with a man from the plane. Never was a word spoken. The doors of the plane opened, he exited the plane, looked me in the eye, handed me an envelope, and returned to the plane. I feared this man. Being in his presence made every hair on my body rise and my heart beat so fast I thought I would pass out in front of him. In this envelope was a check that I deposited on my way home. I never asked who this man was or why he was giving us money. I knew not to. When Mama started getting sick, she told me *this would soon be a responsibility that would be expected of me. She told me to do as I was told and to never ask questions.*

I spent most of my time alone after Mama died. I missed having someone to talk to. She always made me feel better. Daniel, Voula, and Mekel were my only friends now. As my father grieved, I spent my days exploring the many nooks and crannies of the island, looking for different herbs and flowers to cook and heal with. Mama used to say, "The island will take care of you. It gives us everything we need for health and wellbeing. Always respect her." I decided to follow in her footsteps and become a healer too.

Today I noticed that old cement building a couple miles away from the house sitting on the edge of a cliff overlooking the deep sea. I had seen this building before but never really paid much attention to it. Today, with the heat bearing down on me, I took refuge in the shade it provided. As I sat there feeling sorry for myself, I noticed this building was made from newer cement, not the ancient red dust cement filled with tiny pebbles that was normally seen in these old buildings. It was sturdy and solid, with no signs of aging. The other side of the building jetted out from the cliff into the sea, as far as I could tell. It had two large 4'x6' metal doors that had rusted from the salty sea air. The front opened onto the old dirt highway that wrapped around the entire island. The highway was the only way to get from one side of the island to the other without hiking the treacherous canyons and dangerous shale drop offs. There was no way around it.

There were no handles to open the doors, only two holes; one in each door that had a very thick, heavy chain going from one to the other. I slid my fingers into the holes and tried to pull the doors open, but they did not budge. The door was locked from the inside and there was no light penetrating from the inside out. After a while, my curiosity was gone and I had cooled down from the hot sun, so I returned home to find Papa in his chair reading, oblivious to me or anything else. I feel as though my life has taken a turn for the worse. I love this island. I feel her breathing through me, but my connection to her has dampened since Mama died. She gave me the curiosity to always want more, know more, be more, have more.

Now my joy is when I am with Daniel. He makes me feel things in places of my body that tingle with excitement whenever I am with him. When I am alone, I touch these places and dream of him touching me in the same spots. So many times, I have needed someone to talk to about these things, girl things, like this. Voula was the only one I could talk to that understood me. I thought about calling her, but she left the island to go to school in Athens. She and Mekel are so busy now planning their wedding that I do not dare call her with my grief; it would only worry her in a time she should be concentrating on the wedding. I am so happy for her. I love her so much and miss her terribly. Maybe we can have a double wedding. Now that would be something. Mama would have loved that!

Daniel and I spend most of our time together when he is not working with his father. He is learning the trade of masonry like his father and has become quite skilled in a short period of time. Together, he and his father are never without work. The developers and archaeologists on the mainland are always on the island carrying tubes full of architectural designs for them to bid on. I am so proud of him. It is funny now to think I believed he would turn out to be another starving fisherman and amount to nothing. I was so wrong. Daniel is so smart and talented and is becoming very handsome. His body is lean and muscular, and his dark, shiny hair is slightly longer than most. He has mesmerizing crystal blue eyes, and he stands about a foot taller than me. I am only a little over five foot tall. At night I have to massage my neck from spending most of my day looking up at him. I dream of the day he looks down at me and kisses me long and hard. I know my knees are going to buckle and I cannot wait. I love to watch him work. I sit and fantasize about the day we marry and become one. I daydream just like Daniel did when we were in school. It makes me smile to think about those days.

Today he caught me staring at him with big puppy dog eyes, twirling my hair, biting my lower lip in pure bliss as I fantasized about him kissing me. He said, "Whatcha thinkin'?"

I said, "It is a secret. Someday I will tell you."

Daniel replied, "You know you make me crazy, right?"

I blushed, "Good!" He gritted his teeth with a grin, shook his head, ran his fingers through his hair, and in a low rumble, forced out an animal growl. I smiled as the depths of my groin yelled for him.

On a recent outing for herbs, Daniel went with me. He is becoming quite good at recognizing the many plants, and at times teaches me things that I did not know, which surprises me. He says he spends his nights learning as much as he can so he can impress me. And he does. I am so proud of him. One evening not long ago as the sun set over the Aegean Sea, he took my hand and gently pulled me around in front of him. With one hand around my waist and the other at the back of my neck, he slid his hand up into my hair, gently pulled my head back, and held my body tightly to his. He looked deep into my eyes and kissed me for the first time with such passion that it made my body shiver. I could feel his erection against me. My mother had told me of such things when she explained what sex was, but I had had no idea what a pleasing feeling it would be to have the power to bring him to such desire. I will never forget that first kiss with Daniel. It was intoxicating.

He said, "Julia, I want to do that over and over again for the rest of my life."

With no words in my head, I smiled at him, wrapped my arms around him, and held him tight. "I want to do that every day for the rest of my life too," I told him. From that day forward, every time we are together, we kiss a lot.

That night when I got home, I asked my father about the cement building. He said, "For as long as I can remember, it has been there."

I asked, "If one side is against the sea, the other is along the road, and it is a solid structure, how can it be locked from the inside?"

He did not reply. I had gotten used to his silence. His whole life had been wrapped around Mama, Sophia, and Dimitri's lives, and with them gone, he had lost who he was and had drifted to a place in his mind that he did not care to share. His days were spent reading and staring out into the sea.

One evening he asked me to get him a box of books from the storage room upstairs. Over the years he had stored old blankets, furniture, and heirlooms up there. I had never been in the attic before nor had any curiosity about it, which is strange since I am curious about everything. He told me where to look and what the box looked like. I climbed the rickety stairs, found the old light switch, and searched for the box. As I searched, I found two boxes of my mother's journals under several very old barn blankets. There must have been twenty of them. I had wondered what happened to them but never dared to ask Papa. I was not sure if he even knew they existed. I pulled the journal boxes to the side, searched for the box with the red tape wrapped around it, and slid it to the stairs. It was too heavy for me to bring down alone. With Papa's help, we managed to get it down the stairs. That box of books kept him entertained for days. I was relieved he had something to keep him busy besides staring out the window as if someone important was arriving soon.

When Papa left for town today, I snuck back up to the attic and took two of Mama's journals to bed with me. When I was done, I replaced them and took another two. She had journaled everything; from the time she had her first haircut to her first kiss with Papa, the only man she ever loved. I loved reading about my mother's life. It was not something Mama had shared a lot of. She told me of her many shenanigans as a young girl and how strict her parents were, wanting only the best for her, and how she and Papa met, but the stories never had any real depth to them. It was like telling stories of events, not of emotions. As far as I could see, all her journaling was done after she met Papa. There was one journal that was locked. It was different. It had 'Sophia' embossed on it. I left that one alone. Something told me not to try to open it. I started with the other journals, and when I got to the ninth journal, I began to get scared. Page after page I was engulfed. I could not put the journal down. It read:

Without George and Dimitri knowing, I followed them to work. When I agreed to marry George, he sat me down and said he would only marry me on one condition, and it was that I never ask him about his work. What he and Dimitri do is secret and classified. All he said was that it was a good and honorable job. I was never to ask where we got our money, and that it would arrive on the first of every month at a secret location. He said we would have enough money to never worry, but not enough to make the townspeople curious. I trust George. He is a good man from a good and prominent family. George said only he and Dimitri knew what this secret classified job was. But after all these years, my curiosity has gotten the best of me. I know what secret and classified is. I too have a secret that George does not know about. I understand what it means to need some things to be kept silent. But the fact is, the two men spend what seems like every waking moment together, yet when we are all together, they say absolutely nothing about what they do all day. The fishing boat motor broke down and is being repaired, yet they still leave the house each morning. So today I followed them. They went to the far tip of the island where only a square cement building sits with a large iron chain hanging from the outside. There is no lock. For an hour I secretly watched George and Dimitri as they sat on the rock ledge next to the cement building that disappeared down into the ocean. They seemed to be waiting for something. They did not speak. I hid behind the rocks where they could not see me. My heart was racing. I felt as if they knew I was there watching them. I sat back against the rock wall I was hiding behind, trying to figure out how to get back home without them seeing me. When I looked out again, they were gone, the chain still in place. They had disappeared into the rocks.

I had to read this part twice. I wondered why Papa lied to me. What was the secret? What was Mama's secret? Whenever we had our long talks and I asked her certain questions about her past, she always stopped me by changing the subject. I figured it was a painful part of her life so I left it alone. I continued reading:

I ran back home as fast as I could. I started cleaning and cooking dinner even though it was still before noon. I needed to calm down. By the time both men returned, I had had all day to get my nerves under control. What were they doing in the rocks? Are they fishing from this point? Tomorrow they will be in the village checking on the boat motor. I plan to go to see what is down those rocks.

This ended the journal, and I immediately opened the next journal, but it was out of sequence. I needed to go back to the attic to get the next journal, but I could not tonight without Papa knowing. I lay there staring through the window into the night sky, wondering what the cement building was. What was this classified job Papa and Dimitri had and why did Papa not tell me when I asked him about it? This morning, Papa said he was not feeling well and that he would be staying in for the day. I told him I would brew him a healing potion and he would feel better in no time. After he drank his tea, he went to his chair in view of the stairs to the upper room. I knew I would not be reading the next journal tonight, so I decided to ask Daniel to take me on a boat ride. It was his day off and we had already planned to spend the day together. I had never asked him to take me on a boat ride before. I asked him to take me to the spot just in front of the old cement building so I could see it from the ocean. Maybe there was a clue from that side.

He asked me, "Out of curiosity, my love, why this particular place and what are you interested in? It is mostly a jagged rock coastline with waters that are very deep. There is no beach to have lunch or enjoy our afternoon."

I did not know how to answer him. I thought quickly and said, "It is in these waters my father used to fish. I just want to see what is there. Can a girl not be curious?"

He said, "OK, to the far side of the island we go." When we got to the spot that I thought was the back side of the cement building, I looked up, studied the rocks, and finally saw the upper edge of the building. The rest of the cliff looked like all the others; jagged, treacherous, and steep. I asked Daniel to slow the boat to a stop. He did and sat back on the seat, watching me. I studied the side of the cliff and the water below. It was deep and very dark. I glanced back at Daniel. He had stretched out, crossed his legs and arms, and with a curious smile and knitted eyebrows he stared at me. I smiled back and expressed my thanks for him bringing me here as I looked over the edge of the boat casually. As the boat drifted, I noticed that there was a channel under the water, and just beyond the channel the sea was much shallower. Then I saw what looked like large numbers on the side of something gigantic. At first, I thought it was a huge shark, so big I could see its eyes. It scared me to the core. I gasped and put my hand to my chest, and as the boat rocked at that very moment, I fell onto the boat floor.

Daniel jumped up and came to my side and said, "Julia, what are you up to? What is going on?" I looked at him, feeling faint, and asked him to take me back to the docks. He helped me up carefully with worry in his eyes. He held me close and as he did, he looked over the side of the boat without saying a thing. He helped me to the seat and returned to the docks. Neither of us spoke the whole way back.

When we got back, it was still early. I made an excuse to go home and check on my father. He did not want to let me go and used every excuse to walk me home. I smiled and explained that I needed some time to myself and would call him a bit later.

He said, "Julia, I know you – what are you up to? What is going on?" I had no words for him. All I could think about was whatever was down there in the water was big and it was put there by someone.

Somewhat discombobulated and petrified, I ran home. Papa was not in the house, but a note was on the table. He was feeling better and had gone to town to buy more books. I ran to the stairs and rummaged through the journals until I found the next one in sequence. I ran to my room then closed and locked the door. I opened the journal as fast as I could and started reading:

As soon as Papa left, I ran to the cement building. I looked all around where they had been sitting before they disappeared. To the right side of the building, the stones looked different, almost in a line. I noticed that this line of rocks looked like each rock was sitting in a shallow hole, almost like a steppingstone path, yet it had been very stealthily covered up. As I moved each rock to the side, I realized it was a stepping path that wound around to the back of the building. As I rounded the building, removing each rock as I went, I slipped and fell about four feet down the jagged face of the cliff, only to be caught by my belt which prevented me from tumbling over. I found a foothold and climbed back up. I was bleeding and had badly scraped my elbows and knee on the very unforgiving shale rock. My heart was racing. I had almost plunged into the sea. If I had, I would have been dead and George would have never found me. I was so scared trying to climb back up, replacing every rock as I had found it. I ran home and cleaned myself up. What am I going to tell Papa? He is going to ask

*me what happened. I have never lied to him, but today I am going to
have to.*

*I put Mama's journal aside and planned. It was just past 1:00 p.m.
and I knew I had a lot of daylight left to explore. I packed a small
bag, just in case, and brought some rope, adhesive bandages, water,
an extra pair of clothes, and a pair of gloves. I put on my best hiking
boots, a thick sweatshirt and a heavy pair of jeans, and ran to the
cement building.*

*Daniel knew I was up to something. He saw what I saw, and
from the sea he figured out where I was headed. He had already found
the perfect spot to hide and wait for me, though at the time I did not
know he was there. He could see me in front of the building from every
angle from where he hid. I arrived faster than he expected so he quickly took his hiding spot and watched. I took out the rope, wrapped it
around my waist, and tied a strong fisherman's knot. Watching me do
this made Daniel very uncomfortable. He said he was afraid and kept
asking himself, "What is she planning to do? She cannot scale that
rock face. I could not scale that rock face. Whatever was in the water
is too deep and too big. If she plans on getting in the water, she will be
killed from the waves throwing her against the jagged rocks."*

*Daniel later explained to me that he was becoming very uneasy
as he watched me. At this point he did not care if I got mad at him or
not. He almost came out of hiding when he saw me searching the
ground on the right side of the building. Daniel knew I had found some
kind of path. I was studying the ground, searching for the rock path,
and when I found what I was looking for, I began removing rocks.
With each rock I removed, I took a solid step down. When I disappeared, Daniel walked closer to the building. As I came to the same
spot my mother had, I realized the path was becoming much narrower
and closer to the building. I found a large metal ring that was cement-
ed into the lower corner of the building as if it were put there to lock
into to prevent someone from falling. I quickly tethered myself to the
ring, gave myself about four feet of rope, and began to examine a
large, out-of-place rock standing vertically against the backside of the
building. The rock was hiding a larger door that was clearly the entry
point into the cement building. When I leaned against the rock, it*

moved effortlessly, pushing me away from the path and over the edge. I screamed as I fell and was slammed into the jagged rock, face first. Dazed, I hung limply from the rope as it began to synch tighter around my chest.

In a flash, Daniel began pulling me up. My forehead was bleeding badly, and blood was gushing down my face. Daniel was beside himself. He was yelling my name, "Julia, I am here. Hold on, I am here. Julia! Julia!" As he pulled me to his level, he reached down and, with one swift move, threw me up and over his shoulder. He quickly untethered me, ran up the rock path, and put me in the shade of the building. He went through my bag, found the water, and began pouring it on the cut. It was a small cut, but the amount of blood was immense and had saturated my shirt. Every time I breathed out through my nose, the blood bubbled then popped, spreading it even further down my face. A large purple mound was beginning to form on my forehead. As he poured the water over me, my dizziness began to clear, and the pain began to pulsate around the cut. I realized that if he had not been there, I would have died trying to find out what this building was and no one would have ever found me. I grabbed Daniel and held onto him as if I was still hanging over the edge and cried. My whole body was shaking.

When I finally calmed down, he asked, "Julia, what were you thinking? What were you doing? Oh my goodness, you could have died!" He held me tight and began to sob. Reality was now hitting him. He could have lost me forever. We sat in each other's arms for what seemed like forever. When we came to our senses and calmed down, he picked me up and carried me to his truck a mile down the road then took me to his home. He put an ice pack on my head, the pressure making me wince in pain. He made me a cup of tea, sat down, and crossed his arms while staring at me intently as he waited.

I knew what I did was dangerous, but I thought I was prepared. I looked at him shyly, knowing he was not going to let me go until I fessed up to my intentions. Slowly, I told him about the story in the journals and my father's secret life. He listened and as I continued, he softened his posture and began to really hear what I was telling him.

When I was done, he said, "I saw what you saw in the water."
We still had not talked about it. When I first looked over the edge and
saw the thing, I thought it was a giant shark or whale or I do not know
what I thought I saw. But what I did know was that thing scared me to
death and by the looks of it, it scared Daniel too.

We began to sift through the story when Daniel told me what his
father had heard. The villagers knew Papa and Dimitri were not
fishermen. Fishermen never fished that side of the island. There were
stories or myths that circulated around the towns years ago. It was
said that many years ago, Naval officers died working the same cliffs
near the same spot. They said God's hand had something to do with it.
The villagers took that as an omen that the far side of the island was
cursed. They never ventured into that area of the island or the sea.

I explained to Daniel that for years my father spent every day in
this cement building and that I must know what was in there – what
was in the water and what was in the cement building – and that I
would not rest until I found out. Daniel had to admit that he too was
curious and agreed to help me, but not today. We agreed to meet at the
cement building on his next day off. With that, he helped me concoct a
story for Papa to explain my injuries. I was thankful that Daniel was
going to help me get to the bottom of what Papa and Dimitri had been
up to. Daniel helped me clean up, put on my extra pair of clothes, and
took me home.

That night when Papa went to bed, I continued to read. There
had to be more in the journals. Did Mama know? I settled in to bed
with my flashlight, opened the journal to the last page I had read, and
continued:

I went to town today. I went to the church and asked the old priest
about the rumors I had overheard the villagers talking about, rumors
that the far side of the island and the waters were cursed. He told me
the story was not a myth but was truth.

"During the war, Ikaria was a safe haven. Many refugees
escaped the mainland and took refuge here. The island was considered
too treacherous and dangerous to develop, and the people simple-
minded. The people were not a threat and the island was off the radar.
The people of Turkey decided to build a stronghold here. It was a very

secret mission. I know of this because a few of the Turkish men came to me for spiritual help. It was a tragedy, really. When they were digging out the cliffs to build a secret base of some sort, a terrible wind hit only in the spot the Naval officers were digging, literally smashing the men into the jagged rocks, shredding them to pieces. Later, their dead bodies were plucked from the sea by local fishermen. Ever since, that area of the island has been considered cursed."

I asked him if he thought the area was cursed. He said "No, as you know, the winds are unforgiving and, in that year, we had a very unusual and never again seen hurricane. The Naval men had been tethered in, so they were unable to escape as they were slammed into the shale rock face over and over until their bodies broke free of the ropes and they drowned in the sea. It was a freak of nature for sure, but cursed? No, I do not believe in such things. Nature is powerful. It was the wrong time of year to be doing what they were doing, whatever it was."

As I traveled back home, I decided not to return to the cement building. Curse or no curse, I have never been that scared in my life. Whatever the secret is, I think it is best for me not to know!

As far as I could tell, Papa had never found out about Mama's secret trip to the building. I told Daniel what I had read in her journal. Together we strategically planned our next trip to the building. We collected everything we would need based on the last trip, and this time we brought a camera. When the coast was clear and Papa was visiting the village, we set out to discover what was really behind that door. Daniel cleared the path, tethered himself in, and moved the large rock covering the entrance to the cement building. He realized it was purposely put on a hinge, making it easily movable back and forth over the hidden metal door, camouflaging it. The metal door had no handle, only a small keyhole. Daniel looked up the path at me and yelled the bad news, "There is no way in, Julia. It needs a key. Do you have the key?" I remembered Papa having a special key that he had worn around his neck for years, but where that key was, I had no idea.

We headed back to the house to figure out where he might have hidden the key. I walked in circles around the house in deep thought trying to remember, not really looking at anything, but trying to find an old memory that would trigger the possibilities. Then it came to me. He always sat in the same chair in the living room next to the fireplace, and he was always fiddling with a small ring that hung from the inside of the arm of the chair. One day while he was reading, a small key had dropped to the floor. He quickly picked it up and replaced it in the arm.

I went to the chair, found the ring, and pulled it. Out popped a 2" key. By the looks of it, it was the right key. We returned to the building and started the safety procedures all over again, Daniel first, clearing the way, then I followed. Daniel placed the key in the lock, and it turned. When the door opened, it too opened effortlessly and set off a series of lights that lit up the entire chamber. I followed Daniel in. It was a large room with cement walls and floors. To the left of the room, a metal staircase descended to another level. In the middle of the room, sticking out of the cement floor, was the top of a gigantic cylinder with markings on it. Daniel explained that it was a large canister full of hydraulic fluid used as a source to move objects up and down. The size of this one could move a mountain – literally. To the right of the canister's top were gauges and levers registering a stable pressure. Whatever this was fueling was still intact and ready to operate.

As I studied the gauges, I asked him what they were for and Daniel answered, "This amount of hydraulic fluid is what is holding in place and hiding whatever it is that we saw underwater." We looked at the stairs then back at each other. As before, Daniel went first. The stairs had lights under the railing going all the way down, and with the number of stairs it took to get to the bottom, Daniel figured we were underwater. At the bottom and left of the stairs was a closed metal door. To the right of the stairs was a blank wall, and directly in front of them was a giant black curtain. Daniel estimated that it was at least 10'x10'. I noticed the door to the room beside the stairs was just like the one on the outside of the cement building; no handle, just a keyhole. I tried the key we had found in the arm of the chair, but it did not fit.

Daniel stood in front of the curtain, looked at me, and with one giant swoop, he pulled back the curtain. I gasped, covered my eyes, *and froze. Daniel's eyes widened, then he stepped back and told me to go upstairs NOW! We ran to the top of the stairs, out of breath and scared. We started for the door to the outside, but before we got to the door, I fell to my knees, winded, and started crying so hard I could not catch my breath. It was as if that gigantic thing in the window was a great white shark with its mouth open, ready to crash through the window. It was that big and that scary. I reached for Daniel, grabbed him, and held him as if it was going to be the last time I would ever see him. He sat on the floor in a daze next to me in total disbelief. We held each other tight, trying to wrap our heads around what was behind that curtain.*

I was the first to talk. When I looked up at Daniel, he was as white as a ghost. I asked him what that was resting on the ocean floor. He looked at me and said, "It is a giant nuclear submarine, and by the looks of all of this, it is active." Neither of us talked for a while as we sat while mentally absorbing what we had just seen.

I started to panic and asked Daniel, "By active, do you mean it is a live nuclear submarine? Are there people in it? Who is running it? How is it active? Do you mean my father has been guarding a giant bomb?" Fear raced through me.

Daniel's only reply was, "Yes." I asked what would happen if it went off. Daniel said, "There would be no Ikaria on any future maps." I was stunned. I did not know what to think. Daniel got up and started pacing the floor. How were we going to deal with this knowledge? Not thinking, I reached up, grabbed and pulled one of the handles to help myself up and when I did, the whole building started to rumble, knocking me and Daniel back to the ground. The noise in the room was deafening. We immediately covered our ears and started shouting. Daniel crawled to where I was, grabbed the handle, and pushed it back into place. The rumbling and shaking stopped, but the crashing of waves and rocks falling outside was still being heard.

Daniel told me to stay put as he ran back downstairs. All alone, sitting over a giant bomb, I was petrified. I had pulled the handle. Why did I do that? I could not move, breathe, or speak. All I could do was hug my legs while rocking back and forth, praying Daniel would come back up the stairs and get us out of there. It became silent. All I could hear were my own sobs as I clutched myself into a fetal position. I knew at any moment the island was going to blow up and we were going to die.

Daniel yelled from the bottom of the stairs, "Julia, it is OK. We are going to be OK." The view from the window showed that the rocks were falling away from the cliff, landing on both sides of the submarine, opening a path for the vehicle to rise to the top and move forward to launch itself. There was still no light coming from the surface. Whatever damage was done, it had not exposed the craft. As he turned to run back up the stairs to get me, he noticed the metal door to the room to the right of the stairs, the one without a key, was open and there was a light on. He stood frozen. He did not move or make a sound. He listened, and after a few moments he realized no one was coming out from behind it. He went to the door, slowly pushing it open as I heard him calling out, "Hello, is anybody in here?" When the door was completely opened, he looked inside then fainted.

Papa had returned from the village and was out taking a walk when the rumbling began. He knew exactly what was happening, and started running toward the building. After about thirty seconds the rumbling stopped, but he could hear the crashing waves. He ran down the exposed rock staircase next to the cement building that he had become so familiar with that he could travel it effortlessly in the dark. He stepped into the room to find me frozen on the floor, hugging my knees and hyperventilating, tears streaming down my face. When I saw him, I yelled, "Papa, help us! Papa!"

He picked me up and put his coat around me, wrapping me like a cocoon inside his jacket. All he said over and over again as he scanned the gauges, "It is going to be all right, you are going to be all right. It is going to be all right."

When I finally felt safe in his arms and stopped crying, he looked down at me and asked if anyone else was in the building. I nodded up at him and told him that Daniel was down there while pointing to the staircase. Papa grabbed my arms, shook me abruptly and said, "Julia, look at me. Stay here, do not move. Do you understand?" I nodded and he ran to the stairs. When he arrived at the bottom, he found Daniel slumped in a pile in front of the open door. When he looked inside, he gasped, stumbled back, and fell to

*his knees. He bent down onto all fours to catch his breath. Sitting in a
chair inside the room was Dimitri – dead.*

*George shut the unhinged door the best he could, grabbed
Daniel and, like a man of 20, he hoisted him up and over his shoulders
and carried him back upstairs. When I saw Daniel's limp body
dangling from Papa's shoulders, I started screaming. He lowered
Daniel to the floor, grabbed me, and yelled at the top of his lungs,
"He is all right; he fainted. Julia, he is all right."*

*I pushed him away with the strength of a man and climbed on
top of Daniel, listening to his chest, moving his arms, and slapping
his face. I had killed Daniel! "Wake up! Wake up!" I screamed while
hitting him, but he did not respond. Finally, he started moving. I lay
on top of him crying, "I am sorry, Daniel! I am sorry! Do not die,
Daniel!" He wrapped his arms around me and held me until I calmed down. Papa was sitting on the floor watching, trying to catch his
breath.*

Daniel spoke first, "Did you see him?" Papa nodded.

*Still shaking, I looked from one to the other then asked Daniel
in a voice I did not recognize, "See who, Daniel?"*

*Papa spoke next. He looked at me and said, "Dimitri is down
there in the room. The shaking unhinged the door and it opened."*

*I did not understand, "This whole time he has been in that
room? Where is he now?"*

*Daniel leaned back, ran his fingers through his hair and said,
"He is dead. By the looks of it, he has been down in the hole since the
day he went missing."*

*I could not believe what they were telling me. Dimitri's body
was dead downstairs. What did that mean? Dimitri is downstairs. My
Dimitri? Dead? I was in a building with a dead man? I covered my
mouth and started rocking back and forth again, crying softly yet
hysterically, my eyes darting from left to right, trying to figure out
how to get out of there. Daniel pulled me close and held me tight
until I calmed down. We all just sat there on the cement floor staring at each other, our minds swirling with questions.*

Papa finally said, "No one can know about this."

*Daniel's whole body stiffened and he sat up, looked at Papa
with anger in his eyes and said, "There is a bomb under our island!*

Why is it there? What the hell, George! You better start talking, and you better make it good because right now I am inclined to take you to the authorities and turn you in. Do you know what would happen if the villagers found out about this?"

Defeated, Papa raised his hands and said, "I know, I know. Just stop, Daniel. For just a second, stop and listen to me." For the first time I saw an exhausted old man sitting on the floor. He took a big breath and explained the secret that he had been carrying all these years. He began with, "There is a myth that—"

Daniel interrupted him abruptly, "Yes, we know. A bunch of Naval officers died while trying to carve out the rocks below us. We know the myth."

Papa lowered his eyes and started again, "The army protecting our island realized it would take specially skilled men to do this dig, ones who were proficient with TNT and had the skills of the ancient builders in building rock walls above and below the ocean surface. The first crew of men obviously did not have the skills and they all died. Dimitri and I were the only two who were skilled in every area. We were trained by our fathers beginning at the age of 12. We learned to repair the ancient sea walls of the fortresses along the seacoasts all throughout Europe. Around the world, there were only nine of us skilled enough to do this kind of work. The others refused the job and they were killed for their knowledge of the job. Two of those men were our fathers – Dimitri's and mine. Dimitri and I took the job when we were 20 years old. The choice given to us was to build what the Turkish government demanded from us or die like our families did. We were paid well, looked after, and monitored for five years while we built what you now see. We were promised normal lives when we were done if we forever continued to man the station, this station. We had to be ready, day or night, to launch the sub on a moment's notice. We did not ask questions. We believed – believe – this sub would only be launched if our precious island and people came under a fatal siege. In the dead of the night, a little over 20 years ago, the submarine was set in place.

When we were done, Dimitri and I were allowed to venture into the villages to find wives. We never stayed in the village long enough to make friends, so when we found Sophia and Katrina, we fell in love.

They were best friends, inseparable, shy with no friends but each other. They understood mine and Dimitri's relationship. It was perfect. We moved them to this side of the island, and we lived happy lives until Katrina died." He took a big breath, wiped his face with his hand, and looked at us with a blank stare. I was about to go to him when he started talking again. "When she died, he was heartbroken, making us his only family. God, that was so long ago. Anyway, this station is now operated manually from somewhere in Europe." Papa leaned over, put his head in his hands, and said, "We will be hearing from them after this incident. But I am an old man now. I will make my excuses. Do not worry. I have been loyal all my life."

I asked, "What are we going to do about Dimitri?"

He replied, "Daniel and I will give him a proper burial." He asked Daniel to take me home then to return and help him clean up the mess.

I looked at them, from one to the other, "No, Papa, I am staying with you. Do not leave me alone, please, Daniel. I am afraid!"

Daniel touched my shoulder and looked at Papa until he unwillingly agreed to let me stay. Papa said, "Stay here, I will be back," and descended the stairs once again.

Daniel held me, sitting on the cement floor, until I calmed down and got my wits about me. I asked Daniel what he had seen. He said, "When I opened the door, I saw Dimitri sitting in his chair. It looks like he has been down there a long time; it was shocking to see his corpse. Julia, I think he has been dead in that room since they found the fishing boat adrift. The last thing I remember seeing is that there was a lot of gold on Dimitri's desk in front of him."

After a while, Daniel and I went downstairs. Daniel told me to wait at the base of the stairs. When he looked in the room, Papa was reading a final letter from Dimitri. He had draped Dimitri in a blanket, and on the desk were millions in euros, gold coins, precious jewels, and a golden dagger engraved, "For my love, wear it in peace." Papa handed the letter to Daniel while he paced the outer room, trying to remember the days Dimitri had written about, trying to wrap his head around the words. He took no notice of me. He was swimming deep in his mind for memories of days gone by. I got up and slowly entered the room. Daniel had pushed Dimitri, in his chair,

across the room behind a small wall, away from the desk. Daniel
handed me the letter and sat next to me until I finished it.

George, my dearest friend,
I am an old, tired, and lonely man. My dreams and memories are all I
have. There are many things I have done that I am not proud of, but
Katrina knew my lifelong secret and she forgave me. The summer I
left with the son of the royal sheik, I did willingly and joyfully. I met
Qaseem when I was 18. We loved each other deeply, a love like I had
never felt before. He taught me many things, gave me lavish gifts, and
showed me a life I could only have if I stayed with him, but our love
would have to remain a secret. When we were together, I was happy,
but when we were apart, he loved others to honor his people.

Over time I became lonely for his attention and became jealous
of those around him, although I kept these things to myself. He gave
me a choice; I could stay and be his lover by night, but during the day,
I was nothing to him but a friend. I was extremely tormented. I left
quietly and never told a soul. The year that I left you alone to man the
submarine, I planned to return to him. But it was not long after I left
that I realized I had made a mistake. As my heart was torn, I knew my
life was with Katrina. She was a good wife to me. She gave me her
love willingly and she gave it all.

In time, Katrina found the many love letters between Qaseem
and I, and the gifts, but she did not tell me of her knowledge until two
nights before she died. She cupped my face and said, "Dimitri, life
brings us many loves. The love you decide to end your life with is true
love. You are here with me. You chose me. I have no ill will. You are
my husband, and I am your wife. You are a whole man in my eyes.
You lived your truth and I respect you for that. You are 'love' to me."
She kissed me deeply and those were the last words she spoke to me.

George, you, Sophia, and Katrina, you are my family. You three
are my best friends. You three loved and respected me all my days. I
am sorry I kept these secrets from you. I regret that now.

These are gifts from Qaseem. I will now give these gifts to you
and Julia. Little Julia is like a daughter to me too. She might not
remember me, but she lives in my heart. The only gift I ask in return

is your forgiveness, George. You are my brother and I have always loved you as my brother.

Dimitri

I sat down, dropped the letter into my lap, and stared at the desk. I looked at Daniel, "There is a fortune here." Daniel nodded and left the room. I followed. Daniel joined Papa on the stairs as I sat on the floor in front of them while they talked. I listened for hours as Papa recalled his stories about his life with Dimitri and his absence of knowing Dimitri's true heart. As I watched my father speak, I saw an old, tired man full of loneliness now that Mama and Dimitri were gone.

When he was finished, the room became silent again. Then I remembered what he had said a few hours ago, "Papa, you said we will be hearing from them. Who is 'them'?"

He sat up straight and looked at Daniel. "You will help me replace the rocks that have fallen. I will teach you underwater skills as I have learned them. We need to start now!"

He collected all the gifts and pictures on the walls, and all the remnants of the years the two men spent underground together. With the help of Daniel, he brought Dimitri to the top. We gave him a proper burial near the house then they began the underwater work.

I spent my days cooking and cleaning after the men as they worked day and night in the sea. Every day I was in fear that the people Papa called "them" would come. After four months of work, the wall was repaired and they sealed the building. No one came.

Pearl put down the journal, looked at Alex, and said, "Oh my god! This is intense! My whole body is nervous reading this. Jeeez Louise! How are you doing, Alex? I need a break, how about you? Hungry?"

"Which one did you just finish?" he asked.

"Where they found the submarine and Dimitri. Yikes!"

"Yes, I found that one both humorous as well as disturbing. It brought tears to my eyes. Dimitri, my father who I have longed to know all my life, died alone and miserable. This will never sit right in my soul. A part of me wishes I had not pushed so hard to know. When I read that part, I wanted to get up and leave, go back to Qatar.

My heart aches knowing he died in that cement hole alone with a broken heart. I wanted to know about his life and how he lived. I now have the answer I was looking for. Maybe not in the way I wanted it, but I got it.

The more I thought about leaving here, Pearl, the more *something* told me to stay – my work here is not done. This feeling has been overwhelming for several hours now. The more I get to know Julia, or Nonnah as you call her, the stronger this feeling is. Something tells me she, this family, is why I am here. Has this feeling occurred to you? Do you not think this is strange? We have known each other for only a couple of days and here we are as if we have been friends forever. Never have I found myself in such a situation. Never have I felt such a strong connection like this, with anyone, in such a brief period of time. For some extraordinary reason, my intuition is telling me that I am here for a vastly different reason. I cannot shake it. But knowing my father died alone, in a cement room, forlorn with a broken heart truly makes me wish I had never come. So, what am I to do with these feelings, Pearl?"

Pearl lowered her head and wanted to die inside. She looked at Alex and said, "Yes, Alex, I feel the same. I never connect at this level with *anyone* this quickly, but for some reason I do feel like I have known you forever. I feel very comfortable in your presence. Alex, I was totally not thinking when I brought up Dimitri's death. It was a horrible death. I feel terrible for being so insensitive." She got up and hugged Alex, apologizing profusely.

Alex returned her hug and gave her a big fatherly pat on the back. He then leaned back in his chair, stretched his legs with his arms over his head, and let out a big cleansing breath as he elongated his whole body in his recliner. He looked down at the pile, "Pearl, this story is exhausting and intriguing. I need to know more, but I think I need a break." He looked down at the piles and counted, "We have read about ten books so far? Look at the pile. We still have a few to go. And to answer your question, yes, I am hungry. What do you say we make lunch, grab our backpacks, and hike over to where the cement building used to be. I think this might give us some perspective."

Pearl agreed and together they made sandwiches, yogurt sprinkled with honey and walnuts, added a jar of olives, two bunches of grapes, two bottles of water, and a bottle of wine. It was a beautiful day and the sun was sitting at 2:00 p.m. Pearl told Alex to grab a few layers; sweatshirt or sweater and a jacket due to the unforgiving headwinds at the tip of the island where the cement building was. This area is notorious for chilling-to-the-bone winds that come in without warning. Regardless, a hike to the very spot that consumed the storyline in the journals felt like the perfect idea to clear their heads and contemplate the story so far.

It was about a two mile walk to the site. Pearl packed the meals then ran to her room and carefully placed the brass jar into her backpack. Maybe it was time to tell Alex about her mysterious gift. As she packed, she noticed that the spot on the back of her neck was itching as if it was beginning to heal. She tried to look at the spot again with her small hand mirror, without luck. *Maybe Alex can look at it for me,* she thought. At least it was not burning any longer. She tucked her hair into a bun and headed to the kitchen.

With lunch packed and ready to go, they headed to the very spot where Dimitri died. They walked for a few minutes in silence, breathing in the fresh, crisp air while admiring the terrain. Pearl spoke first, "This is where Nonnah and Mom spend most of their time when they are not traveling the globe on speaking engagements." Pearl extended her hand and motioned to the whole island. "You never really know where on this beautiful rock they are going to be, but if you really want to find them, my dad, Mathias, will know. Somehow my parents have a connection that transcends time. It is kind of like remote viewing. It is really cool, actually. I call him up and say, "Hey, Dad, where is Mom?" He will close his eyes, take a big breath then slowly let it out. When all the air is out of his lungs, he sits on empty breath until she pops into his mind. When this happens, her exact whereabouts pops into his mind's eye. Every time he is right. Have you ever heard of such a thing?"

Alex chuckled, "Really? No joke?"

"Really. I used to tell people about his gifts all the time, but it did not take long to realize that was not a good idea. Once, at school I told the class about it. That night a TV reporter showed up with about a thousand people wanting him to find their lost loved ones. It was a disaster! It seems his gift is only reliable with our family's energy field. He can do the same with Nonnah and me. I have to laugh because it took about a year for people around the world to stop showing up on his doorstep begging for help."

"That is interesting. I will admit I do believe in the paranormal and these kinds of unique gifts. I have always been fascinated with the occult. Our ancient texts talk about these types of gifts. History shows us in our ancient writings that such out-of-the-box ideas are found all over the planet, in every civilization known to have existed. Tell me about your mom and dad. I read Charlee's journal. It was a Cinderella story with a sad beginning but a happy ending. How did you feel about what you read?"

Pearl stopped when Alex asked this question. She said, "It hurt my heart to read her journals. I am a bit surprised they agreed to let us read them, to tell you the truth. But for some reason I have a feeling there is a higher power in charge here. For example, I do not know why I trust you or feel this kinship to you. It is as if you are a part of this family, just not biologically. You know, like that made up 'uncle' moms and dads introduce you to that are not really your uncle, like Dimitri was to me. You know what I mean, right?" Alex nodded. She continued, "There is a peace inside me being in your presence. I feel the same when I am with Adeem. And I do not trust ANYBODY!"

Pearl laughed as Alex replied, "I feel the same and I think Adeem does too."

"I hope so. I think I like him. He kind of reminds me of Grandpa's and Nonnah's story – Daniel and Julia on the playground. I hope it does not take a stick of gum to find out if he is worthy or not." They laughed as they reached the spot where the cement building once stood. They walked to the rock steppingstone path and sure enough, it was there in plain sight, but no loose stones were sitting in the bowl of each rock step.

Alex traversed the path down as far as he could without falling over the cliff. Pearl, a bit intimidated by the path, chose to watch from the top. Alex turned and said, "The remnants of the building are down there. I can see them. They are in a huge pile. That must have been some feat to build a cement building of this size on the side of this cliff. Amazing, to say the least!"

Alex returned to the top and watched Pearl lay out a blanket and place all the lunch items on top of it. She asked, "How are you feeling about Dimitri's story?"

Alex took a long drink of his water then reached for the wine, opened it, and poured two glasses as Pearl filled the plates. "To tell you the truth, by reading his story in his own words as well as Julia's and George's, I am beginning to feel closer to Qaseem now. I guess I was hoping to find out that Dimitri might have really known about me. I was hoping to give justification to these years of feeling abandoned. But as I see it, he did not know about me. It is such a shame. He might not have died a broken and lonely man if he knew. I am thankful he had George. I am thankful he had your family. It really is a tragic story.

I would like to know what is in Sophia's journal. She comes across as quite meek in Julia's journals, but my memories and stories from home make her quite the warrior. She saved Qaseem's life and most likely Dimitri's too. Anyway, cheers! Here is to new beginnings!" He raised his wine glass, they clinked, and both took a long, slow drink, letting the wine settle in their mouths before swallowing.

Pearl held up her glass to the sun and admired the color. She explained which grapes were used in her wine and how the grapes were raised high in the cliffs to achieve the perfect flavor. She said, "It is called Angel's Blood. It is the color of blood, the source of life, and Angel because only the angels could grow anything on this shale-ridden island."

Pearl looked out over the calm sparkling ocean absorbing the midday sun. She looked at Alex, looked away, then looked back at him and began to speak, stopped, and took another drink of wine instead. "Pearl, what is on your mind?" Alex asked as he enjoyed the bowl of olives drenched in olive oil that left a lingering spicy, peppery aftertaste.

She said, "Alex, when I was at the conference, on the first day a woman, or at least I think it was a woman, came to my hotel room. It took me a while to recollect her. Everyone in that conference room Friday night has lost their memories of the incident that occurred when the sarcophagus was opened. It is the strangest thing. I did not remember this woman in detail at all until she showed up in my dreams last night. She repeated what she had said to me at the hotel and reminded me of the metal pot I am to give Julia but not before you translate it. After she left my dream, I woke up to the smell of your great breakfast. Before I went to the kitchen, I rummaged through my bags and found the metal pot. My mind was so confused that night. In my dream, when I answered the door, a woman was standing there covered in a black hooded garment. She handed me a metal bowl and told me to give it to Julia. She said it was imperative that she receive it immediately. She said, 'Julia is looking for this. You must have Alexander translate it prior to giving it to Julia. He will know what to do. Do not show anyone this artifact. It is priceless. Do you under-stand? Tell Alexander that no one is to know about this and if you tell anyone, your lives are in extreme danger. This is what Julia has been looking for. She has been chosen. You have been chosen.' She put the bowl in my hands, and as I looked at it then looked back up to express my understanding, she was gone. It was like she had disappeared into thin air. I took my eyes off her for one second and she disappeared. There were like ten rooms on either side of mine, but she literally disappeared.

Alex, I had not yet met you when she gave me this artifact. Anyway, I was so sick to my stomach and on the edge of throwing up when she arrived at my door that I vaguely remembered her the next day. I did not think anything of it at the time. I guess I assumed this person was just another speaker at the conference looking for Julia. Everyone knows Julia is obsessed with this pharaoh. People are always sending her artifacts and bits and pieces about him. The more I think about this and how I am feeling with you, I am assuming you are the Alex I am supposed to give it to."

Alex stopped eating and sat up tall as Pearl told him the story. Pearl reached for her backpack and pulled out the metal bowl. It was brass in color with all kinds of symbol inscriptions circling the edge. In the center was an etched bird with its wings spread like an eagle. It weighed about two pounds. She handed it to him. He carefully took it in his hands then looked back up at her. "No one knows about this? No one?"

"No one. What is it?"

Alex examined the bowl and after a few minutes he said, "There are four different languages inscribed on this outer shell. They are very old languages, but I think I can translate them. Are we allowed to open it?"

"She did not tell me not to."

Alex carefully tried to twist the lid open. It didn't budge. He turned it over and over, looking for some sort of way to get inside. In the center of the bottom was a tiny hole. "Do you have anything in the backpack that is sharp like a pin?" Pearl had a large safety pin holding together a tear on the inside of her pack. She released it and gave it to him. He took it and slowly inserted the sharp point into the small hole. The top clicked and slightly raised. He turned the lid carefully and it came off. What he could see inside were four small metal scrolls and a clear glass container filled with a white powder that shimmered when the sun hit it. Wrapped around the entire contents was a copper wire. Alex looked at Pearl, "Tell me everything you know about this Silver Pharaoh. Why was he important?"

Pearl began, "Well, most of the stories were like wild adventures, somewhat like Indiana Jones movies. I did not take the stories seriously, I thought they were just made up. The underlying story theme was always the same; The Silver Pharaoh knew the recipe for immortality. But in these adventure stories, he was always looking for a missing ingredient, a special water or frequency that started the alchemy process. So, when Nonnah told me his sarcophagus was found, I was intrigued that indeed the stories could be true.

After the sarcophagus was found, a large team of scientists were employed, Julia being one of them, to study the contents of the tomb and eventually the actual pharaoh. For the past seven years they have worked nonstop on this archeological find. Now the interesting and most confusing thing is that Nonnah asked *me* to represent her at the conference, along with her research paper on him. This has been her life's passion, and she is not going to be present when the sarcophagus is opened? I had one week to absorb ten years-worth of information on this guy and get prepared to present her peer-reviewed paper at the conference. This was big for me, but a bit controversial for the other academics to understand. When I questioned her, she acted strange, almost panic-stricken. Why did she not stop the world from spinning to be present when the lid of the sarcophagus to the infamous Silver Pharaoh was finally removed? When I pressured her, she answered me by saying, 'Pearl, I need to be in Egypt, darling. I need help at this point in my research and it is in Egypt that I have been mysteriously requested. I was told in a dream '*He* will find you, the one who will help'. When I told your father this, he told me to step back and let whatever is going to happen, happen. He said he also had a dream that you would find a way, or *he* would find a way.' So, Alex, I am a bit confused. Nonnah would not tell me who HE was. All I know is that she is in Egypt looking at some hole in the ground, some *staircase to nowhere* they call it. When I talked to her yesterday, she told me to give you the metal pot. What now?"

Alex was studying the inscriptions on the outside of the jar. He asked for a pen and paper, which Pearl handed to him. He spent a good hour writing frantically on the pad of paper, then canceling out his work and starting over again. Each scribble was a different language combination. When he was done, Alex looked at her, his face in sheer shock. He carefully replaced the lid, stood up, and got out his cell phone. He paced the ground around the blanket until the phone connected. "Adeem, I need you here now. Can you come tonight? Yes. Yes. Yes, I know. This is an emergency. I need to be in Egypt. No, you are staying here until I get back. Julia, Charlee, and Mathias. I will explain later, just get here – I need the helicopter. Call Yusuf and have him prepare the plane in Athens for a midnight departure. How long can you stay here? Yes, I can have the helicopter sent back to you. OK, great. See you in a couple of hours. Thank you, son!"

He looked down at Pearl who was looking up at him while slowly eating her sandwich as he spoke to Adeem. "What the heck, Alex. What is going on?"

He said, "Let's get back to the house. I want to unroll at least one of these scrolls right now to confirm my suspicions. Pearl, if I am reading this right, what is in this box and on these scrolls is the recipe to turn off the genes that cause aging. It has been theorized that our genome was manipulated over two hundred thousand years ago, may-be even longer, by whom we do not know. But if what is in this box is what I think it is, it *is* the secret to immortality."

Pearl lowered her sandwich and with knitted eyebrows she sarcastically asked, "Are you kidding me?"

Alex began frantically gathering all the stuff on the blanket and stuffing it into his backpack without a concern of breaking or squishing anything on the way in.

Pearl stood up, put her hands on her hips, and yelled, "ALEXANDER, STOP!" He about jumped out of his skin. "Tell me what is going on! And thank you for asking whether I was OK with Adeem coming tonight. There is a lot I need to do to prepare for him to come here."

Alex looked up at her and said, "It is OK, he is OK. He does not mind if your hair is dirty or not," as he started stuffing his backpack again. Pearl stepped on his hand and put all her weight on it. He couldn't move. He once again looked up at her, "OK, OK! Just a minute, my heart is racing. First, I need to talk to Julia. I need to know where she is."

"No, first you need to tell me what is going on."

He looked at her intently, "Pearl, what is in this box changes the molecular makeup of every cell in the human body. I want to get back to the house and carefully open a scroll to confirm this. You do have a few pairs of tweezers and some gloves for both of us?"

"Sure," she replied.

"OK, Indiana Jones," Alex said with a smile, "Let's go find out what we have here. Please call Julia and get her on the line for me." As Pearl bent over to pick up her backpack, Alex noticed the bright red burn mark on her neck. He slowly asked, "Pearl, what is that on the back of your neck?"

She said, "I do not know, but it had been hurting, actually burning for a while, but it is not too bad now. I was going to ask you what you thought it was. Is it OK? Is it infected? What is it?"

"When did you notice this?"

"I noticed it when I woke up after the conference. It felt like a burn, but I do not remember being near anything hot or falling against anything. I figured it was a big pimple or something."

Alex handed her the metal pot. "It is this same bird. You have the Phoenix burned into your neck."

She replied as she touched her neck, "The Phoenix? The bird of destruction and resurrection?"

Alex nodded saying, "This is getting stranger by the minute. When we get back to the house, I will fill you in on this bird and its 138-year cycle. I am not sure what is going on here, but I think we just confirmed that I am not here to learn about Dimitri, I am here for a very different reason. Please get Julia on the line for me."

Pearl said, "Alex, I am worried. What is going on? First, I am 'chosen', then I am 'safe', now a phoenix is burned into my neck. What is happening?"

Alex dropped what he was doing and reached for Pearl, "Come here." She walked over to him with tears in her eyes. He could tell she was really scared. This was a Pearl he had not seen, and it brought out his paternal instincts. He hugged her gently and said, "I am sorry. I wish I had more answers for you. But right now, this is as confusing to me as it is to you. Listen to me." He pushed her away gently and looked into her eyes, "I will get to the bottom of this. Some *thing* or some *one* needs us and as long as that is so, we are OK. Pearl, I truly believe this is something special we have been asked to do. It is in the scrolls; this is about new beginnings and what I can gather, it is based on a loving vibration. So, we are OK. I want you to look forward to some time with Adeem. Do not lose your sassy charm now, girl. That boy needs a woman, a woman like you – strong, smart, capable, beautiful, and not needy. OK? I promise you I will figure this all out with the help of Julia and your parents. So, are you OK? Do you trust me?" Pearl cleared her throat and nodded.

As they walked back, Pearl called Julia, and before Pearl could say anything, Julia answered and said, "Alex?"

"No, Nonnah, it is Pearl. I—"

Julia cut her off, "Pearl, put him on the line please – now!" For the rest of the walk home, Julia and Alex talked. The conversation was so fast back and forth that it was like they had been colleagues for years. The conversation was geared completely toward biomechanics. Alex was using terms only a PhD of biology or quantum mechanics would use. The implications of the conversation were mindblowing.

When the conversation was over, they were back at the house. Alex quickly cleaned off the table, wiped it down with a wet cloth, and dried it. He took the gloves, tweezers, and the Ott light Pearl gave him and placed them strategically on the table with the metal pot in front of him. He put on his gloves and asked Pearl to do the same. He poked the bottom of the jar with the same pin and the lid once again opened. He took out the scroll that was tucked in on the far right of the pot and slowly started to open it.

Pearl asked, "Why did you choose that one? If we are only opening one, why that one?"

"Good question, Pearl. Esoterically speaking, when you write from the left to the right or organize thoughts from the left to the right, it signifies that which is outside of you; people, places, objects, or subject matter. When you write from the right to the left, it signifies that which is within you. Does that make sense? It is a secret code the mystic teachers used." Pearl nodded so he continued, "So, what I am reading on the outside of the jar here is a puzzle, an esoteric puzzle, a read-between-the-lines kind of thing. If I am right, this is the first scroll to read, and we will then move backward. Got it?" Pearl nodded.

Alex ever so carefully and slowly opened the first scroll. It was delicate and fragile yet easy to unroll. It looked like a tiny sheet of very thin copper. It was patinaed but still decipherable. When Alex saw what was inside, he slowly said, "Pearl, please get up and move away from the table." He dropped his tweezers, took off his gloves, and he too walked away from the table.

Pearl looked at him with a frightened look, "Alex, what is it?"

Alex took a big breath, wiped his hand over his mustache and chin, then bent over and let out all the air from his lungs. When he stood back up, he had a big smile on his face and started laughing, "Holy shit! Holy shit, Pearl. Oh my god!" She didn't know what to do. It was as if he was having a nervous breakdown. He kept running his fingers through his hair, leaning back, staring at the ceiling, and saying holy shit over and over again. She sat down and watched him until he finally acknowledged her again. She waited patiently. He leaned back over again, putting both hands on his knees, staring at the floor before he began to speak.

"Pearl, in the beginning, before writing, there was a language based only on sounds and vibrations. Each vibration and sound had a different meaning. Later, letters and numbers were assigned to each vibration and frequency. For example, A=1, B=2, C=3, D=4, and so on. When it comes to the vibrations and the frequencies they carry, that gets really complicated. Each number has its very own special meaning or information embedded within it, just as sounds and vibrations do. This goes for letters of the alphabet too. For instance, we put a bunch of letters together to make a word, right?" Pearl nodded as Alex continued, "When the alphabet was designed, each letter had many meanings, spiritual meanings, and its own frequency. Let's use, for example, the letter P, for Pearl. The letter P means *mouth* and *divine spark of light within our physical bodies.* Pretty cool, huh? A for Alex means *father or alpha.* There have been minor changes over the centuries on alphabet meanings, but not many. For example, the letter A was thought to mean *beast of burden* or represent the Ox, but later it was given the meaning of *alpha* or *father* and the number one to represent it. You understand?" Pearl again nodded her head. "Good. OK now, when we put letters together with positive meanings, the final word will have a positive frequency, such as the word *love.* Our bodies will response positively when it hears the word love. And the opposite happens too; for example, the word *hate.* Our bodies will respond negatively to that word.

Now this is where it gets good. When we put letters or sentences together with a negative frequency, the whole body will react negatively, and disease or dis-ease takes place. The opposite happens to the body when we use words filled with good intentions; kindness, health, and balance, then cohesion occurs. We have become so numb to this esoteric teaching, but the human body has never forgotten, it is tuned in 24/7. The human body and every cell in it, to this day, continues to respond to negative and positive words in a negative and positive way. Again, positive words and vibrations create health, coherence, and balance. Negative words and vibrations create disease or dis-ease. Do you understand?"

"I do. I have heard about this phenomenon as well as witnessed it. I have worked with people who were given three months to live, all doom and gloom. They decided in their last three months of life that they would finish everything on their bucket list. They experienced their adventures with joy and happiness, surrounding themselves with people who love them, only to find out at the end of the three months that their disease had disappeared."

"EXACTLY! RIGHT!"

"Why did we need to leave the table?" Pearl asked.

Alex took a breath and said, "Because the writing on this scroll was made in a frequency format. It is very powerful and I just wanted us to step away from it while I wrap my head around this. Pearl, this form of communication was given to us by the angels before time. No one knows where it originated, but we know it exists. This metal pot and what is in it is extremely old – I mean before time, old. It is impossible! Whoever wanted us to have this is not of this world. Or maybe they are and they need us. It will take me hours to decipher this. No one in their right mind would just hand this over to you. Is there anything else you can remember about the woman who gave this to you?"

Pearl closed her eyes and squinched her face while thinking then said, "OH MY GOD, yes! Alex, she did not have a lower body. She did not have legs or feet. She was only a physical body from her waist up!"

Alex clapped his hands together so hard it stung and he started laughing. "I knew it! Pearl, you met a Watcher. We have been chosen. I knew in my gut that this journey was so much more than Dimitri. I just needed to get out of my own way to get here." He started gathering his things throughout the house.

Pearl was on his heels asking him question after question. "Alex, what did Julia say to you when you were talking to her? And what is a Watcher? You mean like in the biblical sense? Julia used the same word when I talked to her. Alexander?"

Alex was in his own head, not listening. He continued to check the bathroom and the rest of the house for his belongings. Pearl stood in front of him to stop him from leaving the living room. She crossed her arms waiting for a reply as she stood in the middle of the walking path through the house. He finally looked at her and said, "Julia said she had a dream, and your parents had the same dream a few nights ago. They were told in their dream that a translator named Alexander from Qatar would have something for them. Julia was told that she needed to get to Egypt to retrieve the water. She was given the coordinates by Mathias from a dream he had had the same night. I am on my way to Egypt, Pearl. Julia, Charlee, and Mathias are waiting for me. Oh, and I am really sorry about Adeem. I mean really, you two are made for each other. Look at it this way – you now have the place to yourselves." He didn't wait for a reply, he just bopped her on the nose and gently pushed her aside. When he was done packing, he went back to the table and slowly lifted each scroll out of the metal container and placed them on the table. With Pearl's help, he carefully copied everything from the scrolls onto a writing tablet, then carefully replaced the scrolls and the lid.

As Alex put the scrolls back into the metal pot, Pearl called Charlee. "Mom, what the heck is going on? Alex is frantically packing."

Charlee answered, "My love, something's happening, and it's much bigger than us. I'll get back to you as soon as I can. In the meantime, Adeem is on his way. Your father has spoken to him and so has your Auntie Melena. You're safe. Enjoy, Pearl. I can't talk, honey, we're boarding a plane right now. I'll call soon," and she hung up.

Pearl stood motionless, staring at her phone, trying to take it all in. Everyone was moving in fast motion, and she felt as if she was in the eye of the tornado with everyone spinning around her. What was happening? At that moment she felt the pulling from both worlds; her passion for the world of science and intrigue, and the passion brewing inside her as a woman. A man was coming to stay with her, in her home, all alone, and she didn't know him. Then she realized the whole family had talked to Adeem prior to asking her if it was OK if he stayed with her alone. *How old am I, two years old?* she wondered. Her next thought was, *Oh my god, I need to get ready!*

She asked Alex when Adeem would be arriving. No answer. Again, she asked with no response. She was mentally transported back to the days when her father did the same thing to her while he read the newspaper. She rolled her eyes, knowing there was no talking to Alex.

At one point she stood in his path hoping to block him to get more answers, but not knowing she was directly behind him, when he turned around, he ran smack into her, sending her scurrying backward onto the floor. She yelled at him, "ALEXANDER, slow down! OH MY GOD! When will Adeem be here?"

He apologized profusely as he helped her up and said, "In an hour or so. Can I take Sophia's journal with me?"

"There is no key. How will you open it?"

"I am hoping Julia will tell me where the key is, I will have one made or carefully break into it. Any of those options will work, right?"

He didn't wait for an answer as he went to the pile of journals and found the embossed book belonging to Sophia and stuck it in his backpack. Pearl decided the best thing to do was to leave him alone, and the best thing for her to do was to get ready for Adeem.

She asked one final question, "Are you going to tell me about The Phoenix?"

"Pearl, it will have to be a story for another time. Maybe Adeem can help you with those answers. Ask him. If not, we will talk when I return. By then I should have the information to answer any question you have."

Chapter Sixteen

Alex didn't wait for Adeem to power down the helicopter. As Adeem jumped out, Alex threw his bags into the bird and took his place in the warm seat. He looked at his son and yelled over the top of the swirling blades, "This is huge! I will call and explain when I can. I will be in Cairo for a while, I think. Pearl has the numbers. I am stopping in Qatar and planning an early flight out tomorrow morning. Is the plane ready?"

Adeem's hair was being violently tossed with his tie swirling around his neck as the chopper's blades screamed down at him. He cupped his hands and yelled back up, "Yes, Yusuf has you covered. I will have the bird returned tomorrow morning. Good luck," then he made the gesture for Alex to call him. Alex nodded, shut the door, and lifted the helicopter up and away from the island. Adeem stood there staring up as Alex sped away.

Alex had the metal pot safe in his luggage and copies of the four scrolls in his briefcase. Three of the scrolls he knew were written in three different ancient languages; Sumerian, Coptic Egyptian, and Sanskrit. The fourth scroll was a musical composition written in a style he hadn't seen before. It was as if it was written in a mirror style. Leonardo Da Vinci used this technique a lot in his work. It was a musical bar without notes but with number and letter combinations. This scroll would require some help. He had never worked with frequencies, but by the look of it, this journey was going to be all about frequencies. He figured the first three scrolls would take several hours to decipher, and the trip from Athens to Qatar was about three hours. The trip from Qatar to Cairo was about four hours, giving him seven hours to complete these three translations. Hopefully Julia would know how to contact a musical translator. He texted her with the request and as a heads up that he was on his way. Fingers crossed she would have a contact for him by the time he arrived.

Alex's first stop was Athens. As soon as the helicopter landed, he shut down the machine and ran from one tarmac to another to jump into his awaiting private jet. He asked the ground crew to return the helicopter to Ikaria's regional airport and to notify Adeem that it was there. Just in case the situation with Pearl didn't turn out well, he wanted Adeem to have an escape plan.

Alex sat in the cockpit of his private jet with Yusef, his pilot, as he went over his itinerary for the next few days. When Yusef understood the plan, Alex left the cockpit and took a seat with a large table in the passenger section. He leaned back into the plush leather seat, closed his eyes, and took a big breath. There was an element of exhaustion as well as excitement swirling within him. What had he gotten himself into? It was an incredible story and it was just beginning. For the first time in a long time, he felt alive. He felt needed and wanted, and it felt great. He carefully prepared the table in front of him with his open briefcase to the right, his laptops to the left, and his writing pads in front of him. He spread out the copied pages, opened his two laptops, and began his translation process with the easiest translation first; Sanskrit.

As the first scroll began to take on meaning, Alex began to feel as though he was being watched, as if someone was looking over his shoulder. He looked around the plane, but he was alone. There were no other passengers on board except for a flight attendant he saw in the galley at the back of the plane. He had never had an attendant on board before but was grateful she was there. He had her bring him a glass of wine. He took two long sips, tipping his head back while feeling the wine warm his esophagus all the way down. A split second later, he was sleeping.

An hour later he was startled awake, completely drenched in sweat, a pen in his hand and the copied music composition laid out in front of him. The scroll had been deciphered for him while he slept. By the looks of it, he did the writing himself while he was asleep. *Impossible!* he thought. He got up to find the attendant, but she was nowhere in sight. He looked in the back of the plane, the bathroom, and the cockpit. Yusef was flying the plane alone. Alex asked Yusef where the attendant was. He looked at Alex funny, knitted his eyebrows, and said, "Boss, it is just you and me on this flight. I did not have time to bring in help for you, but the galley is stocked with all your favorites. Your meal is warm, sitting in the side-by-side, and the cold box has some choices too. Help yourself. We should touch down in just under an hour."

When Alex returned to his seat, a tray of food was waiting for him. Steam was coming from the meal and a new glass of wine had been poured. Sitting on top of the glass was a piece of paper that said, "You are welcome. You are chosen." He stood staring at his food and the note in his hand as he scanned the plane again. What the hell was going on? He looked up as if looking for Allah and said, "Thank you. I hope I do not let you down. I have no idea what you want from me, but I hope I am the right guy."

Loud and clear, he heard her voice, "You are. I never make a mistake."

Alex started shaking, sat down, and drank the entire glass of wine in one gulp. Adeem's mother used to say this to him all the time when they were together. Was she the angel helping him?

He closed his eyes and smiled as he was transported back in time, remembering her soft hands against his chest and her sexy, girlish smile as she bit her lip while she made love to him. Her skin was soft against his. She was his everything. They had met at the university in a physics class when her long black hair caught his attention. She sat two rows in front of him with her hair shimmering in the overhead auditorium lights. Each toss of her head caused him to want her more. He couldn't help fantasizing about running his hands through it then grabbing it and holding her head back while he gently kissed her neck as she moaned, wanting him. All he could think about was her silky, shiny strands dancing over the top of him as she looked into his eyes, her beautiful breasts cupped in his hands as she slowly moved with him. He had totally lost interest in the professor and the lecture being presented. Completely ensconced with this image, sitting in the lecture hall staring down at her, he closed his eyes and brushed against the erection in his pants.

He shuddered and every hair stood up on his body when he heard a whisper in his ear, "Your thoughts are distracting me."

When he opened his eyes, she was sitting next to him. She was leaning in so close he could see the blue and yellow flecks in her eyes.

He sat up straight and pushed his coat down over the raised mound in his pants. No one in the class paid attention to what was happening; it was as if they were the only two in the room. In shock and red with embarrassment, he said, "Ummmm, what? Excuse me?"

She said again, "Your thoughts are distracting me," as she raised one eyebrow while looking down at his pants with a coy smile. He was completely lost for words. She said, "OK, I see those thoughts are calmed down now." She looked at his paper, saw his name, and said, "Maybe we can finish class now, Mr. Alexander?" He nodded. She replied, "Good," handed him a piece of folded paper, and returned to her seat. When he opened the paper there was a street name on it, Jupiter St, #9. No time or date, just half an address. He sank down into his seat and smiled.

After class he tried to follow her out, but as the traffic jammed up at the classroom exit, he looked down for one second then back up and she was gone, seemingly vanished into thin air. It took him over a week to find her. He found out she was editing the class; she was a visitor, not a student. Eight torturous days later, he found another note on his windshield. This time there was a phone number on it. It said, "Do I bother you? If I do, then call me. I am assuming by your fantasies about me, which were quite nice I should say, you might want to see me again." He called her immediately and from that moment forward they were inseparable.

Alex smiled as he reminisced about his love affair with Adeem's mother. Alone on the plane, he could feel her. He became overwhelmed with emotion. He was so lonely. He still needed her to this day, even though she had been gone for so long. With his eyes closed he could see her. He could smell her. And he was thankful for that. As he collected his thoughts, he began to go over all the supernatural phenomenon that was taking place around him; dreams, collaborating with strangers, impossible translations, and dinner served by a ghost. Whatever was happening was big. As he ate the meal she had made for him, he started talking to the invisible woman on the plane. She never answered any of the questions he asked her, so after a few minutes he resigned himself to the fact that he was alone again. She was gone, whoever *she* was. He finished his dinner then studied the fourth scroll's translations that she had helped him with while he slept. It was a partial translation and seemed to be the last paragraph of the puzzle. What it said made him shudder. If this was the end of the puzzle, what the hell was the beginning?

Chapter Seventeen

Pearl stood in front of a pile of clothes on the floor with every hanger in her closet empty, yet nothing seemed to be just right; no cute skirts, no cute dresses. Every outfit seemed to say, *Look at me, I am frumpy!* She was truly a jeans and T-shirt kind of gal. She slept in a T-shirt, men's boxers, and usually a pair of socks. Half the time she slept in the same outfit she had worn that day, only because she was so exhausted by the time she got home. She stood in front of the long mirror staring at herself with slumped shoulders, a big sigh, and a huge "UGH!" moan. *What am I doing? This is ridiculous!* She was so nervous.

While the hot water filled the tub, Pearl gathered her nail clippers, nail polish remover, a bottle of pink nail polish, her favorite facial scrub, a razor, tweezers, and an exfoliating hand glove. She put everything on her footstool and scooted it next to the tub. About ready to step into the hot steaming water laced with lavender essential oils, she realized she had forgotten the most important thing. She left the bathroom, headed to the kitchen, and returned to the tub with a water glass full of wine. *The bigger the better; I think I am going to need it!* She spent the next hour preening, grooming, plucking, and polishing. She applied light mascara to her lashes and a soft pink lip gloss to her lips. She let her hair hang free in small, soft curls down her back.

After a long deliberation in front of the pile of clothes, she chose a soft pink off-the-shoulder blouse she had found in a bag of clothes she had planned to give to Goodwill months ago. She put on her favorite pair of tight jeans that casually flared at the bottom which made her look like she had a smaller waist than she did. She was the perfect weight and took pride in her toned body. She placed a small drop of vanilla essential oils at the back of her neck, between her breasts, and behind each knee. *No socks tonight*, she thought as she looked down at her tiny, cute feet all dolled up with pink polish. With one last look in the mirror, she decided that if he didn't like what he saw then so be it – it wasn't meant to be. Life is too short to worry about whether a man thinks you're beautiful or not. As far as she was concerned, she had everything a man should want; beauty, brains, spunk, and desire. Period!

Next on her list was to prepare the bedroom and change the sheets. Was it too presumptuous to think they were going to have sex? If they did, she would be prepared. If they didn't, she knew it would be a lovely evening regardless. Knowing he was going to be on his best behavior might put him into the gentleman category on their first night together. She thought about it and decided to change the sheets in both bedrooms, hers and the guest bedroom where Alex stayed, just in case. She fluffed the pillows, turned down the beds in both rooms, and lit four vanilla candles in each room. The flames danced on the ceilings. It was perfectly romantic.

Next on the list were dishes and to prepare a tray of hors d' oeuvres in case Adeem was hungry. She put two bottles of white wine and a bottle of champagne into the fridge and placed three different reds on the table next to the hors d' oeuvres. Not knowing his pre-ference, she felt prepared no matter what his choice. Agnes had taught her to always have a shot of ouzo ready in times like this, so she put two shot glasses and a bottle of ouzo in the freezer. She dimmed the lights in the house and took a last-minute look around. Pleased with her work, she snuggled into her chair and contemplated how the even-ing might go. She thought of every scenario – good, bad, and ugly. Never had so much thought gone into a date before, but for some reason she felt different about this man. The whole situation was beginning to feel like fate, and according to Auntie Melena, this was how she was supposed to feel about the man she was going to give herself to.

When the whirling of the helicopter was within earshot, Pearl began to sweat. OH NO! She ran to the bathroom and put on more deodorant, freshened her lip gloss, fluffed her hair, and drank the last big gulp of wine in the water glass. When the helicopter left, she waited and waited and waited. What was Adeem doing? She peeked out the window thinking maybe he was on his phone, but he was nowhere to be seen. She went to the peephole in the front door and there he was, sitting on the porch with a duffle bag next to him. She slowly walked away from the door and took a seat in her chair and waited. With no knock, she started feeling the butterflies set in. She knew he was thinking about what he was going to say, and most likely he was rehearsing his lines before he knocked. This was his make-it or break-it moment. After a few more minutes, she got up and went to the back of the house and fussed with anything she could find to fuss with so it didn't look like she was too anxious. *Jeez, the games we play in relationships*, she thought!

After a good fifteen minutes, he knocked on the door. Without waiting for her to open it, Adeem walked in and there he was – tall, dark, and handsome. Pearl decided to play the *I didn't hear you arrive* card as she lingered in her bathroom trying to slow her pounding heart. Adeem stood in the entrance foyer and softly said, "Hello?" With no answer he looked around. To the right was the hallway of bedrooms, straight in front of him was a large living room, and to the left was the kitchen. Seeing she was not in the latter two, he headed down the hall. The first bedroom was hers and he entered. He smiled when he saw the candles and the bed turned down. The room was so elegant, so feminine. He had a glimpse of the girly side of her through her bed-room décor. After seeing this, he saw her differently. A soft belly with a tough shell. He set down his bag and ventured down the hall and found another bedroom that was just as feminine. It too had candles burning and the bed turned down. At that moment he rushed to her room, grabbed his bag, and went back to the hallway entrance. "Shit, that was close!" To assume he was staying in her room was a hopeful assertion, but possibly a deal breaker too.

A minute later, she emerged from the bathroom and found him standing in the foyer waiting. She acted surprised, "Oh my gosh, you are here. I did not even hear the helicopter. The fan in the bathroom is so loud. Here, let me take your bag." Wondering which room she was going to take it to, he handed her his duffle bag. She took it and put it on the kitchen chair.

He jumped for joy inside, knowing exactly what that meant – *she* didn't yet know which room he was sleeping in either. Depending on how she felt about him at the end of the evening would decide where he slept tonight. He thought, *Game on! But what if I fuck it up?*

Oh jeez! He ran his fingers through his hair, took off his jacket, and put it over his bag. He stood there waiting for his next cue. He was terrified to speak. He had proven in the past few days that his seduction skills were a bit rusty and, as Alex said, embarrassing. He had practiced what he was going to say during the entire trip over to Ikaria, but succumbed to being quiet and smiling until he had to talk.

Feeling his nervousness, she asked, "Are you hungry? Would you like a drink?" He answered yes to both. She handed him a wine bottle opener and encouraged him to pick the bottle of his choice. She said, "To be perfectly honest, I am a glass ahead of you. There are two shot glasses of ouzo in the freezer too. Please feel free to slug 'em both down! It is Agnes' cure to calm one's nerves. After a day like you have had, I am sure you need it, right?"

He smiled and said, "Right. Would you like one too?"

She said, "Sure," and gathered up the hors d'oeuvre plate and wine glasses then headed to the living room where she had made them a nice sitting area on the couch. She had placed throw pillows and throw blankets on each end of the couch. To break the ice, she figured she would tell him all about the discoveries in the journals and what had happened up to this point.

While she arranged the food in the living room, Adeem had two generous shots of ouzo and let them settle in for a second, thanking Agnes as he stood in the kitchen as nervous as hell. He had been with a woman before, so why the nerves? Granted, it had been a while, but it wasn't like he didn't know what to do. But Pearl was different. She didn't want anything from him. Most women wanted his money or family prestige. They were of little substance with minimal educational backgrounds, and intellectual conversations were always absent. He was used to talking about his jets, his job, how famous his family was, how much money he had, and shopping. Never did he leave a date that he hadn't spent enough money to buy a car with. You could say they were superficial women and he was tired of it. He hadn't met a woman his equal, ever. He yearned for a woman he could talk the night away with and never pull out his wallet. His life was refined, intense, and competitively ruthless at times. But it was also champagne, caviar, appearances, and a lot of small talk. In his world, if a woman couldn't hold her own, she was considered a mistress, a plaything, insignificant.

Adeem didn't feel that way about women. He adored them, he needed them, and he longed for a woman who could see him and know his true heart. He wanted a woman who would challenge him, a woman he could leave in a group of men and know she would come out with respect and admiration, to be considered equal and impressive. In the Middle East, that was almost unheard of, but it was what he longed for.

He loved bantering with Pearl. She had a great sense of humor and wit about her, but mostly he *saw* her. He saw her light and wanted to be a part of it. Being in her presence made him feel vulnerable, excited, scared, sensitive and, unbeknownst to him, he liked it. The more time he spent with her, the more he craved and desired her.

Thank god for the wonderful ouzo, the perfect drink to calm his nerves and stomach, especially in times like this. He closed his eyes and listened to Alex talking in his head, *This one is special. She is not pretentious or greedy. She is exciting and interesting. When she speaks, she amuses you with charm and a witty sense of humor. She is infectious. Do not screw up this one!* He was so thankful for his father's advice. Without a mother figure in his life, he had learned how to wing it with women. This one could not be winged.

He took in a big cleansing breath and walked in with a bottle of Zinfandel, her favorite, and poured two nice glasses of wine, four fingers instead of the usual two fingers you get in restaurants. She gave him a thumbs up and took a long sip. He went back into the kitchen and brought back two more shots of ouzo. They helped themselves to the food tray and, after a brief, awkward moment of silence, Adeem noticed the pile of journals on the floor.

She looked at him, then at the piles. She said, "Yes, that was an all-day project and most likely another day to finish the job." Pearl explained the method of reading, "I read one, Alex read one then we switched. The neat, stacked pile over there is the done pile. The big messy one in the middle is waiting for their pages to be turned." He asked her if she had read anything that surprised her or if anything about Dimitri had come up. She shifted her eyes to the floor, and an overwhelming sorrow filled her mind regarding her mother's history.

She knew this was a story that needed to stay within the closed pages and bindings of her journal, so she contemplated which story to start with.

Adeem sensed her sadness, reached over, touched her hand, and said, "If it is too painful, we do not need to discuss it."

She looked up, smiled, and decided to tell the story of how Daniel won Julia's heart with a piece of gum. They laughed when Adeem said, "I think I would have liked Daniel. Tenacious but kind."

She smiled and agreed then moved on to the story about the nuclear submarine and Dimitri being found dead after years of being in the cement building. While she was telling Dimitri's horrific death story, Adeem's face scrunched up and he looked like he had just eaten something bad. She looked at him and said, "Right? So gross! And unfortunately, this story was very painful for Alex. It actually brought him to tears. He had hoped for so much more."

For the next two hours, she filled him in on the many stories buried in the pages of each journal. He laughed at the many shenanigans of her family. They talked and listened to each other's stories about life, the past, girlfriends and boyfriends, and immediate plans for their futures. The conversations were effortless, as if they had known each other for years. But Adeem sensed a deeper secret that Pearl wasn't ready to tell.

She could feel his silent curiosity about what she was hiding. She was very intuitive. At times it was a frustrating gift, but she needed a bit more time before she could tell him about the metal pot and who gave it to her. She wasn't sure what his take was on the supernatural and wasn't ready to end the evening if he was a non-believer. She fidgeted a bit then picked up one of the journals and skimmed through it as she talked. The journal belonged to Melena. When she realized it, she smiled, kissed it, and held it to her heart before she put it back on the table. He asked her why she had kissed that one. She explained, "This is Melena's journal. Melena named me. She is my hero, my godmother, my best friend, my auntie."

Adeem took that precise moment to ask, "Do you think you can have two best friends?"

Pearl quickly replied, "Oh yes, probably. I am not very close to many people. I find them conditional, which does not allow for a deep connection, you know. I think that is why I love research so much. Just me and the books. They do not seem to care if I open them or not. You know?" She laughed. He did not. She looked at him and his face was blank. He was just staring at her. Then it hit her – he was asking if she could allow someone else into her life. She smiled as she continued, "Well to be honest, if I had a person in my life that was more exciting than the books and has the heart Melena does, then yes, another best friend would be lovely. Do you know anyone like that?"

Adeem looked at her, transfixed. She was sitting on one end of the couch with her legs and feet in the middle. He was sitting on the opposite side of the couch with his legs and feet alongside hers. He loved the connection they were making and how it felt to have half of her body against his. He reached down and took one of her delicate feet in his hands and started rubbing it. Her favorite thing in the whole world was having her feet rubbed and tickled. She was in heaven. She said, "I will give you a half hour to stop that." He smiled.

She reached down to touch his feet and he jumped two feet off the couch and squealed like a little girl. It startled her. She put her hand to her heart and said, "OMG! What? You scared me." They broke out in a wave of laughter.

Between breaths he said, "I am so ticklish. *I* cannot even touch my feet. When I was young, my dad used to hold me down and tickle me for hours. Oh my god, I hated it but loved it. We would laugh for hours. So, no foot rubs for me, please!"

Feeling the wine and the ouzo going to her head, she leaned forward, grabbed his hands, pulled him to her, and kissed him gently. When she tried to lean back, he tightened his grip and held her in place and looked deeply into her eyes. She smiled and said in a sweet, soft voice, "Hi."

He reached under her arms and with one swift, gentle move, raised her up and over his legs until she was lying on top of him. He gently turned sideways, and they were comfortably spooning. He said, "Do you mind if we snuggle as we talk?"

She turned around, they were now face to face, legs entangled. Her reply was, "I thought you would never ask." He wrapped his arms around her as she tucked her head into his shoulder and chest and relaxed into him. Before they knew it, they were asleep.

At 1:00 a.m. she awoke. He was asleep, gently snoring. She slowly pulled away from him and slid to the floor. He didn't move. She took his bags into the guest bedroom, blew out the candles, and turned off the lights. She went into the kitchen and put together a bowl of fruit, made two tall glasses of lemon water, setting one on each of the nightstands next to her bed. She changed into a soft, long, pink, see through T-shirt then brushed her teeth. She closed down the house then went to him on the couch.

He was so handsome. He looked like a little boy laying so peacefully on the couch, gently snoring. What was going to come of all of this? Was this a man she could spend the rest of her life with or was he going to be like the others; a problem after a one-night stand, needy, wanting to move in or live off her. Her second thought was, *That is not going to happen. He is a wealthy businessman from Qatar. This is one guy that will not be mooching off me. Plus, it would be one hell of a long-distance relationship.* It was obvious this was not going to be a long-term relationship. When he explained his future plans earlier, his future description didn't include a relationship commitment and there was no way she was moving to Qatar.

As far as she was concerned, her future was working with Julia. Julia had plans for her and those plans included taking over the business and her speaking engagements. But for right now, she felt like a schoolgirl; vulnerable, sexy, and wanted. She thought about the last 48 hours and realized he probably hadn't had any sleep since the last time she saw him. She touched his lips with her finger and ran her hand through his soft black hair. It felt like silk. She reached up and felt her own hair, "I need to ask what he uses; damn his hair is nice." She could stare at him for hours, but since the wine and ouzo had made its way to her head, she knew herself well enough that if she didn't get in bed now, she would be asleep on the floor shortly.

She gently stroked his hair and woke him, "Adeem, it is time for bed." He stretched and took her hand. She escorted him down the hallway to her room. He didn't say a word. She brought him to the side of her bed. The candlelight was the only light in the room and it flickered dimly on the walls. The soft scent of vanilla permeated the air. She stood in front of him, looked him in the eyes, slowly reached up and unbuttoned his shirt, gently pulled it from his shoulders, and let it drop to the floor. "I would like it if you would share my bed with me tonight. Will you stay with me?" He nodded, smiled, and kissed her gently. She continued to undress him. He watched her and followed her commands. She unbuttoned his pants and lowered them, along with his briefs, to the floor, her eyes following his belly, down his waist, past his groin, and all the way down to the floor. What she saw was the most beautiful man she had ever seen. He was strong, muscular, and chiseled. As her eyes passed his groin, inches away from his penis, she smiled then blushed and collected herself quickly. He was exceptional. She wanted to put him in her mouth and pleasure him right then and there, but she refrained.

In that split moment, the events of the day came swirling into her mind. She was glad she was not alone tonight. As she stood up, she ran her hands along his outer legs until she was standing before him, looking up into his eyes. With every ounce of his being, he concentrated on not getting an erection as he felt her breath and her soft hands on his skin. He was being undressed and touched by the woman of his dreams. His body was in complete turmoil, yet his control was impeccable. He wanted to throw her on the bed and make sweet, unbridled love to her, but he knew better. As she stood slowly, she noticed he had very little hair on his body. This pleased her. She could smell his faint cologne. She had smelled this scent before, long ago, but couldn't place it.

She looked up and smiled, "Would you like to rest beside me?"

He nodded, and before she knew what was happening, he picked her up and took her to the other side of the bed, laid her down, and gently pulled the covers over her. He returned to his side of the bed, blew out the candles, and slid in beside her. He pulled her in close and wrapped his arms around her, "Pearl, thank you for inviting me to your home and to your bed. I hope to make you as happy as you make me." Pearl smiled as she snuggled into him. He gently inched closer to her, and they fell back to sleep.

Being an early riser, when Adeem's internal clock hit 4:00 a.m., his eyes popped open. When he awoke, the sun hadn't yet graced the sky, nor was it interested in doing so at this hour. Adeem was used to getting up before the sun. It was the early, peaceful morning hours he loved the most. He got most of his work done in these dark hours of the morning. When he heard the birds start to wake up, he knew he had forty-five minutes before the sun made its appearance. This was the time he showered and went over his itinerary for the day. But today, instead of jumping right up to start the day, he watched the woman of his dreams sleeping soundly in bed next to him. He smiled as she purred such a gentle, quiet little snore, like a happy cat in the arms of its favorite person. She was beautiful. He wanted to pull the covers back and admire her body and all its wonders, but he refrained. He let her rest.

Usually, he stayed in bed to read and catch up on work, but today he went into the living room and let her rest peacefully. When he was done with emails and looking over the new merger documents, he headed to the stove. He had made a promise and he was going to deliver. Still naked, he saw an apron hanging from the hook on the wall and decided it might be a good idea to cover up some delicate parts just in case the grease splattered on him. He rummaged through the fridge, picking and choosing the best ingredients. He was happy to see she had a fully stocked fridge with many things to choose from. He got out the cutting board and a knife and began to prepare her a breakfast of champions.

Pearl woke to the most delicious smells permeating from the kitchen. Adeem was obviously making her that breakfast he'd promised. When she walked into the kitchen, what she saw made her laugh out loud; a naked man wearing her apron with a sexy, bare butt facing her. He didn't turn around; instead, he wiggled his behind at her and continued cooking. She smiled, crossed her arms, and leaned against the wall to watch. He hummed as he decorated each plate with the fruit from the bowl she had brought to the bedroom. He lifted the lid off the frying pan and smelled his creation, a perfect omelet with melted cheese on top. He turned around, smiled, and said, "Good morning, my Juliet. Would you like coffee or fruit juice with breakfast?"

She put her hand to her mouth and laughed again. He was wearing an apron that depicted him as a big bosom woman in a string bikini. He looked down at his apron, "What? You do not like string bikinis? What is wrong with you?"

She bent over laughing and said, "Oh my god! No, you look fantastic in a string bikini. And coffee sounds great. I think I should gift that apron to you. It looks better on you!" She was still in her see-through T-shirt. He kept his eyes glued to hers, but every time she looked away, he stole a glance. Once again, he was doing everything possible to not get an erection, but she was exquisite. Her nipples were hard against her shirt as it flowed over the top of them and down to her mid-thigh. He wanted so badly to taste them, to hold her breasts in his hands and love them. His mind was swimming with so many thoughts, but at the same time he was scared to death to open his mouth. He was notorious for saying all the wrong things at the wrong moment and he didn't want to disappoint her or embarrass himself. So far everything had been perfect. He gestured for her to sit down as he poured her coffee and juice and set them in front of her. Pearl was starving. All she had in her belly were remnants of wine and ouzo from the night before, and Adeem's creation had her belly rumbling. On the table was a sweet and spicy hot sauce, salt and pepper, and napkins folded into tiny triangles. Pearl was impressed.

She took a sip of her coffee and said, "This is delicious! What did you do to the coffee to make it so creamy and tasty?"

He said, "Well, I am not sure if I should tell you, I might have to kill you if I do."

She giggled and said, "No really, this is really good!"

He said, "It is a recipe that Qaseem used to ask for. In a blender, you put in a half shot of olive oil and, by the way, you have great olive oil, thank you for that. Then you put in a dash of cinnamon, some heavy cream, and half a teaspoon of honey. When the coffee is done brewing, pour about two cups of coffee in and blend for ten seconds. Wha-la – you have the perfect cup of coffee! I am glad you like it." Like a game show host, he waved his hands at the coffee cups and smiled, showing off his perfect pearly white teeth. He was so proud of himself.

Pearl giggled, "It is delicious, thank you! I will definitely make this again. Or maybe you can make it for me again sometime."

"That I will do!" he replied with a wink.

Over breakfast they talked about Adeem's work and what his goals were for the year. He explained that flying back to Ikaria last night had caused a small crimp in his meetings with some huge clients, but with a little finesse he was able to finish the two-year deal and get the contract signed before he boarded the helicopter here. He said, "Pearl, it was a two-billion-dollar deal. And now that it is finally secured, this gives me more time to explore other options I have been thinking about." Pearl's jaw dropped when he said *two billion*. He looked at her and smiled, "Do not be too impressed; in the East we only work in the billions. I know that number is hard to wrap your head around, but there is so much money it should be a sin."

She stared at him then said, "I guess you do not need to worry about putting your kids through college."

He quizzically looked at her as he took a bite of his omelet, "I do not have any kids and, to be honest, I am not interested in having any, at least not anytime soon."

She dropped her head then looked back up at him with a smile and said, "I do not either. I love my work and, I have to admit, I am a bit selfish. I do not want the responsibility of another human life. The thought of it scares the hell out of me. Plus, I am working on a program that will take at least seven years to complete, if my trajectory is correct. So having children is not in the cards for me anytime soon either."

He didn't flinch, he just continued to eat and treated the conversation with no interest or emotion. He said, "Alex gets it. It is our work that made us happy. We both love what we do. We do not get in each other's way and we both grew up in unconventional circumstances. We both turned out great! I mean, look at us." He stood up and twirled, showing off his string bikini apron and his cute white butt.

Pearl laughed and looked up at him. She shook her head and said, "OK, handsome, sit back down."

He said, "Just saying." She watched him take his next bite and realized – she was about to embark on a relationship with a man-boy.

Adeem took several more bites of food then asked her what she was working on and what was going to take seven years to complete. She looked at him, put her fork down, and took a long drink from her coffee cup. She said, "Adeem, did Alex tell you why he wanted you here last night?"

He sat back and said, "No, not really, but I am used to that. He is a passionate man and when he gets excited about something, he never makes sense. I am glad he has me as a sounding board because if he acted this way with his shareholders, he would be without a board, you know what I mean?"

Pearl nodded, "I understand completely. Mom and Julia are exactly like that. Sometimes they make me crazy."

Adeem said, "Right! Now what was he supposed to tell me?"

She looked at him then at her plate, "I have an idea – let's finish breakfast, take a shower, then go on a nice early morning walk. I can fill you in then." They agreed and decided to finish breakfast on a casual conversation about Qatar.

Adeem told her about his home, the chateau he spent most of his time at. He explained his upcoming business ventures, his future business plans, and his love for the Arabian horses. He said, "You have never felt power until you have had an Arabian horse between your legs." He said it so nonchalantly as he cut off another piece of omelet and put it in his mouth.

Pearl sat back and wiped her mouth with her napkin then said, "Well, I guess every woman should feel an Arabian horse between her legs before she dies."

He looked up, realizing how that sounded and started laughing. She just smirked at him. He looked her in the eye and said, "I really want to say something right now, but it will sound as bad as what I just said."

She leaned in and said, "Yes, Adeem, I do."

He cleared his voice and asked, "Do you read minds?"

She answered, "Yes, Adeem, I do."

All he could muster was, "Oh boy, that is not good. There is a lot in there I am not responsible for. I want you to know that."

"I doubt that very much, but I will give you the benefit of the doubt," she said with a sly smile.

Adeem added, "Men cannot be held responsible for anything swimming around in their heads. It is a fact of nature. It is assumed that males have but one brain and it does not reside in their heads. It is not fair! It is *my* assumption that it is that way to ensure that the human population never dwindles."

She laughed, "Put whatever spin on it you want, but us woman have another theory about that. God was originally called Dog, and his fascination with his genitals became so ridiculous that the female was created to snap him out of it. She changed his name to God so he no longer fiddled with the wonderment between his legs, and now looks up and enjoys the world for what it is."

He busted up laughing, "You made that up!"

She laughed, "Yes and it was funny!"

Through his laughter he said, "Yes it was and quite witty too." He raised his hand in a high five and she laughed as she met his hand with a loud smack. Pearl felt so comfortable at this moment. It was nice to have a gorgeous, half-naked man in her kitchen.

With breakfast finished, Pearl started to get up and clear the dishes. Adeem walked over to her side of the table, held out his hand, and said, "Will you join me in the shower?"

"Well, who will do the dishes?" she asked.

"I called the maid earlier and she will be here shortly." She smiled as he winked at her then said, "Shower? With me? I will wash your back if you wash mine."

She took his hand and followed him down the hallway. Her thoughts were completely in chaos, *Oh my gosh, I am going to be naked in front of him in a minute. Am I ready for this? What if I hate it? What if I love it? Maybe this is not a good idea. Maybe we should take it slower. Wait, I do not have to do anything I do not want to do. OK. But look at him. He is so handsome and he wants me. And my parents approve, so what the hell. I am doing this!*

When they got to the bathroom, she reached for the shower and turned on the water. Adeem took off his apron and stood before her, naked and semi-erect. He couldn't control it any longer. He wanted her and the way she was looking up at him, he knew she felt the same way. She raised her hands while looking into his eyes. He slowly slipped off her T-shirt then bent down and kissed her gently at first then passionately as her naked body rested against his. She wanted him. She had wanted him since the day she met him. She was completely drawn to him. She would give herself to him freely, with pleasure.

He felt her relax into his arms as he kissed her. He looked into her eyes and said, "Yes?"

Pearl nodded and said, "Yes." He reached between her legs and felt her wet essence waiting for him. She took a breath and dropped her head back as his fingers lingered over her clitoris then back up her belly to her aroused nipples that were calling him to play. He kissed each nipple tenderly then returned his mouth to hers. He was losing himself in her. His thoughts were racing and his body was fully aroused, holding her as close as he could get her.

She reached down and found his hard phallus and wrapped her hand around it then slid down to her knees and put it in her mouth. He let out a sigh of pleasure as her tongue toyed with it. He could feel himself building up to an ejaculation. He carefully pulled away, helped her up, and took her into the shower. The hot water felt good running down his body and jolted him back out of almost ruining the moment between them. As the hot water relaxed their passion, Pearl put on two shower gloves and asked him to turn around and face the wall. She washed his back then his legs as he moaned with pleasure, feeling the slightly rough surface of the gloves clean his body. No one had ever washed him before and he was in heaven. The stimulation felt so good.

When she was done, she slipped off the gloves, put soap on her hands, and reached in front to wash his waiting semi-erection. When she touched him, his erection became hard and powerful. He turned, faced her, and kissed her passionately, tenderly. He reached down and parted her legs and gently entered her. She moaned as he penetrated her deeply. Their rhythm was slow and methodical at first, rising quickly to passion and a hunger for each other that neither expected. He pulled her hair back as she exposed her mouth to him. He plunged his tongue into her mouth as she cried with pleasure. He whispered in her ear, "Pearl, should I stop?"

She said, "No, Adeem. I want you!" He exploded, his whole body quivering as he pulsated inside of her. She held him tight as his legs began to buckle.

When he regained his composure, he looked down at her, "Pearl, oh my god! You are so beautiful. I need you. I want to do that over and over again." He held her tight and kissed her as the warm water rained down upon them.

Pearl was brimming with desire. She needed the same release. Adeem could sense her wanting. He stepped back and looked at her body. He loved what was standing in front of him, but he knew better than to say that out loud. Instead, he took the washcloth and carefully washed her body as she had his. He asked her to face the wall and when she did, he washed her hair as she tipped her head back for him, enjoying his gentle touch.

When they were done, he dried her body, picked her up, and took her to bed. He lay on top of her, kissing her mouth, her neck, each nipple, sliding down to her belly then between her legs, his mouth finding the warm place he had just entered. Pearl arched her back and let her legs fall apart for him, his tongue exploring her opening. He teased her lotus flower, feeling every inch of her desire and tasting the soft honey she made for him. When she began to move with his rhythm, he lingered over her clitoris until she exploded as he had. He looked up at her with her head back, mouth open, and panting to catch her breath as her legs quivered in ecstasy. He tenderly caressed her inner thighs as he slowly moved up and positioned himself next to her. He wrapped his arms around her and pulled her in tight, "Pearl, I would like to do that again and again if you will let me."

She kissed him gently, smiled, and softly replied, "Yes." In complete peace, they fell back to sleep. If the phone hadn't rang, who knows what time they would have woken up.

Pearl answered the phone. It was her mother. Her first question was, "Good morning, my Pearl, is Adeem with you?"

"Well good morning to you too. Yes, he is, do you want to talk to him again?" she said sarcastically.

"Oh, you're funny. You know it's in my nature to make sure you're always OK, and you must admit, no one knew Adeem. Now we do. And yes, I want to talk to him." Pearl handed him the phone.

Adeem sat up, looked at her as she shrugged her shoulders saying, "I have no idea."

"Hello?"

"Adeem, this is Charlee. Listen, your father will be here soon, and Julia is here with me. You are on speaker phone. Adeem, at the chateau in Qatar there is a stream of water that flows through that property, right?"

"Yes, but Alex closed off the stream years ago. I am sure it is still viable though. Why?"

"Good. I need you and Pearl to meet us at the chateau on Sunday, three days from now, and I need that spring to be open and flowing. Can you make that happen?"

"Sure, I think. That spring runs in a very unusual arch. It runs very deep, like a tap root, then shoots straight up under the house then straight back down, parallel to the first leg of the water route. Does that make sense?"

"Yes. Is that a problem?" Charlee asked.

"Well, yes it is. It will require me to tear up the marble floor and I am sure Alex will not appreciate that. That marble came from Dimitri's family quarries. It is very special to the chateau and to this family." Adeem sat to the side of the bed and ran his fingers through his hair, moving it out of his eyes and continued, "Plus, there is an ancient myth surrounding that water. You might want to ask Alex about it. It was a long time ago when he sealed it up."

Charlee said, "Embellish me."

"Well, it is strange, really; the water reaches the surface in a spiral, actually three spirals. What I mean is, as it reaches the surface it separates into three separate wave forms or connecting spirals, like what you would see on ancient petroglyphs in the Americas. But the kicker is, whatever it meets, it heals. Qaseem used to make us drink it whenever we started to feel ill. After one glass, illness was averted. Qaseem drank it for years off and on through his many illnesses. He should have died 20 years before he did.

Charlee, this brings back an interesting memory from when I was a child. At one point Qaseem had the water tested. After it was tested, a woman showed up unannounced at the chateau and asked for a sample of it. I think I was six or seven. I could not take my eyes off her. She did not scare me, but I felt like I better listen to her. She looked down at me and said, 'I will not take no for an answer. Be a good boy and bring me to the water,' as she patted my head. I was home alone so I showed her the stream and gave her a large jar of it. But the interesting thing is, the woman did not have legs. She was standing in front of me, but with no legs. I kept looking for them, but they were just not there. It was as if she was floating. Is that not strange?" He laughed then quickly said, "We can keep that part of the story to ourselves. I have never told anyone that part of the story. Probably a six-year-old with a big imagination. Charlee, I do not know why I just told you that. This is a bit embarrassing."

Pearl immediately sat up and looked at Adeem in a panic. Adeem looked at her and gave her a pat on the leg like, *It's OK, nothing happened.*

Charlee probed, "What else do you remember about her, Adeem?"

"Well, she said the water was to remain in our care until otherwise notified. She told me I was very special and that someday this water would change my life. If I remember correctly, she said it would give life to the dead but needed a catalyst. I did not understand that word at the time and to be perfectly honest, I am not sure what she meant by that to this day. When Alex returned, I told him about this woman. He told me to keep it to myself. The next day he had the stream closed off, which was quite a feat to close off. It was as if the water was fighting to stay exposed. I have an engineer with sonar equipment, and I can try to get a hold of him. I cannot promise you anything at this short notice. Why the urgency?"

"We have the catalyst, Adeem. Listen carefully – we have three days until the next full moon, when the light of the evening is brightest and its energy stays one with the sun merging into day. This is the energy we need to create the perfect alchemy and release it. These next six days are crucial. Please get up, pack, and take the helicopter back to Athens. There is a jet waiting for the two of you. I will see you on Sunday with an exposed spring in the chateau. Make it happen."

Hesitantly he replied, "OK, I will. Can you tell me more about this?"

Charlee quickly explained why they were in Egypt, "There is a staircase 'to nowhere' as it is called in Abu Rawash. At the bottom of the staircase is a mythical river of spiraling waters. Depending on what Alex has uncovered, it is our understanding that we must combine the spiraling water from Abu Rawash with the spiraling water from your chateau. This is the reason I am asking you to expose the stream, so we can collect water from it. There's so much more to this story, but I don't have time to explain it all right now." She told Adeem about the hooded woman that showed up at Pearl's hotel room the night of the Silver Pharoah's unveiling. She said, "This woman, or whatever she is, gave Pearl a metal pot that was embedded in the body of the mummy that was unveiled at the conference Pearl attended. Alex has this pot and is translating the contents of the scrolls he found inside. Everything connects together." Then she abruptly hung up the phone.

Adeem looked at the phone, "Hello? Charlee?" With no answer, he hung up. "I guess we lost connection."

He looked over at Pearl who had gotten up and was frantically dressing and packing at the same time. Adeem leaned back in the bed and watched. "That was an interesting phone call, Pearl. What is going on here?"

Pearl sat on the foot of the bed, put her head in her hands then looked up and shook her whole body like a little kid would do getting into a cold pool. He smiled and crossed his arms and legs. Pearl said, "Meet me in the kitchen after you shave and dress. I have a lot to tell you." She left the bedroom, went to the kitchen, and put the dishes in hot water while she waited for Adeem. When he arrived, handsome as ever, she handed him a cup of coffee and motioned for him to sit down.

He did, took a sip of his coffee, and said, "OK, what is going on? Are you OK?"

She nodded and started from the beginning, "Nonnah has been researching and studying a certain subject for most of her adult life. Her mother, Sophia, used to tell her bedtime stories about a pharaoh that lived a long time ago. The story goes that in antiquity there was a pharaoh called The Silver Pharaoh. His sarcophagus was made of solid silver. No other pharaoh had ever been buried in this manner. The Egyptian government dated this pharaoh to have lived around the time of King Tutankhamun. What we have come to realize is that the Egyptian government will not budge on its flawed dating system because if they do, history will need to be rewritten. There is evidence that many of the structures on the Giza plateau are much older than they have been dated. Anyway, Sophia's stories said mythology dates this pharaoh to be over a million years older than the pyramids. He is not of this world and what he possesses is the secret to immortality. Literally the ability to stop aging in ANY carbon-based life form. This

Silver Pharaoh's sarcophagus has been hidden until recently. I guess when Sophia told Julia these bedtime stories, she also mentioned that a certain family would present itself to Julia in the future and *he* would need her help. I think *he* means Alexander."

Adeem looked at her and said, "And you think she was referring to my dad? I find this hard to believe."

Pearl nodded, "I know, but I – we – do not know of any other Alexander. The coincidence is mind blowing to say the least."

Adeem stood in silence as he tried to wrap his head around what she had just told him. Pearl let it sink in for a minute then Adeem said, "OK, who found the sarcophagus?"

"An archeologist found his tomb right before WWII then hid it, knowing it would be confiscated. It has been in hiding since 1939 and was found again recently. It was on display at the conference I was attending."

Adeem stopped her, "Why was Julia not at the conference if she has waited a lifetime to find this silver guy?"

"Well, that is the million-dollar question. I asked the same thing, but she did not answer me. She just said, 'Pearl, sometimes we know things that we do not know. I need you to do this for me.'" Pearl told Adeem the entire story then added, "But it was not until the woman in the hooded cloak without any legs showed up to my hotel room handing me a heavy metal pot that this got strange."

Adeem's eyes got big. Pearl looked at him with conviction and said, "Yes, Adeem, she came to me too. I believe your story. When Alex heard my story, he was in shock. It seems the series of synchronicities our families are experiencing together was planned a long time ago. I know that does not make sense, but each one of us is being told by these entities that we are 'the chosen'. First it was me. I was at the conference when the Silver Pharaoh's sarcophagus was opened.

Adeem, when the lid came off, I was dangling from a scaffolding directly above the sarcophagus to get the best view. The Pharaoh was alive! He had been in the box for who knows how long, but I am telling you he was alive. He telepathically said to me as our eyes met, *You are the chosen one, Pearl. Thank you. We will meet again when The Phoenix returns. Find Alexander,* then he turned into vapor and shot through my body, and up and out into the ether. Look at the back of my neck. This is what he left behind. He burned a phoenix into my neck. He said, 'We will meet again when The Phoenix returns.'"

Adeem looked at the mark on the back of her neck then just stared at her. Pearl continued, "Nonnah has been told she has been chosen, and Alex has been told he has been chosen. I assume Mom, Dad, and you are next. Here is a riddle – Alex called the hooded woman a Watcher."

"Holy shit!" Adeem stood and ran both hands through his hair as he looked up at the ceiling. "Where is the metal pot now, Pearl?" Adeem asked in a demanding tone.

"That is exactly what Alex said, 'Holy shit,' over and over again. He has the pot."

"Did you look inside of it?"

"Yes. It had four thin metal scrolls, a jar of white powder, and a piece of copper wire in it. There was something under the powder, but I did not see what it was. Alex unrolled each scroll and copied them then carefully replaced them in the metal pot to keep them safe. He says he can decipher three of them but will need help on the fourth one. After he replaced the scrolls, he frantically said he needed to get to Julia. Frankly, after that he was pretty much in his head, running around the house packing and mumbling."

"This is all very strange," Adeem said. "Charlee wants us up and out of here ASAP and headed back to Qatar to unearth the old stream that used to run through the chateau. She wants everyone there on Sunday."

"Is this the same chateau where Dimitri and Qaseem had their affair?"

"Yes, and it is where I live. It is my home now. It is a beautiful place, and the marble floors are exquisite. There is still a lot to tell your family about those marble floors. I would be shocked if Alex would be OK with me tearing them up."

Pearl said, "Alex told me about the quarries and Nonnah's inheritance. I also read about the chateau and its beauty in the journals. I look forward to seeing it. Do you think Alex knows about Mom wanting to expose the spring?"

He looked at Pearl and sat back down, "I am not sure."

"Well, he took off like a bat out of hell, so I am assuming they are in contact. At least I hope they are. What is the plan?" Pearl asked.

"We need to get to Qatar, but I need to make some phone calls first, like within the hour."

While Adeem was making his calls, the helicopter showed up. Yusef had a driver with him. Adeem met Yusef outside, gave him the keys to the car, and went back inside.

Pearl made them each a sandwich and refilled the coffee. She said, "Here – eat. Let's take a quick minute to fill up; I am not sure when we will get to eat again. Before we leave the island, I need to check in at the Sacred Rock Healing Center. We can land on top of the parking garage. You can continue with your phone calls while I pick up a few things."

Adeem replied, "That is a plan. We need to get out of here as soon as possible. It is my understanding that Julia, Charlee, and Mathias are in Abu Rawash, Egypt. They are at some ancient site in the middle of the desert that has a very interesting staircase to nowhere. Charlee said Mathias was given the coordinates in a dream. I guess this staircase was cut into the limestone and descends almost straight down hundreds of feet. At the bottom of this staircase – by the way, no one has any idea how old it is or who carved it – is a river. They say the water has a different molecular structure than any other water on the planet. What is interesting is that this water surfaces in a three-spiral pattern and has a frequency of 7 to 10hrtz. This is the frequency of healing. This is the same pattern and frequency of the water in the stream at the chateau. I took a minute to look it up before I shaved. Anyway, by putting the pieces together, I think the Abu Rawash water is comparable to the water under the chateau. Charlee wants me to unearth the spring under the chateau and have it exposed by the time they arrive on Sunday."

Chapter Eighteen

By the time Alexander touched down in Qatar he was exhausted. He had called the estate earlier and had his best Arabian horse, Trojan, waiting for him. With his head in a fog and a long journey still ahead of him, he needed the rush of Trojan's speed and the sea air to wake his senses before his next flight. He mounted Trojan, and for the next hour he rode him fast and hard through the fields, to the daring edge of the cliffs, and straight to the chateau. By the time he arrived, he and Trojan were both soaking wet with sweat. Alex felt invigorated. As he rode, he tried to figure out the puzzle of the white powder, copper wire, and spiraling water. There must be a formula that combines these things together to achieve this immortality concept. Mix the powder with water and charge it? Until the other three scrolls were translated, he would still be at a loss. He dismounted Trojan and met Clem at the doorstep. Alex was surprised to see him. Clem was the environmental engineer that had sealed off the stream in the sunroom years ago.

"Hello, Clem, nice to see you. What is up?"

Clem followed Alex inside and told him he had gotten a call from Adeem, asking him to uncap the water supply to the indoor stream. He said, "Adeem told me to be careful with the floor – if you tear it up, Alex will kill you. He said that to me." Clem started laughing then quickly changed his smile to a serious look and asked, "That is not true, right?"

Alex sat down, ignoring the question and said, "Clem, do you know anything about this water? Do you remember working with this spring back then?"

"Oh yes, I do! What is interesting about this water is that it exits the ground in a three-spiral pattern. It was the strangest thing I had ever seen, and to this day, I have never seen water act like that except here and in the stable arena at the estate. I assume it spirals in the house too?" Alex nodded so Clem continued, "Also, when I tested the water before I sealed the stream, it did not match any other water on the planet. Its molecular makeup is very unique. That always stayed with me. I did a little research at the time about this spiraling water pattern. It seems that all over the planet there are ancient spirals like this carved in stone. For the longest time, it was assumed that they represented or depicted the universe, but that is not so if you look at the ancient writings. The three spiral pattern represents water. I am assuming that it means water is here; water can be found in this spot. I do not know. But what I do know is that this particular three pattern spiral is found in very few places."

Alex sat listening while rubbing his chin as he contemplated Clem's words. "I have not talked to Adeem about this yet, but we are onto something here, and I think this is much bigger than us. Clem, whatever Adeem asked you to do, do it. Did he say anything else?"

"Yes, he said he would be here late this afternoon. I guess he is flying in from Greece with a young lady? Anyway, Alex, if you have a minute, I would like to walk around the sunroom with you and look at where I originally capped off the water. I might be able to tap into the water from the inside easier than from the outside. The spring supplying this water shoots straight up, curves, then plummets straight down, a very narrow arch shape. To expose the water from outside means I would need to dig a channel under the house to get to it. It would be a lot less invasive to expose it from the sunroom."

The men headed to the sunroom and walked on the path where the stream used to run. Clem had a long walking stick with a rubber stopper on the end, tapping the marble as he walked. When he heard a certain sound, he stopped. "Alex, I think I can carefully remove these six marble slabs and get to the spring from here. If I am very careful, I think I can do this without damaging the stones. I know how much this floor means to you."

Alex replied, "It is not so much what it means to me, but it meant a lot to Qaseem. So, I respect that." He gave his permission and left Clem on his own to do the work.

In a hurry, Alex jogged to the old library hidden within the giant maze behind the gardens of the chateau and shut the door. He used to spend hours here reading in solace. Qaseem had the secret library built years ago and stored some of the most valuable treasures there. Some of the rarest books in the world were hidden in this room.

Many times, Dimitri had hidden in this secret hideaway when the gossip became too much. Qaseem had the secret door built out of Australian Buloke, the hardest wood in the world. It was carved in a way so that ivy would grow on it, hiding its presence amongst the manicured shrubs that made up the elaborate maze. Through this door a staircase led down to a 1,200 square foot room. The room was windowless and dark with wall-to-wall shelves full of books from antiquity, many still not deciphered. Qaseem could never get enough history. He was fascinated by it. So much of it had been lost to thieves and natural disasters.

There was a bathroom concealed in the wall behind one of the bookshelves, a small sitting area with a large couch, matching chairs, and an antique desk, all sitting on a Persian rug that filled the center space. Candles and small, ornate lamps softly lit the room. It was a comfortable little hideaway filled with secrets hidden from the world. This is where Qaseem safeguarded his treasures and book collection. No one knew it was there, not even Adeem or the gardener.

Alex concentrated on the section comprised of old manuscripts. He searched the shelves until he found *The Book of The Fallen*. He had read this book many years ago and it fascinated him. Within the binding was an explanation of the language that was used by the ancient angels, or Nephilim, in the Bible. They used a frequency-based communication system that was in the 7-10 hrtz range, communicating with song. When they sang, their songs could be heard throughout the universe. Every living cell on the planet responded lovingly to it. It was said that this frequency kept the souls connected to the gods, the planet, and all its inhabitants. It is also said that humans went into a trance whenever the angels sang. During this trance, the cells reconfigured, realigned, and healed themselves. He needed to read this book again and find the connection.

By the time Alex had found the book and browsed through it, his helicopter had arrived to shuttle him back to the airport. He stopped in to check on Clem and let him know he was leaving. Clem had already removed the first gigantic slab. Alex was impressed; the slab was not harmed. By the looks of it, Clem was still confident he could keep the entire six slabs intact. Alex said his goodbyes, left Adeem a note on the table, and headed to the helicopter.

When Alex arrived in Athens, he exited the helicopter and quickly ran to the nearby tarmac where his jet was waiting. For the next four hours, without the help of his previous ghost, he translated the last three scrolls. When he was done, he was speechless. *What in the hell is going on, or rather, why me? Why us? How are we all connected? This cannot be random*, he thought. He put all the information into sequence and wrote it out so Julia would understand it.

The first scroll:
Vibration of the heavens, the song of transformation. The beginning. The awakening of memory. Restoration.

Second scroll:
The formula must be strict. Do not deviate from the formula. Restoration of balance of an imbalance. Death will no longer exist. Now is the beginning of truth, the veil will be lifted. The chosen will learn. The chosen are six. The chosen were chosen eons ago and this is fixed. Let no oils from hands beyond the chosen soil the alchemy.

Third scroll:
On the third day after the new moon, alchemy must begin. This is fixed. Combine the spiral waters from the abyss of Abu Rawash with the spiral waters of Dimitri's secret. Mix with the white gold of the gods. Place copper energy in liquid. Expose to the sun and the vibration of the angels.

Fourth scroll:
The alchemy will spin. First to the west, then to the east, then rise to the rim. This life-force will reverse death. The ends of 46 will be whole. This is fixed. The light in the cell will shine, repair, restore, and fulfill its purpose. The eye will see, the ear will hear, the heart will remember. All will be one with ALL. Feed the planet. The light will vibrate and expose its true identity. Keep safe this path to ALL.

When he was done, he closed his eyes and began to mentally prepare himself to meet Julia. He never would have guessed this was how he would meet her. Should he tell her about her inheritance from Qaseem first or should he tell her about the metal pot and the scrolls first? He decided to trust that whatever happened was meant to happen.

When he landed in Giza, he hoped Julia had a car waiting for him. He grabbed his carryon and headed to the front of the airport. Julia was waiting for him with a sign in her hand that said *Alexander* on it. He was taken aback by her beauty. She was wearing a snug pair of khaki cargo pants, a dark brown belt with a crisp white blouse, hiking boots, and turquoise beads around her neck and wrists, with her long chestnut hair pulled back in a ponytail. He chuckled, realizing they were wearing the same outfit, but his cargo pants were olive green, and he too had his hair pulled back in a ponytail. She wasn't wearing a stitch of makeup, yet she was beautiful. Swarming her were local taxi drivers gawking at her and pulling at her, begging to take her wherever she wanted to go. When Alex approached her, she grabbed his free hand, pulled him around, settled her hand into the crux of his arm, and pulled him forcefully to her awaiting car. When the locals saw the Emir, they quickly backed off, bowed to him, and left her alone.

When they got in the car, she turned to him, blew a curl of hair away from her face and said, "Hello, Alexander. I am Julia. Nice to meet you. Sorry about the abrupt approach, but I had been standing there for thirty minutes dealing with those foul men!" She stuck out her hand and addressed him with a pleasant handshake. She said, "I would love to sit and have coffee with you and spend some time getting to know one another, but frankly we do not have any time for that today. Though I am intrigued by your presence in Greece; I have been told it was me that you came to meet regarding Dimitri?"

Alex smiled and said, "First, it is a pleasure to meet you, and yes, this is true; we have a lot to talk about, Dimitri being part of the equation. But for some reason I feel that something much greater than us has a different idea on how this meeting is going to go, which is extremely foreign to me. I do not usually delve into the supernatural, but there is no other explanation for what has brought us all together."

Julia nodded as Alex spoke. When he was done, she put the keys in the ignition and quickly said, "Yes, Alexander, I am looking forward to having that conversation with you about Dimitri and whatever else is on your mind, but I just left my daughter in the middle of nowhere to find men to help us. And let me tell you, they all looked pretty shady, so please understand that my mind is fully concentrating on getting back to her. Mathias is with her, thank god! I am very thankful you are here. You speak the language, I am told?"

"Julia, I speak more than the language; there is not a soul in Giza that does not know me. Let's just say, it would not be wise if they hurt your daughter or her husband. She will be fine."

"Well, that is a comfort, Alexander, but to be safe we need to get going. By the way, I like your style." She pointed her finger and drew an invisible up and down line from Alex's head to his toes.

Alex chuckled and said, "Thank you, I like yours as well, Julia. And yes, we do have a lot to talk about. Please call me Alex."

She smiled, started the car, and like a bullet she darted out of the airport traffic jam with no qualms about hitting someone or something. Alex's smile turned to concern. He reached to put on his seat belt as he laughed out loud, "Whoa there, turbo! We have plenty of time!"

Julia turned, looked at him, and replied, "Oh, but we do not have plenty of time. We have but little time to get what we need and get back to Qatar, to the chateau."

Alex raised his eyebrows, "Well, I guess that explains why my floor is being excavated right now."

"Yes, it is my understanding that we need to combine the water from both sites in some sort of ritual. I assume you have figured out that part?" Alex started to speak when Julia hit a pothole, thrusting him forward and slamming his nose squarely onto the dashboard." She stomped her foot onto the brake pedal, coming to an abrupt stop. Again, Alex was thrust forward, this time jamming his elbow into the dashboard as he reached for his now bloody nose.

He yelled, "Julia, stop!"

Julia was mortified, "Oh my gosh, Alex! Are you OK?"

Alex reached forward, putting both hands on the dashboard and looked at her in a daze. He'd hit the bridge of his nose so hard it stunned him. He felt as if he was going to pass out. He slowly got out of the car, opened the back door, and took a T-shirt from his bag. Blood was dripping from his nose and down onto his white button-down shirt. He carefully put pressure on the bridge of his nose and leaned against the car. Julia didn't know what to do. His face skewed into a grimace as he felt the large knot forming.

Julia was out of the car next to him, apologizing profusely. She had him sit down to examine the soon-to-be black eyes.

When she reached for his arm to move it, Alex moaned in pain, "I think you broke my nose and my shoulder."

Seeing that he was OK, even with a bloody nose and sore shoulder, she started to laugh. She couldn't help it. He was like a little boy who just fell off his bike and was whining.

He looked up at her as she covered her mouth, trying not to laugh. "You think this is funny? Jeez, Julia, slow down!"

"No, I do not think it is funny, really I do not." she said as she tried to hide her smile.

"Well, you could have fooled me. I am in pain here, have some sympathy. And give me the keys – you have lost your driving privileges!"

She started laughing out loud, "Oh my god, you sound just like Daniel!"

"Yes, well I know all about Daniel. Obviously, he was a saint! No chewing gum for you, young lady!"

She put her hands on her hips and shook her head at him with the biggest smile he had ever seen. "You are right, he was a saint. And god, I miss him! So, are you too broken to push forward?"

"Really, that is all I get after you crippled me? You know this is going to turn into two black eyes. How will you explain that?"

She bent down and kissed him on the nose, "There all better. I will tell the truth – you were not paying attention. You were staring at me instead of looking at the road. You can see this road is riddled with potholes. And for your information, I might have hit one, but I missed a thousand!"

"You sound just like Pearl. The apple does not fall far from the tree, does it? Now hand over the keys."

She dropped the keys in his hand and helped him clean up the rest of the blood smeared all over the lower half of his face. When she was done, she said, "There, brand new." She was looking into his eyes and for the first time since Daniel's passing, she felt that feeling – that curious feeling that makes the heart take notice. She took a step back but continued staring at him. She had an overwhelming feeling she had met him before.

As she looked into his eyes, he noticed her expression change. He knew that look and he too felt something. Pearl's words came rushing to the forefront of his mind, *You will love her, everyone does.* He quickly stood up and said, "OK, so why the rush? Why are you in such a hurry?"

He took off his shirt and reached for another from his bag in the back seat. As he removed his shirt, his hair tie fell to the ground, releasing his hair. Standing before her was a gorgeous body. Not knowing his age but assuming he was at least seventeen years older than she according to the timeline Pearl gave her, she was amazed at how fit and sexy he was. He had the body of a man half his age. He was well over six feet tall and his muscles were very toned, as if he spent hours a day in the gym. There wasn't an ounce of fat on him. His full head of black hair, slightly streaked with silver stands, lay against his shoulders. His face was chiseled with a slight five o'clock shadow, and his nose, well, it was swollen so that was a distraction. She giggled as the thoughts ran through her head.

Alex watched her out of his peripheral vision. When she giggled, he turned and stood half naked in front of her. She couldn't help it – she looked him up and down and put her hand over her mouth again. He said, "So this is how it feels to be gawked at?"

Julia rolled her eyes and said sarcastically, "Yep – you look pretty good for your age."

Alex threw his dirty, bloody shirt at her and smiled back, "Thanks."

Collecting her thoughts she said, "We have about an hour's drive to Abu Rawash. As we speak, Charlee and Mathias are trying to find a guide to hire that will take us to the bottom of an ancient staircase. It leads to a spring or river, I am not really sure which. We need a large sample of water from it. So, do you think we can be there in an hour, mister, *I am in charge of the driving now?*"

This time he rolled his eyes at her as he settled into the car, readjusting the seat and rearview mirror.

"Put on your seatbelt or you will undoubtedly be my twin with the same pair of black and blue eyes." She put on her seatbelt and turned to him as he continued, "What is so interesting about this water and staircase?" he asked.

For the rest of the trip to Abu Rawash, Julia explained the dreams that she, Charlee, and Mathias had had. She began with the story about The Silver Pharaoh. Alex watched the road and her as she talked, barely taking a breath between sentences. He saw the passion in her that Pearl had talked about.

Julia spent half of her time watching the road and the other half connecting with Alex. "The important and most concerning issue right now is that we need to perform a ceremony of some sort with this water and whatever you have in the metal pot Pearl told me about. The kicker is that this ceremony needs to take place during the new moon cycle, which only gives us a couple days to gather what we need and return to the chateau before Sunday. Alex, I am not sure what this is all about, but what I do know is that it is important, I mean biblically important. What did you learn from the scrolls?"

It was Alex's time to shine. He navigated the potholes the best he could as he continued down the bumpy dirt road. His head was pounding in discomfort and his nose had swollen shut. He spent the next twenty minutes explaining everything that had transpired since he had met Pearl, ending with the translation of the scrolls, but leaving out the part about the flight attendant helping him during his flight. Julia asked him if he had any idea what this was all about. He shrugged his shoulders and shook his head. He said, "I have no idea. I came here to share Qaseem's will with you, but I am beginning to believe this is not the true purpose of our connection. Once we finish whatever this is, Julia, I do have another issue to discuss with you and it is big."

She nodded, "Yes, Pearl alluded to an inheritance from Dimitri. We can discuss that later if that is OK. For now, let's concentrate on collecting this water and getting back to Qatar."

Alex nodded and said, "I agree."

When they arrived in Abu Rawash, they truly were in the middle of nowhere. For as far as the eye could see was dry, loose sand, with no life anywhere. There were no trees, no bushes, not even a stump; just dusty, dry, yellow sand that was delicately picked up by the incremental passing breeze flowing like a river over the surface of the dry earth. In the very distant perimeter were dilapidated and crumbling ruins. Soon they would disappear back into the sands of time too. The heat coming off the sand was both blinding and scorching.

In the middle of nowhere waiting patiently were two guides along with Charlee and Mathias. The guides were talking under their breath, smiling as they stared at Charlee. When Alex saw her, he too found himself staring. Pearl was the spitting image of her mother. There was no doubt that Pearl was her daughter. Charlee ran over to the car and as Julia got out, she said, "You will not believe this; to hire these two imbeciles I had to raise my shirt, exposing my breasts to them before they would agree to help. Mathias is livid. I am afraid if he is in the presence of these men for too much longer, they are not coming out of that hole alive!" She turned to Alex, "Hello. You must be Alexander. Nice to meet you. I am Charlee and that is my husband, Mathias," she said, pointing in the direction of Mathias. She looked back at Alex, "Jeez, what happened to your nose?"

Julia smiled at Alex, shrugged her shoulders then took Charlee's hand as she helped her out of the car. Julia hugged Charlee and said, "Are you kidding me? I am so sorry you had to do that, honey. Let's just get this done and get out of here. Did they bring a container for us?"

"Yes, they brought a five-gallon bucket and some strange device in a box they claimed we needed to excite the water."

Alex touched Julia's arm, "This is making more sense now. I will explain later. Let's go. Oh, and by the way, Charlee, your mother-in-law's fantastic driving skills rearranged my face. I am sure it is only going to get prettier." He then turned to Julia and gave her a sarcastic smile. Julia rolled her eyes at him.

Charlee looked at them both, smiled, threw her hands in the air, and said, "Finally!" as she walked toward Mathias. When she reached him, she said, "Do you see what I see?"

Mathias nodded with a huge grin, "I do, my love, I do, and they are in so much trouble when they figure it out."

Charlee reached up and kissed him, then rested her head on his chest and said, "Mathias, I love you." He returned her words and hugged her deeply. When they turned around, Julia and Alex were standing next to them. Mathias and Alex shook hands and introduced themselves then Alex abruptly said, "Excuse me for a moment," and turned. With anger in his eyes, he walked over to the two guides. His paternal instincts had kicked in. It wasn't but a second later that the guides fell to the ground bowing and mumbled profusely in Arabic.

When the conversation was over, both guides approached Charlee and apologized for their behavior. Charlee, disgusted, spit at their feet. Mathias walked up to them boldly, expanding his chest with his hands in a fist. Both men dropped the box they were hold-ing and ran away.

Mathias turned to Charlee as she stood and watched the scene unfold. When he reached for her, he held her tight and kissed her gently, "Babe, that will never happen again. Being alone out here with them, I did not know what to think. Exposing your breasts to them or them possibly taking you from me raced through my mind. I am so sorry, my love."

She hugged him tight and said, "I was as frightened as you were. It's OK now, it's OK." He gently caressed her face and kissed her on the forehead while holding her tight. Julia looked at Alex and mouthed *thank you* to him. When the moment passed, they all looked down at the box Alex was holding, the box the guides dropped before running away. Inside the box was a large cylinder glass tube with a filament in the center. On one end of the very fragile glass cylinder was a hole that a copper wire could fit into snuggly.

Alex said, "While they were face down in the sand, the men explained that they were given this box to give to you, Julia. The amount of energy produced by the heating filament in the middle of this cylinder is the amount of energy the water needs to be exposed to. When asked who gave them the box, they pointed at a woman behind them, standing in the distance. I looked to see what the guides were pointing at. It was she, the hooded woman without legs. I look-ed back at each of the men then back toward her, but she was gone."

Before anyone could say anything, Alex motioned to the hole in the ground, "We should go."

Chapter Nineteen

The staircase to nowhere was an elongated hole, flush with the earth. If you didn't know it was there, one could walk into it and disappear. Mathias dropped a stone into the hole and at about the four second mark, they heard the stone hit the bottom. Alex said it was roughly two stories deep by the distance the stone dropped. The width of the opening was about three feet so they would need to descend single file. The sun reached approximately ten feet down before it became pitch black.

They carefully made each step down the staircase into the darkness. Alex went first, hoping no one was claustrophobic and that nothing was at the bottom that might want to eat them for dinner or, worse yet, torture them and ask for a ransom then eat them. He knew he could fetch a pretty penny, but the poor soul who might have thought this would be a good idea would find himself hanging in the town square. Alex cleared his mind of these thoughts, stopped, and looked back to make sure everyone was still following him. No one said a word. The tension descending with them on the long, dusty staircase was palpable. When it became too dark to see, they pulled out their cell phones, turned on the flashlight app, and continued down.

As they reached the halfway mark a few feet past the darkness, the tunnel opened into a massive cavern. Alex couldn't see the entirety of the cavern, but what he could see looked to be about the size of a professional football stadium. The reflection from the flashlights bouncing off the walls and ceiling made the cavity look like it was made of crystals. When Julia took a closer look, she realized it wasn't crystals illuminating the cavern like she had assumed, it was total vitrification. The ceiling and walls surrounding the entire cavern were glass and as smooth as silk. They acted like a mirror, reflecting the lights from their cell phones back out into the enormous cavity.

They stopped and brushed their hands along the walls, amazed at what they were witnessing. As their fingers met the stone, the walls burst into life, creating welcoming colors of light that resembled fireflies in a dark meadow. The colors danced on the walls, on the staircase, and on them, filling the room with sparkles like a rotating disco ball. The lights illuminated the path down to the underground river. They could hear the movement of water flowing through the river in the distance.

As they continued to make their way down the staircase, the air became alive, gently swirling around them; there wasn't a breeze, yet it was alive. It was crisp and clean, filling their lungs with energy, as a sense of love surrounded them. The feeling was overwhelming. Each of them, at the same time, took a breath as the tears started flowing.

Alex wept as he looked back and witnessed the surge of emotions each were experiencing. Mystified and unable to speak, they sat down and watched the colors dance around them until they regain-ed their composure. When the feelings subsided, they joined hands as if saying, *we are in this together* before continuing down the staircase.

When they got to the bottom of the stairs, they could see the river in the distance. When they reached the water, it was spiraling like thousands of tiny vortices. Alex said, "I have seen this only twice before; from the spring under the chateau and in the pools of water on the estate. The water swirls like this in my bathtub and in the horse arena pools. I have always thought it was just a coincidence."

Julia and Charlee said at the same time, "*That* is why we are going to the chateau." They each bent down and put their hands into the cool, gently flowing water. As they did, the water crawled up their wrists and danced around as if it were alive, rubbing itself on them like a purring cat. The water welcomed them and slightly tug-ged at each of them to enter. The sensation was friendly and inviting. They looked at one another, wondering if they should enter the water. Something intrinsically told them that it was OK, no harm would come. Julia went in first and when she reached the center of the river where the water reached her shoulders, she began crying as if being cleansed by God.

Charlee cried out, "Mom! Are you OK? Get out!"

Julia said, "No, my darling, come to me. Feel what I am feeling. It is beautiful. Come here."

They each followed, and when Alex entered, he knew what to do. He lowered himself until his bruised and swollen face was completely submerged. He could feel the water healing his nose and shoulder as the pain disappeared. He stayed under for as long as he could. If he could have taken a breath under the water, he would have. When he surfaced, he looked at Julia. She smiled, with tears flowing down her cheeks. She reached for him and sank into his arms and together they sobbed.

Charlee and Mathias were doing the same. When the tears stopped, they each lay back into the water and floated, fully releasing their trust to the river, which supported them in place. With their eyes closed and ears submerged, they listened to the melodic music coming from the water as it gently spiraled around them. The notes were peaceful and gentle, like love in motion. The water rubbed against their bodies, loving it as if it had hands, slowly caressing every inch. They could feel their insides tingling. Every cell in their bodies were alive, talking, conversing with the water, healing them and laughing as though they were playing like children. The dancing lights of the cavern surrounding them lit up the water as if asking to play too. They were completely engulfed in love.

When they had fully released their trust to the river, it spoke to them, "Welcome, I am Psusennes, I am the water. And I am Priya, I am the light," two gentle voices spoke. "We have been waiting for you. Your true mission in this incarnation has now begun. We have been with you always, through all your lifetimes. Together we are ALL and we live within you and through you. It is time to usher in a new paradigm. It is time to fulfill your destiny, to end the cycle of reincarnation. It is time for souls to live in harmony with one another on Mother Earth. You were chosen to fulfill this prophecy and you each accepted this task before you eons ago. It is time for you to remember. The Watchers will be with you and will guide you through this journey from this moment forward. Trust them. You are safe. We thank you. We love you."

They had no idea how long they had been effortlessly floating in place in the river. It was as if they had been hypnotized into a trance state, listening to the most beautiful voices they had ever heard. When the voices finished, they woke up to find themselves in the sunroom of the chateau in Qatar.

Chapter Twenty

When Adeem and Pearl arrived at the chateau, Pearl was in awe of the beauty surrounding her. Dimitri's description didn't do it justice. It was the most exotic and lovely place she had ever seen. She walked around and smelled the flowers as she touched every plant she passed, connecting spiritually to each one. She had never before seen so much life and so much color in one place. She thought, *If there is a heaven, this is what it must look like.* It was spectacular.

Adeem smiled as he watched her delicately cup the flowers in her hand and talk to them as if they had ears. He saw in her what he saw surrounding the chateau; love, color, life, and beauty. *Could she see herself living here?* he wondered. It was a hope he was keeping close. When they entered through the front door into the sunroom, they were immediately drawn to the exposed spring.

Pearl quickly scanned the room, the ceiling, and the indoor gardens as she slowly walked to the stream. The chateau was just as beautiful inside as it was outside. Adeem smiled down at her and took her hand as they stood at the water's edge and watched the spirals dancing on the surface.

Without talking, they instinctively removed their clothes and got in. They experienced the same profound love as the others did within the sacred river at Abu Rawash. Even though they were separated by miles of land, they were all together in an energy field that held them as if they were in the same place, sharing the same space, together as one, with ALL, while listening to the same two voices speaking to them. They held hands as they floated in the caressing water, listening to the spring's music playing in their ears. They fell into a trance state as they listened to Psusennes and Priya's loving words. When they were done speaking, Adeem and Pearl woke up and stepped out of the water in a daze to see Alex, Julia, Charlee, and Mathias looking at them with blank expressions.

They all stood staring at the stream as it settled down into gentle, peaceful spirals again.

Julia was the first to move. She handed Pearl and Adeem a couple of throw blankets to cover their naked bodies. No one spoke as they embraced and held each other in a tight circle, silently weeping tears of love, their minds trying to make sense of where they were, how they got there, and how much time had elapsed. As they stood in silence, rays of warm light beamed in from the tall windows and engulfed them with palpable energy. They were transfixed by it, and instinctively stepped back and held hands in a circle around the open spring, captivated by its spiraling action. As if in a dream, they stood staring and waiting for what they didn't know.

Suddenly, the woman in the hooded cloak without a lower body appeared in the center of the circle, hovering over the water. Alex had referred to her as a Watcher. Was she an illusion? An apparition? Her head was tipped down, hiding her eyes from them.

She shimmered, almost ethereal, as if you could put your hand through her. At that moment the rays of sun from the window began swirling around them, all-encompassing like a tornado, yet nothing in the room moved. They were transfixed by the woman's facial features which were delicate and transparent, almost opalescent, like a rainbow moonstone. Her hair was long and white, each strand glistening in the sun's rays. She slowly raised her eyes to them. They shone like brilliant emeralds with a million suns behind them. The center of the circle was bathed in a brilliant green. They couldn't release their hands; they were glued together, hypnotized before her.

She slowly rotated, gazing deeply into each pair of eyes and connecting telepathically as she moved. When she had completed the circle, as if in a trance Pearl, Alex, Adeem, Julia, Charlee, and Mathias closed their eyes, arched their heads back, and listened. In a sweet, breathy voice she spoke, "You are the chosen. You were chosen eons ago. A contract was created for each of you with The ALL. This contract was to return the *knowing of* the ALL, and the *connection to* the ALL, back to the souls within this universe. The ALL was curious and desired to experience emotions and did so through the human senses. The ALL lives consciously within and through every living organism in this universe. Everything in this universe is alive within The ALL.

The ALL has completed the journey of curiosity, and the desire to experience the senses is complete. It is time to restore order to the field of possibility. Within order there is cohesion, the return of scattered particles back to source. Together you are the source; you are The ALL. But you were asleep. This was deliberate, intentional by The ALL so it could experience without distraction, through you. The ALL is returning the gift as unconditional love which is what The ALL is. Everything that has been created will now know love in its purest form. There will no longer be sickness, sorrow, pain, loneliness, hatred, revenge, anger, strife, war. The universe and everything in it will grow and experience unity and cohesion through love.

Love is found in light. Your light is located in the photon at the core of each living cell. This light carries the memory of The ALL. It was programmed to vibrate at a lower frequency, creating amnesia of The ALL. The sacred water or plasma and blood of the human body holds the memory of The ALL. It too was programmed to vibrate at a lower frequency, creating a finite existence – mortality. Both the light and the blood will now vibrate at the same higher frequency. Only then can the channels open to the lost connection. This frequency matches the songs of the angels. This pairing will lift the amnesia, turning the off-switch back into the 'on' position. This higher vibration will create perfect harmony and connection to every cell in the universe. Immortality.

The sacred metal pot that I gave you, Pearl, contains a combination of Mana and Ormus. Together they give and sustain life. Together they expand the mind and open the channels in every cell in the body, the channels to the higher self which is known as The ALL. Combine them with the sacred spiraling waters from Abu Rawash and the waters spiraling before you. These two waters together contain the memories of this universe throughout time. Sing the musical notes within the first scroll as you combine the two with the electrical current. This alchemy will merge the memories in the waters with the memories in the cells through a coherent vibration. When ingested, this alchemy will open the cell wall and awaken the photon. The combination of sacred waters of Gaia with the sacred waters of the body, fed with Mana and Ormus, will stimulate the light within the cell. This will then restore the telomeres on the ends of the forty-six chromosomes within your DNA and stimulate the pineal gland at the same time. Memory will be restored and the amnesia will be lifted. The combination will create a vibration that will unite in perfect harmony with The ALL. You will once again remember unconditional love and enjoy eternal life. Every living cell will stop aging and begin learning to cohabitate lovingly with self and nature. This is your purpose in this lifetime.

Within Sophia's locked journal are the instructions to the alchemy, as well as the earthly coordinates where the elixir is to be placed. You will drop the elixir into several bodies of water around the planet. Mother Gaia will, by evaporation and tears, seed the skies, the soil, the oceans, and the ground water. The air, the soil, the water, and all of nature will be healed. All living organisms will heal through consuming the food, breathing the air, and absorbing the water that was changed and made new. A higher frequency will permeate the planet and extend out through the universe. The universe is ready, the time is now, and you are the chosen ones. Your cellular structure is now one with The ALL. When this circle is closed, you will have the ability to astral travel with your bodies. This is how you will seed the planet. You will complete your contract by the next new moon. I will be with you until your contract is complete. This transformation and rebirth will happen to all living vibrations within the universe. It will take two years to complete the process once the waters are seeded. The frequency and vibrational changes will be subtle and gentle to all living organisms.

The ALL is within you. The ALL will guide you. Your meal has been prepared, so eat. We are grateful to you for fulfilling your destiny, and we will protect you in the days to come. Your rings will protect you.

Julia, we ask you to trust thyself. Alex, within two weeks the global financial institutions will fail. All assets will disappear within the corporate banking system, and all corporate communications will cease. Your system operates on a monetary venue and will continue to do so. Transfer all your assets out of the international banking

system immediately. The Council of Seven will help you when
the time is right. Both your and Adeem's assets will be needed for
what is to come. Now, open Sophia's journal for further instructions."
And she was gone.

They slowly opened their eyes and dropped to their knees
with heavy breaths. Alex was the first to rise. Still stunned, he went
to the kitchen. He left the others alone until they were ready to join
him. On the dining room table was a variety of cooked vegetables,
fruits, and grains. He stared at it. His mind was quiet; it had no
thoughts. He put his head in his hands and sat there in disbelief.

Slowly, Julia, Mathias, Charlee, Pearl, and Adeem joined
him. No one said a word. In silence, they slowly began to eat from
the banquet of food as they were told. With each bite, they began to
feel more awake and aware of their surroundings and each other.

Julia spoke first, "Where is the metal pot?" Alex got up and
retrieved the pot from his luggage. It was sitting next to the door in
the sunroom alongside the box containing the glass tube and the five-
gallon jug of spiraling water from Abu Rawash. He placed it on the
dining table along with his notepad with the translations inscribed
on it.

The first scroll:
Vibration of the heavens, the song of transformation. The beginning.
The awakening of memory. Restoration.

Second scroll:
The formula must be strict. Do not deviate from the formula.
Restoration of balance of an imbalance. Death will no longer exist.
Now is the beginning of truth, the veil will be lifted. The chosen will
learn. The chosen are six. The chosen were chosen eons ago and this is
fixed. Let no oils from hands beyond the chosen soil the alchemy.

Third scroll:
On the third day after the new moon, the alchemy must begin. This is
fixed. Combine the spiral waters from the abyss of Abu Rawash with
the spiral waters of Dimitri's secret. Mix with the white gold of the

gods. Place copper energy in liquid. Expose to the sun and the vibration of the angels.

Fourth scroll:
The alchemy will spin. First to the west, then to the east, then rise to the rim. This life-force will reverse death. The ends of 46 will be whole. This is fixed. The light in the cell will shine, repair, restore, and fulfill its purpose. The eye will see, the ear will hear, the heart will remember. All will be one with ALL. Feed the planet. The light will vibrate and expose its true identity. Keep safe this path to The ALL.

Alex opened the metal pot and pushed it toward Julia. Julia took the metal pot into the sunroom and placed it on a round table in front of the large windows flooded with sunlight. She removed the scrolls and placed them methodically around the pot, facing the four cardinal directions: north, south, east, and west. She placed them six inches from the pot that sat in the middle, resembling the sun with rays bursting from it. She removed the jar of powder, and underneath were six thin gold rings sitting on a parchment along with two clear crystals. She placed the two crystals above and below the north and south scrolls. She put the six rings on the table and each ring moved effortlessly by an invisible hand toward its owner.

They each put on their rings; the only finger that would accept it was the wedding finger, and when they did, a surge of energy ran through them from the base of their coccyx to the crown of their heads, putting them into a trance state. They intuitively stood and held hands in a circle as they had around the spiraling spring earlier. When their hands connected, a bolt of energy surged through them from ring to ring and the hooded woman appeared in the center of the circle, again floating and rotating slowly, connecting with each pair of eyes as she did before.

In her breathy, sweet voice she said, "On the parchment are six coordinates. These are the coordinates where you will place the water around the planet. You each know what to do, and when you are done with the alchemy process, each will take a glass jar and fill it with the healing waters. When you have emptied the water from your jars into the oceans of the planet, stand and repeat, 'And it is done'. We thank you and we are grateful. We will be with you always." Again, she was gone.

They dropped hands and looked down at the rings that were glowing on their fingers. Julia left the circle and returned to the dining room table. Sitting at the end of the table were six glass jars that would each hold three quarts of water. They each knew what to do. Julia got the jar of Ormus and Mana and sat next to the spring in the middle of the sunroom.

Alex retrieved the box with the glass tube and placed the copper wire in the hole at the end. He took the tube to the table, set it next to the metal pot, and placed the end of the copper tube into the pot. He then sat next to Julia. Julia open Sophia's journal and read the instructions out loud carefully.

Mathias brought the five-gallon jug of water from Abu Rawash to Julia and sat next to her. Adeem took the scroll with the musical notes on it and sang the song out loud for the others to hear and imitate. Pearl placed the six jars next to Julia and sat next to Adeem. Charlee wrote each coordinate from Sophia's journal onto small pieces of paper and placed them at the end of the scrolls and crystals around the metal pot on the table then sat next to the spring with the others.

When they were all in front of the spring, Mathias poured the water from Abu Rawash into the spiraling water of the chateau as Julia poured in the Ormus and Mana. Together they sang the notes from the scroll. The water began to glow and gyrate, spinning faster and faster while rising in the center then pouring over like a fountain. They each took a jar and filled it with water from the fountain and returned to the round table. Following Sophia's instructions, they simultaneously poured a small amount of water from each jar into the metal pot then placed the jars on top of the coordinates. They held hands and began to sing the notes again, over and over. The filament began to shine brighter and brighter until the water in the metal pot spun and rose like the water in the spring. As it rose, it grew six long fingers of water that reached out to each of the six jars and added a small amount into them from the pot until it was empty. The water in the jars began to spin faster and faster. The sun became dark and the water in the spring and jars glowed as if the sun had set inside them. They held hands and continued to sing as the energy surged through the rings, through their arms, and up through their heads, followed by a loud flash-bang. A split second later, they were gone. The sun returned, shining through the window, the waters settled, and the room became still. The table was now empty. The chosen had disappeared.

Chapter Twenty-One

At midnight, the floor in the chateau over the spring began to heal itself. Each slab of cherry marble tile replaced itself back into its original space, sealing off the spring and repairing the hole. At dawn, a flash-bang once again rang throughout the sunroom where Julia, Pearl, Charlee, Alex, Adeem, and Mathias reappeared in a circle holding hands, with rings and bodies glowing. They remained in this position in a trance until the rings dimmed and the sun's first morning rays peeked through the windows and shone onto them. When they opened their eyes, they looked at each other, stunned, tired yet younger in appearance. Alex and Julia didn't look a day over thirty-five, and Charlee and Mathias looked as they did on the day they first met at the rock wall below Agriolykos twenty-four years earlier. Adeem and Pearl were radiant. Their eyes were bluer, their skin flawless, and their hair longer.

They released their hands and took huge cleansing breath. With each breath their minds cleared. They began to move, taking a few steps backward, away from the circle. Their bodies radiated, full of pulsating energy. When the light died down, they all started talking at once, touching each other as if trying to find out where the years of age had gone. Next to the fireplace was a large mirror. Each took turns staring into it, shocked at what they were seeing.

Adeem looked at Alex and said, "Wow, Dad, you look great. You look like me!"

Alex chuckled, "Thanks, son."

"No, you know what I mean, I look like you, or you look like me... Oh jeez, you look great. How do you feel?"

"I feel great!" Alex moved his body around, trying to see if that sore, stiff back was still present – it wasn't.

Julia just stared at him then back at her own reflection while shaking her head, "This is unbelievable!" They spent the next few minutes staring at each other, trying to wrap their heads around what they were seeing. Julia said, "I am not sure about you, but what I just did was unbelievable." She wanted to share her story first. "Let me tell you what happened to me."

As they sat to listen, they noticed there were six glasses of water sitting in front of them with a note that said, 'Drink'. When they drank the water, their eyes glowed for a split second and the clarity of what they had just accomplished was profound.

Julia began, "I found myself in the Azores in the Atlantic, standing on a rock platform on the edge of the ocean, alone with my jar of water. There was not a soul in sight. I intrinsically knew what to do. I carefully submerged the jar into the salty ocean and watched the swirling spirals exit their confinement. As the two waters merged, that from my jar as well as the ocean before me, I swear every form of sea life appeared in my mind's eye. I could not see them, but I could hear them. The message was of gratefulness and love. As I bent over the water, the feelings I was experiencing were so intense that I began to cry, and a tear dropped into the water. From this tear the water became illuminous, like millions of diamonds all sparkling at once. Then the ocean became so clear that I could see through it like a glass of water. I stood and said, 'And it is done', then I was back in the sunroom."

As Julia told her story, they each nodded their heads as if in agreement that her story was the same for them. Pearl posed the question, "Where did the coordinates take each of you? Mine took me to the island of Hilo in the middle of the Pacific Ocean."

Alex's coordinates took him to The Ile Saint-Paul in the Indian Ocean. Mathias's coordinates took him to Iquitos on the Amazon River in South America. Adeem's coordinates took him to the New Siberian Island in the Artic Ocean.

When it was Charlee's turn, she lowered her eyes and spoke, "I went to the Antarctic Ocean. At first, I didn't feel the cold of the Antarctic, but when I stood and looked around, I found myself completely alone. The cold began to overtake me and I panicked. I almost dropped the jar of water on the rocks. At that very moment, the hooded woman was standing next to me. She took my hand, which filled me with warmth, and helped me to the water's edge.

Together we placed the water from my jar into the ocean and to-gether our tears dropped into the spiraling water. We too saw the water clear and heard the sea life thanking us. It was so surreal. The hooded woman then turned to me and took my hands. She told me to close my eyes, and when I did, she introduced me to my biological parents in my mind's eye. My parents explained why they gave me up for adoption. It was because of all of you and my connection to this destiny. It was a beautiful and cathartic moment. As soon as that deep-seeded emotion of abandonment left my soul, the hooded woman was gone and I was once again freezing cold.

Through the wind she said, 'Speak your words' and I said, 'and so be it' and here I am." As the smile returned to Charlee's face she said, "I am so glad we are all back here together where it is warm." She looked at Mathias and said, "Babe, I have no desire to return to James Ross Island in the Antarctic Ocean."

They all laughed as Mathias stood up, went to her and held out his hands, raising her from her chair and hugging her deeply, "Oh, my love, I will warm you tonight, do not worry," and kissed her tenderly.

As they shared their experiences, delicious aromas permeated from the kitchen. Mathias walked Charlee to the dining table, pull-ed his chair closer to hers, and helped her fill her plate from the hot meal that was waiting for them. The table was covered in a banquet of dishes they had never seen. Famished and thirsty, they enjoyed the variety of foods in silence, each in deep thought about where this journey had taken them and grateful for the love they shared, knowing they were the chosen ones, chosen to change the world back into a beautiful paradise. But the big questions in their minds were, *What now? How is all this going to play out?*

Chapter Twenty-Two

After the meal was done, the women retreated to their rooms and took long hot showers while the men gathered back in the sunroom. Alex built a nice fire in the floor-to-ceiling stone fireplace. They each found a cozy chair, sank into it, and stared deeply into the dancing flames. The reality of what they had done was weighing on their minds. They had changed the world with six jars of a highly volatile water. What if they had just destroyed humanity? What if the water poisoned the oceans? And they did this because an apparition told them to? Why? No one had questioned her. What if they had made a huge mistake? Nothing made sense. Neither family knew of each other a few days ago, yet there was an undeniable trust between them. The one thing they did understand was that they were now a bonded unit that must stay together and share the consequences of their actions. The thought of separating and going back to life as usual was now out of the question.

Adeem spoke first, "Mathias, this experience leads me to believe that we are connected for life, yet I do not know much about you. Would you care to share your story with me then I will do the same?"

Mathias smiled and continued to stare into the fire as he listened to the question. He put his fingertips together in front of him and rested his elbows on the armchair. He glanced over at Adeem then back to the fire, "Adeem, my life before Charlee was typical. I worked very hard alongside my father, Daniel, excavating, building, and repairing dilapidated ruins throughout Greece and the islands. I started working with my father seriously at twelve years old. He also taught me English, mathematics, business, and to appreciate women. He loved my mother Julia desperately, everyone does. She is a woman to fall in love with."

Alex was staring into the fire as Mathias reminisced, and when he heard this, he smiled and let out a chuckle. "Funny, Pearl said the same thing. She said, 'You will love her, everybody does.'"

Mathias acknowledged Alex with a return smile and continued, "It is amazing how wonderful my mother is. She is tough but soft. She is passionate yet playful. She is tenacious yet cautious. She loves deeply and gives generously. I used to dream that if I could ever find a woman even remotely like Julia, I would marry her. I was twenty-three when I felt her – Charlee. I literally felt her before I saw her. I knew the moment I heard her voice behind me that she was the one. I had spent my whole life working and studying. Relationships were not my thing. I was raised to be a successful man, one who could provide for his family no matter what the circumstances were. So, I had no clue about women except through my sister, Melena. She too is a wonderful woman." Mathias looked over at Alex and said, "You will love her too. She lives with a broken heart but has the gentlest soul."

Alex smiled then returned his gaze to the fire as Mathias continued, "I remember the day Charlee showed up in Therma; fearless and so full of life. I immediately felt her energy pulsating with unimaginable possibilities. It was so overwhelming. I could not speak or move. I was paralyzed on a twenty-foot scaffold with my father next to me. I think if he had not been there, I would have fallen off. It was Melena, who my mother called for backup, that prepared me to meet Charlee properly for the first time." The men chuckled at this.

Mathias said, "No, I am serious, she actually flew over to Therma from Athens on a quick jump-over just to help me dress for the occasion. I guess it worked because Charlee and I have been inseparable since. She is an amazing woman. There is something about her that makes me want to be better, you know?" He turned and looked at Adeem.

Adeem said with a big smile, "Mathias, I get it. I do! I fell in love with Pearl the first time our eyes met. I do not think she felt the same way, but I was hoping. She has given me grief and she has challenged me to the core – to the point that at times I think my head is going to explode. And she has shown me more love and tenderness than any woman has ever given me. In such a short time she has me walking two feet in one shoe, and I love it."

Mathias smiled and said, "These women are very special to me. I hope you both realize this. I see in their eyes, especially my daughter, that there is potential here. The way they love rests deep in the core of a man's being. My father loved Julia from the moment he met her on his first day of kindergarten and his love never faltered from that moment forward. Now theirs is a story you should hear."

Alex smiled as he remembered her story in the journal, but he stayed silent.

Mathias continued, "The day we had Pearl, ummmm, that day changed me forever. She is the joy that makes me want to live. Charlee and I have had a great life. We spent the first years of our marriage building The Sacred Rock Healing Center. It is our second baby, the jewel of the whole family. These days, we spend most of our time in The Center, enjoying the people who come from all over the world, all looking for healing.

It is actually Charlee's baby. She saw that old ruin of a hotel and became obsessed with it. She has a connection to it that is indescribable, and what she has made of it is truly incredible. She changed the lives of the people of Therma, giving a share of the business to each family. They all built it with her, and it is considered one of the best healing centers on the planet. Julia, Charlee, and Pearl truly have the gift of healing. They have saved many lives with their talents. You will have to stop in – the food is great too!" He laughed as he adjusted himself in his chair.

"To answer your question, Adeem, I am just a skilled mason, by way of my father, who gives his wife and daughter whatever they want. I spent many years in the beginning traveling and building my career to support them in their endeavors. Now I support their dreams and fix whatever breaks. I am now the handyman. And I am wonderfully grateful for that.

Adeem, I can see that you love my daughter. Are you prepared to be taken to the ends of the earth and back, experiencing every emotion known to man and love her no matter what? Because it takes a strong man to love the women in this family. You do not get to love just one, you must love them all. They are a package."

Adeem said, "Mathias, I respect you and after what we have been through, whatever this was or is going to be, I am all in. Now that is not to say I will not come to you for help when I am in the doghouse! I hope your door is always open, yes?"

Mathias replied, "Always – and that is a promise!" as he reached over and shook Adeem's hand then looked at Alex. It was hard not to stare at him. He was so young looking, so different than he was hours ago. Alex was in deep thought, staring at the flames, not participating in the latter part of the conversation. Mathias said, "Hey, man, you in there?"

Adeem smacked him on his arm and Alex jumped as if someone had just slammed a door. "Yeah, what?" Both men laughed out loud. "Sorry, I was in my head."

"We can see that!" laughed Adeem. "What is up?"

"I was thinking about how to start the conversation with Julia about Dimitri's inheritance. And to be perfectly honest, the ladies' strong connection to the healing center concerns me. I assume neither Pearl nor Julia would want to leave Therma?"

Adeem sat up, looked at Alex then at Mathias. This was a question he had been contemplating for the past few days. Mathias cocked his head and raised his eyebrows saying, "No, they would not. If you want to be a part of their lives, it will most likely need to be shared on Ikaria. I am sure they would not have a problem visiting Qatar if that is what you are implying, but moving to Qatar – it would have to be for a very special reason and not just about falling in love. They have been approached before about moving. Many potential investors have offered them extremely great deals. They do not even take a minute to think about it. The answer has always been no, and they have never regretted their answers. After what we just went through, I have a feeling a whole new project is in store for them. Julia is going to research the heck out of this. Her research lab is in Therma, and she is going to need it more now than ever. Within the next two years, total healing of the planet will occur and immortality of the human race sets in? Have you even thought about what all this means? This is big, much bigger than whatever the heck it was we just went through. Julia's research lab is in

Therma and she will most likely be in that lab for months trying to figure out all this."

Adeem let out a huge sigh and slumped back in his chair as he stroked his hair back with both hands. He started tapping his foot like a little boy in trouble at school.

Mathias smiled, "Gentlemen, you have a situation here, do you not?"

Alex looked at Mathias, "I have a royal position in Qatar that requires me to live in my own country. Being away these past few days is about all I can give up. I guess I underestimated the situation. It was presumptuous of me to think she would even consider leaving Ikaria. We do not even know each other, but after all this, I do not believe I could choose any other woman to be by my side. I have a lot to think about. So, if Julia had all the money in the world and could move her lab anywhere, you do not think she would give up Therma?"

"Alex, this family is not about money. We have a lot of it. It might not look as though we do, but we are a very successful family. A humble family. We have ties all over; Greece, Turkey, and parts of the Americas – especially Julia. She is quite famous and accomplished. Her passion, as well as Charlee's, is research. Pearl brings a whole other aspect to the table. She is brilliant in physiology and chemistry. The dynamics surrounding us now is about a changing world and as I see it, we all just did that. We changed the world and they are going to want to examine the changes we are about to experience. I am not sure what this means for us as a group, but we will always have each other. This is a given. So to answer your question, no, I do not think Julia will leave Ikaria, especially now. But I do know what we have as a group is very special." Both men nodded their heads.

The three returned their gazes to the fire as they heard the ladies' voices coming down the hallway. Julia stopped in the kitchen, happy to see it was clean and the food was put away. She smiled and entered the sunroom with Charlee and Pearl. "Thank you, gentlemen, for cleaning up. That was so kind of you," Julia said as she sat down on the loveseat next to Alex's chair. Pearl sat in Adeem's lap and Charlee sat in Mathias' lap. The men said nothing about the kitchen. How it got clean was anybody's guess.

300

Alex and Adeem were not receptive to the women at first. Pearl looked at Adeem then at Alex, "OK, what is up? What is going on?"

Alex said, "Julia, I am sorry. I am still trying to wrap my head around all of this. It is a lot to think about and we still need to sit and go over Dimitri's inheritance. What time is it?"

Julia answered, "1:00 p.m."

Alex replied, "OK, I am going to go and take a shower. Do you think we could talk about it when I am done?"

Julia looked quizzically at him, "Sure, but I think we have a lot more to talk about than Dimitri's inheritance. I am finally formulating a million questions in my head about the past few days. I feel like I have a box of puzzle pieces in my head that need putting together."

Alex got up and with a half-smile said, "Yes, me too. I know we need to come up with a game plan, and I need to get back to Qatar. I had not planned on being here for five days. My mind is overloaded. This metaphysical apparition that has entered our lives – and I am assuming she is the one who cleaned the kitchen – has my mind whirling. Makes me wonder if our involvement in changing mankind and the planet is truly done. We were chosen eons ago? This is a bit overwhelming. But right now, I need a shower and to clear my thoughts. Julia, do you mind if I pour myself a glass of wine and take it to the shower with me and we can talk after?"

Julia stood up and said, "Yes, that would be fine. I will bring you a glass of wine. Go ahead. It is OK. I understand. It is a lot to take in. I am overwhelmed too. Go ahead, go." She shooed him off with her hand while asking, "Do you want red or white?"

Alex stood to leave, turned back and said, "Red, always red."

Julia left the others to themselves in the sunroom and headed to the kitchen to pick out a bottle of wine. She opened it, poured herself a glass, walked over to the window, and admired the beautiful gardens that blanketed the landscape. It was a breathtaking piece of property, and the chateau was exquisite. Her mind was restless. She knew what was going on with both men. It was palpable. She had been here before. This is a place no one wants to be, a place in time that requires a decision that is not conducive to both parties.

Pearl had told her about Alex reading her journal and the many questions he had asked. Pearl had implied that Alex had fallen in love with her through her journals, and after all they had just gone through, what was a man to do? How could he trust another when so much was opened in him by her, let alone the universe? Only the six people in that circle, in this house, would ever know or understand what was about to happen.

Julia stood twisting the ring on her finger. It was on her wedding finger. She then realized everyone's rings were on their wedding finger. They were wed, together as one with The ALL. She tried to take it off, but it wouldn't come off. She went to the sink and put soap in her hand. No matter what she did, the ring was on to stay.

As Julia poured herself and Alex a glass of wine, she began to see him as a man, a very handsome man, not just a guy who showed up looking to give her information. It had been a long time since she had looked at a man that way. Daniel was the love of her life. She missed him terribly and still spoke to him, asking for his advice or his ideas when she needed it. Sometimes she just carried on a one-way conversation with him, knowing what he would say if he were in the room with her, but lately she had gotten lonely. Her work kept her head focused, but her body longed for a man's touch. She now found herself longing for Alex's touch.

She drank the wine in her glass and refilled it. Hesitantly she walked to the bathroom door, questioning whether she should enter or not. The bathroom door was ajar, so she let herself in. She sat on the stool on the white fur rug and watched Alex. He had both hands on the shower wall below the faucet, head down and eyes closed as he let the water run over his head onto his back. He was crying. She felt as if she had made a mistake and got up to leave when he said, "Stay, do not go." She sat back down and just watched. He finally stood, took a washcloth, put soap on it, opened the shower door, and turned around, his back facing her. She got up, went to the shower, took the washcloth and washed his back, his buttocks, and down his legs. His body was beautiful, reminding her of The David in Florence, Italy. Standing in front of The David had changed her just as it had everyone in the room. She felt the same feeling at this very moment. It was as if she were inside of him, as if they were one person. She could feel his emotions, his pain, almost empathic. Her emotions welled up inside her as she stood behind him, staring up at his shoulders with the soapy cloth in her hand dripping onto the floor. He slowly turned, his eyes meeting hers. He reached for her, placing his hands on either side of her neck, bent down, and kissed her tenderly, longingly, slowly introducing his tongue into her mouth. She dropped the washcloth and placed her hands on his chest, returning the kiss, paralyzed in front of him. The energy surging through them was one of pure love as neither had felt in a long time. She started to enter the shower, but he stood strong in his stance, kissing her, penetrating her mouth deeper and deeper as she willingly returned his affection. When he withdrew his lips from hers, he looked into her eyes and said, "I love you, Julia. Thank you for the wine. I will see you shortly. Please go now." He closed the shower door and returned to the same position she had found him in.

She took one slow step backward, turned, and walked out of the room into the hallway. She closed the bathroom door and leaned against it. In that kiss she heard his thoughts and felt his pain. He didn't want to leave her. She felt his thoughts as if they were her own. She looked down at the ring – it was glowing.

Alex looked down at his ring – it was glowing. They both watched the glow slowly fade away.

Julia had left her glass of wine in the bathroom and didn't dare go back in to retrieve it. When she got to the kitchen, everyone was at the sink with soapy hands, trying to remove their rings. She said, "They do not come off." At that moment, four pairs of eyes were on her. As Julia opened another bottle of wine, without looking at them she said, "I want you to do something for me. Will you kiss each other passionately? I want to see what happens to the rings." She poured her wine and when she looked up, all four were engaged in a long, romantic kiss and all four rings were ablaze. Julia saw the passion in each of their rings as she did in hers after kissing Alex. Her eyes welled up again as a tear rolled down her cheek as she realized they were all bonded for life.

Charlee and Mathias left the kitchen, saying goodnight to everyone before heading down the hall to their bedroom. They were exhausted and had no idea when the last time it was that they had slept. A soft pillow was all they could think about.

Pearl's eyes were full of tears. She heard Adeem's thoughts and could sense his grief when she kissed him. She looked up at him asking, "You are leaving me. Why?"

He looked into her eyes and said, "Pearl, I cannot stay in Therma with you. My world is here. I have responsibilities that do not allow me to be away for long. I know I cannot ask you to stay here with me."

Pearl said, "Why can you not ask me?"

He said, "Pearl, will you stay here with me, live here in Qatar with me and be my wife?"

She looked at Julia. Julia looked down and left the room. For the first time, Julia realized that there was a huge possibility that her granddaughter might not be returning with her. Her dream, hers and Daniel's dream, was to create a place of healing, to create a place where Charlee and Pearl could continue her studies, and together they could make a difference in this world. Sharing that dream with the girls was her greatest blessing. She now realized that Pearl might not follow in her footsteps. She had been grooming her since she was a little girl just as she did with Charlee after she had arrived at Agriolykos.

With a full glass of wine, Julia went out into the gardens and walked the pebble paths, meandering around the roses, vines, and fruit trees. She found herself so deep in thought as she walked through the gardens that when she turned to walk back, she realized she had lost her way. It became a maze just like the Longleat Maze in England, a path of no return if people didn't pay attention. She picked leaves along the path, dropping them as she walked, thinking the breadcrumb method should take her back to the entrance. If not, she knew another path was warranted. She did this for almost an hour and still hadn't found the way out.

Alex was standing in the window looking down at her as he made a few phone calls. From here he could see into the entire maze and witness where she had made her mistake at each turn. He dressed and headed to the gardens to rescue her before she started yelling for help. He called her name out loud. She bent over, putting her hands on her knees and thanking god that someone knew to come and look for her. She answered pitifully, "Alex, please help me out of here. I am lost."

Alex chuckled and replied, "Yes, I am aware of this. Stay put and listen to my voice as I get closer and closer to you. You are OK. There are not any wild animals in here that can eat you." With that he was standing in front of her with a wine glass in one hand and a satchel over his shoulder that contained a bottle of wine, a bag of grapes, Qaseem's will, and all the treasures that were now hers. "Come with me." He took her hand and they walked deeper into the dark maze, rounding corner after corner of the tall, lush boxwoods until they reached the middle. It opened up into a large courtyard decorated with a colorful array of flowering pots, Koi ponds, and bird feeders. The tall hedges blocked the sun, leaving a dark shadow over the entire area.

Alex looked down into Julia's eyes and said, "The magic awaits you. Stay still, do not move." He let go of her hand and walked into the center of the open area. Within seconds the whole area lit up with tiny white lights illuminating the white, sparkling pebbles beneath them.

Julia gasped, "Oh my gosh, this is lovely, Alex." A beautiful pink marble water fountain with an angel resting in the middle filled the center of the white and pink pebble patio. Water delicately flowed over the angel and into the pool surrounding the statue. The gentle pattering of the water was serene. There was a small metal table designed in a filagree pattern of roses, along with two chairs that were waiting for them. Alex set the wine bag on the table, pulled out a chair, and motioned for Julia to sit. They took a seat. He carefully poured her a glass of wine and placed the grapes on top of the bag. He raised his glass and Julia did the same as they clinked the two together and took a long swallow of the warm, rich Zinfandel.

Alex began, "Julia, my main purpose a few days ago was to deliver to you what is rightfully yours. I had no idea the extent of your inheritance until a few years ago. I had been searching for Dimitri, my father, for a very long time. Qaseem suffered from a long illness, and as he got closer to the end of his life, he confided in me about his true relationship with Dimitri. In my world, if his secret had gotten out, he would have been tortured to death. It is considered the worse offense to Allah that a man can commit. Only one person knew of their affair: my mother, Gabriella, Qaseem's sister and Dimitri's one-night stand.

Qaseem was a gentle and kind man and took me under his wing when my mother died, and raised me like a son. I am not sure if you knew that Dimitri and George's families were murdered?"

Julia answered, "Yes, I am aware."

Alex continued, "The night Dimitri and George's families were killed, it was all over the news, *Several famous masonry families killed in horrendous accidents over a few days' time,* was the headline on all the newspapers and news stations. You see, George and Dimitri's families were very well connected with every building contractor and architect in Qatar. They were the best of the best in the field of stone work. The authorities in Qatar became alarmed when they heard about the accidents. This loss was of great importance to them when the headlines read the families of Dimitri and George had been among the dead. For years the Qatar government had purchased all their marble stone slabs from the two quarries owned by the families. All the marble here in the estate as well as the chateau – even these pebbles – come from their quarries." Julia looked around, took a drink of her wine, and nodded as Alex continued, "It was assumed that Dimitri and George were also killed. By morning, the site of the bombings had been cleaned and all evidence removed. No bodies were found. Eye-witnesses stated the boys were seen with their parents at the time of the accidents. The boys were never seen again so the assumption was considered fact after a few days.

Qaseem was heartbroken. He learned much later that Dimitri was still alive, but he was never able to find him. And the one and only time Dimitri returned to Qatar to reconnect with Qaseem, Qaseem was gone on business. Dimitri left leaving only a note, but did not share his whereabouts. Qaseem never truly recovered from losing Dimitri. He died a broken man. He had loved only one person in his life and that was Dimitri."

Julia lowered her eyes and swirled the wine in her glass, "Yes. The letter that Dimitri left behind expressed his undying love for Qaseem. I read it when I was young. It was beautiful and very sad."

Alex stood and paced as he talked, "After the news died down and no suspects were charged, the quarries went up for sale. Qaseem bought both family businesses, keeping the businesses and employees for years, operating at profit levels beyond belief. He quadrupled the profits by selling the marble around the world, and he made a fortune. He sold the quarries twenty plus years later. Both quarries were still producing at maximum levels, even after twenty years. The money he made from the sale now belongs to you. It resides in a bank account here in Qatar. You are the sole bene-ficiary, and you are welcome to have it transferred to any bank of your choosing." Alex pulled an envelope from the satchel and handed it to Julia.

She took it, turned it over and over then looked at Alex, "Do I open this now?" He nodded then watched as her delicate hands carefully opened the envelope. She pulled out a slip of paper and on it read *$922,000,500.00 Paid in Full to the recipient Julia A. Kaya.* Her social security number, date of birth, and home address were printed on the bottom of the paper. She stared at it in dis-belief. With one hand on her chest and the other holding the note she gasped, "Oh, oh my god. Oh my god, Alex, is this real? I mean, there are a lot of zeros here. Oh my god!"

Alex sat back in his chair, "There is more, Julia. Gabriella was to inherit many of the jewels from Qaseem's collection. With her death, Qaseem hid many of the jewels and several other pieces from the monarchy, and he saved three pieces for you. Pearl has one of the pieces on her finger, a ring that is priceless. I am not sure if you noticed it. It is going to be hard for Adeem to top that one." He laughed out loud.

Julia didn't laugh, she just stared at him in disbelief; she was in shock. Alex cleared his throat and regained his serious com-posure. He reached into the satchel and pulled out a box the size of a small loaf of bread, put it on the table, and pushed it over to her. She looked at him and he nodded for her to open it. Inside were two small boxes and two thin jewelry boxes. She opened each one. The first small box was a five-carat diamond ring paired with a studded ruby band. Julia let out the huge breath of air she had been holding. She took the ring out of the tiny box and looked at it closely then looked at Alex and said, "This is the most beautiful ring I have ever seen." He took it from her and before she could say no, he put it on her finger next to the gold band. When the two bands touched, to their surprise the gold band began to glow as it did earlier, and it fused itself to the diamond ring. In a panic, she quickly tried to take it off. As the gold band proved to be forever stuck on her finger, now both were stuck. Alex smiled, "Why am I not surprised?"

Julia looked at Alex, frightened, "Alex, I cannot wear this all the time. I cannot wear jewelry in my profession. Most of my work is done in sterile environments. We need to get this off!"

Alex shrugged his shoulders with a smile saying, "I do not know what to tell you. Maybe in time, maybe the spell will wear off. I do not know, but for now, enjoy your gift. Open the rest." The large box was heavy and contained the breathtaking necklace that matched Pearl's ring. It was a choker with a matching bracelet. Each had seven strands of one carat diamonds linked together, and the clasp was made of rubies. Alex said, "It too is priceless."

She carefully ran her finger over the stones, admiring its beauty. She left it in the box and opened the second thin box. In it was a string of white, flawless pearls with two large rubies and an eight-carat heart diamond hanging from its center. "Priceless too?" she asked.

He smiled, "No, but it is on the top side of $1,000,000. Now you might ask why you were given these jewels." Julia nodded as she gazed at the necklaces. "Qaseem said he was told to give them to you. He never said who told him and I never bothered to ask. The fact is, there is much, much more. Qaseem was a very rich man and now I own his estate. It is hard to believe how much money circulates throughout this country. We use money to build great empires, not to hoard and covet as most people do around this planet. We have come to realize that as you spend to build, more money comes to you. The wealth has become so vast that it is sinful, really."

Julia watched Alex talk. She had no words. He pushed the last small box over to her. In it was a key.

She looked at Alex questioningly, "This looks like the key to my front door. Do you know what this is for?"

"Yes, I do. It belongs to a research center here in Qatar. That box is from me. The center is vacant right now, and state-of-the-art equipment is being installed this week. This facility can employ and house twenty-five interns, scientists, or whatever type of employee you need. It also houses conference centers, restaurants, daycares, and a gym. And it comes with a bottomless budget."

Julia looked at him, knitted her eyebrows, and by the look on her face, he knew she was about to rebut the offer.

He knew she would think this was a means to get her to stay in Qatar with him. Before she could speak, he said, "You can manage this research center from Therma, if you wish. I will provide you with transportation back and forth to Ikaria. This is an opportunity to finish what we started here. We were told the planet would take two years to completely heal, so you have two years to study the changes that we put into place when we seeded the oceans. The planet is about to undergo a transformation that will stun the world. I still cannot wrap my head around the fact that we, us six, were chosen eons ago to save the world. I do not think any of us have come to realize the extent of how this has changed us as well. Look at us, Julia. We are young again. People are going to notice. We have a second chance. We can make a difference. You will be ahead of the game just by what you know now. This alchemy needs to be studied. I do not know about you, but I feel better than I have in years. I can feel every cell working as if I were a machine. It is like I can feel them talking to each other, if that makes sense."

Julia enthusiastically said, "Yes, I can too. I did not know how to describe it."

"Julia, these rings are not coming off, and there is a reason for that. We need to be open to receive more information from the apparition. I believe there is more expected from us. I believe there is more to do. I know it, I feel it. What about you?" She looked down at the rings and nodded. He added, "You can do this, Julia. I believe in you. Accept my offer. There are no strings attached." She stared at him, looking for the right words. "Look, Julia, I am not giving you this key in hopes that you will stay here with me. To be honest, I spend a lot of my time traveling. I am responsible for many lives and many businesses around the world. I know you are a driven scientist and your research is your baby. As I see it, your baby just got a whole hell of a lot bigger. So, what do you think? Will you accept my offer?"

Julia was listening as the possibilities were swirling in her head. The vast amount of research she could do with this kind of opportunity was extraordinary. She reached for the grapes and slowly peeled the skin off one of them. She ate grape after grape, not talking, just deep in thought. Alex gave her time to consider as he too picked a grape, peeled it, and ate along with her. Finally, she said, "I need to talk to the girls first. How much time do I have?"

"You have all the time in the world. I must tell you that Adeem and I need to leave by noon tomorrow. We need to fulfill the request to move our money and assets out of the global banking system. That is going to be quite tricky considering the amount we are talking about, and it will most likely take a few days to accomplish. I will leave you the number to the bank where your money is being held as well as my private contact numbers. After I set up the new accounts, I will notify you so you can do the same. When you are ready, just call. OK?"

Julia nodded, looked down, and asked, "Where exactly is the research center?"

Alex replied, "It is next to the Arabian center on the same property as my home. It is exactly one-hour's horse ride from the chateau. It is safe and it is guarded. No one will be able to enter without being vetted first."

This gave her peace of mind. Then she looked at him, "Tomorrow, huh?"

Alex nodded as he pulled a few grapes from the vine and popped them into his mouth, "Julia, this has been so much more than I expected when I got off that plane in Greece to find you. I have no idea the extent of what we have done, but when I placed the water from the jar into the ocean, the water began to glow and spiral away from me at great speed. The ripples it formed were huge. It looked as if I had just dropped a large boulder from a mountaintop into the water. I could see the bottom of the ocean for miles. It was pure, clean water, as if I were standing in a glass of water. I climbed up on the rock behind me and looked out over the sea. For miles all I could see was pure, clean water moving in every direction. The water from our jars were merging and it happened very fast. Did you see that too?"

Julia said, "Yes, Alex, I did. Quite frankly, I am afraid to go to sleep tonight. What are people going to say tomorrow when they see the oceans around the world as clear as a glass of water? What are they going to say when they see us? Alex, you look like you are thirty years old. Yesterday you were an old man!"

Alex smirked at her, "Old man? For seventy plus I was not so bad, but I do like the new and improved me. I spent at least 30 minutes after my shower just staring in the mirror at the image looking back at me. It is quite amazing!"

She smiled back at him, lowered her eyes, and with great concern said, "I am not being facetious. You know what I mean. And yes, you do look great. But Alex, the apparition said the rings will protect us. What does that mean? Will we be targeted for this? This could turn out to be a very grave situation. We need to seriously think about the implications here. The world is going to take notice. The amount of chaos that is about to ensue on this planet is going to be astronomical. Corporations are going to tumble, the healthcare field will become obsolete, insurance companies will go bankrupt, pharmaceutical companies will go under, and banking systems will topple? I mean, can you imagine this to be true? Not to mention that the oceans will be tested and all ocean life will be studied. Hell, it could cause a mass killing just to get to the fish. People are crazy. If they believe the fountain of youth is in the fish, that could be catastrophic!

Alex, I am nervous. If at any point the authorities find out it was us that changed the planet, we will be hunted like wild animals."

Julia got up and started pacing, "If I agree to accept your offer to use the research facility to study this phenomenon, I am going to need bodyguards around the facility and a staff that lives, breathes, and eats there. A compound like the Vatican. We will need to camouflage the research and make it look like we are studying herbal tinctures, which is my specialty. We can compartmentalize the research so the employees are safe."

Julia was pacing so fast and becoming so paranoid that Alex began to wonder if her concerns were valid. He got up and stood in her path. He stopped her, held her hands, and said, "We will figure this out. We were all in such remote places, no one saw us. I believe we are safe. I cannot believe the powers that be would put us in danger after what we did. *We* were chosen to heal the world. Maybe that is why these rings are stuck on us. Do they have protective properties? Hell, I do not know. We can talk about it sometime next week. In the meantime, talk to the girls, decide what works best for you and go from there."

Julia dropped her head forward and rested it on his chest. Alex raised her chin, bent down, and kissed her as he did in the shower. Julia responded passionately. When he pulled away, Julia asked, "Why were we chosen for this job?"

Alex kissed her again, this time longer. When he lifted his mouth from hers, she started to say, "But—" Alex kissed her again, but this time he picked her up while kissing her and opened the hidden door in the maze. He walked in still kissing her, and when she looked around, they were inside a room. It was a very old library with wall-to-wall bookshelves. By the looks of it, they were ancient books. Julia wiggled to get down. He gently set her down to wander around the room then poured them each a glass of whiskey. Julia was like a little girl in a candy store, picking up book after book, "Oh can I borrow this one, oh and this one? Oh my god, Alex, I need this one, and this one over here." In a split second her arms were full. "Where did you get these? I really should read them all. Look at these! These are full of alchemy from antiquity. If I could get my hands on some of these ingredients, I could cure the world."

Just as the words left her mouth, they both laughed out loud. Alex took the books from her arms and handed her the whiskey tumbler, "You are welcome to read as many as you want, but they must stay here and no one is to know about this place. Not the gardener, not even Adeem." He took her hand, escorted her to the couch, and began to tell her the story of the great family collection dating back several generations. Alex said, "Many of the books were saved from the great burning in 1933. Do you know this story?" Julia looked at him with a blank stare, took off her shoes, settled cross-legged into the couch, and listened.

"In 1933 the Germans invaded homes, libraries, and educational institutions, confiscating – actually stealing – books by the greatest writers and intellects of the world, then they burned them. You could say they claimed they were heretical. The concept creeped all the way to the Americas. Most of our greatest history was lost to these imbeciles and their radical ideas, but my great-grandfather was a revolutionary. He and others snuck around at night, perusing personal libraries and stealing some of these great works before they were burned. These midnight capers started well before the Germans began their burning parties. The stealthiness of my grandfather and his team of characters is well defined in this room. They got their hands on some of the most amazing, shocking, and mind-blowing books ever written and they are all in here. The men in my family were thieves by night and emperors by day." Alex let out a chuckle, remembering the days of yore. He repositioned himself on the couch and continued, "The books you see here are from countless hours of sneaking around in the dark. We call them spooks."

Julia was intrigued. Alex continued to talk for over an hour, and while Julia listened, she got up and scanned the many pictures around the room. Her eye was caught by one photo in particular. It was a black and white photo of a young woman who stood alone in a garden.

When Alex was finished and the whiskey was gone, Julia handed him the photo. He looked at it then took a double take. "Do you see what I see?" she asked.

Curiously, Alex looked at the picture, "Yes, I do."

"Who is she?"

"I do not know, but she is wearing your necklace and bracelet. I will take it with me and try to find out who she is." Alex walked around the room, noticing this woman was in many photos wearing different dresses but wearing the necklace and bracelet in each one.

On the desk was a magnifying glass. Julia took one of the pictures and looked at the woman closer. "I tell you what, Alex, this woman looks just like Melena, my daughter. Look."

"I have never seen a picture of your daughter, but to me she looks like you. That is an unnerving coincidence, do you think?" Alex said.

Julia turned it over and used the magnifying glass to see the name written on the back. The name was Julia Kaya 1838. Julia gasped as she put her hand over her mouth, "Oh my god, look at this."

Alex took the magnifying glass again and looked at the picture with much more interest. "I do not know what this means, but the resemblance is uncanny. I have a few photo albums somewhere. I will look for them and get to the bottom of this."

Julia sat down and looked up at Alex, "This is beginning to freak me out!"

Alex poured another whiskey and sat down on the couch next to her, "Tell me about your daughter."

Julia lit up with a big smile, "My Melena, oh my goodness. She is my precious jewel, she is. Do you have an hour? If so, I will tell you about her."

Alex chuckled, "I am all ears."

Julia swiveled on the couch facing Alex, crossed her legs, propped the pillow behind her then leaned back with a big smile and began, "You will love her. Everyone does. Oh my gosh, OK, so, Melena was a small child, her lungs took years to really develop, so playing was hard on her. She would get breathless and weak easily, but over time her health and immune system became stronger. She tried her darndest to keep up with her brother; they were inseparable.

Mathias never let Melena out of his sight. I taught Melena all about nature and the importance of respecting life and its beauty. As she grew, she taught Mathias how to see the beauty in nature just as I was teaching her. It was so cute. He was never allowed to kill anything or stomp on any living creature like many of the boys in town did. If she caught him even looking at a bug wrong, she would give him a look – you know the one that says, 'You better not or else'."

Alex smiled and was entranced watching Julia come alive telling the story. "She is kind and gentle to everyone. In her presence, she changes you. She is a listener. She *hears* what people say and responds without advice but with understanding. She never talks out of turn, and she finds joy in everything.

I will never forget one hot summer day when Hollywood came to the island to shoot a movie. It was a love story which included the healing waters of Therma. Some of the biggest stars were there. The village was chaotic, taking care of the many people who showed up to film. Melena was bound and determined to meet a movie star, so she packed a bag for the day and went to town in search of fame. The filming days were long and the actors were not used to the heat. The story goes, she was watching the star actress saunter around the set speaking her lines when she noticed the actress was not doing well. She could tell that heat stroke was getting the best of her. When the director yelled cut, Rose Monroe, the biggest female star of Hollywood, left the set quickly. Melena followed her. When she rounded the corner of the building, Rose was on the ground. She ran to her, pulled her into the shade, unbuttoned the upper button on her blouse, and raised her long skirt. She took off Rose's shoes and placed Rose's head in her lap. She grabbed the water bottles and a cloth and began to moisten her skin as she blew on it.

When Rose opened her eyes, she looked up into the face of the most beautiful girl she had ever seen and asked, 'What happened?'

Melena said sweetly, 'You had a heat stroke and you are dehydrated.'

Rose asked, 'How do you know?'

Melena held her hand and pinched Rose's skin, telling her, 'See how the skin stays pinched and does not fall back down like mine does?' Rose nodded. 'This is a sign of dehydration. The heat and humidity here is unbearable to most people who are not used to it.'

Rose asked how she knew these things so Melena explained, 'I was a sensitive child and I too have suffered dehydration. My mama taught me what to do.' Julia giggled. Those two girls are best friends to this day."

She smiled at Alex who was still listening, so she continued, "They were inseparable after this. Rose was 23, only six years older than Melena, and they got along famously. Rose stayed with Daniel and me for most of the summer and into the early fall months while the film was being made. When it was over, Rose asked to take Melena to Paris with her. She promised she would be well cared for and never allowed out of her sight. The trip would be for one year. Daniel and I were beside ourselves, wondering if we should let her go." Julia sat up, fluffed up her pillow and began with excitement in her voice as if she was there, in the story, her hands dancing in the air like an Italian. "Rose was into fashion, and the great fashion season of Paris was about to begin. Melena was now 17, and after great deliberation, we allowed her to go. For a year she traveled France, Italy, and all of Europe. She wore the most exquisite designer clothes, enjoyed the most delicate of cuisine, frequented the opera and stage theaters, and danced with the most famous men in the world. She spent a year learning different languages, seeing great works of art, and enjoying the museums.

Through all this, Melena never changed. She was a special soul who stayed true to herself. Men tried to seduce her and the film industry tried to hire her, but she had no desire to become a star after she saw what the industry did to young girls. She stayed behind the scenes and let Rose enjoy the accolades of her stardom.

One night while strolling through the museum, she saw Maximus. She had seen his pictures all over town; on magazines, billboards, and theater posters. He was the heartthrob of film. She said that while she was walking around admiring the new paintings that had been added, she suddenly realized she was alone, the busy museum was void of people. She stepped behind a wall, looked at her watch, and realized it was still midafternoon. The museum was usually full this time of day, but only she and Maximus were present. When she peeked around the corner to see if he was still in the room, he was gone.

At dinner that evening she asked Rose about him. Rose had worked on a few movies with him. She said he was a kind man who had never married, and as far as she knew had never had a girlfriend. I guess he took care of his parents who lived next door, on the outer edges of town. At the time he was the top paid actor and model in Hollywood. They even designed a line of suits named *Maximus*. And of course, she bought one for her father. It was a nice suit. They were all the rage!

Melena called me that afternoon, talking a hundred miles an hour. She was going to some fashion show that night where he was promoting his clothing line.

When they arrived at the fashion show, Rose found the table with their names on it. In Melena's seat was the painting she had been admiring earlier that day. It had a pink bow wrapped around it with a note that said, 'You are never too far away from home.' Rose searched high and low until she found Melena, then dragged her to the table and pointed to the painting in the chair. Melena looked down at it then around the room. She knew who it was from, but Maximus was not to be found. Throughout dinner and the fashion show, she said she looked over her shoulder nonchalantly as she scanned the room. No Maximus. She was grateful for the picture but tired so she decided to take a taxi home.

When she left the grand ballroom, she rounded the corner to the coat room and ran directly into him. She said she almost peed her pants!" Julia and Alex laughed as Julia continued, "I know this is kind of a long story, but for you to understand Melena, I must tell you what happened. It is such a great story. I remember it as if she was telling me yesterday. I hope you do not mind."

Alex said, "I am loving every minute of this. Go on."

She smiled, adjusted herself, and continued, "Well, she said she was speechless as her body was next to his and she was looking straight up into his blue eyes. Neither said a word, they just stood there entranced with each other. He had her coat and wrapped it around her, and before she knew it, he had swiftly put her in an a-waiting car with him, but not before pushing through a sea of woman begging for an autograph.

He took her to a lookout above the city skyline. She said looking down into the valley was like looking at a Christmas tree; millions of colorful lights everywhere twinkling like stars. When she looked up it was even more beautiful. She was taken aback. She was transported back to Ikaria and the many stars we see every night. She thanked him for the painting, but knowing it was probably very expensive, she felt uncomfortable about it. He told her that all museum paintings have replicas, and she now had one too. That painting is hanging on the wall in Agriolykos. I will show it to you, Alex, when we return. Anyway, she asked why he bought it for her and he told her it was because it made her smile. He gave Melena her first kiss and she fell in love that night. He was a gentleman, took her home and said his goodnights, then she called us in the middle of the night to tell her father and me that Maximus gave her the best first kiss ever.

When Rose awoke the next morning, she heard Melena talking downstairs, with a male voice in the background. She covered up and bolted into the kitchen, and there sat Maximus, Melena, and their guardian, having breakfast and coffee. She was speechless. It was at that breakfast table that Rose watched Melena and Maximus fall in love.

Melena and Maximus had dated for only two weeks when all of Hollywood and Europe became abuzz about the new couple. It became hard for them to hide from the crowds. They were constantly asked to do movies together, both always refusing. Then one day the perfect script was put in front of them, and shockingly Melena agreed to make just one film. Their love for one another came across on the movie screen and every girl in the world had a new idea of the perfect man, the perfect love, the perfect kiss. After that film was released, hair-styles changed, clothing styles changed, and every woman wanted to look just like Melena.

My Pearl was the largest grossing film of all time. The last line of the movie was on everything from perfume advertisements to jewelry advertisements to the sides of buses; *When you see the stars, they are heaven's pearls. You are my pearl.* The biggest Hollywood kiss was shown on the movie screen only a few inches from their faces. There was no imagination necessary; it was real, passionate, deep, and lingering. Women passed out in their chairs, fanning them-selves, and the men were trying to copy Maximus's moves. Everyone wanted to be Maximus and Melena. It was epic and no one saw the movie just once.

After that, they lived together, traveled together, and were the center of attention wherever they went. They were in love. Between Melena's new perfume line, *Pearl,* and Maximus's clothing and cologne empires, they decided to leave the world of Hollywood behind and move to Europe. But three years into their retirement from Holly-wood, Maximus received a script he could not turn down. It was some sort of period piece that was to take place in the desert, *The Sands of Midnight* it was called, or something like that. The script intrigued him enough to say yes. He told the press that this was his final film. When Maximus left, Melena spent a few weeks doing girl things with Rose, who was thrilled for Melena. The women made a pinky swear promise to stay in touch."

Alex interrupted, "What is a pinky swear?"

Julia intertwined her pinky around Alex's pinky and said, "Now make a promise; this gesture means you swear to keep that promise. Hence, pinky swear."

Alex said, "I promise to make you happy. Pinky swear."

Julia giggled, "I am going to hold you to it. Pinky swear."

Julia continued, "Melena packed and called saying she was coming home for a week to visit and I was so excited. I had not seen her in a while. While she was packing, in a hidden drawer in the dresser she found a ring that Maximus was going to give her with a note saying, 'Melena, I have traveled through time to find you. We are one and always will be. Will you marry me?' The ring was a perfect pearl set in gold with three diamonds on each side of the band. She was thrilled and I was elated! I loved Maximus. They were perfect together, and I was so happy for them. She put the ring and the note back in the drawer exactly as she had found them and spent the rest of the day calling me, all her girlfriends, and her brother Mathias, telling us she was getting married. She could not get home fast enough. I think as soon as she hung up the phone, Daniel and I were already making plans for an outdoor wedding at Agriolykos. It was an exciting time for us all.

The day before she was to board the plane home, Rose made an unexpected visit. Melena was thrilled.

She ran to the dresser, pulled out the note, and showed Rose the ring. Rose smiled softly, watching Melena bask in the joy of love. When Melena realized her friend had not said a full sentence since her arrival, she stopped talking long enough to notice the tears streaming down Rose's face. She went and sat next to her and asked her softly, 'What happened?'

From her purse, Rose handed Melena a sealed envelope addressed to her from Maximus's lawyer. She stood up, staring down at the envelope then back at Rose. She slowly opened the letter and began to read it. Paraphrasing the best I can, it read:

Dearest Melena,
We regret to inform you that during the filming of *The Sands of Midnight*, Maximus was thrown from his horse and sustained injuries which took his life two days later. During this time, I spent every waking moment with Maximus. Knowing we could not get a message to you in time, he dictated his last will and testament to me.

My Melena, behind the center door of my aunt's antique dresser is a hidden drawer. Within it you will find a token of my everlasting love. I bought this for you two days after I bought you the painting, the night of our first kiss under the pearls of the sky. I knew that night we would be together for eternity...

My darling, I should not have left you. I should not have agreed to one more film. I can no longer dream of our future together, but I can ensure that your future will be spent on your terms, with no worries. I bequeath all that I own to you. You were my true strength. You let me feel life and pleasures as I have never felt before. My world became colorful and fragrant the night I saw you close your eyes and smile at a dream inside the painting. Forgive me, my love. Forgive me. Know I am always with you, forever.
Love, Maximus"

Alex straightened and said, "Oh my god, Julia. This is terrible. What happened next? I am so sorry."

Julia lowered her eyes then looked back up at him with a solemn face, "Thank you. Yes, it was horrible. The news crushed her to the core. When Rose called that afternoon and told me what happened, it devastated me. The hardest part was not being able to hold her in her time of need. We were mortified when we heard the news. It was so unbelievable.

After, Melena fell into a deep depression. She would not eat and she could not sleep. Mathias and I went and got her and her things and brought her home. Mathias, Daniel, and I took turns taking care of her, making sure she ate, slept, and bathed. On the night she found out Maximus had died, she went back to the hidden drawer, got the ring, put it on, and she has never taken it off. It took months for her to begin to recover. In time, she entertained many suitors, but she has never married, nor has she ever brought anyone home. She is now a tycoon living in Europe – mostly France and Greece, depending on the time of the year. I am very proud of her. Melena and her brother Mathias are still very close. He has tried to pair her with a few men he felt worthy. She shares a meal or two but has never fallen in love since Maximus.

We all get together twice a year to share and update everyone on each other's lives, and the shenanigans are priceless. Melena gave Pearl her name. Those two, when they are together, are like two peas in a pod. It is fun to watch them together.

So that is Melena's story. She is a beautiful soul and a tender woman. She makes me proud every day. All my kids do, Charlee being one of them now."

Alex was stroking Julia's hair as she finished her story. He felt closer to her and felt she might be feeling the same toward him. He had been listening intently to every word and when she was done and looking up at him he said, "I am looking forward to meeting her. Thank you for sharing her story with me. I am proud of your family too. I admire the relationship you have with one another. It is very interesting that I have known this family all of five days, yet I feel as though I have known you a lifetime. Julia, I have not been with a woman or in a relationship with a woman in many years. I must admit, I really like being a part of this family and I know Adeem does too," he chuckled.

Julia sat up, "You know, I have not read my journals in years. You liked what you read?"

"Yes, I did. You had a very interesting childhood and through your writing, I truly enjoyed feeling the tenacity and love Daniel had toward you. I am sorry I did not know him, but I am thankful to know he was a good man, a good father, and a good husband. You are quite a remarkable woman. I see a lot of you in Pearl. I know Charlee is not your daughter, but it is amazing how much you three are alike. You talk alike, your mannerisms are alike, your humor is very much the same, and the fortitude within you three is admirable."

Alex stopped talking and looked into her eyes. He wanted to ask her a question but couldn't find the words without sounding too vulnerable. Julia smiled up at him and searched his eyes. She felt an uneasiness about him all of a sudden. She sat up and waited for him to find his words. Slowly he said, "Julia, will you lay here with me for a few minutes? Let's just take a moment to absorb everything we have gone through over these past few days. If you do not mind, I feel like holding you." She lay next to him with her head on his chest and before long they were sleeping.

A few hours went by before Julia woke up. She watched Alex resting peacefully. *Who is this man? How did this all come to be?* She still couldn't wrap her head around all of it. It was like a big dream they were all going to awaken from.

Having to go to the bathroom, Julia searched for the knob in the door, thinking she could find her way back to the house while Alex rested, but no knob could be found. She sat on the coffee table in front of Alex and stared at him. He woke, yawned, and stretched before he realized she was sitting there looking at him. "Are you willing me to wake up?"

"Yes, I am. Alex, I want to go to bed in the house. I cannot find the door. There is no handle."

He laughed out loud, "I told you it was a secret!"

"Well un-secret it please. I need to go to the lady's room."

"Well, we cannot have you soiling this antique rug, can we?" he said with a chuckle. He got up and showed her to the bathroom inside the library. It too had a secret door. When she was done relieving herself, he waved her over to the wall, "Here, I will show you. See this little knob? Push it back then to the right." When she did, the door opened effortlessly. She started out the door when Alex reached for her arm. He looked down then back up at her and said quietly, "Julia, may I join you in your bed?"

Her face flushed, she turned her back to him, "Alex, I have not been…"

He interrupted her, "We can just sleep. I need to hold you, if you are OK with that. We can just lay together and sleep – that is all I ask." She nodded and went outside. It was dark, the only light coming from the moon. Alex closed the door and said, "Go ahead, I will follow you."

She turned and hit him on the arm, "Very funny!"

He laughed and said, "Here, climb on. I will give you a piggy-back ride back to the house."

She grabbed the satchel from the table, giggled, and climbed on as she said, "I bet you could not have done this yesterday when you were an old man!"

"Have faith, woman, I am stronger than you think. It did not take a miracle to build these muscles." She giggled and held on tight, feeling like a little girl while enjoying the walk along the maze back to the house.

When they got to the chateau, the lights were off and the others were nowhere in sight. Julia got two glasses of water, squeezed half a lemon into each one, and headed to the bedroom. Alex walked around the house, making sure everything was turned off then joined Julia. She had changed into a sheer white negligee that went to her knees. Small thin lace adorned the edges of it, and as she fluffed the pillows, one of the straps gently fell down her arm, exposing her breast as she bent over. He could see her entire naked body peeking through the material.

Alex immediately felt himself becoming aroused. He turned, left the room, and headed to his bathroom. Standing in front of the mirror, he smiled at himself and thought, *Oh boy, this is not going to be easy.* He hadn't been with a woman in many years and Julia was the woman he wanted to 'break the curse' with, as Adeem called it.

He returned to Julia's room and said, "Julia, it might be a better idea if I sleep in my own room tonight."

She had seen what he was trying to hide before he left the room. She smiled at him, sank down into the sheets, and said, "OK, no worries. If you change your mind, you can return. Will you turn out the lights for me please?"

He did and left the room. A part of her was thankful he decided not to stay. She thought of Daniel and the years they'd had together. Her love for him was so deep, and losing him took her years to recover from. She smiled thinking of the days when he drove her crazy with silly notes. She remembered the day she truly, unconditionally fell in love with him, standing in the cement building believing he was dead. She knew she truly loved him right then. Isn't that the way the story goes – you don't know what you have until it's gone? She wondered if he would approve of Alex. No sooner did this thought appear that she heard him say, *Julia, he is a good man. Let him in, he will love you as I did. My love, choose to be happy.* This settled her mind as she closed her eyes and fell asleep.

Alex lay in his bed tossing and turning. Sleep was nowhere in sight. Exhausted yet alive with emotions of wanting her next to him, he ached inside. He began to realize this opportunity might never happen again. He needed to go to her. He needed her to know he wanted her. If he had but one chance, it was now.

Alex made his way into the kitchen and was surprised to see Pearl sitting in the dark with her head in her hands. He started to turn around when she asked him to stay. He sat down and waited. She began with, "Alex, I believe I am in love with Adeem. I have never felt this way before, but the thought of leaving Mom, Julia, and my studies behind is tormenting me. I do not know what to do. Why can I not have both?"

Alex took a long breath of air in and slowly let it out before saying, "Pearl, I am wondering the same thing. I do not have an answer for you. Julia has some things to decide herself that might make everyone's decision easier. Think on it tonight and revisit it in the morning. You can talk with her then and let her know how you feel. What did Adeem have to say, may I ask?"

"He wants me to stay here and live in the chateau with him. He wants to marry me."

"And you? Do you want to marry him? Our way of life is a bit different than the Greeks, especially our customs and how we believe. Now, I know your generation has changed the scope of customs and religion for most of the world, but society here has not."

"Yes, but I can stay here and not venture into society, right?" she asked.

"Pearl, you cannot look at this home as a compound. It will wear on you. You are a trained scientist and you will miss your studies. You will become bored, maybe even bitter. A life of love is a lifetime of work. Do not be jaded by love. It will destroy you in the end if you leave your dreams behind for it. Let's wait until morning and see what Julia has decided. She has a few opportunities that might change the dynamics of this whole situation. OK?" Pearl felt a bit of relief. Alex's calm demeanor gave her hope. She smiled, said goodnight, and went back to bed.

Alex sat in the dark, realizing he was possibly pulling this family apart. Would he regret it? He helped himself to another glass of whiskey as he pondered losing what he had just found.

At 4:00 a.m., Julia woke up and went to check on Alex, but he was not in his bed nor his bathroom. She found him asleep with his head resting on the kitchen table. She whispered his name to wake him and asked him to bed. He followed her willingly. She turned down the covers on his side of the bed, turned to him and motioned him to sit down. She sat next to him on the bed and brushed his hair back away from his eyes and kissed him gently.

Alex reached up and ran his fingers through her hair, gently pulling her forward and kissing her like he did in the shower. He said, "Lay with me, Julia. Let me hold you. I need to feel you in my arms."

Julia smiled, walked around the bed, and crawled in next to him. His body felt so strong next to hers, and her body felt so soft next to his. He slowly pulled her into him, and she willingly let him. He raised up on one elbow and with the other hand lowered her silk strap down, exposing her breast. He kissed it gently, feeling her nipple stiffen on his tongue. She arched her back and moaned softly, giving herself to him. She felt alive. He felt love, a deep love, and knew he would protect this woman with his life. She was his and no one would ever take her away from him. He wanted her, he wanted to be inside her. She took his hand and slowly brushed it down her chest to her belly and down until it reached between her legs. He caressed her inner thighs, teasing her as he passed from one thigh to the other. She watched him gaze upon her body as he raised her gown, exposing both breasts and the soft spot between her legs. He carefully entered her with his two fingers as he kissed her passionately. She moved beneath him as he moved his fingers in and out of her. Her body was aroused and wet, wanting him. With his thumb, he found her clitoris and gently massaged it as she moaned with pleasure. The rhythm was intoxicating. She wanted him and she was ready. He moved his body up and over hers, never leaving her mouth as he placed his hard penis inside her. She arched her head back and raised her hips as he gently moved rhythmically in and out. She pulled his waist in as she relaxed her legs, wanting all of him. He raised his chest and looked into her eyes, never leaving them as he began to move faster and faster, deeper and deeper. She ran her hands over his flexed and engaged muscles, exciting her even more. The coming orgasm welled up inside of him. Her breathing became labored as she moved in unison with him. Harder and harder they moved until he exploded inside her, letting out a visceral moan. He reached under her and swiftly pulled her hips into his as he pulsated, feeling every inch of her insides squeezing his pulsating erection. His muscles were engaged, strong, and in control. She felt his body slowly relax on top of hers as he looked at her with tender love. She smiled and moved his hair behind his ear to see his eyes. He gently pulled out of her and lowered his body down to her awaiting soft spot. He caressed her clitoris with his tongue as he penetrated her with his fingers until she released herself to him as he did to her. He drank in her juices and her intoxicating smell. He felt complete satisfaction and a complete connection to her. He carefully raised his body up and over her and kissed her. He tenderly loved her mouth with his tongue, sharing the nectar of their lovemaking with her.

She knew then she would stay with him, she would stay in Qatar. She could love again – she *was* in love again. Alex positioned himself next to her. She rolled over on her side facing him, placing her head on his shoulder and her bent leg over his groin as if claiming him as hers. They fell asleep.

Alex was up early and Adeem was not far behind. Together they made a huge breakfast of nuts, yogurt, and luqaimat with plenty of syrup and sesame seeds, sweet breads, and fruits of all kinds. Adeem made a pot of coffee and placed it on the table. As they prepared breakfast, Alex told Adeem about his decision to transpose the Arabian medical facility into a research center for Julia. He explained that the transformation was already in progress. Adeem asked, "Did Julia agree to this?"

"No, not yet, but I am hoping she will accept my offer. Her plans are to talk to the girls this morning."

Adeem said, "I asked Pearl to marry me."

"Yes, I know. I met her in the kitchen late last night in her hour of distress over the question."

"Oh, and what advice did you give her? I assume you did since that is what you usually do."

Alex laughed, "I told her Julia has some news of her own and that her decision might be made easier after she talks to her."

"In your heart of hearts, what are you hoping for, Dad?"

"I am hoping she takes me up on the offer and stays here with me. I know the healing center is Charlee's baby, but they have such a strong bond and the work they are doing together is important to them both, and Pearl too. I offered to supply her with transportation between the facilities as needed. I anticipate that her research is going to take a complete one-eighty now. So, giving her a state-of-the-art facility as well as security to do the work she needs to do will hopefully entice her to stay. Plus, son, I am in love with her, as strange as that might seem. Five days ago, I would not have entertained this. I was in my seventies, but who knows how old this body is now, thirty? Look at me, look at her. We can get away with it now and I can love her like she wants and needs to be loved. She can love me and see me as her equal now, not as some old man."

"Dad, it is pretty wild looking at you. You look like you did when I was a kid, maybe even better. It is mind-blowing looking at my own reflection. Pearl and I have a big age gap between us too. I was a bit worried about that, but not now, thank god. If Julia accepts the offer, that will make it easier for Pearl to stay here and continue her work with Julia. Let's hope this works out for both of us." Slyly he added, "How was your night?"

Before Alex could answer, Mathias and Julia walked into the kitchen. Hearing the question, Mathias said, "Well, I have a comment on that subject – Mom, you need to figure out this formula and bottle it. You will make millions!" Adeem and Mathias did a high five as they passed each other in the kitchen.

"How old are you two – ten?" Julia said grinning as she looked at Alex who was looking at her with the same grin. Julia said, "OK, boys, enough of that. Behave. Remember you are gentlemen."

Pearl and Charlee walked into the kitchen together and chimed in, "Last night they were not!" and everyone laughed out loud.

Breakfast was filled with innuendos, pet names, and tender moments between each couple. Love and lust were in the air and it was charming.

The conversation quickly turned when Alex and Adeem announced they needed to leave to take care of business. Julia looked at Alex and said, "I have a question I think you two need to contemplate before you leave." She began with the most obvious question, "What are you going to tell your colleagues when they ask about your new appearance, looking significantly younger than you did five days ago?" When the question was broached, everyone sat back, realizing this was going to get complicated. Alex got up and looked at himself in the mirror hanging on the wall behind him. Every wrinkle, mole, freckle, and grey hair was gone. He stood taller and his body was leaner. Even with clothes on, he looked like a bodybuilder and so did Adeem and Mathias.

He turned to Adeem and said, "This is a legitimate concern. What is our story going to be?"

Adeem thought for a minute then replied, "Julia Kaya is a healer who develops miracle tinctures made from multiple herbs that grow on the island of Ikaria, an island where people never die. Is that not the motto on Ikaria, a blue zone – that people never die?"

Charlee said, "This is true. Ikaria is a blue zone and it is touted that people never die, which is wrong, but we can go with that. It is a start. But with this type of validation, *Julia's fountain of youth in a bottle takes years off you*, the healing center is going to be booked solid for the season before we know it. Everyone will truly believe this island does contain the fountain of youth. But we can take into consideration what the apparition told us, that the process of rejuvenating the planet will gradually happen over the next two years. People are going to notice themselves getting younger by the day. I do not think we will be singled out for long. At least I hope not." It was the best plan they could come up with, *miracle tinctures*. The advertising was already in place, *Ikaria, the island where no one dies* which was established when Ikaria was named a Blue Zone in the year 2000. So, it was decided, miracle tinctures from Ikaria – they work!

When breakfast was over, Julia asked Pearl, Charlee, and Mathias to join her for a walk in the gardens. The sun was high in the sky and the air was crisp and welcoming. For the next two hours, Julia shared with the others Alex's offer to live and work in Qatar and commute back and forth to Ikaria as needed. Her argument to stay in Qatar was that it was safer to do this type of research in a secure facility and the estate provided just that. She explained that if living in Qatar part time didn't work for the family, she wouldn't accept the offer. And if that was the case, the lab in The Sacred Rock Healing Center would need to be renovated to accommodate Julia's new work. After long deliberation, it was decided. Charlee and Mathias would continue to manage and run The Sacred Heart Healing Center, and Mathias would update the research lab at the healing center so Julia could travel back and forth from lab to lab. Pearl was given everyone's blessing to marry Adeem, if, as Mathias demanded, she finished her studies at the university and continued her research with Julia. Pearl agreed to the conditions with great joy.

Julia was thankful for Mathias's fatherly concerns and demands. Pearl was the best student she had ever had. Her unique observation skills and intrinsic knowledge of physiology in both plants and animals was a gift. Julia had relied on Pearl many times to troubleshoot problems she couldn't figure out, and every time Pearl contemplated a scientific conundrum, she 100% produced perfect mathematical solutions with commonsense outcomes. She amazed Julia daily. It was decided that both Julia and Pearl would relocate to Qatar part time. Pearl would reside at the chateau with Adeem, and Julia would arrange to stay in one of the wings in Alexander's estate next to the research center.

When the meeting was over, it took one second for Pearl to jump up and run to Adeem with the wonderful news. Alex heard the commotion in the kitchen and joined in the excitement. For the first time in decades his heart was full of love, and knowing Julia and the family had accepted his offer made his heart race with excitement. This was the woman of his dreams. The woman he would spend eternity with.

Julia was already in research mode and asked everyone to join her in the sunroom. They each found a chair and gave Julia their attention. "OK, before you men leave, I have a few questions. Alex, what do you know about the water here in the chateau; where does it originate?" she asked.

Alex had asked Clem the same question the day he found him pulling up the marble tiles. He stated, "There is a large aquifer under the Arabian estate property. This is why it is so green in that area.

Actually, it was Dimitri's father who built the conduit system that brings the water to the surface. The same aquifer feeds this stream here in the sunroom. It is funny now that I think about it; Qaseem's Arabians are the best in the world. On occasion we would bring in horses that were questionable, not as strong as we would like in the racing world, but after six months of being exposed to the water in the swimming pools, which are fed from this aquifer, they became beasts. I always gave the trainers the recognition, but maybe it was the water I should have been praising."

Julia sat nodding her head as she added, "Yes, I think you are right. I want to know if it spirals in all areas it surfaces."

Alex rubbed his chin as he looked at Adeem. Adeem started smiling and answered, "It does. I questioned this many years ago. The swimming pools in the training center spiral like whirlpools just as the stream does here in this room. I asked if there was a device causing this motion and was told no, it comes out of the pipes that way. I never thought about it until you asked the question."

Julia was ecstatic, "This is great news. Does the new research center have the same water source?" Julia asked.

"Yes, every building on our property uses that same source," Adeem replied.

Julia clapped her hands, "Yes! Good news. I did not want to tear up this floor again," she laughed then continued, "Mathias, do you think you can build a system that will provide enough water to fill two or three small pools in the research center?" Mathias explained that he would need a tour of the center before he could answer the question. To fulfill that request, everyone decided to depart the chateau and head to the new research center for a quick stop before flying back to Agriolykos. Alex called Yusef and within an hour they were all on their way to the estate.

The women were shocked when they saw the research building. Alexander hadn't skimped on anything. Julia looked at him in disbelief, "Your people did this in twenty-four hours?" Alex explained that it was originally used as a medical facility for injured and sick horses, so it wasn't much of a stretch to prepare it for an agricultural research lab.

The new lab was almost perfect. Julia made a list of the additional equipment needed, as well as counter space, cabinets, and storage units for water and materials. Mathias walked around the center with a pad and paper, walking off measurements as he mentally designed the lab to Julia's specs on the grid paper. When they were done, everyone planned to meet again in two weeks at the research center on the estate. Pearl, though disappointed she would be away from Adeem that long, decided to use the time to plan a wedding.

Chapter Twenty-Three

After they completed a walk-through and troubleshooting session in the new research center, Alex asked Yusef to pilot the group from the estate to the Athens airport, pick up one of the helicopters, and fly the group on to Ikaria where the helicopter would stay for Julia to use as needed while he and Adeem took care of their banking business in Doho, Qatar.

Before they left, Alex pulled Julia aside, "I am leaving one of the helicopters at the Ikaria airport. If at any time you need to use it to travel back and forth while you and Mathias prepare and renovate the center, it is yours to use. I have instructed the tower to contact a pilot for you at any time." Julia was thankful for the added convenience as she had already planned a trip to Athens to talk to one of her colleagues about the genetics of the human cell and its systems communication properties. Alex's expression changed as he looked into Julia's eyes. She could see the agita on his face as he told her, "Julia, I had a very vivid dream this morning. I am a little unsure of what I am doing. It feels a bit uncomfortable."

Julia became concerned, "What is it, Alex, you can tell me anything."

He said, "This morning the apparition came to me in my dream. She gave me the name and number of a contact that I am scheduled to see tomorrow morning at 9:00 a.m. in Doho. When I woke up this morning, that same number was written on a piece of paper, waiting for me on the dining room table. I called the contact while you were showering and, sure enough, this woman is well aware of the meeting with me. I have never met this woman or her firm nor have I ever heard of them. This woman's name is Julia Kaya and her firm is called *The Council of Seven*. Does that ring a bell?"

Julia quickly straightened up and with panic in her voice she asked, "What did you say?"

"You heard me right. Her name is Julia Kaya with The Council of Seven."

"Holy shit, Alex! Oh my god! What is going on? Do you think it is the same woman in the picture?"

"She has the same name, that is all I know right now," he replied.

Julia said, "The kids had some interesting dreams last night too. Charlee called it a 'premonition' on what is to come. In their dreams they saw rioting in the streets and people hurting each other. They are putting up a front, but I can feel their apprehension. I am glad we are going back to Agriolykos to regroup. It will give us some time to wrap our heads around all of this. Funny thing is, Charlee and Pearl brought up the fact that we are now immortal and asked me what that means. I mean, they understand the definition, but the actuality of truly being immortal is too much to comprehend. It is not a concept that the human brain can easily process. It is crazy to think we are never going to die. I have so many questions about what this means myself. Alex, have you realized that we really do not know what this is all about? We have been chasing an apparition around the world but have no clue why. I will have to admit, being told we are the chosen does not answer any questions, it only brings up a million more."

"Yes, I have been festering on that thought myself. There is so much we do not know." Alex stepped back and ran his fingers through his hair. "Julia, I understand you want to decode the water, but what then? What is our role in this shift going forward? And why us? These are my questions. I had a perfectly content life, full and busy with a side hobby of investigative journalism – trying to find Dimitri – and now I am immortal. What the hell?!" Alex let out a deep, cleansing breath. "Did you dream last night?"

"Yes, I did. I was shown how the cells are dividing in our bodies right now; yours, mine, and the others. As our cells die off, as they do in the millions every day, ours are being replaced with cells that will never age. Instead, they are creating new communities in our immune system, causing us to vibrate at a different frequency. It is vibrating at the same frequency as our planet and the other planets in our galaxy. Somehow, I am not sure how yet, we are being influenced by the magnetic field that connects the outer planets to ours and to the invisible energy field surrounding us." Julia let out a sigh, dropped her head, raised her hands, and waved them in the air, "I do not know, Alex. I am as confused as the rest of you. I have a feeling the answers will be presented during your meeting tomorrow morning; at least I hope you find some answers. Whomever you are meeting with, ask a lot of questions please." Julia put her hands together as if praying, "Do not forget to ask a lot of questions!"

"Well, I hope this 'Julia Kaya' has the answers to give. I do not normally do business this way. Usually, I vet my business associates quite extensively before I agree to meet with them. I *hope* I get some answers tomorrow morning," he replied. Julia leaned against his body as she looked up at him with a loving smile. He bent down, kissed her gently then looked into her eyes, "Thank you for last night. It was beautiful and so are you, my love. Are you ready for whatever is to come?"

"I do not think we have a choice at this point. I believe we are all in this together whether we want to be or not," she answered.

"Can I ask you to consider us a couple?" he asked as he hugged her tight.

Julia smiled, "I will consider it, yes. But you must know, when I am in research mode, my brain shuts off the outside world until I can successfully form a scientific method and present my conclusions. It is a process that requires most of my time, Alex. And *this* is something I have never done before. I have never been in a scientific predicament like this before. My life's work has been wrapped around healing. There is nothing to heal now, or shortly there will not be. So, I am in a learning phase here, like a fish out of water." Julia stepped back from Alex and paced the floor in front of him as she started to comprehend the totality of it all. "I figure I will start the experiments on the plants and water then work up to the human aspect of it. Alex, knowing I am going to be preoccupied for quite a while, are you OK with that?"

He reached for her hands and when she took his hands in hers, he looked deep into her eyes and said, "I will wait a lifetime for you, Julia. I will help you in any way I can. I am not a scientist, but I can make you a mean hot meal at the end of your day. I can rub your feet and listen to your scientific methods until you fall asleep. I can make love to you when you need to be loved. That is what I can offer. Will you accept my package deal; me, food, and sex?"

Julia laughed out loud and said, "Deal!"

He held up his pinky finger. She laughed, intwined hers with his, and together they said, "Pinky swear!"

He kissed her gently, assuring her, "Thank you! I will not let you down!"

Chapter Twenty-Four

At 8:30 the following morning, Alexander's driver arrived to pick him up for his 9:00 a.m. mystery meeting in the Aspire Tower in Doho, the capital of Qatar. Alex had never been in this building before, but he had flown over the top of it on hundreds of occasions and always admired its extraordinary architectural design. The fifty-story hotel tower that was shaped like a tall, thin torch was the tallest building in Qatar. It was surrounded in glass and reflected the sun in rays of rainbows, making it quite spectacular at sunset. The tower's location and multipurpose use made it a destination hotspot for international tourism. Whether it's as a hotel, a restaurant mecca, or a shopping experience, this tower was iconic.

The car arrived at the Aspire Hotel. Alex started to open his car door to get out but was greeted by a man in a black suit who opened the door for him and motioned him to enter the building. Once he entered, he noticed a thin, tall woman, much taller than he, smiling and moving toward him. She had the look of an American model in the 1970s; tall, thin, and pale, but stunning. She was wearing an indigo-colored pantsuit that shimmered as the sunlight from the towering windows in the main lobby rested upon it. She was beautiful with her long chestnut hair, blue eyes, extremely white teeth, and a flawless, pale complexion that shimmered like her suit. It looked as if she had dusted herself with a powder made with tiny sparkles. She was wearing soft pink lipstick, but not a stitch of other makeup. She looked American but with accentuated features. Her eyes were bigger and her nose and mouth just a bit smaller. Her smile and presence were calming.

She quickly welcomed him, "Alexander, it is a pleasure to meet you. We have been waiting for this meeting for very a long time." He didn't recognize her accent. It sounded like a combination of European and Australian decent. She extended her hand and smiled as she

greeted him. Alex shook her hand and was taken aback by the
warmth and size of it. It felt as if she had just been holding a hot
cup of coffee and his hand dwarfed hers. She motioned toward the
elevator that was open and waiting for them.

She introduced herself as they entered the elevator, "Welcome.
I am Julia Kaya. You can call me Kaya, for lack of confusion as we
move forward." He turned to look at her again, this time trying to put
the face with the black and white aged photos he had found in his
library. She said, "I look better in color – at least I think I do." She
smiled and looked Alex in the eye. "Those are great photos of me in
your library, but just a little dreary don't you think?" she said with a
sweet laugh as she looked up at the elevator numbers increasing by
each floor. A strange feeling started to arouse in his stomach, a feeling of nausea. He swallowed hard as the saliva started building in his
mouth. He could feel the blood draining from his head, and knew he
was going to faint. She watched until his eyes began to roll back in
his head then reached up and pressed on the center of his forehead –
and he was out.

When Alex awoke, he rubbed his eyes as they slowly adjusted
to the extremely bright room he was sitting in. He started to stand,
but the residual dizziness didn't allow it. He dropped his head, took
a deep breath, and waited until he regained his composure. When he
did, he quickly scanned the room. It looked to be entirely made of
multi-faceted glass resembling large sheets of crystals. Alex watched
the prism of opalescent colors bounce from the floor to the ceiling
and back to the walls as he adjusted himself in his chair. Even the
floor was clear. The room appeared to be floating in thin air. It was
completely illuminated from all directions as if floodlights were
beaming in through the walls. The ceiling was so high, it looked as
if there wasn't one. The space appeared to be about the size of a
small auditorium and completely sterile. As the walls and floor
shimmered, seven people materialized in front of him, all sitting
behind a clear C-shaped desk. He sat up, trying to focus on the faces,
but only Kaya's was clear. They were all radiating a lavender
opalescent energy. It likened to scorching heat waves undulating
off white desert sand, but in a glimmering pattern that blotted out
the facial details. Though they were sitting, they seemed to be in subtle

constant movement. As Kaya moved in her seat, the lavender energy moved with her in perfect harmony like a delicate ballerina dancing all around her. No one said anything as they watched him. Alex turned and looked at the room behind him. There was nothing else in the room, not even an elevator door, no way to exit if he wanted to. He was sitting in the center of the room in a metal chair facing the desk that was about twenty feet away. There were three men to Kaya's right, and two women and one man to her left. She was sitting in the center.

Kaya spoke first, "Hello again, Alexander. Welcome. How are you feeling?"

Alex answered, "Besides feeling dizzy, nauseated, and extremely confused, I would like to know where I am and why you have drugged me!"

Kaya adjusted herself in her seat and replied, "We're sorry for the confusion. It's understandable. Where you are I cannot explain other than it's a place not of your world. There's a lot to explain to you today and much of it will be hard to wrap your head around, but at this point, I assume you'll not be too astonished about the information we're about to share with you. We ask that you listen and keep an open mind. We're here because of you and your family and what your presence means to the galaxy. If at any point you need time to reflect or have any questions, please let me know. Do you have any questions at this point?"

Alex looked around the room again and scoffed, "There are millions swirling through my head, but first, who are you?"

Kaya smiled, expecting a more confrontational moment, but appreciated Alex's calm presence considering this was the Emir of Qatar they had kidnapped. She smiled and said, "We are the Council of Seven. We represent the seven races from seven different planets that monitor and watch over your Earth. Each of our planets reside within your solar system and are located behind your sun. Your government is aware of us, yet we've not made contact with them. Our vibrations weren't compatible with your planet until now. When you seeded the oceans with the spiraling waters full of nutrients and healing powers, it raised Earth's vibration enough for us to meet with you here today without hurting our energy fields. We represent a peaceful and nature-loving star system. We're just one of many star systems that make up the Galactic Federation. The Galactic Federation is an alliance of extraterrestrial leaders from a conglomerate of planetary systems located throughout the Milky Way galaxy. We work together to ensure harmony and unified peace within the universe.

For eons we've been communicating with your family, Alexander, as well as Julia's family. You, Julia, Adeem, Charlee, Mathias, and Pearl have all incarnated together for many lifetimes. The seven of us are part of your soul group. Soul groups, which there are billions of, share a strong emotional, mental, and spiritual bond with one another that transcends time. During each incarnation, The ALL, or who you call God or Allah, prepares the soul for its final mission. The mission is to ascend into a higher level of consciousness. This doesn't mean, like most believe, that you've made it to heaven and are one with God; it means that your soul has experienced all the emotions this dimension has to offer and the soul no longer yearns for experience but yearns for love. To return to pure love, a soul must intrinsically learn the difference between love and hate, evil and good, and all the levels in between. It's necessary for the soul to go through many lifetimes to achieve this. Reincarnation was set in place at the beginning of the first soul's incarnation, its first separation from The ALL. When this separation occurred, with each incarnation a mental blank slate was established, a deletion of the brain's memory of prior lifetimes. What you call amnesia. To be honest, we don't agree with this method but understand that The ALL needed time to learn and experience emotions through us without conflict. Alexander, is this making sense?" Alex set up straighter in his chair and slowly nodded.

Kaya continued, "Alexander, through each incarnation we, The Council of Seven, have prepared you for this time in history. Each of us has incarnated with you, in this lifetime, to ensure a physical bond was created between us. This was necessary to build trust due to the amnesia of our prior lifetimes together.

I'm going to explain to you a different perspective of your planet, and why Earth is so special to us, particularly at this time.

This is where I need you to keep an open mind. Earth is a very special planet to every species in the universe, and there are thousands. It's the only one of its kind. Unfortunately, throughout her history she's been bullied by several nefarious intergalactic species wanting to exploit her, and pelted by the celestial bodies in her own solar system. She's been crying for help for millions of years. We're all connected, everything in this galaxy, and we all felt her and her pain. Much of her pain was caused by several catastrophic geological events which in turn caused extinction events, many more than your geologists are willing to admit. All these extinction events were caused by celestial bombardment. The most destructive bullying of planet Earth has come from our own sun."

Kaya got up and walked around to the front of the C-shaped desk. She sat back against it, standing directly in front of Alex. She crossed her arms, took a deep breath, and said," Alexander, once again an extinction event is upon us. It took Earth over 1,200 years to recover from the last event, this being the Younger Dryas Period, as your scientists call it. That event happened only 13,000 or more years ago. The planet's surface was ripped apart by solar flares in the form of plasma bolts, or what your astrophysicists liken to solar flares. Plasma bolts, unlike your typical lightning, hit the earth with a magnitude of heat and energy of one hundred Hiroshima atom bombs. When this happened, a giant shockwave shot through your atmosphere in a matter of seconds, instantaneously toppling everything in its path. Many of your ancient sights prove this. At the same time, volcanoes erupted around the planet, glaciers melted, and the skies went dark for many centuries. Planet Earth was thrown into an Ice Age in a split second.

During this tumultuous time, the planets in your solar system had a very different alignment that contributed to the sun's highly charged particles becoming unstable. Since then, your planets have rearranged themselves into the alignment they now hold. It's a much more conducive and harmonic alignment, but still a vulnerable one. Because Earth is part of our universal family, we felt the earth's pain and suffering each time she went through these extinction events. It was like a child crying out for help. We knew it was time to step in and help her.

It was decided that by stabilizing the magnetic fields and the energy fields around Earth, this would help minimize the violence. We put in place the Van Ellen Belt to protect the planet from the sun's solar bombardments and we placed artificial moons around each of your planets. These moons locked onto each planet they were designated to mate with and stabilized the magnetic fields around them. This was done not long after the great flood 5,200 years ago.

Alexander, the galaxies are constantly moving through the Universe which has many energetic layers. All of us here in this room, as well as the entire Galactic Federation, have been collaborating and preparing Earth for this next moment in space and time.

Our galaxy is about to travel through the most powerful energetic band of space that we've ever encountered. This powerful new energy will create chaos within the human body. Earth's humans no longer resonate with the energy fields inside or outside her atmosphere. In the beginning, the human body was created from the Earth and synchronized with her vibration and energy field so you could live and survive together symbiotically. It was the most perfect pairing ever created. But over time, humans have been so polluted with toxic chemicals and false ideologies, which in turn changed and separated the frequency connection between Earth and humans. The human body can no longer physically handle the molecular changes in the new energy field we're heading into. Your planet and race of people have become very ill, disconnected, and aggressive due to the greed and the toxic warfare your governments have inflicted on you.

Unfortunately, a long time ago, your government created alliances with outside entities who had selfish agendas for planet Earth. Alexander, how're you doing? Are you following me?"

Alex nodded and said, "Yes, continue."

"Good. Now your history teaches that Earth experienced chaos and darkness after the dinosaur's extinction, but so did many other planets. The black hole in the center of the Milky Way holds this galaxy together, but an event occurred millions of years ago that caused this black hole to become violent and unstable. It sent out multiple shockwaves from its center that destroyed the nearby planetary systems. Many of the technically advanced civilizations lost their entire planets, making them space-faring people looking for another planet to inhabit. The Galactic Federation decided to find a new planetary system, far away from the black hole, that could meet the needs of all species.

During this early time, planet Earth was inhabited by a waring reptilian species of giants that were well over eighteen feet tall. This species conquered your planet after their planet was destroyed by the black hole's shockwave. When they arrived, they created a large family of dinosaurs for pets and food, and lived alongside them for many years. Ironically, a piece of their home planet, in the form of a large asteroid, made its way into Earth's atmosphere and collided with her, eliminating most of the species on Earth, causing it to become a beacon once again, calling out for help. The Galactic Federation decided to explore this part of space and find the source of the distress call. It was considered fringe space, so far out on the edge of the galaxy that no one really noticed her, but your planet continued to reach out for help by sending vibrations of pure love into space until someone noticed.

When we, the seven planets that make up the Council of Seven, arrived, Earth was a fireball." Kaya stood up and walked around to the back of the desk. Alex watched her ethereal body shimmer as she sat back down in the center of the C-shaped desk. She continued, "Alexander, everything in the universe is connected energetically, just as all souls are connected energetically. We deeply felt Gaia's pain. We reached out and helped your planet, putting out the fires and terraforming the surface back to the paradise it once was. When the plants and waters returned and the sky was healed, which took thousands of years, the Galactic Federation decided that Earth would become the ark to all species within the Federation. Humans were created and DNA from every species in this galaxy was placed within your DNA. It was to remain dormant until the great reset occurred. We knew this time was coming and we needed a safe haven to store our genetic profile. Your bodies are the ark, Noah's Ark as you refer to it. The allegory of a boat or vessel was made to confuse you. You are the boat – you are the vessel. It surprised us when the genetic program between 1860 and the 1950s blatantly called most of the DNA within the human genome 'junk DNA' and disregarded it. That 'junk DNA' belongs to the many civilizations that helped save Earth 65 million years ago then again 13,000 and 5,200 years ago. What we didn't realize was that a large portion of this 'junk DNA' belongs to war-faring species. At the time, we didn't know that many of the members of the Federation were from rogue planets hiding under a ruse to become part of the new human race. The abundance of this 'warring gene' created a war mentality within the human genome. Over time, these genes became more dominant, and compassion for Earth and one's fellow man was lost. In its place, a conquering humanoid, homosapien sapien emerged, filled with greed and power-mongering ideals. During this time, a lower vibrational blanket of darkness engulfed Earth and created great illness within her once again. This lower vibration has come to a peak and is now affecting the entire galaxy.

Alexander, we have finally made our presence known because we need to change the molecular chemistry and energy fields within your planet and your immune systems. This is necessary for both the human body and Earth to handle the transition into the higher frequency field we are heading into. We've been waiting and preparing for this transition for thousands of years, but Earth has been preventing us from moving into this new expansion because of her lower vibration. By seeding the waters of your planet with the healing properties combined in the alchemy you created with the spiraling waters – and we thank you for your help – your civilization will no longer feel the need to war or conquer. When ingested, it will remove all the toxins from the body and destroy the negative war mongering genes that promote lower vibrations and disease. It will also reverse the aging process, as well as reconfigure your energy fields to pair with your new galaxy placement. You'll be immortal as we are. We're all connected and it's now time to adjust and begin again. *This* is the time of the great reset.

Alexander, this next part will be even more difficult to comprehend so listen carefully."

Alex thought, *There is more? I am already confused and have so many questions.*

She said, "Yes, and we'll answer those questions as we go."

Alex's next thought was, *She can read my mind?*

"Yes, we all can, Alexander, now listen. Many humans won't be transitioning with us. Those who aren't ready for the vibrational changes and those that reject the water will return to soul and return to source. Understand this isn't a punishment. The souls that don't transition chose to temporarily incarnate during this time to experience the lower vibrations one last time before they're gone. It's what souls do; they incarnate to experience emotions. Some have called this the Rapture, the immediate disappearance of a mass of people. We don't recognize your religious beliefs, but it's a way of explaining to you what's about to happen to life on your planet. Many humans will stay, those who see through the veil and have come to terms with it in a positive and loving way. The Galactic Federation vowed not to interfere with Earth's progress and have left you to your own vices, but now we have no choice. We're all in this together. To cross over into this new energy field, only the higher vibrational species and planets can enter. If one planet with lower vibration enters, the field will collapse. When the transition occurs, we'll all live together as one vibration in the universe: the vibration of love, kindness, and unity. We won't see each other as different though we'll look very different.

Immediately after the transition, the entire Galactic Federation will expose themselves to you. We'll share planets and technology for the betterment of all. We'll truly become one with the universe, traveling and exploring together as one mind. Alexander, do you have any questions?"

Alex was staring at each member of the council one at a time. He felt as if he was in a dream. He was grasping everything they were saying yet the reality of this was unbelievable. He shook his head, raised his hands, let them drop to his thighs, let out a loud sigh then shook his head NO.

Kaya continued, "We know this is a lot to handle and comprehend, but there's no time for you to 'think' about this or 'contemplate' it until it makes sense. Many of your governmental institutions are about to fail. Your food supply is about to diminish exponentially. No one will know why at first except you, Julia, Pearl, Mathias, Charlee, and Adeem. The domino effect has begun. The waters of your planet are changing and the life within the water is waking up to a new paradigm. Your oceans have already recovered from the pollution dumped in her. There will be a spontaneous global awakening. The questions humans ponder – who are we, what's our purpose, and what's our true history – will now be answered. The veil and amnesia will completely dissolve through a massive download, but only to those who remain on Earth. It's imperative that Julia, Charlee, and Pearl immediately put into place a system of growing new crops of food. The new bodies won't be able to handle any animal products or animal by-products. To merge into the new field, no death from an animal source can dwell inside the body. Consumption of this infected toxic flesh has lowered the vibration of the humans as well as the animals on your planet. The new diet will be sourced from what the planet itself grows. The waters are connecting with the soil as we speak, and the ecological root systems are healing. Alexander, you'll use your monetary riches and status, along with Julia, to build and perfect the new food supply for the new planet. Once the transition is complete, but not until then, can we unite our planetary systems and work together, sharing all technologies and resources. Until then, temporary systems need to be put into place. You'll have support from many countries and the Galactic Federation. The rest will gradually fall into place.

After this meeting, we won't contact you again, but we will be with you always. Be prepared; the corporate systems will fall like a house of cards in the next few weeks. We've moved your investments to a new banking system that's run by the council inside this building on the ninth floor. You're privy to it at any time and for any use. We have no desire to withhold from you what's yours. We are asking for you to change your focus on how you use it. We ask that you use it to feed and educate the world. We ask you to teach and serve your fellow man during a very confusing time. Will you help us help you save the universe and every species that ever lived within it?"

Alex stared at the council, knitted his eyebrows, and asked, "Why us? Why this family? Why me?"

Kaya stood up and walked around to the side of the large desk the council was sitting behind, "Alexander, stand up please." Alex got up and stood in front of the council. Each council member stood, walked around the desk, and stood in front of Alex. They each extended their right hand. Alex began to tremble as he shook each hand. The first hand belonged to George. The second hand belonged to Daniel. The third hand belonged to Dimitri. The fourth hand belonged to Gabriella. The fifth hand belonged to Julia Kaya, the sixth hand belonged to Qaseem, and the seventh hand belonged to Sophia. Alex dropped to his knees before them and wept with his whole body shaking. Gabriella and Dimitri approached him, reached down, and helped him to his feet. Gabriella held his hands while Dimitri put his arm over his shoulder and said, "We love you, son. We are so proud of you, and we thank you for your help." Alex hugged Dimitri and Gabriella as he cried like a little boy. He had his parents in his arms. He tried to talk, but the lump in his throat and the shock to his system was too much to bear. He couldn't form words.

Kaya said, "We've been on this journey with you for a long time."

Qaseem walked over and stood in front of Alex and said, "Each of us were a part of your life, my son. We chose to incarnate with you this time to feel the human experience. We needed to understand the human condition to understand the implications of what this transformation and energy shift would have on the planet. I will admit, human emotions are quite exhausting." Each of the seven smiled and nodded in agreement.

Kaya asked the question again, "Will you help us help you, help us?"

Alex said yes. She asked him to return to his chair and The Council of Seven returned to their seats behind the desk. Kaya explained, "It will take two years for the higher vibrational transformation of this planet to be complete. This transformation began when you seeded the water. There will be great turmoil for a period. Ignore this and stay focused. Remember what the end results will be; a planet of health, joy, love, creativity, trust, and connection. We've set in motion for the seven leaders from the seven continents to meet with you one week from now. You all know what needs to be done. All resources are available to you. You'll be contacted again when the transformation is complete. We love you very much."

Alex asked, "Can I ask a question?"

"Yes."

"I know each of you," he said as he nodded toward the others, but I do not know you, Kaya. Who are you?"

"I am your Julia, Julia Kaya, from another space time continuum. We've been together through many lifetimes. This is why your Julia has my necklace. It's her necklace, our necklace.

It's time for you to leave now. You'll remember all that's taken place here today. Adeem is waiting for you at the estate, and you'll both go to Agriolykos when the rains end in three days. Pick up Julia and Pearl and return to Qatar. Julia will be shown the new science and physiology of quantum mechanics based on frequencies. In one week, you'll meet with the seven leaders back here on level nine. The great exit will begin two days after the meeting with the other leaders. Stay focused. We emphasize this because billions of people will disappear in one afternoon and that will be hard to come to terms with. Remember, all exiting souls from the planet will return to source. No one will suffer, no one is left behind, and no one is judged. There's no such thing as karma. The Source doesn't judge itself or anything else; it lives within us and through us. It loved, played, and experienced all emotions through us. It's now ready to let us live without interference. It's released us so we can be one and not separated by our amnesia. Everything is entangled with Source. We are Source. We are one. This concept will be a knowing amongst all species."

In a split-second, Alex was sitting in the car, his driver ready to take him home. It was close to midnight. The last thing he remembered hearing was, "We are one." He sat back and closed his eyes, reliving everything that had just been said to him. Realizing what was to come saddened him, but knowing that no *one* or no *thing* would be harmed gave him comfort. The driver of the car asked for directions. Alex said, "Take me back to the estate."

Chapter Twenty-Five

When Alex arrived at the estate, the door to the new research center was open. The lights were on, but no guards were on duty and Adeem was wandering around inside. Alex walked in and was shocked to see the lab was completely finished with everything on Julia's wish list in place. The men looked at each other and shook their heads, "I am not surprised by anything any longer. What happened at the meeting?" Adeem asked.

Alex told Adeem everything and when he was done, Adeem said, "They sequestered me also. I was in the same crystal room you describe. They told me the same things and I too met Dimitri and the rest of the group. Dad, they told me Pearl and I are going to have twins, a girl and a boy. It seems she is pregnant. These children are going to usher in a new paradigm to the new Earth. It was explained to me that The Silver Pharaoh, Psusennes, the original god of chaos, and his escort Priya, goddess of love and goodness, will be reincarnated into the twins. Together they will restore universal balance and usher in the higher vibrations and energy fields of the new planet. I was told that in 2040 The Phoenix will return, and the twins are the only ones who can close the portal of chaos. What this means, they would not say. Pearl has asked me many times about The Phoenix. We have done some research on this phenomenon and the return of this bird is not a good thing. It is the bird of destruction and resurrection and seems to be on a 138-year cycle. The next cycle ends in 2040.

Kaya said Pearl will be told what the connection is when the twins are three months old. So, I guess we will wait and see. I asked her about the rings. She told me these rings will protect us from the chaos and interplanetary frequency changes that are about to take place. She said the changes will be difficult for many to experience but we, us six, will be unaffected as long as these rings stay on us.

Kaya explained then showed me that they are wearing the same rings."

Alex looked down at his ring and spun it around on his finger. He thought about trying to remove it just to see if he could then changed his mind. He looked back up at Adeem who continued, "Kaya also told me that planet Earth will bifurcate. The old Earth as we see it today will remain in this realm, and the new Earth will travel into the new space-time continuum ahead of us. Kaya went into great detail to explain that the souls that chose to stay on this original Earth wanted to stay. Those that go, chose to go. At the end of two years, the old planet will implode on itself and die, no longer existing. It is all such a mind-bending concept."

Adeem let out a huge sigh as he ran his fingers through his hair. "I wonder if Pearl knows. Anyway, I asked them why they told me about the twins. They said, 'Your job is to teach the children love and kindness and to help them find joy in every living thing.' I am to teach them the laws of nature and to appreciate the beauty in the world. They said that when the children turn ten, they will change the world. That is all they would say about the subject.

The next thing I knew, I was back here standing in front of the research door, nauseated and scratching my head, feeling like I had been hit by a truck! When I arrived, the lights were on and I could see movement. My first thought was, *Oh shit, we are being robbed*, but when I walked in fists up and ready for a fight, what I saw were celestial-looking beings all working together, manifesting all this equipment out of thin air. Interestingly, they had no lower bodies, just a gentle swirl of white dust that sparkled as they moved about. Alex, they were hovering in midair. Even their upper bodies were ethereal in nature, but they did have faces. Most of them appeared to be men. There was one being that acknowledged me with a nod and a smile when I entered, but then held up his hand, motioning me to stop. When I did and lowered my fists, he returned to business at hand. I watched this whole lab appear one piece of equipment at a time until it was, as you see, perfect. All the equipment is state-of-the-art. I do not think NASA even has this equipment! It was amazing to watch. The last thing they did was install the three pools over there and the water system in it. Look at this water. Here – you gotta taste it. One of the beings, before he left, gave me a full glass of it and waited for me to drink it."

Adeem filled a glass of water from one of the ponds and handed it to Alex. Hesitantly, Alex looked at Adeem before he took the glass. He held it up to the light, examining it for scary particles. "I drank from it and I am fine," Adeem added.

Alex drank the whole glass and within seconds his body was glowing in the same type of field as the Council of Seven. Every hair on his body was standing on end, even the hair on his head. Adeem stepped back and watched, and when it all died back down, Alex dropped to his knees.

Adeem said, "You are OK. Stand up. Is that not the coolest thing ever? The water spoke to me. It explained that it had rearranged the final sequencing of our DNA for immortality. My understanding is that a series of genes that controlled our cortisol levels and our fight or flight systems have been turned off. These genes are also responsible for triggering anger, restlessness, depression, and several of the personality disorders that create illness and inflammation in every organ of our bodies. These genes, along with the manipulated aging gene, kept our vibrations static or lower such that any joy or love that entered our fields would not register as a true feeling but as a cautionary emotion. This in turn prevented us from truly knowing what love feels like. By turning them off and removing the emotion of unexplainable fear and emotional distress, we can now handle the new energy field we are about to encounter. This field is a high vibrational field that only love, or higher vibrations, can enter. I do not know how else to explain it. The weirdest thing is that no one told me this, it just appeared in my thoughts after I drank the water."

Alex held up his hand as if to say *quiet please*. After a minute, he looked at Adeem and said, "Yes, I understand. It is as if the water is talking to us, reminding us of knowledge we all lost long ago. The water also spoke to me while I was floating in the river in Abu Rawash. I assumed it talked to you as well when you were floating in the stream here in the chateau?" Adreem nodded his confirmation.

"This has become so confusing and intense. Julia and Pearl are going to have to make sense out of all of this," Alex said as he looked around the research center in disbelief. "What I do know is that Julia is going to love this center and what they did with it."

Adeem looked at him with a big smile, "I agree. Alex, after I drank the water, well, all I can say is – I feel like a million bucks. I was feeling totally out of sorts before I drank it, but the clarity came blasting in. It is amazing! Are you hungry?"

It took a minute for Alex to collect himself, but admittedly he too felt great. He said, "Wow, this is incredible! Adeem, I am as confused as you are, but I must confess, I am ready for this change and what it means to humanity. And yes, I am hungry!"

Adeem laughed and said, "I know, right? I am SO hungry."

They closed the research center doors, talking at the same time as they headed to the house. Their biggest concern was how to feed the world. As they plotted and planned, they went through the cupboards and refrigerator, trying to piece together a late-night meal. As they cooked, they became silent, working together like perfect dance partners around the stove, both in their heads as the visions began. Visions of times long ago. Past life memories flooded in. They stood in a catatonic state for several minutes as the emotions and scenes in their minds came in waves, playing out lifetime after lifetime like an old movie. Tears rolled from their eyes then turned into laughter then turned into sorrow then laughter again. When the memories stopped, both men turned and hugged each other. They had experienced several lifetimes together as different family members, friends, and foes.

Alex said, "This is exhausting. I wonder how long this is going to go on. I am not sure how long my head can endure this kind of information all at once." Adeem nodded, held up a bottle of wine as he looked at Alex for a yes or no response. Alex said, "Absolutely! Make it a double, please."

Adeem gave a quick thumbs up with a big smile as he poured two glasses of wine and delivered them to the dining table. Alex filled their plates with rice, steamed vegetables, and stuffed cabbage leaves.

As they took their first bites, a thunderous roar of hail fell from the sky. It fell so quick and hard that it sounded as if the entire Arabian racing team was running across the roof. Both men ducked when it began then got up and ran to the windows in the sun-room. They watched trees snap and break under the weight of the ice stones. Quickly, it turned into rain and gusty winds. Debris flew past the windows as if a tornado was approaching. What started out as a peaceful night turned into a Class 5 tornado in an instant.

Alex pointed to the barns. The back doors had swung open, and they could see the trainers were in trouble. Alex and Adeem ran to the back stairwell and took the underground passageway to the inner arenas. They could hear the men yelling and the horses banging into the walls of their stalls as they reached the end of the passageway. When they entered the arena, it was total mayhem. The trainers and stable hands were trying to calm the horses as they bucked and kicked, knocking down anything and everything in their way. The animals' screams were deafening and the men were shouting as they were being knocked to the ground. The horses snorted and whinnied, front legs fighting the air, pulling to break free from the ropes that were attached to posts in each stall. You could see fear in the animal's eyes as if something was hurting them. Many were able to break free, running in all directions and knocking over everything in their paths. They were frantically looking for an open door, a way to escape. The wind and flying debris smashing into the sides of the building elevated the thun-derous banging sounds inside. Alex bolted the doors shut as Adeem ran to the medical supply room and grabbed the drawer full of tran-quilizers and syringes.

Adeem loaded the syringes full of tranquilizers as fast as he could as Alex and the trainers fought to inject the serum into the haunches of the spooked horses. Everyone was yelling at once as the total chaos continued. By the time they had gotten the last horse down and secured, two trainers were left with bruised ribs and several gashes to the head. After a brief regroup, it was time to deal with the injuries. The weather was getting worse, so there was no going anywhere. The local emergency room was miles away and it was assumed that by now many of the roads were washed away, so it was up to the men to stitch up each other. Everyone was exhausted.

Adeem filled bottles with the healing waters from the pools for the injured men to drink. When he gave them the water, each drank, but nothing happened. It was if they were drinking normal water.

There was no hair raising, no goosebumps, and no cells communicating so loudly that you could hear them talking in your head. Adeem and Alex realized at that moment that these men were not moving into the new energy field; their time on Earth was almost over. When the barns were under control and the trainers and stable hands were stabilized and resting with the animals, Alex and Adeem returned to the house through the underground tunnel. The storm was not letting up and the rains and winds were relentless as debris continued to smash into anything in their way. It was now well into the early morning hours and the men were exhausted. They closed all the curtains in the house to prevent glass from flying in before they went to bed. They lay in their beds worried about the women. Were they OK? Were they safe? There was no knowing.

Sound asleep at 6:00 a.m. the next morning, Alex's phone pinged. It was a wi-fi emergency message alert. He sat up in bed and read the message, *Rain has engulfed the entire planet. It is being heralded as an Atmospheric River.* Alex got up and went into the sunroom, looking out the window to see the pouring rain and violent winds thrashing about just as it was before he went to bed a few hours earlier. There was no reprieve on the horizon. He turned on the news and indeed, torrential rains had engulfed the planet, but no flooding was occurring. The planet was absorbing the rainwater as soon as it hit the ground.

For three days Alex and Adeem watched helplessly as the tumultuous weather anomaly spun out right on top of them. They tried calling Julia and Pearl, but all lines were down. The only access to the outside world was through an emergency news outlet streaming 24/7 with updates on what was occurring around the world. It didn't matter where you were located, the entire planet was experiencing the same weather pattern. At the end of the third day, every lake, every stream, every aquifer, and every living thing on its surface had been exposed to rainwater. The same water had evaporated from the seeded oceans carrying the new blueprints, blueprints that would change the molecular structure in every living cell. Alex realized it had begun. The planet was now preparing for a successful navigation through the energy field that would establish Earth's new placement in the universe.

Chapter Twenty-Six

When the girls and Mathias returned to Ikaria, they spent the first day collecting herbs, flowers, fruit trees, small insects, and reptiles from all over Therma. The plan was to study the specimens and monitor the changes in their molecular structures after being given the new water. They also collected two beehives and enclosed them in a viewing plexiglass case with a small hole for the bees to enter and exit through. By studying the pollen exchange and the changes in the beehive due to the strict diet of the new water, Julia could determine how to adjust the growing expectations in the food supply after the great reset.

When the rainstorm and the large sea swells hit Therma, Mathias quickly boarded up the windows and secured the doors of the center as well as Julia's house next door. The center was plummeted with crashing waves from the sea. The sea wall protecting the small cove of Therma, directly in front of the healing center, washed away in a matter of hours after the storm began. The sea wall protecting Agriolykos, exposed to the open sea, was taking the brunt of the relentlessly crashing waves.

Pearl realized she was here to stay; there was no going to the other side of the island to her home any time soon. She was raised on the third floor of the healing center, and Nonnah Julia lived right next door. It was like her childhood days all over again when the whole family lived together while working to build the healing center for people around the world to visit. These were some of her favorite memories. But this was different. The environment wasn't peaceful and calm, but hectic and disorganized. They all understood this was crunch time, and there would be no sleep as they prepared to usher in the new paradigm. The job now was to figure out how to feed the remaining souls. The thought was a mind-boggling one that hadn't fully sunk in for any of them.

The day they had returned to the island, prior to the rains, Mathias spent much of the day with a sketchpad and pencil, designing a water collection system. His father had built a huge collection system many years ago for the city of Therma during a horrific year of heat and drought. Mathias' system would be on a much smaller scale but would mimic his father's design. Its purpose was to provide Julia with a collection of fresh water after the first rains. The new water collection system would need storage containers large enough for Julia's research to continue for months to come. Without a true picture of life after the reset, Mathias prepared for at least a year's worth of collection, to be safe. He completed the new system hours before the rains began.

For three days straight, Julia, Charlee, and Pearl worked tirelessly through the rainstorm in the lab at the healing center. It was imperative to figure out what changes to the soil had occurred and what to expect from the seedlings being planted. One big question was, *Did the seedlings need soil or just the rejuvenated water to thrive?* Julia arranged all the collected plants and insects in single units under sterile glass cases and fed them the original water and waited, but nothing happened. She waited twenty-four hours then exposed the same specimens to the rainwater. Within seconds they stood tall and faced her, bowed, and began rubbing themselves on each other as if to say *Hi.* Julia was floored. She couldn't believe her eyes. It was as if the plants and insects were conscious and aware of her.

Immediately, the plant stems grew thicker and began to sprout more and more leaves, reproducing exponentially. When the plant grew to the size of the container it was in, it stopped growing, settled down, and began to love itself again. When Julia picked a leaf, a new one instantaneously took its place. She examined the pruned leaf and tested the nutritional value of the plant as well as the soil it was in. She had noticed, over the past ten years, that the soil on Ikaria had drastically changed. Many heavy metals were starting to appear in the soil, and the lack of water throughout the drought seasons had reduced most of its nutrients to almost zero. One cup of spinach used to give the body 100% of its needed nutritional value, now it took 100 cups to provide only half of its nutritional value. After the exposure to the rainwater, the plants and soil were completely void of heavy metals and pesticides. The nutrients were swimming under the microscope, and the new values were off the charts. She needed to get back to Qatar to use the new equipment in the research center to better investigate the cell structure. For now, she had to stay put until the storms stopped. She figured she had at least three days until she could safely travel. Until then, Julia, Pearl, Charlee, and Mathias basically lived, ate, and slept in the lab as they pushed forward their research.

When the rains stopped, Julia contacted Alex and arranged a flight back to Qatar for her and Pearl. Charlee and Mathias stayed behind, deciding it was best for them to clean up the mess from the storm. Several repairs were needed, and Therma's townspeople needed help as well.

Alex had a helicopter waiting for them the next morning. They were not surprised to see the airport in shambles. The rains had washed away the dilapidated runways in the small Ikaria airport as well as several of the runways at the Athens airport. No flights were leaving from Greece anytime soon. Yusef would chopper them all the way to Qatar.

When they arrived, Alex and Adeem were patiently waiting for them on the helipad. The chopper blades hadn't even begun to power down before Pearl jumped from the bird and ran to Adeem. With a smile as big as the crescent moon, she jumped into his arms and said, "How ya doing, boyfriend?"

He laughed out loud, picked her up, and held her tight as he kissed her passionately, "I am exhausted! I have not slept in three days. I have missed you terribly. Have you missed me terribly?"

She nodded and hugged him tenderly, "Yes, every minute of every day. I am exhausted too, my love. It has been an amazing yet hectic three days. None of us have slept a wink. The new water, as well as the new supercharged vegetables we have been growing and eating, seem to be giving us the energy we need to sustain this work-load. But I must admit, I am a bit more exhausted than usual. My belly seems to be a bit bloated, and my back is achy. Maybe it is too much nutrition too soon? I do not know, but I am looking forward to one of your spectacular back rubs. I would like to put in a request for one now, if I may." Pearl reached up and kissed him tenderly, rested her head against his chest, and let out a big sigh, happy to be back in his arms.

Adeem looked at Alex who nodded and said, "Tell her."

"Tell me what?" she asked.

Adeem looked down at her, spun her around, and pulled her in tight, with her back against his chest. He reached around the front of her and put both hands on her belly.

When he did this, she leaned back into him and then gasped, "Oh my god." She put both her hands on top of his and together they closed their eyes and began to giggle like two kids with a new toy. The joy they felt was palpable.

Julia watched, unable to hear the conversation from the helicopter engines as she continued to unload the bees, bags, plants, and critters. She could tell Pearl was very excited about something. She looked at Alex and asked, "What is going on?" It took all of two minutes for the reality to hit Pearl. She turned and looked up at Adeem then down at her stomach, white as a ghost as she began to sob, "Adeem, are you ready for this? I mean, I never thought about children anytime soon, now two of them? Oh my god, I did not plan for this, at least not now. I have so much to do. There is so much we need to uncover and prepare for. Bringing children into the world now... How are we going to do this?" Pearl covered her face and started to cry.

Adeem reached for Pearl's hands and pulled her in close. He looked into her eyes calmly, with a slight smile, "My Juliet, we were chosen to bring these children into this world. They too have been chosen and will do great things soon. I am so ready for this. I love you to the moon!" Adeem kissed her tenderly on the forehead, the nose and the lips then hugged her.

Julia headed over to see what the commotion was. When she saw Pearl crying, she ran to her, "Pearl, are you OK? What has happened?"

Pearl said, "Come here, Nonnah. Put your hand here." Julia put her hand on top of her and Adeem's hands resting on top of Pearl's abdomen. When she did, she heard the babies talking. Julia put her hand to her open mouth and just stared at Pearl, "There are two babies in there, correct?" With a blank look as if in a state of shock, Pearl nodded her head. Julia looked at each of them, threw her head back, and started laughing as she clapped her hands in excitement.

Pearl cried and laughed at the same time as all three started jumping up and down, embracing each other. Adeem finally pulled Pearl away and said, "Come, let's go inside. I need to tell you a few things. When I am done, we can share the info with everyone."

Julia shooed them away with a big smile on her face and said, "You better tell Charlee or I will! Remember, it takes a village to raise children and you have the best village there is!"

As the two walked off to the house to catch up, Julia returned to Alex and melted into his arms to receive her big welcoming kiss, "I am going to be a great-grandma! You are going to be a grandpa. Oh my god, Alex, this is getting more interesting by the day."

Alex said, "Oh, Julia, you have no idea. I have so much to tell you." After they emptied the chopper and examined the new lab, they all adjourned to the sunroom in Alex's estate with a plate of cheese, crackers, and fruits. For the next two hours, Alex and Adeem shared the outcome of their meetings with the Council of Seven. Pearl sat through the entire story with her mouth open in disbelief. She thought, *History books really need an update!* Between Julia and Pearl, the questions were like rapid fire until they were exhausted. Julia was astonished that Alexander and she had been star-crossed lovers since the beginning of time. Tears came to her eyes as she thought about Daniel and Alex being in the same room together, and the thought that they shook hands awed her. She felt the need to ask questions about him but didn't know how to ask. Alex turned to her and said, "He was a gentle man. Kind and supportive of us. I am thankful I got to shake his hand." Tears gently slid down her cheeks as she listened to Alex's words. She felt light and for some reason, free.

That evening, the dinner table conversation was all about the Galactic Federation, babies, and the upcoming wedding. Pearl and Adeem decided to tell Charlee, Mathias, and Melena via a conference call during dinner. Julia got her cell phone, called Charlee then Melena, placed the phone in the center of the table, and put it on speaker mode for all to hear.

Pearl started out by saying, "Hello, everyone. Adeem has some news for you, and we figured it was best to share our news with you all together."

Adeem looked at her and gave her a surprised look, pointing at himself, and in a whisper said, "Me? You want me to tell them?"

Pearl giggled out loud and said, "Yes, you. Tell them!"

He took a big breath and blurted out, "We are pregnant!" No one said a word for about five seconds then everyone was laughing, clapping, and talking at once.

Melena was overjoyed. She said, "It is going to be a boy and his name will be Maximus! Oh my god, we are pregnant! I am so happy for you both!"

Adeem chuckled and added, "There are two of them." Once again silence then again everyone began talking and cheering all at the same time.

When the commotion settled down, Charlee turned to Mathias and said hesitantly, "OK, two of them. We can do this. Babe, we are going to be grandparents!"

Mathias kissed her gently and said, "Oh boy, yes, we are. Pearl, Adeem, congratulations!" They were elated. They knew Adeem would take care of their baby girl and that he would be a wonderful father. Julia sat back and watched and listened to the love surrounding her. She was so happy for Pearl and Adeem, and she was happy to be back in Alex's arms.

Chapter Twenty-Seven

Over the next few days, Julia and Pearl were in total research mode. Alex and Adeem took turns bringing them food and drinks and checking on them. Whenever they entered the lab, all they saw were two women hunched over computers, typing fast and furious or staring into the microscopes. The two electron microscopes the apparitions provided were gamechangers. Julia was amazed at the results and the molecular changes that were taking place before her eyes. It was like watching God work inside a tiny cell. When the research was complete, Julia dictated the abstract steps while Pearl typed the scientific paper with a conclusion that would shock the scientific world. They also put together the proper food-growing methods to insure a perfect yield to every crop. When they were done they called Charlee, Mathias, and Melena and asked them to fly to Qatar for a family meeting.

When the women finally emerged from the lab, they were exhausted. They had not slept more than three hours a day for several days. Adeem and Alex met them in the kitchen and prepared a snack for them. Both ate then napped for a few hours before the family arrived to hear the conclusions of their research.

At 6:00 that evening, the entire family was sitting in the outdoor sunroom at the estate, waiting for Julia and Pearl to present their findings. When Melena arrived, she walked in the door, looked at Alex and Mathias and said, "What the heck?" her eyes darting from man to man. She approached her brother Mathias and touched his face, "How is this possible? Mathias, you look different, younger. Alex, I assume you are about the same age as my mother, yet you look younger than me. I want some! How?" She shook her head while staring at the men as they stuffed their hands in their pockets and thanked her with big grins on their faces. Melena continued, "No really, what is going on? This is crazy looking at you right now."

Alex answered, "Melena, there is so much to tell you. Bear with us for a few moments. All will be explained shortly. Trust me when I say you need to be sitting down for this."

While they waited for the family conference to begin, Alex introduced himself properly to Melena and shared a short version of the 'Melena life story' Julia had told him. When he was done, she smiled and said, "Oh my goodness, so you know my story; I hope to hear yours with the same amount of detail, Mr. Alexander," as she grinned at him and crossed her arms.

Alex agreed. "How about over a cup of coffee in the kitchen at a later date?"

Melena nodded, "I am looking forward to it." He asked her to sit down next to Mathias and Adeem as he began to explain everything that had transpired over the past week. When Alex took a break in the story, Adeem and Mathias took over and shared their interpretations until the room was abuzz, everyone talking at once. Melena was flabbergasted, to say the least.

When Julia and Pearl arrived in the sunroom, everyone became quiet. Julia was holding seven stapled paper packets and a large whiteboard. She and Pearl were geared up and ready to teach the group what was in the final research report. Pearl handed everyone a packet while Julia started the meeting, "Hello, everyone... oh, hello, my darling!" Julia reached over and kissed the top of Melena's head and said, "This is my Melena. Have you all met?"

Melena smiled, "Mom, yowzah! Look at you! It is unbelievable. Please forgive me as I pick up my jaw from the floor. You look like you did when we were children. Just beautiful!" She got up and gave Julia a hug as she touched her face while examining the amazing transformation. She finally sat down and said, "Of course, we have all met, Mom. We are all caught up. Go ahead and begin your presentation – chop, chop." Melena sat back on the couch as she looked at each of them, and in a whisper said, "Wow, just amazing!"

Julia smiled, winked at Melena, and continued her presentation as if she were teaching a class at the university, "What is immortality? It is the ability to live forever without disease and aging. This simply means that cells are no longer subject to illness or death.

They can ignore and self-correct any negative or potential threat. In layman's terms, every cell is a machine and has an operating manual built inside of it. Every component within and on the cell – and there are thousands – work together like a fine-tuned machine. They monitor and allow organized processes within the cell to happen with deliberate intent. The cell wall, or membrane, is like a revolving door, and this door opens and closes, allowing cells to receive information from the environment then respond to it.

For example, if a bear is in front of you, a mechanism called fight-or-flight takes place. The cells, either way, prepare to stand up and fight or to run. A burst of chemical reactions take place in that split second. The cell wall opens and floods itself with adrenaline and cortisol, stimulating the cells which in turn send signals and energy to every muscle in the body to run or fight. If not in a fight-or-flight scenario, the cell wall will not open itself to a burst of stimuli it does not need. The cell walls' 'monitoring system' of opening and closing also occurs when the cell needs nutrition and oxygen or needs to eliminate toxins, waste or poisons from our bodies – which, unfortunately, we receive from our food supply, air supply, and pharmaceuticals. Our cells also keep our nervous system and immune system in balance. What is really fun is that our cells belong to communities. For example, the heart has its own unique cell community. The liver has its own unique cell community. The skin has its own unique cell community, and so on. These communities live, protect each other, and thrive together. They communicate with each other every second of every day. What is extremely fascinating is the cell's ability to function, communicate, repair, and fight infection all on its own. We do not instruct it to do any of this. Now there is a lot more, but the basic principle is that the human body is made up of trillions of these perfect little machines and communities that run at maximum speed twenty-four hours a day, seven days a week, fifty-two weeks a year for approximately eighty years, give or take.

If we go back in time, let's say biblical times, the human lived up to a thousand years or more, according to scripture. So, what happened to the human body that decreased the cell's ability to live that long? Frankly, we do not know for sure, but we do know that the process of aging relates to an area on the end of our chromo-

somes called telomeres. These are like the little plastics on the end
of shoelaces that eventually will determine our death. As we age,
they shorten until they become so short we die. What we do know
is that our chromosomes were manipulated about two hundred
thousand years ago which in turn caused the telomeres to slowly
shrink. The manipulation occurred in chromosome number two.
Due to this manipulation, our cells age, removing the immortality
scenario. Who changed the policy of living forever to only about
eighty years? Who manipulated our chromosomes? Maybe we will
soon find out.

Now here is where it gets interesting; within the cell is a
photon, a light or energy source. When we take a cell apart and remove all the mechanisms within it, what is left is a small photon,
kind of like a tiny light at the end of the tunnel. A small, brilliant
spark that cannot be destroyed or die. Some call it our spirit or soul.
When the cells die, the body dies, but the photon, the energy or spirit,
continues to live and departs the body out into the ether. What we
have discovered in the lab is that the water at Abu Rawash and the
water in the aquifer under us here in Qatar have a very ancient molecular makeup. It appears that these waters are what seeded the planet
in the beginning of time. This water is pure and highly excitable.
This is the reason for the spirals. When we combined the Ormus
and the Mana to the spiraling waters, it increased the excitability
and increased the vibration of the water molecule ten-fold. When
we introduced the electrical current from the copper wire connected
to the filament and combined it with the vibrations from the musical
notes and the rays from the sun, the electrons within the cells began
spinning at explosive speeds. This stimulated the photon, or the light
energy, at the center of the cell and created a plasma field that perfectly connected and melded itself to *the field*."

Julia raised her hands and circled them in the air and continued, "This field we can call ether. It is the space where no mass
or material is, yet where all the energy of the universal system lives.
It is said that one drop of this energy can boil all the oceans on the
planet. This energy we can call God, Allah, Source, or whatever
you want to name it. This energy is benevolent and perfect. The field
surrounding us, ether, and the energy field in the cell's photon en-

tangled in a split second after being exposed to the new water. Perfect homeostasis of the entire system was established. So, every cell in our bodies, that which makes us – us – is now connected to the ether and they are now cohabitating. We are a machine together as one, and we are now running at optimal conditions. Does all of this make sense?" Everyone adjusted themselves in their seats and nodded.

While Julia was talking, Pearl collected several of the plants from the lab and brought them into the sunroom. She also brought a sickly plant and a vial of the new water. When Pearl gave the water to the sickly plant, the group sat straight up in disbelief of what they were witnessing.

Julia said, "Is this not amazing? I had one of your workers bring a beehive from the chateau gardens to the lab. We encased it in glass and fed the bees the spiraling water. We also brought a hive from Ikaria with us. When we fed the hives the water, they began to vibrate and levitate. The energy from the bee's wings stimulated the field by 100%, if you can even imagine that. There is now enough honey in the lab to feed the entire population of Qatar for a week and it is still growing. After I analyzed the honey, I found it to be the perfect food supply. It contains all nutrients necessary for survival, not just for humans, but for every living thing on this planet. Now what is really amazing is that when *we* were exposed to the water, it connected us to the ether field and a correction occurred within chromosome #2. It will no longer age. As scientists, we call this connection to the field 'en-tanglement'. We are all now entangled with everything. We are all perfectly connected to everything – and I mean everything!"

Pearl stepped in and continued, "The combination of alchemy with the ancient water created the perfect medicine for our bodies. When we exposed ourselves to it, it not only purified our systems, but it created an energy field around us that is now compatible with Earth's frequency and magnetic field. If we are connected to the planet and the planet is connected to us, we can go anywhere it goes without disruption to the mind, body, or soul."

Julia added, "So whatever we are about to go through cosmo-logically, our bodies and this planet are now ready for the new paradigm."

Pearl asked everyone to come into the kitchen. She had poured a glass of the rainwater for each of them. She said, "Drink, it is astonishing what happens!"

Adeem and Alex chuckled "Yes, it is. We have experienced the sensation already."

Everyone drank and then pointed at each other, giggling as the hairs stood on end all over their bodies. When everyone had their giggle, they returned to the sunroom and Pearl asked everyone to turn to the next section in the handout. It was titled, *Hydroponic Gardening*. Julia explained that the best method for growing food in the immediate future would be hydroponic gardening. Pearl chimed in saying, "It took us a minute to come up with this, but the idea is simple; with the significant reduction of humans, there will be a multitude of empty buildings in the next few months. Our idea is to refurbish the buildings into giant greenhouse towers."

Pearl looked at Mathias, "What did you come up with, Dad?"

Pearl had called Mathias the previous day with the tower idea. For the next half hour, Mathias shared his engineering design and plans for each tower, depending on climate. He said, "We can accomplish this quite quickly. The buildings are already there, and infrastructure is already available. Heating and ventilation systems are already in place, so with the right teams in each city, we can put together growing houses immediately. They might be a bit archaic at first, but they will be functional and in time we can perfect them."

Alex held out his hand and asked to see the designs. "Mathias, I have a meeting tomorrow and it is on this topic. Can I take these with me?"

Mathias nodded his head affirmatively. "Thank you for putting this together, Mathias. Julia, Pearl, thank you for the research packet. It will make tomorrow's meeting so much easier for me."

Pearl said, "You are so welcome. We assumed they will want to understand this in scientific terms and want designs that can be implemented immediately. Are there any questions?"

Melena said, "Yes, I have a question. So, you are saying that by just drinking this spiraling water, it resets our systems back to its original frequency that once coexisted and paired with Earth's frequency?" Pearl told her it did. Melena said, "OK, and the mechanism that allows this is the reversal of the manipulated chromosome #2?"

Pearl answered, "Yes, along with the photon's connection to the field. The repairs to chromosome #2 and the balancing of frequencies has allowed the entanglement to happen. This entanglement is omnipresent, it is everywhere. Our energies are one with The ALL, or Source, or whatever you want to call it. We will once again live in perfect homeostasis within a loving, higher frequency energy field that will connect us to planet Earth. We will be one with her again. Her children, stewards of Mother Earth. One big family unit again."

Alex added, "Although not everyone on the planet will be going through this change with us. It was explained to me that every human reincarnates after death. Some souls incarnate back to Earth and some to other planets in the universe. Planet Earth is very special in that it was created like a playground, a place to experience every emotion and sensory connection. It is a place where free will allows a soul to live a life of excitement or despair. Most souls want to experience these things at least once. I am not sure if other planets have the same freedoms that Earth does. But, before incarnation to Earth, we also choose what type of life we wanted to experience. So, my understanding is, if this makes sense, that the souls that are here now knew upon arrival that they were going to experience a chaotic world prior to its higher frequency emergence. They knew this was the last opportunity to feel tumultuous emotions and enjoy free will. Maybe they just wanted to experience being with their ancestors one more time? I do not know.

This being said, when we go through the new energy field, only about half the population will be going with us. The Council of Seven likened it to the concept of The Rapture, but emphasized it was not a punishment but a pre-knowing departure back to Source after playing on the playground one last time. It is quite astonishing, I must admit. I am not sure how this will all go down, but I have a feeling it is going to be big. I am thankful we are all going through this together and that we come out the other side with the support of the Galactic Federation."

After all the questions had been answered, they each sat back in their seats and just looked at each other as they wrapped their heads around what was in store for them.

As Melena sat back in her seat she said, "Wow! I wish Maximus was here to see this."

With that, Pearl stretched, softly rubbed her belly and said, "Adeem, take me to bed, I am exhausted." Everyone laughed.

Julia looked at Alex and gave him a weary smile. He said, "You too, my love? Do you need a foot tickle and a back rub?"

She nodded, "Yes please!"

He got up and said, "I will draw you a bath. Give me five minutes." He left and started the bath water while Julia and Pearl put away their teaching items.

Alex returned to the kitchen and poured Julia a glass of wine, made a cheese, crackers, and small fruit plate for her, and took it to the bathroom. When he shut off the faucet, the water in the tub was spiraling. He put his hands on his hip, shook his head, and said out loud, "This is so crazy!" just as Julia arrived.

She said, "I know! Alex, this was a lot to take in. I am so glad our family is together for this new world, or life, or what are we calling it?"

He stared into her eyes as he thought about the question, "Let's call it a new beginning. We are headed into a new beginning."

Julia smiled and said, "Alex, it truly is a new beginning for us all, not just for this family but for everyone." Alex kissed her tenderly as she stood in front of him and raised her arms with a smile. He slowly pulled her sweater over her head. Reaching behind her, he unfastened her brazier. He softly kissed each nipple as he unbuttoned her jeans and lowered them to the floor. She put her hands on his shoulders for balance as she stepped out of them, and Alex took off her socks. He took her hand and guided her into the tub. She sank all the way into the water, submerged her whole head, and listened. She heard the music playing. It was the notes from the scroll, but the melody was much longer, like the water had added to the composition. It was beautiful.

When she came to the surface she enthusiastically said, "Alex, get in. You must hear this!" He did as he was asked. His head was at one end of the large bathtub for two, with hers at the other. They sank into the water at the same time and listened. It was the same ethereal sound from Abu Rawash; soft and melodic. All of Julia's tension disappeared. She was so relaxed and wanted to stay under, but obviously that couldn't happen. When they surfaced, they did so with warmth in their hearts and smiles on their faces. They shared the wine and treats and talked about what lie ahead of them. Alex watched Julia as she talked to him. He was in love. Julia had filled the hole in his heart that he had succumbed to being empty. He was happy and content, a feeling that had become so foreign to him.

Alex sat smiling at Julia as he listened. When she took a breath, Alex said, "Julia, I love you. It has been made clear to me that you and I are star-crossed lovers and from this day forward, if you will have me, I would like to spend the rest of my life with you. Will you be my wife?"

Julia leaned forward, looked into his eyes, and said, "Are you sure you want to spend a lifetime with me? That is a long, long, long time."

He splashed water at her and said, "I know, I know, I know. So, will you marry me?"

She said, "Where is my gum?" and they both cracked up laughing. She reached for her glass, took a long drink of her wine, and stared at him for a few minutes. She thought about Daniel. Their love was so deep, yet she felt the same intense love with Alexander. They were two different men from two very different worlds, but she was ready to see where the next adventure would take her.

Alex could feel her thoughts. He knew she was reminiscing about Daniel, and he let her have a moment with her thoughts. He rubbed her foot as he kept her gaze.

When her brain had wrapped itself around the idea of being a wife to Alex, she smiled sweetly and said "Yes!" Alex's serious expression turned into a big smile and a sigh of relief. He cupped her face in his hands and said, "You have made me the happiest man in Qatar!" Alex now knew that no matter what happened during this reset, or new beginning, he had the love of his life next to him. *All is well in the universe*, he thought. They washed each other's bodies, lingering in a few places longer than others, and lounged in the spiraling water until it cooled. After, they snuggled in bed and rested for an hour before dinner.

Melena sat in the sunroom staring out the window as the family rested, and thought about her life with Maximus. She wondered how different her life might have been, sharing it with him for eternity. The thought made her smile and shed tears, knowing she was without him during the most important time in history. He had been gone for so long, yet his memory and the feel of his touch was still very much alive in her daily thoughts. She was happy for Julia and Pearl. Seeing Julia so happy with Alex gave her hope. When her father died unexpectedly, Melena watched her mother go through what she had when she lost Maximus, a loss so deep that it makes one wonder if life after death is worth living. But with the love and happiness surrounding her now, she had hope that maybe one day she too would feel love in her heart again for a man. She walked into the kitchen and decided to turn her melancholy into a creation of delicious wonders for everyone when they woke up.

Julia, Alex, Adeem, and Pearl awoke to wonderful smells from the kitchen permeated the air. Julia said, "I hope Melena is cooking. She is the best cook!"

When Melena heard the rustling of sleepy people making their way into the kitchen, she poured them each a glass of wine, and a glass of bubbly water for Pearl. Everyone took seats at the kitchen bar to watch Melena do her magic. She asked question after question about all that had happened over the past week. And boy did she get an earful. When the stories came to an end, she put down her knife and said, "I almost feel as if I should not go home right now. Maybe I should stay here with my family. Would you mind if I did?"

Pearl jumped up, ran around the counter to the stove, and hugged Melena then held her at arm's length and said, "We are having a baby, two babies, and I need you. Please stay." She put her hands together in a prayer position and begged.

Melena giggled and said, "OK, if you insist." Pearl grabbed her saying thank you over and over again. Julia was on cloud nine. To have all her children close to her during this tumultuous time gave her the sense of peace that she needed. If Melena had not suggested her staying, Julia had planned on asking her to.

The kitchen was full of life as the smells wafted up from the pan to the nose. Julia sat back and smiled at Alexander. He winked, blew her a kiss, and said out loud, "All is good in the universe." In unison everyone replied, "Amen!"

Dinner was fabulous and full of life. Everyone shared questions and concerns about the upcoming events, where Melena would stay, and how she would contribute to the journey ahead of them. When the meal was over, Pearl and Adeem, and Julia and Alex went to bed. Charlee, Mathias, and Melena stayed up and talked a bit longer, enjoying another bottle of wine as they stared into the crackling fire while contemplating life.

At 7:00 a.m., everyone's phones began to ping. Alex reached over and read the wi-fi emergency message. He abruptly threw off the covers, ran into the living room, and turned on the TV. Within seconds, everyone was in the living room glued to the news. Alex quickly flipped through the channels to see how widespread the information was. It was on every channel. The pictures being broadcast were of complete chaos. People were running, crying, pushing, stampeding, and yelling.

The reader board on the bottom of the screen read, *Cattle, Poultry, and Swine across the globe disappeared into thin air at 2:00 a.m. Eastern Time. All animal products sold around the world in stores and restaurants also disappeared at the same time. All of our world leaders are in contact to discuss who might be behind this disappearance and when the animals will be returned. All animal husbandry is in shock this morning. 80% of soybean and corn crops around the world are grown to feed livestock, leaving corporations devastated.*

The news anchor was yelling into the camera, pleading for everyone to calm down when he abruptly stopped talking, grabbed and cupped his ear, trying to hear the feed being reported to him through his earpiece. He looked toward the ground, trying to concentrate. Ten seconds later, he raised his head quickly and said, "Breaking news! I have just been informed that all GMO crops across the planet have disappeared into thin air and have been instantaneously replaced with fields of grass." He lowered his head again, cupping his ear then snapped back up repeating, "More breaking news! I have just been

informed that the areas of deforestation in the Amazon have returned to their original state. The forests and vegetation have reappeared!
Also, the many plastic garbage patches around the world are now
empty. They have also disappeared!"

Alex turned the channel. Panic was everywhere. People were
rioting and looting, smashing and grabbing anything they could as
they swarmed the retail buildings. Large groups of religious believ-
ers were chanting on the street corners, holding signs professing the
apocalypse was at hand. Signs proclaiming the return of Jesus were
bouncing around on the screen.

Alex sat back and ran his fingers through his hair, "Oh my
god, it has started." Everyone looked at Alex then back at the TV.
Julia asked him what time his next appointment was. He said 1:00
p.m. Everyone continued staring at the TV in disbelief. Before they
could wrap their heads around the chaos, there was another emergency bulletin, interrupting the news.

The President of the United States popped up on the screen.
He was standing in the Oval Office as his staff fussed around him,
attaching microphones to his collar. Seconds later, presidents and
leaders from around the world were patched into the same feed.
Everyone sat up to see all the leaders of the world on the screen before them. Together they addressed the world.

The U.S. President quickly addressed each leader then took
the lead as he stood behind his podium and addressed the world,
"Good morning. I want to encourage everyone to calm down and
take a breath. This emergency bulletin is being aired all around the
world. As you now know, the livestock around the planet, as well
as the soybean and corn crops, have disappeared. We *will* get to
the bottom of this, I promise you! I'll be meeting with the world
leaders that you see before you at 3:00 this afternoon. Together,
we'll gather information to find out who is responsible for these
acts of terror. We, the world leaders, have made it perfectly clear
that we will *not* tolerate any terrorist attacks on our world governments and international security, and that includes our food supply.
We will incarcerate those involved, demanding they replace what
they've stolen from us. We're a family, and we take care of our
family. We need your cooperation by *peacefully* demonstrating. As

soon as we know more, we'll inform you immediately. Thank you." The scene returned to the local newsroom.

Melena put her hand to her mouth as she watched. The gravity of all this hadn't hit her until this very moment. She couldn't watch the rioting and anger being displayed on the television screen any longer. Her heart was racing and her hands began to shake as she watched people being stomped on, beaten, and pushed to the ground. She got up and left the room to find a bit of solace in the kitchen, her favorite place. She made a large pot of coffee and prepared breakfast for everyone. The rest couldn't pull themselves away from the horror playing out on the screen.

As the morning progressed, the news got worse. Alex finally turned off the TV and said, "OK, we knew this was coming. We are safe here and I want everyone to stay here. And for the sake of our sanity, I think it is best if we leave this thing off. I will know more, I hope, after the meeting today."

Melena called everyone to the table. They sat in silence as they picked at their food. It was one thing to be told the world was going to change, but when it actually happens, the reality is shocking.

Chapter Twenty-Eight

At noon, the same car and driver arrived to pick up Alex for his 1:00 meeting at the Aspire building. Every street was packed with protesters, dumpsters were on fire, and rioters were smashing windows and looting storefronts. As Alex's car tried to drive down the streets, people banged on the hood and windows yelling, "Judgement Day is here! Judgement Day is here!" Alex sat back and peered at the madness outside his window, not believing his eyes. He began to wonder how many of these people would soon disappear. When the car stopped in front of the building, as before a man in a black suit opened his car door and escorted him to the elevator and up to the ninth floor.

This time, no dizziness, no nausea, and no passing out. Alex was ready for it, but thankfully he didn't have to endure that again. The elevator opened to a room that looked like a typical bank with all tellers working as usual. There was no panic, no fear, no screaming, just business as usual. He wondered if they knew what was going on downstairs or if they were a part of the new beginning.

As he contemplated this, a woman approached him, shook his hand, and said, "The others are here waiting for you." She walked him through the calm bank lobby to a large, open door. Alex walked into a boardroom with no windows. The walls and ceiling were made of dark wood and the only light came from a chandelier hanging in the center of the room. Inside was a table that could seat at least twenty. There were three men and three women sitting at the end of the long table furthest from the door. There was coffee, teas, muffins, and fruit in the center of the table, but no one had any food or beverages in front of them. The strangers sat erect in their chairs with their hands clasped together on the table in front of them. Alex introduced himself and gave a brief synopsis of his background and why he was at the meeting. The others stared at him while they listened, then nodded their heads when he was done. No one said anything. He looked around the table and locked eyes with each of them, hoping to get some sort of reaction. Nothing. He addressed each one and asked for their names and where they were from. They each answered simply with two words; what country they came from and their first names only. Alex handed each one of them a packet that Julia and Mathias had made and gave a quick synopsis on what they would find in the packets. Each member took a packet and thoroughly read it. Alex sat observing each one, wondering who was running the show. Never had he been in a scenario quite like this before. His meetings were usually with world leaders dealing with high stake business deals. He sat there strategically watching the group read while trying to feel the pulse in the room. He was at a loss. There were no emotions being expressed, just empty stares.

Before he knew what was happening, the man named James said, "This makes a lot more sense now. At least we have a plan. What is the next step?"

Alexander looked around at the faces staring at him. He quizzically asked, "Excuse me?" He started to get up to leave, thinking maybe the meeting was missing the vital link – that being the one in charge. Maybe the guy in charge hadn't arrived yet.

Then the woman named Pam said, "Alex, we can hear your thoughts. *You* are the man in charge. We met with the Council of Seven just as you did and, like you, we were shocked at first. There is no way to make sense of what is going on. Our understanding is that these sudden changes to the planet are a necessary cleansing that will allow us to survive the new energy field our planet and our galaxy are about to go through. Yes, it would have been nice to know earlier and be more prepared, but it is like an earthquake; you deal with it after it happens. We are here to usher in a new era and a fresh start. Our job now is to understand the new physiology of our bodies, which this paper explains, thank you, and to learn how to replace our food supply in an ecofriendly manner. The ideas you present in this packet are brilliant. It makes sense to turn abandoned buildings into towering greenhouses, and it is completely doable in a short amount of time."

Alex sat back with knitted eyebrows and scanned the table, looking each person in the eye. As he did, he could hear their thoughts. Their thoughts were unanimous, *We trust you.*

Alex spent the next two hours going over the packet and the engineering designs for the hydroponic gardens and new designs for the towers. By the end of the meeting, each representative knew how to begin the process of rebuilding and restoring. Each shared their contact numbers and agreed to meet in the same place once a month. In the meantime, it was agreed to stay away from the media frenzy and concentrate on family. By the time the meeting was over, Alex felt more sure of himself. He was part of a group that would usher in a time of rebirth, rebuilding, and reestablishing connections to each other. The world would soon be free of lower vibrational emotions, those of self-serving motives, and the emotion of love would replace them. It all seemed too surreal.

When Alex left the meeting, he was once again escorted to the lower lobby where his chauffeur was waiting for him. His car was being plummeted with banging fists, bottles, and food scraps. People were running around with blood dripping from their noses and cuts on their heads. The rioting crowds were turning on each other. Alex pushed through them, sustaining blows to his body as he tried to get to the car door. When the door closed, the overwhelming emotion of sheer fear brought panic to both Alex and his driver. They sat for what seemed like an hour as they stared out the windows at the disrest in front of them.

The driver looked back at Alex with fear in his eyes, "I cannot move. If I do, I will run over them! I cannot do that, Emir. What do you suggest?"

As the car rocked and rolled and the ceiling creased from the weight of the crowd jumping on it, Alex yelled, "Look at me. Go slowly and carefully. You can do this. Just go slow." When they turned their attention back to the windows, the streets were suddenly empty. There was not a soul in sight. No debris, no blood, no bodies, just a perfectly sunny day. Both men leaned forward in disbelief, looking through the windows surrounding them. The streets were clean, the trees were greener, and the sun's glow was soft and easy on the eyes.

The driver started crying. He put his head down on the steering wheel and sobbed. Alex thought, *It is happening. It has started.* He got out of the car and walked back into the building.

When he entered, standing before him was Qaseem who was waiting for him. He walked up to Alex, put his hand on his shoulder, and said, "You have got this, son. It is a new world. There is more to come. Be prepared. May love and happiness be your guide," They hugged. The driver entered the building looking for Alex, still shook up. When he saw Qaseem, his mouth dropped open in shock. He stood staring into Qaseem's smiling eyes as he and Alex hugged. Alex turned to look at his driver and when their eyes met, in that second, Qaseem was gone.

Alex and his driver stood side-by-side staring out the glass doors of the Aspire Building into the empty streets, then back at each other. Alex said, "It is time to go. While you drive me home, I have a story to tell you."

And so it began…

Over the next several months, the world lost 4.3 billion people. The remaining spontaneously awakened to their true identity. The questions, *Who am I, Why am I here, and What is my purpose* were no longer thoughts. An understanding of who God/Source is, what the universe is and how it operates was immediately downloaded into the psyches of those remaining. The downloads revealed that our universe is just one of thousands, all connected by hidden frequencies and ancient portals, all teaming with intelligent life. Seven ancient star-gates or portals were opened around Earth and on hundreds of other planets, allowing travelers to move between the planetary systems during peak sunrise and sunset hours. This is when the sun's energy connects with the photons in every living cell on every planet, rejuv-enating and replenishing lost energy.

It was explained that each galaxy has its own incarnation system. Civilizations past, present, and future are all the same souls returning over and over again, simply living through the many scenarios within The ALL. When The ALL reached the point of understanding emotions, it released every species from the amnesia programmed within us. The ALL is simply sentient energy that has no form. It encompasses the space that surrounds everything; every person, every tree, every rock, every planet, every galaxy, and every universe. The ALL is the space where nothing is, what everything swims in. Some call it "Dark Energy," but it is best to be described as ether.

The ALL is now content with its understanding of the human condition. It is our parent and has provided life throughout the multiple cosmos since the beginning of time. No one knows when the beginning was, but it is understood that it has no end. It is and always will be. With every breath, we breathe the ether which is Source that surrounds us and lives inside of us at all times.

Millions of species from every universe began traveling between planetary systems to do business with each other, all sharing their advanced technologies. All technology created for good yet used for war and mind control no longer existed. Many of the species visiting Earth and working with us had to deal with complex atmospheres and the many different forms of nutritional issues, as did we when we traveled to other galaxies. Over time, systems were put into place to provide for these complex issues. It wasn't long before trust and community were gained and celebrated between the different species. When the reset occurred, love, compassion, and creativity were the new driving force within all life forms. The saying 'working to live' became 'living to create'. No longer was 'doing' important. The state of living in the now took its place. Children were taught to embrace their creative abilities and school itineraries transformed into developing passions in students instead of stringent academics. The new Earth kept the old Earth's history available for study. The horrors of its unimaginable past were eventually archived.

In the months that followed the great exit, over two thousand intergalactic species exposed themselves to earthlings. The first to arrive were the humanoids that looked similar to us. The more exotic creatures arrived several months later. There was no shock and awe, there was only love and acceptance. Interplanetary travel and cooperation with the Galactic Federation was now part of everyday life. The joy of living in the 'now' was the new normal. The worldwide web was taken down and rebooted. All algorithms, AI, and social media were removed. The science fields boomed. New technologies based on energy sourced from the field/ether were put into place. The scientists of the world were given new physics for propulsion systems and energy systems that used *the field* for energy. The electrical grid became obsolete. Gasoline, natural gas, wind turbines, and ocean currents were no longer used. Around the planet the air, the oceans, the soils, and the freshwater aquifers were once again clean and rich in nutrients. Plants grew bigger and better, the human condition healed, and the planet thrived.

The legal and political systems became obsolete overnight. There was no greed, no lust, no adultery, no lying, no gluttony, no stealing, no war, and no God-figure that was worshipped. Planet Earth belonged to Source, The ALL, and it was loved and respected. The 3.7 billion people that remained treated each other with love and respect. The material things that the 4.3 billion people who disappeared had accumulated disappeared with them. All species were now a team, working together for the greater good of all. Earth completely healed herself within weeks of the great exit. It was a new planet operating at its full potential, and over the next couple of years, all the new operating systems would be up and running.

The Sacred Rock Healing Center was transformed into a teaching center, becoming The Sacred Rock of Transformation. Cooking classes, gardening classes, and creative arts of all kinds brought people from all over the world to Therma, Greece to share and connect. Life was peaceful, joyful, creative, and fun.

When the traveling and heavy work was done, and the galaxy was in balance and teaming joyfully with a new diverse world family, Melena threw Pearl and Adeem a huge wedding at Agriolykos that made Charlee and Mathias' wedding look like peanuts. Pearl wore a beautiful champagne pink gown that showed off her huge baby bump. The ceremony was small but was televised for the world to view. Adeem and Pearl had become the royal couple who were to give birth to the children that would solidify the new universal frequency that allowed the universe to remain forever in harmony.

One year later, Melena, in a very quiet ceremony, married Alex and Julia. After the ceremony and the guests had gone, Alex and Julia sat in Adirondack chairs in the courtyard of Agriolykos. Holding hands, they watched the most beautiful sunset overlooking the island of Fiori. It was bright orange with shades of reds and yellows shimmering across the bay and up the walls into the courtyard where they sat. Julia asked, "Alex, what do you think the twins are going to do when they reach the age of ten?

Alex answered, "I am not sure, but I know it is going to be something amazing. I can feel it. I had a dream that Psusennes and Priya, at the age of ten, would destroy the lower frequency of the first Earth, the frequency of The Phoenix that has kept us all in limbo and fear for so long. If this is true, Julia, life will only get better and better. It will indeed be magical."

Julia smiled and kissed him gently, "Yes, and we will be here to witness that magic. I am so excited!"

Alex got up and held out his hand. Julia took it, stood up, and faced him. Looking into her eyes he said, "Thank you for being a part of my life. Thank you for loving me. Thank you for being you. Thank you for believing that anything is possible." He kissed her deeply and longingly then escorted her to bed.

Epilogue - The Phoenix Phenomenon

In the first several months of pregnancy, Pearl was able to keep up with her heavy schedule of speaking engagements with Julia around the world. Julia focused on immortality, which was the biggest hurdle for most to adjust to, and Pearl focused on integrating the new intergalactic species to the plants, bees, and all thing nature on Earth. Their seminars were standing room only.

Into the eighth month of pregnancy, Pearl's belly was nearly the size of two watermelons and her back could no longer support the weight of the twins while standing for hours at a time. She returned to Qatar and settled into home life with Adeem at the chateau. It was a peaceful life and the chateau became her sanctuary.

Melena had originally planned a beautiful wedding for Adeem and Pearl *after* the birth of the twins, but when Pearl retired home, her and Adeem decided to wed earlier, realizing a set of twins could prevent them from truly enjoying a wedding night. Melena had been planning their wedding since the two of them announced the engagement. She was ecstatic when Pearl asked her to expedite the event and began the final preparations immediately.

Pearl helped Melena with the wedding arrangements when she could, but her biggest joy was feeling her babies play inside her. She spent hours daydreaming about the days to come, the days she and Adeem would teach the twins about life and nature like Julia and Charlee had taught her. She loved being pregnant and she loved Adeem. She remembered the days when her life revolved around books and PhDs, when the thought of children and marriage were far off her radar. None of that was a priority now. She was happier than she had ever been and having a beautiful world to raise her children in was the icing on the cake. As Pearl traveled around the globe in her first months of pregnancy, all that met her knew intrinsically that she was carrying two very special babies. It was as if Psusennes and

Priya were connecting to the energy field that all information was now imprinted on and shared instantaneously to everyone. Adeem and Pearl were royalty and respected, loved and adored. At first it was hard to adjust to, but over time they did.

One night in a lucid dream, Pearl dreamt that she was in the presence of her children, Priya and Psusennes, in a room similar to the crystal room Adeem and Alex had described. In *this* room, there was a white couch with a large window streaming in warm shimmering sunbeams. In her dream, Pearl was sitting on the couch. She could feel the warmth of the sun shining on her while she listened to the long-awaited answers to her questions, "Who is The Phoenix and why was I chosen?"

Priya sat on the couch next to Pearl as Psusennes sat in the metal chair facing them. Priya was beautiful with long blonde hair, green eyes, and translucent skin. Looking at her reminded Pearl of the hooded woman, the apparition that helped them seed the waters.

Psusennes was just as beautiful. Priya's mannerisms were soft, almost maternal as she reached up and caressed Pearl's face and brushed a small ringlet of hair from her eyes. She took Pearl's hands in hers and said, "Pearl, it is time to tell you a story. This story you will remember tomorrow when you awaken. When you do, place Adeem's hand on your belly and we will repeat what we are about to tell you to him. Are you ready?" Pearl shifted in her seat then nodded.

"In the beginning, The ALL became curious as to what it would be like to interact with someone other than itself. It created Psusennes, and Psusennes created me. Psusennes was chaos. He was created into a world of darkness, and he was created with a conscience. He could sense love all around him, but he could not touch it. He could not feel it. So, he created me out of the darkness so he could feel love. Soon after, many more were created. Your mythology calls us angels.

It was a beautiful time. Singing harmonic melodies was the only way to communicate, and the songs were beautiful. When Earth was first created, we inhabited the planet and lived a tranquil life. Earth was magnificent! So lush and fertile. The entire sphere was a Garden of Eden. We had a very symbiotic relationship with Earth. We sang to her and she provided for us. Your myths also call us the Fallen Ones and paint a dark, demonstrative narrative around us, the story being that we sinned and were thrown to Earth and corrupted her in many horrible ways. This is not true. We are very loving souls who brought peace to a world filled with all kinds of creatures.

Pearl, your family is part of our family, the first original souls, the angels. You are an angel, and your bloodline is very special. You were created from me, along with Julia, Charlee, Melena, Sophia, and Gabriella. The men – Alex, Adeem, Mathias, Dimitri, George, and Qaseem – were created from Psusennes. We are the first souls The ALL's consciousness created.

But there came a time, a long time ago, when Earth's vibration and electromagnetic field weakened. Your sun's magnetic field became unstable and expelled massive amounts of energy in the form of solar plasma bolts, unfortunately aimed at Earth. This bombardment of atomic-like energy burned holes in Earth's protective layers. When this happened, a very negative interstellar species made their way in through the breach and decided to stay for a while. They harvested and took many elements from Earth, leaving behind a desolate surface in many areas of the planet. When they had had enough of what they came for, they decided to leave, but the tears in the protective layers had healed themselves so this group of beings were stuck here. They became hostile and angry. They tried desperately to find ways to tear open the fabric once again. Over time, they created weapons to stimulate the sun into discharging more plasma bolts, thus hoping to escape, but they failed every time. They finally realized they were here to stay. This species is called 'shapeshifters'. They took on the appearance of humans and over time have integrated themselves into your governments, corporations, political parties, religious organizations, television, and social media platforms. They have done this to many civilizations that came before you, and each time they have become more aggressive in their integration.

Anger turned into greed and greed turned into power-mongering amongst them at the expense of the humans. What they did not factor in was the human condition and its intrinsic desire and determination to survive. Time and time again, the population exploded and the masses found strength in numbers and stood up and challenged the powers of this cloaked group in the form of riots and organized demonstrations. What they did not expect was for the human condition to awaken to their potential and fight back. This was not desirable or accepted behavior. So, this covert species turned the humans and Earth into a game, a game they could win over and over again by using time manipulation. They programmed a deteriorating vibration into Earth that lasts 138 years. Each 138-year cycle begins with hope, innovation, reconstruction, advancements in technology, and growth. As the cycle nears its halfway mark, the vibration becomes negative, cataclysmically destructive, with gross manipulation of the human spirit, causing it to turn on itself. They watch and play this game within this cycle over and over again to their own amusement. As generations die off, new generations are born without knowledge of the game and fall into this never-ending trap. The powers that be realized it took exactly 138 years to coerce humans into a fear-based workforce built on slavery and brutal mentality. Thus, never allowing love to thrive. Love is the strongest human emotion and this is not an emotion they understand, nor did they want to.

So, every 138 years the cycle is reset and eventually catastrophic events once again plague Earth, planned and operated by the shapeshifters hiding within the system. Some of these events were extinction events, others were devastating catastrophes that decimated populations. This 138-year cycle is called The Return of The Phoenix. The cycle of birth, destruction, death, and resurrection. The Phoenix is their mascot. What humans fail to realize is that it is *they,* the humans, that are the resilient ones. They are the ones who have endured, survived, and have continued to rebuild from the ashes time and time again. It is this resilience that angers the shapeshifters. Each time The Phoenix, the 138-year cycle, returns, the mental devastation inflicted on the masses is more destructive. They have been slowly lowering the positive, loving frequency to a negative, barbaric frequency. This has been going on for millennia.

Pearl, do you understand what I have just explained to you?"

Pearl sat in disbelief as she listened to Priya talk. She caressed her belly, realizing her child was sitting before her telling her this horrific story. Pearl hesitated then nodded.

Priya continued, "Pearl, Psusennes and I have the power to end the cycle, and only we can end it. This is *our* destiny. We will be born on May 7th, 2030, six weeks from now and exactly ten years and one week prior to the beginning of the next Phoenix cycle. On May 14th, 2040, at the age of ten, Psusennes and I will leave this Earth for the last time. We will capture and neutralize the lower vibration of the malevolent species that still inhabits the old Earth that we bifurcated from. Even though we have broken free of them and are now in parallel dimension of space-time, their vibration is still alive within the third dimensional field. When we destroy the vibration, all dimensions can ascend. The only time this window opens is on the first day of the new 138-year cycle representing the period of 'resurrection'. We had to wait for this time to fulfill the prophecy and end the cycle of The Pheonix. This is our purpose in this incarnation."

When Priya was done, she sat still and watched Pearl digest what had just been said to her. After a few minutes, Pearl began to cry, "Are you telling me that when my children, when you are ten, you will no longer exist? Are you telling me that you are going to die at the age of ten?"

Psusennes came around to the other side of Pearl, sat next to her, held her hand, and said, "Pearl, look into my eyes and concentrate with me. Let me help you remember. But first, let me explain your burn." Pearl reached up and felt the back of her neck. The months of pain was finally gone and her neck was once again soft, yet the scar was still there. Psusennes continued, "The exact moment that my sarcophagus was opened was a pivotal moment in space-time. It was the shift in time that prepares for the destructive vibrational phase of The Phoenix's return. This vibration is very vulnerable during the shift. My role was to capture this vibration, subdue it, and plant it in a vessel that had the strength to hold it without death occurring. I seared The Phoenix's vibration into the mark on your neck, along with the energy of Priya and me the moment our eyes met. We, the three of us to-gether, prepared for that moment eons ago. All three energies were embedded into your neck inside this mark. When the time was right, our energy became the twins you are carrying. By the time Priya and I are born, we will have absorbed The Pheonix's energy from you and it will reside within us until we turn ten. At that time, we will have the ability to destroy it and return to The ALL. Our incarnations will be complete. Now close your eyes and remember with me." Through her tears she did as she was asked.

Slowly, Pearl's eyes began to dry and the pain in her heart softened. She was one with Psusennes, soul to soul, and she remembered. This was the agreement, her purpose in this incarnation: to save the world, to save the universe through her children. She took a quick breath and removed her hands from Psusennes'. She said, "I remember, I understand. I am OK." She gathered Priya and Psusennes into her arms and hugged them.

Psusennes said, "Remember, we never die. We will see you again and we will always be with you. Pearl, you and Adeem will have more children that will live an immortal life with you. You are destined to have a joyful and wonderful life. The universe will reset and the negative vibrations will no longer exist. This will become the new golden age. A time of prosperity, innovation, creation, and connection. As the generations rebuild, let the elders share the stories of how it was before the great reset then show the children love. Live with love and love will live within you. Lower vibrations cannot thrive within love."

Pearl awoke from her dream.

Adeem was sitting next to her quietly whispering, "Pearl, baby, are you OK? Wake up, my love. I am here, you are OK. It is just a dream."

Pearl looked into Adeem's concerned eyes as a tear rolled down her face. She placed Adeem's hand on her belly, and over the next hour Priya and Psusennes told him what they had shared with Pearl in her dream. When they were done, Adeem remembered, as Pearl had, the purpose of this incarnation. They remembered their mission. The sorrow Pearl had felt in her dreams was now subsiding as she lay in Adeem's arms. Together they caressed her pregnant belly and settled the rambunctious twins inside.

On May 7th, 2030, as promised, the twins were born. Pearl delivered them in a warm spiraling pool of water that Adeem, Charlee, Julia, and Melena had prepared for the twins' birth. They stood alongside the pool and helped Pearl through the delivery. It was an easy birth, one that ended in laughter, tears of joy, and clapping as the babies emerged from Pearl's womb and into the healing waters. They were perfect, both with green eyes and blonde hair. Pearl cried happy tears as she handed each child to Adeem to hold and bond with. It was the most beautiful moment in Pearl's life.

For the next ten years, the family played, taught, experienced, and shared in the beauty of life with the twins. As they grew, their wisdom became more profound and the world learned through them. By the time they were ten, through their love, they had taught the world how delicate Mother Earth is and our responsibility to her. May 14th, 2040, the hooded woman returned. Psusennes and Priya were ready. Holding their parents' hands they said, "You will not feel the impact of what we are about to do, but the universe will and will forever be changed by it. We love you. We are always with you, and we thank you for being our parents and fulfilling this mission with us. Remember, your name, Pearl, means, 'Divine spark of light within our physical bodies.' Our light, together with the light within the six of you, was created in the same moment that chaos became form. You, Pearl, held and hold the frequency, the light that our frequency and light connected to. It was planned. You were chosen for this reason. We are one with you, Pearl."

Pearl and Adeem hugged Psusennes and Priya then let them go. They each took one of the hooded woman's hands, turned and smiled at their parents, then disappeared. At that moment, Pearl felt an ache in her abdomen. When she reached down to touch her belly, she knew that she was once again pregnant.

About the Author

Robin A. Clark is a retired cardiac nurse with numerous publications in medical journals. She recently authored *Shhhh, Breathe* and *Battling Adult Philadelphia Positive Acute Lymphoblastic Leukemia: The Real Fight for Those with Ph+ALL*, detailing her and her husband's experiences during a clinical study for a rare leukemia and his bone marrow transplant. These works offer valuable tools and insights for others facing similar diagnoses.

Robin's passion for writing continued with *Naked Without a Hat: An Extraordinary Adventure Through Astrocartography*. After four years of widowhood, she embraced single life and whimsically chronicled her self-discovery journey through Greece, inspired by an encounter with an astrocartographer. Her first novel, *Spiraling Waters: The End of the Phoenix*, celebrates her PhD in Metaphysics. This fast-paced Indiana Jones-style archaeological adventure follows two families, unaware of each other, who travel through space and time via reincarnation on a synchronistic mission to save the human spirit and planet Earth.

Robin also patented a female supplement, Fem-Ease, for Interstitial Cystitis (patent # US6143300A, Sept 2000). In 2003, she owned and operated two successful restaurants in Oregon and rezoned a 216-acre waterfront parcel to develop a high-end multi-unit RV resort at the mouth of the Coos River. She earned her PhD in Metaphysics and a Master's in Divinity in 2009.

Robin is the proud mother of two children: one a decorated Iraq war veteran with two Purple Hearts, and the other a practicing esthetician. She also has two beautiful grandchildren. When not writing, she enjoys golf, oil painting, beading, gardening, camping, and long walks on the beach. She currently resides in Bandon, Oregon, and continues to write.

www.ingramcontent.com/pod-product-compliance
Lightning Source LLC
Chambersburg PA
CBHW030550260626
47157CB00006B/2254